A Mother's Courage

When Eloise Cribb receives the news that her husband's ship has been lost at sea she wonders how she and her children are ever going to manage.

The Constant Heart

Despite living by the side of the Thames, eighteen-year-old Rosina May has wanted for little in life. Until her father's feud with a fellow bargeman threatens to destroy everything.

A Mother's Promise

When Hetty Huggins made a promise to her dying mother that she would look after her younger sister and brothers, little did she know how difficult this would be.

The Cockney Angel

Eighteen-year-old Irene Angel lives with her parents in a tiny room above the shop where her mother ekes out a living selling pickles and sauces, whilst her father gambles away what little money they do manage to earn.

A Mother's Wish

Since the untimely death of her husband, young mother Effie Grey has been forced to live on a narrowboat owned by her tyrannical father-in-law Jacob.

The Ragged Heiress

On a bitter winter's day, an unnamed girl lies dangerously ill in hospital. When two coarse, rough-speaking
individuals come to claim her, she can remember
nothing.

A Mother's Secret

When seventeen-year-old Belinda Phillips discovers that
she is pregnant, she has no option other than to accept
an arranged marriage, and give up her child forever.

Cinderella Sister

With their father dead and their mother a stranger to
them, Lily Larkin must stay at home and keep house
whilst her brothers and sisters go out to work.

A Mother's Trust

When her feckless mother falls dangerously ill, Phoebe
Giamatti is forced to turn to the man she holds responsible
for all her family's troubles.

The Lady's Maid

Also by Dilly Court

Mermaids Singing

Born into poverty and living under the roof of her violent and abusive brother-in-law, young Kitty Cox dreams of working in a women's dress shop in the West End.

The Dollmaker's Daughters

For Ruby and Rosetta Capretti, life in the slums of the East End holds little promise. Despite their humble background, Rosetta is determined to work under the bright lights of the music hall and Ruby longs to train as a nurse.

Tilly True

Dismissed from her position as housemaid under a cloud of misunderstanding, Tilly True is forced to return home.

The Best of Sisters

Twelve-year-old Eliza Bragg has known little in life but the cold, comfortless banks of the Thames, her only comfort the love and protection of her older brother, Bart.

The Cockney Sparrow

Gifted with a beautiful soprano voice, young Clemency Skinner is forced to work as a pickpocket in order to support her crippled brother, Jack.

Dilly Court

The Lady's Maid

arrow books

Published by Arrow Books 2012

2 4 6 8 10 9 7 5 3 1

First published in Great Britain in 2012 by
Arrow Books
Random House, 20 Vauxhall Bridge Road,
London SW1V 2SA

www.randomhouse.co.uk

Addresses for companies within The Random House Group Limited can be found at:
www.randomhouse.co.uk/offices.htm

The Random House Group Limited Reg. No. 954009

A CIP catalogue record for this book
is available from the British Library

ISBN 9780099562559

The Random House Group Limited supports The Forest Stewardship
Council (FSC®), the leading international forest certification organisation.
Our books carrying the FSC® label are printed on FSC® certified paper.
FSC is the only forest certification scheme endorsed by the leading environmental
organisations, including Greenpeace. Our paper procurement policy can be found at
www.randomhouse.co.uk/environment

MIX
Paper from
responsible sources
FSC
www.fsc.org   FSC® C016897

Typeset in Palatino by Palimpsest Book Production Limited,
Falkirk, Stirlingshire
Printed and bound in Great Britain by
CPI Group (UK) Ltd, Croydon, CR0 4YY

For my good friend, Diane.

Chapter One

Maiden Castle, Dorset, September 1854

Zolfina could tell that the gorgio girl's life was ebbing away on a crimson tide. She laid the naked newborn child on her mother's breast. 'You have a daughter, Clara. She is a fine healthy baby – a little small, perhaps, but she will soon grow.'

'I will not live to see it.' The words came out in a hoarse whisper as Clara wrapped her arms around her baby.

'What sort of talk is that?'

'I'm dying, gypsy woman.'

'You are not dying, child. You must put these thoughts from your mind.' A superstitious shiver ran down Zolfina's spine, and she crossed herself as she glanced up at the towering ramparts of the Iron Age fort in whose shelter she had so recently brought two new lives into the world. It was a pagan place ruled by the gods of the ancients, but there was no mystic or magical power that could save the young mother. Zolfina had seen many a newly delivered woman bleed to death. She had skills in making herbal remedies, but there was nothing more she could do for this delicate fair-haired girl who was little more than a child herself. A doctor might have been able to save

1

her, but they were at least a mile from Dorchester, the nearest town, and Clara was slipping away into the world of spirits. Zolfina turned to her daughter, Dena, who was sitting beneath a stunted oak tree nearby, cuddling her own newborn babe. Dena raised her eyebrows in an unspoken question and Zolfina shook her head.

'Come closer, gypsy,' Clara whispered. 'I cannot see your face.'

Zolfina knelt down beside her. 'Save your strength, child.'

'Promise me that you will take care of my baby.'

'You will take care of her yourself, Clara. You have so much to live for.'

'I'm not afraid to die. But I don't want to leave her alone in the world.'

Zolfina clasped her hand; it was cold and bloodless. She knew that it would not be long now. 'I will see that she is cared for, but surely you have family somewhere? There must be someone close to you?'

Tears welled from Clara's blue eyes and trickled silently down her ashen cheeks. 'I disgraced my family. They want nothing to do with me, and her father, Alexander, is dead – killed in action in the Crimea. We will be reunited soon in heaven, but I want you to give our child a blessing.'

'I am not a priest. I am a simple Romany woman – I have no power for good or evil.'

'I'm giving her to you. Promise me that you will find a good family who will love and protect her.'

Zolfina took the mewling infant from Clara's arms.

'You have my promise.' She reached for the bucket of water which she had fetched from the Winterbourne river at the onset of Dena's labour. It was there, on the riverbank, that she had found the exhausted and heavily pregnant Clara. She had helped her back to the hollow at the foot of the earthworks where Dena and her baby now lay on a bed of dried bracken and straw. Romany law said that a woman in labour was impure, and birthing must be accomplished away from the main encampment: Zolfina had acted accordingly, but she had not reckoned on delivering two babies that day, let alone two girls. She beckoned to Dena. 'Bring your babe here. We will name the little ones together.'

It was dusk, and the flickering fire sent a fragrant plume of woodsmoke rising into the opalescent sky above the dark hump of the prehistoric fort. A barn owl flew overhead screeching its hunting call, and in the distance a dog fox barked. Then there was silence.

Zolfina dipped her fingers in the bucket and made the sign of the cross on the baby's forehead. The infant uttered a cry of protest as the cold water trickled down her face. 'I name thee . . .' Zolfina paused, looking to Clara for guidance. She had to bend closer to hear the whispered name.

'Katherine – after my mother.'

'I name thee Katherine. May God's blessings go with you for all of your days.' She gave the baby to Dena, exchanging her for her own granddaughter. 'What name will you give your little one?'

Dena tossed her head. 'I will not have her long enough to name her if you have your way, Mother.'

'Keep your voice down,' Zolfina hissed. 'Can't you see that the girl is not long for this world? Do you want to send her to her maker with angry words in her ears?'

Dena hung her head. 'Josephine. I want to call her Josephine.'

'What sort of name is that for a Romany child?'

'Her father was called Joseph and he was a gorgio. She may never know him, but she will be raised as one of his people. You have seen to that, Mother.'

'Don't blame me, my girl. You left me with no other choice.' Zolfina dipped her finger once again into the water, but this time she was met with a silent, almost defiant stare from the baby's dark eyes. Zolfina crossed herself – that was a bad sign. The child ought to have cried to cast the devil out. 'I name thee Josephine,' she said hastily. 'May the blessing of God go with you.' She gave the infant back to Dena. 'Josephine and Katherine – I renounce the devil and give you both to God. May your lives be long, and may the good Lord give you the strength to deal with whatever ills may befall you.' As the last words left her lips, Zolfina realised that Clara was trying to speak. She leaned closer, taking her hand. 'What are you saying, child?'

'My ring.'

Zolfina looked down at Clara's left hand, which she raised with such difficulty, and her attention was captured by the heart-shaped emerald surrounded by tiny diamonds. 'I see your ring, and it is beautiful.'

4

'It is my engagement ring,' Clara whispered. 'Take it and keep it safe for my child when she grows up. I have nothing else to leave her. Promise me, gypsy.'

'I promise.'

Clara's eyelids fluttered and closed. With her last breath, she whispered, 'Alexander.'

'What did she say, Mother?'

'She's gone to join him – her man. God rest their souls.'

'Poor creature.' Dena stifled a sob. It could so easily have been she who was lying there on the cold ground. She had been spared, but perhaps the pain of having her child taken from her was greater than death itself? She held her baby a little tighter; she was so small, so helpless and so precious.

Zolfina slipped the ring off Clara's finger and crossed the dead girl's hands on her breast. She covered her with a brightly coloured woollen blanket. 'We will never know who she was or where she came from, but those hands had never done a day's work. Clara was obviously a lady and her man was a gallant soldier who gave his life for his country.'

'It's very sad.'

'But she is gone now and we cannot leave her here for the crows to pick at.' Zolfina handed the ring to her daughter. 'Keep this safe, Dena. I must return to the camp and speak to Yoska. He will know what to do for the best.'

Dena closed her fingers around the ring. It felt like a lump of ice in her hand and she shivered. 'It is almost dark, Mother. I don't want to be left alone.'

5

'I won't be long. You will have to stay here and look after the babes until I get back. We leave tomorrow for our camping ground on Hackney common, but at first light I'll take Josephine to the big house, as we agreed.'

'I want to keep her. I cannot bear to let her go.'

Zolfina threw her hands up in despair. 'No one knows about the baby, not even Yoska. Everyone in the camp thinks that you are still working as a maid-servant for the Damerells. If Marko discovers that you have been with another man he won't marry you – no man will have you – and our family will be disgraced.'

'I would rather be disgraced and keep my baby.'

'Don't talk rubbish, my girl. You would be an outcast, reduced to begging on the streets. None of this would have happened if you had not gone with the gorgio. You stay here, and think about what you have done.'

She disappeared into the night, leaving Dena alone with the sleeping infants and the body of the tragic young mother. She laid the babies down side by side beneath the tree while she collected twigs and brush-wood for the fire. A grey mist was sneaking inland from the sea, which was less than eight miles distant; it moved wraithlike between the steep embankments, bringing with it a sudden chill. Looking up at the black silhouette of the earthworks against the darkening sky, Dena could hear the sounds of conflict: the cries of the women and children and the warlike yells of the warrior Durotriges as they fought their fatal battle with the Roman soldiers. She shuddered, wrapping her arms around her body and forcing the images out of her mind. She had inherited the second sight from her maternal grandmother, but it was an unwelcome gift.

A whimpering sound from Josephine brought her back to reality and she hurried over to pick her up. The hungry mouth sought her breast and Dena sat down, leaning back against the gnarled tree trunk. She undid the buttons on her blouse and allowed the baby to suckle. The sensation was strange, but wonderful and yet bittersweet, for tomorrow she knew she must give her daughter up, never to see her again. Tears spilled from her eyes and ran down her cheeks unchecked. She was paying the price for that night of madness when she had lain with Joseph Damerell, the dashing brother of Sir Hector, who had come from London for a weekend shooting party. They had danced beneath the stars and drunk champagne from a silver goblet. He had made her laugh and had charmed her with his teasing smile and soft words. She had known that it was wrong, but at the time it had seemed so right – the laws of purity and the sanctity of marriage had flown out of her mind like a flock of migrating swallows. The result had shocked her; she had not imagined that she could conceive so easily or so quickly. She would never forget that magical night when they had hidden in the summer-house and slept in each other's arms. They had awakened to a cold and frosty dawn, making love again just as the sun was rising, but even as they parted with a lingering kiss, she had known that she would never see him again.

She wiped her eyes on the back of her hand. The baby had stopped suckling and she hitched Josephine over her shoulder, rubbing her tiny back until she gave a satisfactory burp. She had often held other women's babies and cuddled them, breathing in their milky scent, but she had never experienced the flood of emotion and protective love that she felt at this moment. She cradled the infant in the crook of her arm and Josephine stared up at her with a dark unfocused gaze. Who would have thought that this perfect little creature could have emerged from her womb? A shaft of fear stabbed Dena in the heart. She could not bear the thought of giving her beautiful baby to sour-faced, acerbic-tongued Miss Hickson, Lady Damerell's personal maid. It was she who had noticed Dena's swelling belly, and her condition would have warranted instant dismissal but for the servant's determination to help her barren mistress. Miss Hickson had sent for Zolfina, and between the two of them they had worked out a plan to hide Dena away until her confinement while Lady Damerell acted out a phantom pregnancy. The irony of the situation was not lost on Dena; she might not have produced a son, but Josephine was a Damerell. She was being forced to give her baby to another woman, who would pass her off as her own, when all along the child was of the family blood line.

Josephine slept, but now Clara's baby had begun to cry. Dena did not want to suckle another woman's child, but it seemed as though it was the only way to quieten the infant. She was shocked that she felt nothing for this helpless little scrap of humanity, but she could not allow her to starve for want of a mother. She had her own baby cradled in one arm, and Clara's baby at her breast, when Zolfina came crashing through the undergrowth.

'You'll have to stop that very soon or you'll have paps like a cow. I'm taking her to Miss Hickson in the morning. She wanted the babe as soon as it was born, but it's too late to go tonight.'

In spite of everything, Dena could not suppress a giggle. 'I'm sure that my lady will be glad to deliver the cushion that she has been wearing stuffed beneath her corsets these past few months.'

Zolfina scowled at her. 'It's no laughing matter, my girl. You'll be hard put to convince Marko that you're still a virgin when he claims you for his bride. At least the money from the Damerells will give you a big enough dowry to buy his silence if he does realise that you are spoiled goods, but you've still got to play your part.'

Dena licked her lips. She had worked it out in her head and now she must convince her mother that she had the perfect solution. 'Perhaps she will take the gorgio child instead?'

'What are you talking about, girl?'

'No one knows about Clara and her baby. And you said that she was a lady, so why not give her baby to Lady Damerell?'

'Because, you silly girl, Clara's child is going to be as fair as her poor dead mother. The Damerells are all dark-haired, which is why Miss Hickson and I worked out a deal which would benefit us all.'

Tears spilled from Dena's eyes. 'But she is mine, and I love her. I cannot give her up.'

'You have no choice.' Zolfina modified her tone. She did not want to see her daughter suffer, but she must be firm. She must not waver now, for all their sakes. 'Marko is a good man, and it's fortunate for you that his travels have kept him away for many more months, because if he were to find out about this he would seek another bride.'

'I know that, Mother, but I can't give my baby away.'

'You will have many more babies, and they will be true Romany. We will leave tomorrow morning, at first light. You must say goodbye to her, and there will be no argument.'

Dena bowed her head. Her heart was crumbling inside her breast, but she knew that she must obey her mother and Romany law. 'Promise me one thing, Mother.'

'And that is?'

'That you will tell them her name is Josephine. It is the only thing that belonged to her real father that I can bestow on her.'

Zolfina nodded in agreement. 'I will try. Now get some sleep.'

'But what will happen to Clara's baby?'

'I've thought of that and I think I have the solution.'

Dena glanced at the shape beneath the woollen blanket. 'And Clara?'

'Yoska is going to see that her poor dead body is

10

treated with respect. You need not worry your head about Clara. Nothing in this world can harm her now.'

Next morning, Zolfina awakened as the first grey streaks of dawn appeared in the east. She crept over to where Dena lay sleeping beside the two infants, who were swaddled in woollen shawls. There was no mistaking Josephine, with her shock of dark hair, and Zolfina picked her up gently. She made her way stealthily from their makeshift camp, and set off to walk the two miles to Damerell Manor, the family's country home.

As arranged, Miss Hickson was waiting for her in the summerhouse by the lake. The black bombazine skirts of her dress swirled around her skinny body as she paced the floor, and her shawl flapped in the breeze, giving her the appearance of an agitated crow. Zolfina quickened her pace, terrified that the infant would awaken, start crying and draw the attention of the grooms and gardeners who were already beginning their day's work. This transaction had to be done in the strictest secrecy if the servants were to believe that Lady Damerell had been delivered of a baby.

'Where have you been?' Miss Hickson demanded angrily. 'I waited for hours last night, and I've been here since the crack of dawn.'

Zolfina climbed the steps into the summerhouse, panting for breath. 'The labour was long and difficult, but the child is perfect and healthy.'

'And it's a boy?'

'Alas, no. But she is beautiful nonetheless.'

'Give her to me,' Miss Hickson said, holding out her hands. 'This is disappointing. Sir Hector was desperate for a son and heir.'

'No one has a choice in these matters.'

'Apparently not, although I suppose you still want your money?'

'And my lady wants a child to prove that she is not barren and might in future bear a son – so all are satisfied.'

'I doubt if Sir Hector will be.' Miss Hickson took a leather pouch from her pocket and handed it to Zolfina. 'Take your money and go. And tell that slut of a daughter never to come near this house again.'

Zolfina drew herself up to her full height. 'You need not worry about that. We have honoured our part of the bargain; it is up to you to see that the child is well cared for.'

'You are impertinent, woman. This child will have the finest of homes both here and in London, she'll have the best of parents and everything that money can buy. She will grow up with wealth and privilege. She is the most fortunate of little bastards ever born. Now go on your way. Our business is done.'

'Not quite. The baby needs a wet nurse. Have you arranged that?'

'You insult my intelligence.' Miss Hickson drew herself up to her full height. She could not resist the temptation to boast about her cleverness. 'The wife of our head groom is about to be delivered of her fourth child, but in each case her babes have been stillborn. She is staying at present with her father-in-law who manages the home farm, but she will return to London with the rest of the household at the end of the month. Are you satisfied now?'

'Aye, mistress. I am content.' Zolfina was about to leave, then she remembered Dena's tearful plea. 'There is but one thing, Miss Hickson.'

'And that is?'

'The child has been named Josephine.'

Miss Hickson curled her lip. 'I don't think it is any of your business what my lady chooses to call her child.'

'A gypsy's curse will be on this great house if the mother's wish is ignored.'

Miss Hickson's eyes widened and her hand flew to the silver crucifix hanging about her neck. Her lips moved silently, as if in prayer. Zolfina turned on her heel and walked away stifling a chuckle; it was ridiculously easy to frighten gorgios with the threat of a curse. She quickened her step as she headed through the wood. The leather pouch was satisfactorily heavy; it would buy Dena a good husband. One day Marko would take over from Yoska as head man. Dena would have a position of respect, and she would be grateful to her mother for covering up her youthful indiscretion. Zolfina blinked away a tear; she must not weaken now. The baby, her granddaughter, would never want for anything. That was the thought she must hold on to, and she must never admit that parting with the baby filled her with anguish. She squared her shoulders – she must be strong. Now she had one more thing to do and that was to find a family who would take poor little Clara's child. The thin-lipped termagant, Miss Hickson, had given her an idea.

Miss Hickson wrapped the baby in her apron and scuttled across the grass sward to the stone steps leading up to the drawing room. She hurried through the music room into the great hall, with its high ceiling ornamented with gilded plasterwork, and she mounted the flight of marble stairs, glancing nervously around to make sure she was not seen. Her mistress's bedroom was at the front of the house overlooking the gravel carriage sweep and beyond it the avenue of copper beeches, resplendent in their burnished summer foliage. She let herself into the room without knocking.

Marguerite Damerell had been standing by one of the tall windows staring out over the parkland, but she spun round as she heard the door open. Her pale face was transformed with joy when she saw the baby. 'Hickson, you've got him at last.'

'My lady, I'm afraid that it's a girl child.'

Lady Damerell's lips trembled and her eyes clouded with disappointment, but as she took the sleeping infant from Miss Hickson's arms her expression softened. 'But she is beautiful, Hickson. And she is mine.'

'Yes, my lady. She is your daughter.'

'And you trust the gypsy woman to keep silent?'

'She has been well paid, my lady. If she should come back I will have the dogs set on her.'

'I hope there will be no need for that, but you must do whatever is necessary.' Lady Damerell smiled tenderly as the baby opened her eyes. 'She has beautiful brown eyes, just like my husband's. I cannot wait to show her to him, and I must choose a name for her. Until now I had only considered boys' names. I will have to think again.'

Miss Hickson cleared her throat, mindful of the Romany woman's parting words. She did not really believe in gypsy curses, but she was not going to take any unnecessary risks. 'I know that you will not agree, my lady, but the baby's mother expressed a wish that the child be named Josephine.' She clasped her hands tightly behind her back, crossing her fingers.

'Josephine?' Lady Damerell rubbed her cheek against the baby's head. 'Her hair is like black silk.'

'The mother has no right to impose her wish upon you, my lady. I was just passing on the information.'

'My husband's grandmother was called Josephine. I think he will be pleased with the name, and I shall put it to him in such a way that he imagines the choice is his.'

'And when is the master due to return home, my lady?'

'Not until next week, but I will send a messenger to our house in Bedford Square with the good news.'

'Very good, ma'am. Now, may I suggest that you get back to bed while I dress the little one in more appropriate clothes?'

'Of course, we must act out the charade to the end. Everyone will be surprised how quickly I get my figure back after the birth.' Lady Damerell carolled with laughter as she handed the baby back to Hickson. She leapt into bed, pulling the covers up to her chin. 'We must find a wet nurse for her too. That is of the utmost urgency, but I suppose you have it all planned?'

'I have, my lady. It is all arranged. In fact, you might remember the girl. She was a parlourmaid here before her marriage to your head groom, so you know you can trust her to behave in a proper manner and to be discreet.'

Lady Damerell frowned. 'But the baby needs a wet nurse now. Coggins and his wife will have remained in London.'

'Not this time, my lady. Mrs Coggins has produced only stillborn infants during her marriage and I took it upon myself to persuade her husband that she might fare better in the country. Whatever the outcome, she'll be returning to London with us and will tend the baby for as long as necessary.' Miss Hickson rocked the baby in her arms, resisting the temptation to crow. Having had several months to prepare for the happy event, she had worked her plan out in the minutest detail.

'Very well, Hickson. I'll leave it entirely to you, but first I will need a pen and paper so that I can write to Sir Hector. One of the grooms can take it to London. Then you must make all the necessary arrangements with this woman. What is her name, by the way? Not that it is important, but I like to know these things.'

'Bertha Coggins, my lady.'

'Splendid.' Lady Damerell held out her arms to receive the baby, who was starting to protest as Hickson dressed her in a silk nightgown that had been painstakingly embroidered as part of the baby's layette. 'You

16

may spread the good news below stairs too, Hickson. Tell them that I have given birth to a beautiful baby girl.' She frowned. 'I hope Sir Hector isn't too disappointed that it wasn't a boy, but I shall so enjoy having a daughter. Maybe next time I will bear a son.'

'Yes, my lady.' Hickson left the room, wondering if her mistress had lost her mind. It seemed as though she truly believed that she had given birth and could do so again. She headed for the back stairs leading down to the maze of passages and basement rooms – the servants' domain. She took a key from the chatelaine at her waist and unlocked a cupboard in which she had secreted a set of my lady's bed sheets. It was all part of her carefully constructed plan to trick the other servants into believing that their mistress had been delivered of a child, and she smeared the bedding with pig's blood that she had collected in a flask from the meat larder. She locked the cupboard and carried the soiled sheets to the laundry room where the washerwomen had lit fires beneath the coppers and were already hard at work.

Hickson held up the sheets with a triumphant smile. 'The mistress has given birth to a fine baby girl.' She swept out of the steamy atmosphere, leaving the women to chatter delightedly amongst themselves. The birth had been long awaited. Some said that the mistress would never bear a child – now they would have to eat their words. Hickson went to the kitchen to spread the glad tidings. She went next to the stables to instruct one of the under grooms to be ready to take a message to Sir Hector in London, and then she set off at a brisk pace across the parkland towards the home farm.

Robert Coggins opened the farmhouse door and his eyes widened in surprise at the sight of a gypsy woman standing on the step. In her arms she carried a baby swaddled in a coarse woollen shawl. He had not slept that night and he blinked against the bright sunlight. 'What d'you want, woman?'

Zolfina looked him straight in the eye. 'I heard that your good lady was about to give birth, master.'

'Get away from here. I don't hold with your sort.' Robert tried to shut the door but Zolfina was too quick for him and she stuck her booted foot over the sill.

She angled her head. 'I can tell that you've had a bereavement, master.'

'I don't want nothing to do with your black arts. Get away from my door, witch.'

'I'm a true Romany woman, not a witch. But I can help you, if you'll let me.'

'You'll get nothing from me, so be on your way.'

'But I have something for you, master.' Zolfina held the baby out for him to see more clearly. 'I can tell by your face that the birthing did not go well. Am I right?'

The hairs on the back of Robert's neck prickled and he swallowed hard. 'Yes,' he murmured, his voice breaking on a suppressed sob. Exhaustion was making him weak. He had been up all night and had just left his wife semi-conscious after a dose of laudanum administered by Dr Smith. Bertha's labour had lasted for two days and the baby when it finally arrived had

18

been stillborn. She did not know it yet, and he dreaded telling her that their much longed for child had not drawn a single breath. 'Say what you have to say and then leave me to my grief.'

'Your infant is dead, master. This baby girl needs a mother and a father. You are a good man, I can tell. Take her. She is yours.'

Robert stared at her blankly – was he still in the middle of the nightmare? 'What are you saying, gypsy?'

'This child's mother died giving birth to her. I came upon her by chance and did what I could, but I could not save her. She entrusted her baby to me, begging me to find her a good home.'

'This is madness,' Robert said, shaking his head. 'You cannot trade in human life.'

Zolfina bit back a sharp retort, forcing herself to speak calmly. 'I want nothing for the babe. All I ask is that you take her in and bring her up as your own. God will reward you.' She drew the shawl gently back from the baby's face. 'Look at her, master. She is a beautiful little girl, and she has fair hair and blue eyes, just like yours. Would your good lady know any different if you were to put this babe in place of the dead child? Would it not be a kindness to let her think that this was her baby girl?'

He blinked hard. He was not dreaming; this woman was real and so was the child. His dazed brain grappled against the temptation to snatch the baby from the gypsy and place her in the wooden crib that he had made with his own hands. 'I don't know. It don't seem right.'

Zolfina saw that he was weakening. 'Think about it, master. If a lamb loses its mother, would you not put the orphan to another ewe that has lost her own offspring?'

'My wife is a woman and not a sheep.'

'But she would have been a mother, and I hear tell that you had almost given up hope of having a child, just like her ladyship at the big house.'

Robert frowned; he could not rid himself of suspicion. 'What would a gypsy woman know of the happenings at the big house?'

'Am I not supposed to have second sight, master?' Zolfina thrust the infant into his arms. 'Her name is Katherine. Her mother was a lady who had fallen on hard times. Her father was a gallant soldier, killed in the Crimea. She has no one else in the world to care for her. Would you deny her a chance in life? And will you stand by and watch your poor wife die of a broken heart?'

Katherine opened her eyes, staring up into Robert's face. It seemed to him that she smiled, and he was lost. 'I will have to speak to the doctor. I am not sure I can take this decision on my own.' He looked up, but Zolfina had seized her chance and departed.

Hickson arrived at the home farm just as the doctor was leaving. 'Good morning, Dr Smith.'

'Miss Hickson.' He tipped his top hat as he untethered his pony's reins from the hitching post.

'Has all gone well with Mrs Coggins and her baby?'

'She is safely delivered of a daughter, Miss Hickson.

It must be close to Lady Damerell's time too?' Dr Smith bridled, unable to conceal the anger and affront simmering in his breast. 'I suppose that she has her London physician in attendance?'

Hickson was quick to note his displeasure, but she had never liked Dr Smith and it gave her grim satisfaction to see his nose put out of joint. She smiled. 'Her ladyship gave birth last night. All she needs now is a wet nurse for her daughter.'

'I don't know about that, Miss Hickson,' he said icily. 'Mrs Coggins is very weak and must stay in bed for the lying-in period. I have advised her not to exert herself unduly.' He climbed onto the driving seat of the trap.

'Don't worry, doctor. I am sure that Mrs Coggins will be honoured to suckle the heiress to the Damerell fortune.'

Chapter Two

Tavistock Mews, London,
January 1873

It was almost dark, with only the dim flicker of lantern light emanating from the stables in the mews. The smell of horseflesh, leather and saddle soap mingled with the stench of rotting manure from the dung heaps at either end of the narrow street. Snowflakes fell from an inky sky, settling in white lace crystals on the cobblestones and frosting the detritus lying in the stagnant gutters. Kate hurried homeward as fast as the iron-clad pattens strapped to her shoes would allow, and the clink of metal striking stone echoed off the tightly packed buildings. She wrapped her thin shawl a little tighter around her head and shoulders as she picked her way towards the stables and coach house which belonged to the Damerells' grand home in Bedford Square. Having just come from the big house, where she was employed as a housemaid, Kate was even more conscious of the squalor in which the coachmen, grooms and their families were forced to live, tucked away out of sight of the Georgian terraces in the elegant residential squares. She stepped over the carcass of a dead rat, suppressing a shudder although vermin were common enough in the city streets, and thrived in the warm conditions of the stables where food was plentiful.

She let herself into the coach house, and taking care not to wake the stable lads who slept on beds of straw in one of the empty stalls she made for the narrow flight of wooden stairs which led to the room she occupied with her father. She found him, as usual, slumped on his bed, snoring loudly, with an empty gin bottle clutched in his hand. His clay pipe was still clenched between his teeth but it had long since gone out. She removed it gently so as not to disturb him and prised the bottle from his fingers. Having suffered in the past from his drunken rages, she did not want to wake him before he had time to sleep off the effects of jigger gin. She sighed, gazing down at his unshaven face and slack jaw with a dribble of saliva running down his chin. Pa was not a bad man, but he was weak. When sober he was quiet, kind and conscientious, which was how he had managed to keep his job with the Damerells for so many years, but in drink he became a completely different man. He had been like this since her mother died of the lung fever ten years ago when Kate was just eight, and she had kept house for him ever since. Not that there was much she could do to improve their living conditions in the small room beneath the eaves. She swept the floorboards daily and dusted the dresser on which were displayed the plates, cups and saucers that had been a wedding present to her parents and were now prized family heirlooms. Kate handled them with as much care as she did the bone china dinner and tea services owned by the Damerells.

She raked the coals in the grate in an attempt to rekindle the fire, resorting in the end to the bellows.

When the flames licked up the chimney she rose to her feet, holding her hand to her aching back. She had been at the big house since six o'clock that morning and a quick glance at the mantel clock told her that it was getting on for half past ten at night. The family had dined at home that evening and Sir Hector was unlikely to need her father's services until morning when he went to the office in the City where he held an important position, although she was not quite clear exactly what he did there every day.

Kate picked up the smoke-blackened kettle but it was empty, and although she would have loved a cup of tea the communal pump was at the far end of the mews and she could not face braving the bitter cold again. She sat down on the only chair in the room and began unbuttoning her boots. It had been a particularly busy day in the Damerell household and Miss Hickson had been on the warpath, although it was not her business to oversee the maidservants, as Mrs Evans the housekeeper had pointed out to her in no uncertain terms. There was always tension between the two of them and Mr Toop, the butler, had his work cut out to keep the peace. Kate sometimes wondered why the rest of the staff put up with Miss Hickson, but the mistress would not have a word said against her. She pulled the second boot off with a sigh of relief. They were too small for her and worn down at the heel but Pa said he could not afford to waste money on new shoe leather when she had a pair that would go on for years. She rubbed a blister on the back of her heel and grimaced with pain. Perhaps Grandpa would buy her some new boots when the Damerell family removed to their country home for Christmas. Grandpa Coggins liked to spoil her as much as he was able, and she looked forward to the brief period in the winter when they went to Dorset and the long summers when Sir Hector insisted that the whole household decamped to Damerell Manor, despite his wife's pleas for them to stay in town for the London season.

Kate stretched her feet out towards the fire, wriggling her toes and frowning when she realised that there was a hole in one of her black woollen stockings. She would have to darn that before she went to bed. She sighed. She had grown up knowing that there were two worlds, sharply divided. The Damerells lived a life of pampered ease, waited on hand and foot by a small army of servants. Then there was her world, one of servitude and relative poverty. She lived in the rat-infested stables with the smell of horses clinging to her hair and clothes, while Josephine Damerell, the spoilt, petted and over-indulged daughter of the house, dwelt in luxury. It was hard not to envy her and resent the manner in which she took her good fortune for granted, but then Kate remembered Josie's good points: her generous, fun-loving nature and her wicked sense of humour. Josie was a rebel and had always ignored the rules set down for her by her parents, her succession of governesses and the indomitable Miss Hickson. Josie cocked a snook at all of them, and it had been through her that Kate had received a good education.

Friends from childhood, they had played together in the woods surrounding the Damerells' country house, and Josie had insisted that Kate shared her lessons, refusing to study anything unless her friend was present in the schoolroom. Kate had to smile when she recalled those days which now seemed so far off. Josie had been the torment of many a young governess and tutor. She was quick and intelligent but also wayward and argumentative. Kate had been the studious one and it was she who wrote the lines that had been meted out as a punishment to Josie for whatever indiscretions or misdemeanours had occurred during lessons. It was Kate who learned long poems by heart and prompted Josie when she was compelled to stand up and recite them. It was Kate who wrote the essays that Josie could not be bothered to pen, and it was Kate who copied out her own mathematical workings in a fair imitation of Josie's hand so that it appeared as though she had paid attention in class. Her reward for all her efforts was to be embroiled in Josie's wild adventures, which quite often involved Sam and his younger sister Molly, two orphans found abandoned in Dorchester market by Kate's grandfather, who had taken them in and raised them as his own children. She smiled as she thought of Sam and Molly, Sam with his dark hair and blue eyes the colour of speedwell and his strong muscular body, honed by hard work on the farm. Then there was sweet-natured Molly, her baby sister in all but name. She missed them both when they were separated by her return to London.

She was startled from her reverie as her father groaned in his sleep. She thought for a moment that he was going to wake up and demand another drink, but to her relief he sank back into the arms of Morpheus. She was safe until morning, when he would be sober, but morose and complaining of a headache. She took off her stockings and rose from the chair to find the rush workbox that her grandfather had given her for her twelfth birthday. She darned the hole and made everything tidy before turning down the wick in the paraffin lamp and undressing in the glow of the fire. She laid her grey uniform dress neatly over the chair back and slipped her flannelette nightgown over her head. Her bare feet pitter-pattered on the floorboards as she went to her narrow wooden bed in the far corner of the room. She unrolled the straw palliasse and lay down, pulling the old horse blanket up to cover herself. It still smelt of the stables and there were bits of straw interwoven with the coarse material, but it was thick and heavy and if she curled up in a ball she would soon be warm enough to sleep. She closed her eyes, fixing her thoughts on Christmas which would be spent with Grandpa, Sam and Molly, if Mrs Vance, the housekeeper at Damerell Manor, allowed her to live at home instead of occupying one of the attic rooms in the main house. She longed for her comfortable featherbed in the farmhouse and awaking to the smell of roasting goose wafting up from the kitchen below on Christmas day.

Next morning she was up and about before either her father or the stable boys had stirred. Outside the street was covered in a thin layer of pristine snow, and even the steaming dung heaps had a crusting of white, like thick cream on a plum pudding. She grimaced at the thought as she hurried on her way to work, where her first duty of the day was to make tea for the housekeeper and Miss Hickson.

The sleepy young kitchen maid, Elsie, a child of ten recently acquired from the workhouse, stopped raking the embers in the range and turned with a start when Kate entered the room, but her frightened expression dissolved into a broad grin when she realised that it was her friend and protector who stood before her, and not one of the older servants who took grim pleasure in bullying a skinny little girl.

'Good morning, Elsie,' Kate said with an encouraging smile. 'Well done for getting the fire going so early. It makes my job so much easier.' She hung her bonnet and shawl on a peg in the hallway, returning in time to see Elsie puff out her chest, blushing with pleasure at the unaccustomed praise. Kate glanced at the crumpled bedding on the floor by the range. 'You'd better stow that away before Cook comes down,' she said gently. 'You know she doesn't like an untidy kitchen.'

Elsie scrambled about picking up the thin palliasse and blanket that served as her bed. 'Yes, miss. Only I thought I'd best see to the fire first.'

'Quite right, and you succeeded splendidly. Put the bedding in the linen room and then you can have a nice hot cup of tea before the others descend upon us like a flock of hungry birds.'

Elsie scampered out of the room carrying the bundle, which was almost as big as her. Kate made the tea and while it was brewing she set out the trays with the special china which was reserved for the housekeeper, the butler and Miss Hickson. She had observed the strict hierarchy of the servants' quarters from an early age and now it was second nature, but all her sympathies were with young Elsie who had so much to learn. Despite her wiry frame, Elsie bore all the marks of a sickly child who had clung tenaciously to life through the scourges of measles, mumps and scarletina that ravaged the young occupants of the workhouse, taking many of them to an early grave.

Kate took a tray to Mrs Evans and another to Miss Hickson. She hurried back to the kitchen to snatch a quick cup of tea before her next task which was to light the fire in each of the family rooms. She poured the tea, adding a generous amount of milk and a lump of sugar for Elsie, and taking the biscuit barrel from the shelf in the pantry she gave one to Elsie, winking and holding her finger to her lips. 'Not a word to anyone and don't leave a trail of crumbs or you'll get me sacked.'

Elsie gobbled the biscuit, wiping her lips on her sleeve. 'Ta, miss. You're a good 'un.'

'I don't know about that, but I do remember what it's like to be ten years old and always hungry.' Kate ruffled Elsie's cropped hair. 'Don't forget to put on your mobcap. You know how strict Cook is about neatness.'

Elsie swigged her tea, glancing about nervously. 'I'll do it now.'

'Good girl.' Kate took the cups into the scullery and washed the incriminating evidence before the scullery maid could tell tales to Cook. She then set about the backbreaking job of cleaning out the grates in the bedrooms and reception rooms, before hefting coal scuttles and bundles of kindling up many flights of stairs in order to light the fires. After that her duties consisted of carrying ewers of hot water to the bedchambers, and the less pleasant task of emptying and cleaning chamber pots.

Josie's room was always last on the list as she slept late every morning, and was to be left undisturbed until she rang the bell for her morning chocolate. Lady Damerell had given strict instructions that Miss Josie was to have breakfast taken to her room on a tray. It was common knowledge below stairs that her ladyship was convinced that her daughter was delicate, and needed constant nurturing. This, Kate was told, had begun when Josie contracted a fever of unspecified origin as an infant, after which her doting mother had decided that she was too fragile to be treated like a normal child. Kate knew that her friend was made of much tougher material but Josie, always quick to take advantage of a situation, played on her mother's anxieties in order to get her own way in everything.

Kate set the silver chocolate pot on a side table close to Josie's four-poster bed with its silk hangings and Italian-quilted satin coverlet. She pulled back the heavy damask curtains, allowing the morning light to filter in from the square, and was about to leave the room when Josie called her back. 'Kate, come here.' She snapped into a sitting position, beckoning to her.

'Yes, Miss Josephine?'

'Don't call me that when we're alone.' Josie ran her hand through her tangled mass of raven dark curls with an exasperated sigh. 'Stop behaving like a servant, Kate. This is me you're talking to.'

'But that's what I am.' Kate eyed her warily. 'What can I do for you, miss?'

'You can start by acting normally, for goodness' sake.' Josie swung her legs over the side of the bed, stood up and stretched. 'I'm bored to death, Kate. I want to go shopping and you must accompany me.'

'But that's impossible. You know I can't do that.'

'Why not? If I say I want you to come with me, who is going to stop you?'

'Mrs Evans for one. I'm just a housemaid, Josie.'

'It's never stopped you when we're down in Dorset. You and I do all sorts of things together, and Sam used to join in too.'

Kate shook her head. 'That was a long time ago.'

'It was last summer, if I remember rightly.' Josie lifted the pot and poured hot chocolate into a bone china cup. She sipped, gazing at Kate over the gold rim. 'I'll speak to Mrs Evans and make her give you the time off.'

'It won't do any good.'

'Huh. We'll see about that.' Josie put the cup down, her frown melting into a persuasive smile. 'Come on, Kate. Where's your spirit of adventure?'

'It's all very well for you to demand this and that of the servants, but I have to live amongst them, and if I lose my position here I'll be lucky to get a job as scullery maid in a respectable household.'

Josie opened her mouth as if to argue and then closed it again, nodding her head. 'All right, you win. I'll tell Mrs Evans that you're in desperate need of a new pair of boots. And don't argue with me, I've seen you limping about as if each step was agony. I'd give you some of my cast-offs but my feet are bigger than yours. Compared to you I'm a big, clodhopping cow, and you're a dainty little gazelle.'

The comparison was totally unjustified and the ridiculousness of it made Kate chuckle. 'That's utter nonsense.'

Josie did a twirl. 'That's better. Now fetch some hot water and tell Mrs Evans that I want to see her now.'

'You can't summon her to your room, Josie. She'd be furious.'

'See if I care. Tell the old witch I'm waiting, and if she doesn't like it I'll tell Mama that she disobeyed an order and made me ill.'

'You're wicked, Josie.'

'Yes, dear, I know. It's fun, isn't it?'

Tight-lipped and with spots of colour emphasising her high cheekbones, Mrs Evans sailed into the kitchen with her hands clasped in front of her like an affronted Mother Superior. 'Coggins, you're to accompany Miss Josie on a shopping trip this morning. Have you finished your tasks?'

Kate had just come from the scullery clutching a bucket of hot water in one hand and a scrubbing brush in the other. She paused in the doorway. 'I was just going to scrub the hall floor, Mrs Evans.'

'Minnie, you'll have to do it.' Mrs Evans turned to the tweeny, who was mopping the quarry tiles. 'You will take over the rest of her duties until midday.'

32

Minnie's mouth drooped at the corners and she shot an angry sideways glance at Kate. 'Yes, Mrs Evans.'

'But I need Minnie here with me,' Cook said crossly. 'I've got luncheon to prepare for the mistress and some of her friends and the family are entertaining tonight, so there's a five-course dinner to prepare. I can't do without her for a whole morning.'

Mrs Evans raised her eyebrows and Kate could see a vein throbbing in her temple. It was not a good sign. She held her breath, not daring to say anything.

'Well, then,' Mrs Evans said after a moment's reflection. 'The second parlour maid will have to help Minnie.' She shot a searing look at Kate. 'And you will take her place serving at dinner this evening. You will work longer to make up for the time lost this morning.'

'Yes, Mrs Evans.' Kate forced herself to sound meek but inwardly she was seething at the unfairness of being punished for something that was none of her doing. All this fuss had been caused by Josie's habit of riding roughshod over anyone who stood in her way. Such behaviour had not mattered when they were younger, but now things were different, especially in London where the gap between the classes was even wider than in the country.

'Go then,' Mrs Evans said, pointing dramatically to the door. 'Go with Miss Josie, but don't think this is the last you'll hear of this business, Coggins. Servants who get too friendly with them above stairs invariably come a cropper.' She whisked out of the kitchen, leaving Kate to face an irate Cook and a rebellious

Minnie. Elsie poked her head round the scullery door and seeing the looks on their faces she retreated hastily.

Half an hour later, Kate followed Josie out of the house. They set off on foot, Josie having refused Toop's offer to send for the barouche. His expression was one of outraged dignity as he closed the front door, causing Josie to cover her mouth with her hand in order to stifle her laughter.

'Poor man,' Kate said, walking a respectable two paces behind her mistress. 'You've hurt his feelings.'

Josie stopped, proffering her arm. 'He'll recover in time. Walk with me, Kate. I'll not stand for this silliness any longer.'

Reluctantly, Kate took her arm, glancing over her shoulder in case any member of the household happened to be looking out of the window. 'It's not the done thing,' she murmured. 'What will the neighbours say?'

'As if I care.' Josie tossed her head and her dark eyes gleamed with mischief. 'I've been cooped up in that house for days. I feel like a caged bird but now I'm flying free and so are you.'

Her good spirits were infectious and once they were clear of the square Kate began to relax. 'Where are we going?'

'Soho Bazaar. It's in Soho Square, which is only a short walk away. I've heard all about it and longed to go there but Miss Hickson refused point blank, saying that it was not the sort of place for respectable young ladies to be seen. Such nonsense.'

'Why would she say that?'

Josie's dimples deepened and her eyes gleamed

mischievously. 'Because louche gentlemen go there to ogle pretty women. It's considered a fashionable thing to do, so I've heard, and I want to see for myself.'

Kate was not convinced. 'Perhaps Miss Hickson was right this time.'

'She's never right. I hate the old trout, but Mama thinks she can do no wrong, and Hickson trades on Mama's good opinion. If it weren't so ridiculous I'd think that Mama was sometimes a little afraid of the wretched woman.'

Kate tugged at her arm, holding her back as Josie was about to step off the pavement in the path of an oncoming dray. 'You'll get run over if you aren't careful.'

Josie tossed her head. 'They wouldn't dare. Anyone can see by my clothes that I'm a lady. They wouldn't dare knock down a baronet's daughter and her maidservant.'

'Don't be silly,' Kate said, losing patience. 'How would they know who you are?'

Josie gave her a pitying glance. 'They would just have to look at the way I hold myself to know that I'm different from the hoi polly.'

'Do you mean the hoi polloi?'

'You're such a pedant, Kate. Sometimes I don't know why I bother with you.' Josie held up her gloved hand and marched across Tottenham Court Road, causing a carter to rein in his horse. He shook his fist at them, swearing volubly.

'Sorry, mister,' Kate said breathlessly as she was dragged helplessly towards the other side of the street, much to the amusement of a group of ragged urchins.

'Give us a penny, lady.' The boldest boy held his hand out to Josie.

She looked him up and down, taking in his filthy appearance from the top of his lice-ridden hair to his bare feet. 'Go away or I'll call a constable.'

Kate snatched her hand free and opened her reticule. She had three pennies that she had been saving towards a new pair of boots, but she could see the children's bones sticking out like gnarled twigs beneath their grime-encrusted skin. They all looked as though a good meal would do them the world of good. She tossed the coins on the ground and they fell on them, scrapping like wolf cubs over a juicy piece of flesh.

'You're a fool,' Josie said, quickening her pace. 'They've probably got more money than you have.'

'You could have spared them a penny or two.'

'Not me. I look after myself. I don't care about anyone else.' She chuckled. 'Well, maybe I care a bit about you, but don't let it go to your head.'

'As if I would.'

Josie took her hand and tucked it in the crook of her arm. 'No, you always manage to keep calm. I've never known you to have a fit of the megrims. I don't know how you do it, Kate Coggins, but I'm full of admiration.' She squeezed her hand. 'And sometimes I could shake you and tell you to shout and scream and get angry, as I do.'

Kate smiled. 'It wouldn't do if we were all the same. But please stop at the kerb or better still find a crossing sweeper when we get to Oxford Street. I really don't want to end up in hospital with a broken arm or worse.'

'You have no sense of adventure, but I will take care. I don't want to get my new gown muddy or the rakes and libertines won't take a second look at me.'

They arrived at the two-storey bazaar in Soho Square without further mishap and headed straight for the rooms devoted to the sale of items which held a special appeal for ladies. Stalls were ranged on either side of the aisles, selling gewgaws, ornaments, trinkets, gloves, jewellery, millinery and fine lace. Josie swooped upon them like an eager magpie attracted by glitter and sparkle. Kate was more cautious and examined the price tags before replacing the items with some reluctance, having given her last penny to the street urchins. Josie purchased items randomly: a feather fan, a bead necklace and a piece of lace which served no purpose other than being pretty. She bought a blue satin bonnet trimmed with velvet bows and immediately gave it to Kate, saying that she did not like it after all and the colour would not flatter her complexion. She bought a pair of white kid gloves and a china cat with green eyes simply because it reminded her of a pet she had owned as a child.

Kate followed her round dutifully, carrying the mounting pile of brown paper packages containing Josie's impulsive purchases. As they flitted from stall to stall she was aware that they were attracting the attention of several well-dressed young men who lounged casually about, their sole purpose seeming to ogle any female who was neither old nor ugly. Josie paid them little attention until they entered another large room when she stopped, clutching Kate's arm. 'Oh, no. Don't look now, but I know that man.'

Instinctively, Kate turned her head, and received a sharp pinch from Josie's clawed fingers. 'Ouch. What was that for?'

'I said don't look. Pretend that you haven't seen him.'

'But I haven't. I don't know who you're talking about.'

'It's the old man my parents have decided I should marry,' Josie hissed. 'He's filthy rich and owns a castle somewhere in the country as well as a house in town. He's supposed to be quite a catch even though his family made their money in trade.'

'I thought you wanted to marry a wealthy man.'

Josie scowled at her. 'Of course I do, but my parents intend to sell me off like a prize heifer to the highest bidder. I want to love the man I marry.' She dragged Kate back through the doorway. 'Quick, run. I don't want him to see me. If he tells Papa he saw us here I'll be locked in my room until we leave for the country.' She made for the staircase but as Kate attempted to follow her she came to a sudden halt. Her skirt had snagged on a nail sticking out from the trestle supporting one of the stalls, and the parcels she had been carrying flew from her grasp, scattering in all directions.

'Allow me to help you, ma'am.'

Before she had a chance to respond, the stranger had bent down to disentangle the coarse linsey-woolsey material from the offending metal spike. She could see Josie in the distance, gesticulating frantically and shaking her head. Kate could only assume that this must be the would-be suitor whom Josie wanted to avoid and she would have moved on the moment she was free to do so, but if she made a run for it she would have to abandon Josie's purchases.

'Thank you, sir,' she murmured. 'Very kind of you, I'm sure.' She bent down to retrieve the packages, hoping that he would walk away, but he seemed hell bent on chivalry and he scooped up the remaining parcels, holding them cupped in his gloved hands.

'These are yours, I think.'

She raised her head and found herself gazing into a pair of twinkling eyes that were a shade somewhere between blue and green. She stared at him in amazement. This could not be the gentleman who had sent Josie running for cover. He was not exactly handsome but he was certainly not plain. He had quite a pleasing open countenance and a determined set to his jaw, and there was a humorous quirk to his generous mouth. He had the look of someone who might be good company, if given a chance. She took the packages from him and bobbed a curtsey. 'Yes, thank you.' She started to walk away but he caught her by the sleeve.

'There's just one thing I must point out before you run away,' he said, smiling.

Chapter Three

Kate met his amused gaze, resisting the temptation to smile. 'What is that, sir?'

'You can tell Miss Damerell, who is hiding behind that wrought-iron pillar, that she has nothing to fear from me.'

'It might be difficult to pass on the message since I don't know who you are, sir.'

'My name is Harry Challenor.' He angled his head, staring at her plain clothes and down-at-heel boots. 'But you have me puzzled. I can't quite place you, Miss – er . . .'

'I'm nobody, Mr Challenor. Good day, sir.' With as much dignity as she could muster, Kate walked off in the direction of the staircase. 'You can come out now, Josie. He's gone.'

Josie emerged from her hiding place. 'Hell and damnation. I wish I'd never come here today. What did he say to you? And why did you stop and talk to him?'

'I couldn't get away,' Kate said sharply. 'I caught my skirt on something and he unhooked it for me. If I hadn't been carrying all your things I might have done it for myself.'

Josie began to descend the stairs, glancing nervously over her shoulder. 'But what did he say? Did he see me?'

'Of course he did. You were waving your arms like a windmill.'

'I was trying to attract your attention.'

'You told me that he was old.'

Josie frowned. 'Well, he's twenty-five at least and he's got a certain reputation with the ladies. I won't be pushed into marriage with a man I don't know and can't trust, just because he does business with Papa.'

'He seemed quite nice, and he gave me a message for you.'

'Which is what I've been trying to ascertain, you ninny.'

Ignoring the insult, Kate smiled. 'He said that you had nothing to fear from him.'

'And what did he mean by that, pray?' Josie tossed her head. 'Is that a veiled threat that he might tell Papa that I came here when it was out of bounds, or did he mean that I'm too poor and too plain to be of interest to the great Harry Challenor whose grandfather made his money in trade?' She pulled a face. 'I expect he had a whole fleet taking cargoes of slaves from Africa to the West Indies.'

'Aren't you being a little melodramatic?' Kate followed her out of the building into the crowded square. 'You know you'll have to marry one day and I can't imagine you living in a farm worker's cottage or a tradesman's town house.'

Josie stopped, turning on her with eyes blazing. 'Do you really think I'm so shallow, Kate? We've known each other all our lives. Surely you don't believe that I'm so avaricious and unfeeling?'

'No, of course not. But perhaps you should give Mr Challenor a chance. He seemed pleasant enough, and very well mannered.'

'You have him then,' Josie said, flouncing off in the direction of Oxford Street. 'Anyway, I thought we were going to buy you some new boots. I can't have my lady's maid looking like a pauper.'

Kate caught up with her, clutching the packages to her bosom. 'What do you mean by that?'

'If I'm to be treated like a proper young lady I want a maid to look after me. I'm not having Hickson, and I'm tired of seeing you turned into a drudge when we're in London. I'm going to tell Mama what I want and she'll inform Mrs Evans. I'd give anything to see old Hickson's face when she finds out.'

Josie walked on briskly with Kate hurrying after her. 'Stop a moment. I'm not sure about this.'

'Well I am. You're worth so much more than doing menial work, and you're my friend. I wouldn't have been able to do much about it until now, but if I'm considered old enough to be married off to the highest bidder, then I should have some say in who looks after me. I want you and that's that.'

Lady Damerell, as ever, acceded to her daughter's wishes without much argument. Josie had taken advantage of Hickson's afternoon off, and had used all her considerable powers of persuasion to great effect. 'Very well, my dear, you shall have Coggins as your maid,' Lady Damerell said at last, sounding resigned and weary.

Kate had been outside the drawing room door and had heard every word of the mainly one-sided conversation. As she resumed her task of dusting the staircase, she had to acknowledge that Josie was a force to be reckoned with once she had set her mind on something. Kate waited to be summoned to the drawing room.

Mrs Evans' face was a picture when Lady Damerell told her of Kate's promotion. She demurred as far as she dared, but without Hickson to back her up she soon capitulated and agreed to advertise for a house-maid. She retreated to her own private domain visibly put out but unable to relieve her feelings, Kate suspected, until Hickson's return.

Kate took advantage of her new status to slip home for a few moments before she had to help Josie get ready for the dinner party. She was eager to share the news of her promotion with her father as it would add considerably to her wages, and make their lives more comfortable.

Lawson, one of the under grooms, was attending to one of the coach horses when she entered the stable.

'Is my pa upstairs, Mr Lawson?'

He nodded. 'He's up there, but I think he's had a bit of bad news, Kate. I'd go carefully if I was you.'

She hurried upstairs and discovered her father sitting at the table with a piece of paper clasped in his hand. He looked up and his expression was grim. 'The old man's dead, Kate. Passed away in his sleep two nights ago, according to young Molly. She's the one who penned the letter. She says that Sam's working hard to keep things going till we gets down there.' He shook his head. 'I dunno what to do, girl. I ain't no farmer. My life's been spent with horses, not sheep and hens and such.'

Kate bit back a sob. 'Poor Grandpa.'

'He was old, love. Old and tired. It comes to us all in the end.'

'I know, but I'll miss him.' She dashed her hand across her eyes. 'What will we do without him?'

'I dunno and that's a fact. But as there's no other close relation, I suppose I'm the head of the family now. I'll have to get permission from the master to travel down to Dorset as soon as I can be spared. Someone will have to sort out the funeral arrangements and see that things don't go to rack and ruin before the master finds a new tenant.'

Aghast at the thought of another family living in her old home, Kate stared at him in dismay. 'But, Pa, the Coggins family have tenanted the home farm for a hundred years or more. And what will happen to Sam and Molly if someone else takes over?'

He shook his head. 'They ain't blood relations, my duck. They'll have to fend for themselves.' He folded the letter and tucked it back in the envelope. 'Anyway, what are you doing home at this time of day? You ain't got the sack, have you?'

'No, Pa. As a matter of fact I've just been promoted to lady's maid.'

'Don't tell me that old Hickson has got the push.'

'No. I'm Miss Josie's maid. She's coming out next season. Lady Damerell has high hopes that she'll find a rich husband.'

He shook his head. 'I don't envy the man who gets landed with that young bundle of trouble.'

Saddened by her grandfather's death and grieved at the thought of losing the only real home she had ever known, Kate returned to the house where she received a cool reception from Mrs Evans. 'You may have wheedled your way into Miss Josephine's good books, but you'll still have to help serve dinner tonight, Coggins. We're short-staffed until I can hire another housemaid, so don't think you're going to take things easy.'

'No, Mrs Evans.'

'Like I said this morning, you'll stand in for Polly this evening. She took over your duties above stairs when Minnie had to help Cook. Your gallivanting with Miss Josephine put me to great inconvenience, Coggins.'

'Yes, Mrs Evans.'

'I've left a uniform out for you in the linen room. You'd better put it on now.'

'Yes, Mrs Evans.'

'She thinks she's too good for us,' Cook muttered, ripping the skin off a Dover sole. 'I can't be doing with her airs and graces.'

Kate left the room, her cheeks burning and her spirit rebelling. No matter how hard she tried to fit in with the servants in the London house there had always been an undercurrent of resentment amongst them. She knew she was different from them, but she had always put it down to her country upbringing, or maybe her father's moody disposition had tipped the scales against her. She had tried to overcome their prejudices but it was an uphill struggle and now she knew that things were going to get even more difficult. She went to the linen room to change into the plain black dress, starched white pinafore and frilled cap worn by the upstairs servants. The uniform was two sizes too large, and she had to tie the apron strings tightly around her waist to prevent herself from tripping over the hem, but there was no time to do anything about it now and anyway she did not really care. The sudden change in her status within the household and the shock of her grandfather's death had left her feeling slightly dazed, as if she was in the middle of a weird dream from which she would wake up suddenly and find everything back to normal.

Falling back on the years of disciplined training that she had been forced to endure, she put her personal problems to the back of her mind as she tidied the linen room, making a bundle of her discarded garments ready to take to the laundry room for washing and ironing ready for the next housemaid. She stood for a moment, taking deep breaths and using every ounce of self-control to put a brave face on whatever difficulties she might encounter above stairs. Moving like an automaton, she made her way to Josie's bedchamber.

Josie was sitting at her dressing table, brushing her hair when Kate entered the bedroom. She gave a hoot of laughter when she saw Kate's reflection in the mirror and she spun round on the damask-covered stool to stare at her. 'Good heavens, Kate. It's not fancy dress.'

'I'm glad you find it funny. This is Mrs Evans' way of putting me in my place. I'm to help serve at dinner this evening.'

'Oh, Lord. I'll never keep a straight face with you hovering behind me at table,' Josie said, chuckling. 'If you dare so much as look at me when I'm speaking to hateful Harry, I'll collapse in a fit of giggles.'

Kate took the hairbrush from her. 'I shan't do anything of the sort. I'll have to be on my best behaviour as Toop and the rest of the servants will be watching me like hawks, just waiting for me to make one little slip so that Mrs Evans can get me sacked.'

'Ouch, that hurt.' Josie jerked her head away as the hairbrush tugged at a particularly knotty tangle. 'I'll sack you myself if you can't do better than that.' She met Kate's troubled gaze in the mirror and smiled. 'Don't look so tragic. It will be all right. I promise to be on my best behaviour tonight, if only for your sake, although I've no intention of encouraging Harry's advances no matter how much it would delight Papa if I caught a rich husband.'

Kate began twisting Josie's gleaming black curls into a coronet on top of her head, fixing them in place with tortoiseshell combs and hairpins. 'I'm sure that Sir Hector has your best interests at heart.'

'And I'm certain that my happiness comes second to a new roof for Damerell Manor. Pa may work in a bank, but we're paupers compared to some of the county families.'

'Sir Hector owns the bank, and you're not exactly living in poverty.'

Josie held up her hand. 'Correction. The Board of Governors own more than half of the shares. Pa told me so himself. He's always saying that he's got one foot in Carey Street.'

'Then accept Harry Challenor if money means so much to you.' For a moment Kate had let her guard drop. She had not meant to speak sharply and she bit her lip. 'I'm sorry, Josie. I spoke out of turn.'

Suddenly serious, Josie gave her a searching look. 'What's the matter? You can't keep anything from me, Kate. Have the servants been beastly to you? There's something wrong, I know.'

'Pa had a letter from Molly. Grandpa Coggins died in his sleep two days ago.'

Josie leapt to her feet and enveloped Kate in a warm embrace. 'I'm sorry. I know you loved the old man, and he was always good to me whenever I visited the farm. Has anyone told Papa? I'm sure he'll be grieved at the news.'

Kate shook her head. 'I don't think so. Pa said he was going to ask for permission to go down to Dorset so that he can sort out the funeral arrangements. It's not fair to leave it all to Sam.'

'Of course not, although I'm sure Sam is more than capable, but he's not a blood relation.' Josie slipped off her silk wrap. 'Help me into my gown. I'll speak to Papa before the guests arrive.' She held her arms up to allow Kate to slide the ivory satin gown over her head without disturbing her coiffure, remaining motionless while Kate did up the tiny mother of pearl buttons at the back of the garment. When she had finished, Josie turned to examine her reflection in the cheval mirror, adjusting the waterfall of Brussels lace that fell from a décolletage to her waist. 'My pearls,' she said, pointing to a leather jewel case on the dressing table. 'The necklace and earrings. And my long cream satin gloves; you'll find them in the top right hand drawer.'

Kate fastened the treble row of milky pearls around Josie's slender neck. 'I'll never get used to all this, Josie. Perhaps you should have someone who's trained to be a lady's maid.'

'Nonsense. I'll teach you. There's nothing to it. Remember the days when we used to sneak into Mama's bedchamber and try on some of her ball gowns, even though they were far too large for us? It's just the same, only now the dresses are made to fit me and the pearls are mine. Although I must admit I would love to have some emeralds. Green is my colour, don't you agree?'

'I think perhaps rubies would suit you better.'

Josie frowned and her red lips pursed into an ominous pout. 'You must never disagree with me on a point of fashion or taste. I know exactly what I want and need, and now I'm going to buttonhole my father and tell him to let Coggins go to Dorset.' She moved towards the doorway, leaving a trail of gardenia perfume in her wake. She paused with her hand on the doorknob, a slow smile spreading across her face. 'We'll go too. I'll tell Papa that I will represent the

49

family at the funeral, as is only right and proper, and that you must accompany me. After all, it is your grandpa who is deceased and I can't travel without a lady's maid. This way I can escape the attentions of hateful Harry. It's all coming together wonderfully well.' She breezed out of the room leaving Kate to clear up a mess of discarded silk stockings, soiled undergarments and a dressing table littered with hairpins, pots of rouge, cut-crystal perfume bottles and combs.

Kate set everything in order before hurrying downstairs to take instructions from Toop, who had the footmen and maids lined up in the dining room while he inspected the covers on the huge mahogany table. Lady Damerell had adopted the relatively new fashion for dining *à la russe*, which consisted of several removes, rather than dining in the old style *à la française*, where all the dishes, both savoury and sweet, were put out at the same time. Cook had taken a while to come round to the idea and Toop had complained that there was insufficient cutlery to cope with the current fad, but Lady Damerell had insisted on ordering the recently invented fish knives and forks, which included special forks for oysters; and to confuse matters even more there were also different forks for salad and cakes, which according to her ladyship they simply must have. Sir Hector, it was said by his valet, had borne the cost of the silverware without complaint, and dinner parties at the house in Bedford Square had become more frequent. Hickson had put it about that Lady Damerell was now the most sought after hostess outside Mayfair, or would be if Sir Hector did not insist on retiring to the country while the London season was in full swing.

Even though she had been low down in the hierarchy below stairs, Kate had been aware of all this going on, and now she was seeing the revolutionary changes for herself as Toop went round to each place setting with his measuring stick, making minor adjustments until he was satisfied that everything was perfect. He spotted a glass that was not polished to diamond brightness and berated the senior footman soundly. He then detailed each of their duties, insisting that the guests should be served quickly and efficiently and in such a way that those waiting on the table were to all intents invisible. Kate was familiar with the military precision with which Toop instructed his staff but she had never actually served at table, and she was extremely nervous.

When the guests started to arrive it was Toop who ushered them into the square entrance hall with the cantilevered flight of stairs rising elegantly to the first floor. Huge urns of hothouse gardenias and clove-scented carnations filled the air, mingling with the perfume worn by the ladies and the liberal amounts of cologne used by their escorts. The newly installed gaslight fizzed and popped in the gasolier, Toop's pride and joy, which was lowered to the floor daily and polished until the brass gleamed like gold.

Kate's first task that evening was to take the gentlemen's cloaks, hats and gloves while the senior chambermaid saw to the ladies. She stood at a respectful distance, keeping her gaze lowered as they shed their outer garments, only allowed to speak if anyone addressed a remark to her, which no one did until the last guest arrived. She averted her eyes quickly as she recognised Harry Challenor. Little thinking that he would remember her or if he did that he would say anything, she could hardly believe it when he walked past Toop and came to a halt in front of her. 'Why, if it isn't little Miss Nobody.'

She held her breath, hoping that he would go away if she did not respond, but the shiny leather shoes remained in her line of vision, stubbornly immovable. She knew that Toop was watching her every move and she kept her head down.

'You can't have forgotten me, Miss Nobody. We met this morning at the Soho Bazaar.'

She shot him a glance beneath her lashes. 'Please go away. You'll get me into trouble.'

He clicked his heels together and inclined his head in a formal bow. 'Certainly. But at least tell me your name. I like to know to whom I'm speaking.'

'Coggins, sir.'

'That's a damned ugly name for a pretty girl.'

Toop cleared his throat. 'Would you care to follow me to the drawing room, sir?'

'In a minute, my man. I've asked this young lady a perfectly reasonable question. Is there any reason why she should not answer it?'

'No, sir.'

Kate could imagine Toop grinding his teeth in annoyance, and suddenly in spite of everything she wanted to laugh. She wished that Josie were here to share the joke. She raised her head and looked Harry in the eye. 'My name is Kate Coggins, sir.'

'Kate. That's better. It suits you.'

'Thank you, sir.'

He put the fancy box he was holding on a side table while he divested himself of his gloves, cloak and top hat, which he placed in Kate's outstretched hands. 'Thank you, Kate. I'm much obliged.' He picked up the box and turned to Toop. 'I'm ready to join the others now. Lead on.'

Toop marched off with his head held high, and having given Kate the full benefit of his charming smile Harry strolled after him. She was left holding his opera cloak and hat, and a pair of the softest peccary leather gloves she had ever seen. His garments had retained some of his body heat and smelt of lemon scented verbena, expensive pomade and just a trace of a Havana cigar. She could only guess that the box, which obviously contained expensive chocolates, was a gift for Josie. She suspected that Harry Challenor was living up to his reputation of being a confirmed lady's man and a hopeless flirt, but she had glimpsed a hint of steel beneath the well-mannered charm. She could not help feeling that Josie had met her match.

Dinner passed without incident. The staff moved swiftly and silently, serving and clearing without mishap, and Kate was relieved not to have disgraced herself. Josie was apparently on her best behaviour, although she drank a little too much wine and instead of treating Harry with disdain she flirted with him quite outrageously. Kate had witnessed Josie's sudden changes of mood so often in the past that she was not surprised by this about turn, but she could see that Lady Damerell was completely fooled by her daughter's behaviour. She positively glowed with satisfaction, and Kate suspected that this was part of Josie's plan. She wanted to lull both parents into a false sense of security so that when she asked if she might depart for their country estate earlier than planned they would willingly accede to her wishes. Despite the melancholy that gripped her heart, Kate had to smile to herself and secretly congratulate Josie on her cunning.

Flushed with the apparent success of her dinner party, Lady Damerell rose to her feet and invited the ladies to join her in the withdrawing room. Following Toop's instructions, Kate went to serve them with coffee. She waited until they were seated, watching with a degree of curiosity as this was her first opportunity to see how the wives of wealthy men behaved when their husbands were not present. The ladies took their time arranging their voluminous skirts, each of them chattering nineteen to the dozen as if they had been suddenly released from the circumspect behaviour expected of them by their spouses. They reminded Kate forcibly of a flock of starlings coming home to roost.

Josie took a seat on the sofa beside her mother, clutching a box of Cadbury's chocolates. 'Look what Harry gave me, Mama. Do try one.' She took the lid off the box and offered it to her mother. 'Wasn't that sweet of him?'

Kate almost dropped the coffee pot as she filled the cups set out on a silver tray. She glanced at Josie and looked away quickly as Josie winked at her, grinning wickedly. She knew then for certain that this was simply one of Josie's ruses in order to get her own way.

'He's a handsome young man.' Mrs Horton, the plump wife of one of Sir Hector's banking associates, eyed the box greedily. She had already eaten three desserts and Kate could almost hear her corsets creaking as they strained to contain her bulging flesh.

Josie leapt to her feet and wafted the box in front of her. 'Do try one, ma'am.'

Mrs Horton's piggy eyes gleamed. 'Just the one then, dear.' She selected the largest and popped it into her mouth.

Josie handed the chocolates round to the other ladies, who declared that they could not eat another morsel while taking their time selecting their favourite centre. Kate served the coffee and then stood back, hands folded in front of her, waiting until her services were needed.

'Might we hear wedding bells ringing in the near future?' Miss Bourne asked, trilling with laughter. Unmarried herself but a notorious matchmaker, well known to the servants for complaining about anything and everything, she had apparently found no fault as yet but was determined to make at least one person blush.

Kate stared into space, hiding a smile. It would take a sharper person than Miss Bourne to embarrass Josie, who was patently enjoying the situation.

'It's a little early to speculate,' Lady Damerell said hastily.

'You were always one to speak first and think later, Miriam Bourne.' Mrs Horton glared at her over the top of her lorgnette. 'Spare the girl's blushes.'

Miss Bourne bridled visibly. 'Harry Challenor is a good catch. Any girl would think herself lucky to attract his attention.'

'And I do,' Josie said smugly. 'But I don't want to appear too forward.' She took her seat at her mother's side. 'That's why I think it would be politic if I were to go to the country soon, Mama. Absence makes the heart grow fonder, so they say.'

Lady Damerell almost dropped her coffee cup, spilling some on her purple shot-silk gown. 'I don't know about that, my love.'

'Out of sight, out of mind,' Mrs Horton added, shaking her head.

The two ladies who had so far been silent nodded in agreement, but Miss Bourne sat upright, waving her spoon at Josie. 'I think that is an excellent plan, my dear. Keep the young man dangling. There are many eager unmarried girls out there, and we all know that it's the gentlemen who like to do the hunting. The excitement is all in the chase, as anyone here who has ever followed the hounds will know.' She glanced round with a superior smile as if she was well aware that none of the women present had ever taken part in blood sports. 'I,' she added grandly, 'used to hunt when I was a girl.'

'But she never caught a husband.' The more senior

of the two who had so far not contributed to the conversation spoke in a stage whisper, which Miss Bourne affected not to hear.

'That put you in your place, Miriam,' Mrs Horton said, chuckling.

Josie turned to her mother with a pleading smile. 'Mama? May I go to Dorset tomorrow with Coggins? Papa gave him leave to make the funeral arrangements and now I have a maid of my own it would be perfectly proper for me to travel with them.'

A worried frown puckered Lady Damerell's forehead. 'I don't know what your father would say to that, my love. We'll need the carriage when we travel next week. Can't you wait until then?'

Josie's lips trembled and tears welled out of her eyes. 'But Mama, I've got my heart set on it, and I don't want to stay here and look as though I'm chasing after a rich husband. You know how horrid some people can be.'

Lady Damerell held her hand to her head. 'Oh, dear. Now I don't know what to say. Where is Sir Hector? Why do gentlemen have to take so long over their brandy and cigars?'

'You'd better do something to stop her crying before they join us,' Miss Bourne said, glancing anxiously at the doorway. 'No man likes to see a girl with red eyes and a blotchy face.'

'There speaks the expert on men.' Mrs Horton rose to her feet and swayed over to sit next to Josie on the sofa, which creaked beneath her weight.

Kate hurried forward to rescue the coffee cup and

saucer from Lady Damerell, who looked as though she was about to collapse.

'Fetch my vinaigrette from the drum table,' Lady Damerell moaned. 'I feel faint.'

'Nonsense.' Mrs Horton reached across Josie to poke her ladyship in the ribs. 'Take deep breaths and pull yourself together.' She gave Josie a nudge for good measure. 'And you, girl. Stop that snivelling. I can hear the gentlemen coming. Do you want to ruin your chances?'

Josie stood up, almost tipping Mrs Horton off the sofa. She brushed her hand across her eyes and snatched the silver vinaigrette from Kate's hand, thrusting it in front of her mother's face. 'Say yes, Mama, or I'll go to my room and to hell with Harry Challenor. I hate being treated like a bitch ready for mating.'

'Josephine.' Sir Hector's angry tones rang out as he strode into the room followed by Harry Challenor and the rest of the male guests.

Kate froze to the spot, her gaze fixed on Josie's horrified face. Judging by the looks on the faces of the other ladies, it would take more than a silver tongue to get out of this one.

Lady Damerell rose shakily to her feet. 'Don't blame, Josie, Sir Hector.' She pointed a trembling finger at Kate. 'It's that girl. She's a bad influence on our daughter. I want her sent back to the country immediately.'

'I say, that's a bit harsh.' Harry strode forward. 'I don't know what I've done to offend Miss Damerell but she's not the first young woman to tell me where to go,' he grinned ruefully, 'and I doubt if she'll be the last.'

Sir Hector held up his hand. 'Generous of you, Challenor, but it won't do. Josie, go to your room, and you, girl, go back to the kitchen. Both of you will go to the country tomorrow with Coggins. I won't have such language in my house, Josephine. You will remain in the country if it takes a year or even two, but you will learn manners or you'll remain there forever. By God, you will.'

Chapter Four

Dorset, September 1874

Kate stopped for a moment, setting her willow basket on the ground and leaning over the parapet of the bridge to look down into the fast-running waters of the River Frome. The first signs of autumn were mellowing the Dorset countryside: beech mast tumbling from the trees, hedgerows groaning with blackberries, and clusters of orange berries hanging from the rowans.

It was almost ten months since Josie's fall from grace, and she was still in virtual exile. She had refused to apologise to Harry Challenor for her behaviour at the fateful dinner party, and as a consequence had missed the London season. What was even worse, Kate had been forbidden to associate with her, but if Sir Hector thought that this would prevent them from keeping each other company he would have been disappointed to learn that it had had the opposite effect.

Josie was under strict instructions not to mix with anyone from the village, but she had declared from the outset that rules were made to be broken, and she was a frequent visitor at the farmhouse where Kate now lived with her father, Sam and Molly. Robert had somewhat reluctantly agreed to take over the tenancy of the home farm, but to Kate's relief it seemed to have been the making of him. Back in the house where he had been born, he was a new man, and his heavy drinking was a thing of the past.

Kate worked long hours but she had no desire to return to the miserable mews in London and the dire living conditions above the stables. She was content, but she worried constantly about Josie. Her banishment had only served to make her more rebellious and had encouraged her wild ways. She often came to the farm in order to escape from the strict regime instigated by her chaperone, Mrs Wardle, whom she described as a prison warder sent from hell to try to make her behave like a lady. Lady Damerell, no doubt influenced by the indomitable Hickson, had employed Mrs Wardle, a widow of good birth but reduced circumstances, to give her wayward daughter lessons in etiquette, deportment and the social graces that would stand her in good stead in the next London season. Infuriated and determined to get her own way, Josie had delighted in making her chaperone's life as difficult as possible. Instead of behaving like a well-bred young lady, she took every opportunity to roam around the countryside on Sheba, her bay mare, with Kate following more slowly on an aged pony that Josie had long since outgrown.

Josie loved nothing better than to gallop across the fields, urging her steed to take fences and hedgerows like a steeplechaser, while Kate's mount trotted sedately or at most broke into a canter. Sometimes, if Kate was too busy, Josie persuaded Sam to leave whatever he was doing on the farm and accompany her on one of her escapades. The fact that he did so willingly was also a cause for concern. Kate was painfully aware that Sam's childish devotion to Josie had matured into something deeper, and she feared for him. Josie would take his heart and, if it suited her, she would break it without giving him a second thought.

But despite all this, it had been an almost perfect summer. Kate plucked a dandelion head and tossed it into the water, watching it bob about and float downstream, a tiny golden boat heading for the open sea. Life, she thought, was good. The sun was pleasantly warm on her back and winter seemed far away. She turned her head at the sound of an approaching horse-drawn vehicle.

'Good morning, Miss Coggins.' Squire Westwood drew his horse to a halt, tipping his top hat and smiling.

'Good morning, Squire.' Kate bobbed a curtsey.

'Are you on your way to market, Miss Coggins?'

'I am, sir.'

Edmund Westwood steadied his horse with a light touch on the reins. 'I'm going there myself. I could take you the rest of the way, if you so wished.'

Kate hesitated. It was little more than a mile to the market place in Dorchester and she was used to walking. Tongues would wag if she were seen driving with the squire. She knew that she ought to refuse politely and continue on her way, but she could not resist the temptation to arrive in style. She smiled up at him. 'That's very kind of you, sir.'

He leapt down from the driver's seat, issuing a

command to stay to his two black Labradors who were preparing to spring out of the dog cart, their tails wagging and their pink tongues lolling out of their mouths as if they were grinning. The dogs obeyed him instantly. 'If only my two daughters were so well behaved,' he said smiling as he picked up Kate's basket and tossed it in the back of the cart. He handed her onto the seat and climbed up beside her. 'My girls miss a mother's guidance, the poor darlings.' He flicked the whip so that the horse moved forward at a spanking trot.

Kate was well aware that the squire had been a widower for many years, but such a frank confession from a man in his exalted position was embarrassing, and she did not know quite how to respond. 'I'm sorry,' she murmured, clutching the side rail of the vehicle as it tooled along the lane, its swaying motion causing her to slide too close to him for comfort. She held on for dear life as he encouraged his horse to go even faster. She suspected that he was trying to impress her, and she was beginning to regret her impulsive decision to accompany him into town. She shot him a sideways glance, and was relieved to see that he was concentrating on the road ahead. He was a large, undeniably handsome man, with craggy features and a leonine mane of auburn hair, but he was twice her age and almost as far removed from her station in life as Sir Hector Damerell. He seemed to sense that she was staring at him and he turned his head to give her a beaming smile. 'Miss Coggins, I have a confession to make.'

'A confession, sir?'

'I came this way in the hope of meeting you.' He was silent for a moment, concentrating on his driving as they met a farm cart lumbering towards them from the opposite direction. Farmer Coker tipped his cap at the squire, but his expression changed to one of frank curiosity when he glanced at Kate. He nodded his head to her as the two vehicles squeezed past each other. She could imagine him telling his wife that he had seen Robert Coggins' little maid sitting up beside the squire as bold as you like.

'It will be all round the county now,' she said, chuckling. 'Kate Coggins was seen out driving with Squire Westwood.'

'They will have to get accustomed to it, if you accept my offer.'

'Squire?' She stared at him in surprise and suddenly it was no laughing matter. There was only one sort of proposition a man in his position might offer a girl from her walk of life, and if the dog cart had not been travelling at such a speed she might have leapt to the comparative safety of the grass verge. She sat bolt upright, hardly daring to breathe.

'I'll come straight to the point, Miss Coggins. My daughters have reached an age when they are no longer children but are not yet young women. Without a mother's guidance they are running wild. Miss Morton has been an excellent governess, but she will be leaving soon to take up another position with a younger family, and my girls need a companion who is close enough to them in years to understand their wants and needs. I think you would be exactly the right person.'

Relief swept over her in a tidal wave. 'You are offering me a position in your household, Squire Westwood?'

'That's about it, Miss Coggins. If you accept my offer I would pay you a good wage for your services and you would live as one of the family.'

'Live in, sir? Oh, no. I mean, I thank you very much for considering me, but I might be returning to London with Miss Damerell in the very near future.' This was not exactly true, but it gave her a valid excuse for refusing his offer.

'I don't wish to offend you, but it is well known that you act as unpaid housekeeper for your father, and that you work in the dairy and on the farm as well. It's no life for a young woman who had the benefit of being educated at Damerell Manor.'

'I was extremely fortunate, and for that reason I must remain loyal to the Damerells who have done so much for me. I must also help my father while I can. He needs me.'

They had reached the market place and Edmund guided his horse to a shady spot beneath a horse chestnut tree. 'Whoa, there.' The wheels of the dog cart crunched on the crisp fallen leaves as the vehicle came to a halt. He turned to Kate and his expression was serious. 'Your father is still a relatively young man, Kate. May I call you that?' Without waiting for an answer he took her hand in his. 'One day he might take another wife, and you will find yourself a stranger in your own home.'

The pressure of his fingers and the intense look in his piercing blue eyes both scared and angered her. She snatched her hand away. 'My father has no such intentions, Squire Westwood. He loved my mother dearly and he would never look at another woman.'

'My dear girl, your mother has been dead for many years. A man needs a companion and a helpmate in life, and one day, in the not so distant future, you will find a husband.'

He had gone too far now and she was angry. 'Thank you, sir. I appreciate your concern, but it really is none of your business.' She scrambled down from the cart, reaching in the back for her basket. The dogs licked her hand and raised themselves, looking at her expectantly, but she was too upset to make a fuss of them. She backed away towards the bustling centre of the market place. 'Thank you, Squire. But now I have business in the market. Good day.'

'I did not mean to upset you, Kate. Won't you at least give my offer some consideration?'

'I've given you my answer. I won't change my mind.' She quickened her pace, glancing over her shoulder to make sure that he was not following her, and was relieved to see that his attention had been claimed by one of his tenants. Her thoughts and emotions were in turmoil as she made her way between the market stalls, automatically nodding and smiling in acknowledgement of the many familiar faces that greeted her. Squire Westwood's words had disturbed her more than she cared to admit. It might be due to her vivid imagination, but she had sensed an underlying motive in his sudden desire to have her living in his house. There were plenty of middle-aged widows with limited means who would have filled the position much more ably than she. The squire had deliberately placed ideas in her head that would never have come naturally. It had never crossed her mind that Pa might remarry, or that their way of life would change now that he was settled on the farm. During the past few months she had not minded how hard she worked in the house, and in the dairy where she made butter and cheese. She had tended the chickens, collected their eggs and taken them to market, accepting her new way of life without complaint. Whether she would be called upon to act as lady's maid to Josie and return with her to London was a matter for conjecture, but she doubted if it would happen. Josie would almost certainly marry well, and her promise of eternal friendship would be forgotten when she embarked on her new life.

Until now Kate had never questioned her lot, but the squire's offer of employment had made her stop and think. It was true that she had received an education well beyond her station in life, but there was always someone waiting to remind her that she came from humble beginnings. Josie might treat her as an equal when it suited her, but her moods were capricious and Kate was ever conscious of the difference between them.

She quickened her pace. Dawdling in the sunshine and worrying about what might never happen was a waste of time. The reason she had come to market in the first place was to purchase the ribbons and lace she needed to embellish a cast-off gown of Josie's which she intended to wear at the harvest supper. She made her way through the press of country folk. The sturdy women proudly sported their best cotton-print frocks, starched white aprons and sun bonnets, and their husbands were dressed for practicality in coarse linen smocks, boots and gaiters. This was the day when people from the outlying villages got together to buy and sell, and also to chat and exchange gossip. The market place was filled with the sound of cattle lowing, the bleating of sheep and the occasional grunt from pigs snuffling at the straw in their pens. The stall holders had to shout even louder to advertise their wares, but Kate was not interested in buying fruit and vegetables, pots and pans or willow-pattern china. She had come with a single purpose and she went straight to the stall that sold ribbons, lace, pins and needles, coloured silks and spools of cotton. She had just paid for her purchases when a voice at her elbow made her jump.

'Good morning, Kate.'

'Sam, you startled me.'

He dragged off his wide-brimmed felt hat and brushed back a lock of dark, curly hair, eyeing her with a teasing smile. 'You was so intent on them snippets of ribbon and lace, you wouldn't have noticed if a brigade of soldiers had marched up behind you.'

She could not help smiling. It was hard to be cross

with Sam for any length of time. He had been her friend and playfellow during her visits to her grandparents' farm for as long as she could remember. It was more than fifteen years ago that her grandfather had found Sam and his sister tied to a cattle pen and abandoned. Sam had been six years old then, and his sister Molly little more than a babe in arms. Gradually and with much coaxing, Sam had been able to tell Grandpa Coggins that his father, a journeyman carpenter who travelled the countryside looking for work, could no longer care for him and his sister after the untimely death of their mother. He had left them in the market place in the hope that some kind soul would do exactly what Ezra Coggins had done.

Sam, she thought fondly, had grown into a fine-looking fellow, all muscle and bone with the wickedest twinkle in his eyes that were such a deep shade of blue that they sometimes looked black. His smile could charm the birds from the trees, of which he was very well aware, and he was a dreadful tease. He gave her bonnet strings a playful tug. 'What's the matter, Kate? Cat got your tongue?'

'Never mind me. What are you doing here? Pa didn't say he was sending any animals to market.'

'There was a small matter of some hens' eggs. Someone, mentioning no names, forgot all about them in her hurry to buy folderols and frippery to make herself pretty for the harvest supper.'

Kate frowned. It was true. In her haste to get to market she had forgotten all about the wretched eggs. 'You could have reminded me, Sam.'

'You was off like an arrow from a bow this morning. I thought I'd catch up with you on the highway, but you must have had winged feet for I never saw you on the road.'

'Squire Westwood offered me a lift in his dog cart, if you must know. But seriously, did you or did you not bring the eggs to market?'

He jingled a leather purse in front of her eyes. 'Biddy Madge took the lot for her stall. Said as how there'd been folk clamouring for eggs all morning. What say you to a tankard of cider in the King's Arms afore we sets off home?'

'I'd say you are a bad influence, Sam. Pa would kill me if I were to set foot in a public house, and you are supposed to be working.' She tempered her words with a smile. 'You may drive me home though.'

'Thank you, my lady. First off it was dancing with Squire Westwood last Christmas in the village hall, and now he has you sitting up beside him in his dog cart. It's enough to give any girl airs and graces.' Sam placed his hand on his hip and tossed his head in a fair imitation of a flighty female.

'Hold your tongue, you cheeky monster.' Kate gave him a gentle shove, but she could not help laughing at his antics.

He rammed his hat on his head and proffered his arm. 'It would be a pleasure to escort you home, Miss Coggins. But there is a condition.'

'Which is?'

'That you promise me the first dance at the harvest supper.'

'You drive a hard bargain, Mr Loveday, but you have my word on it.'

'And I promise not to tell Pa Coggins that you forgot to take the eggs to market.' He handed her the leather pouch. 'You'd best keep this. With a bit of luck the gaffer won't notice that I'm not off ploughing the ten-acre field, which is where I was supposed to be this morning.'

Kate linked her hand through his arm. 'Then we'd best get home as quickly as possible.' She glanced over her shoulder, just in case the squire should have followed her, but he was nowhere to be seen. Perhaps she had misread his intentions after all.

Kate's bedroom was situated at the back of the house, overlooking the orchard. It was large and airy with a beamed ceiling, whitewashed walls and chintz curtains. In winter it was warm and cosy beneath the thatched roof. In spring the birds warbled from their nests beneath the eaves, and the scent of the apple blossom wafted in through the open window. In summer her room was deliciously cool, and now, in autumn, she could look out at the trees heavy with ripening fruit and the grass beneath them studded with rosy wind-falls. She closed her window as the evening breeze freshened. Taking a last look in the mirror, she was more than pleased with the result of her labours. The deceptively simple blue silk gown fitted her slim figure perfectly; the addition of lace and ribbon had made it feel as though it was her own and not a hand-me-down from Josie. The low neckline, puffed sleeves, nipped-in waist and full skirt with a bustle at the back were the very latest fashion, or at least they were the latest fashion in this part of Dorset, which was probably two or even three years behind society in London, but Kate did not care – she felt like a princess. She went downstairs to the kitchen where Molly was busy sweeping the floor with a besom.

'Why, Kate. You look beautiful.' Molly's eyes misted with tears and her lips trembled. 'I ain't never see'd a dress like that in all me born days.'

Kate did a twirl, almost bumping into her father who had come downstairs behind her. 'What do you think, Pa? Do you like my gown?'

'You look good enough to eat, love.' Robert raised his chin, tugging at his cravat. 'Now if only I could tie this confounded thing, I'd be a happy man.'

'You are so impatient, Pa.' Kate pushed his hand away and deftly knotted the material, arranging its folds beneath the stiff points of her father's shirt collar. He was very red in the face and perspiring heavily. She kissed him on the cheek. 'There, now don't you look handsome? We are going to be the envy of everyone there tonight.'

'I wish I was coming too,' Molly said, sighing heavily.

Kate pulled on her lace mittens. 'There's no reason why you can't. Is there, Pa? You don't mind if Molly has a few hours off to join in the fun? Sam could take her.'

Robert shrugged on his jacket. 'I've no objection, so long as she don't touch anything alcoholic and behaves herself. I won't have us being shown up. So you bear that in mind, young Molly.'

'Wash your hands and face,' Kate said, shooing Molly out into the yard. 'You can borrow my pink and white dimity, but don't you dare spill anything down the front of it. And make sure Sam brings you home early. Pa and I are going to walk up to the big house now, and you can follow on when you're ready.'

As they walked arm in arm through the farmyard and down the narrow lane towards Damerell Manor, Robert patted her hand. 'You look like a proper young lady all dressed up, Kate. You ought to be riding in a fine carriage and not walking with your old pa. You'll like as not ruin those pretty dancing slippers.'

She smiled up at him. 'It's only a harvest supper, Pa. We won't be going into the big house, just one of the barns. It will all be done up nicely, of course, but we're not exactly hobnobbing with the gentry.'

'I wouldn't say that. The squire will be there for certain, and the parson. Maybe Sir Hector and Lady Damerell will join in the celebration later.'

'And maybe they won't.' Kate looked up at the darkening sky. The sun had set, leaving a trail of flame-tipped clouds floating on a turquoise sky, misting to purple at the horizon. 'It's going to be a lovely night, Pa.'

The hay barn had been made ready for the harvest supper. Festoons of greenery were draped from the rafters and the fiddlers were tuning up their instruments ready to entertain the revellers. Trestle tables had been laid with white cloths and decorated with swags of ivy. The air was redolent with the mouth-watering fragrance of pork pies, fruit tarts and apple cakes. A silver punchbowl on loan from the big house was brimming with cider cup, and judging by the rising tide of laughter and the buzz of conversation, some of the early arrivals had already been sampling it. The twanging of the fiddle strings competed with the sound of the harmonium as the parson's daughter, Emmeline, warmed up by practising scales.

'Can I get you a cup of punch, Kate?' Robert had to raise his voice to make himself heard.

She nodded her head. 'Thank you, Pa.'

He left her side and strolled off towards the table where a crowd of men had gathered around the punch-bowl. She was about to make her way over to speak to Parson Daleymount and his wife when she was accosted by the squire's housekeeper, Miss Stamp, whose overly plump body was tightly corseted into a scarlet taffeta gown. 'My dear Miss Coggins. How lovely you look.'

'Thank you, ma'am.' Kate glanced over Miss Stamp's shoulder, wondering if the squire had arrived. She could see his two daughters, Amy and Letitia, but there was no sign of him.

'If you're looking for the squire, he will be along later.' Miss Stamp gave her an arch look. 'I believe that he has offered you a position in our household?'

'I have no intention of leaving home, ma'am.'

'But you will one day, my dear. You will marry and have a home of your own.'

74

Before Kate could reply, Robert came up to them holding two punch cups. 'Good evening, Miss Stamp.'

'My, aren't we formal this evening, Robert? It was Honoria when we last met.'

Kate was quick to notice that Miss Stamp's plump cheeks had flushed rose-red, which clashed rather badly with her gown, and she was fluttering her pale eyelashes at Pa in a quite ridiculous manner. It might have been attractive in a young woman, but Miss Stamp was a spinster well past the first flush of youth.

Robert cleared his throat noisily, staring down at his hands as if trying to decide what to do with the glass cups. 'Will you take a glass of punch, Honoria?'

'Thank you, Robert. That would be delightful.' She flashed him a coy smile as she accepted the drink.

He offered the other cup to Kate, but she had had enough of watching Miss Honoria Stamp attempting to flirt with her father. She shook her head. 'No, thank you, Pa. I really ought to circulate.'

Honoria laid her gloved hand on Robert's arm. 'That leaves just you and me, Robert. Shall we sit together at supper?'

Kate moved away, intending to greet Parson Daleymount and his mousy little wife, but there were so many people who claimed her attention that she was only halfway across the barn floor when Sam and Molly caught up with her. Molly held out the striped skirts of the dimity dress and she did a little dance. 'See how it fits me, Kate. But I had to stuff some kerchiefs up here.' She patted her chest.

'That ain't no way to talk,' Sam said firmly. 'If you don't behave proper I'll send you over to play with the youngsters.' He pointed to the end of the barn where the younger children sat on bales of hay, swinging their legs and giggling as they waited for the signal to begin supper.

Molly scowled up at him, pouting. 'You are so mean to me, Sam.'

'You look very pretty,' Kate said hastily. 'Look over there – Farmer Cobb's daughter, Sal, is waving her arms like a windmill. I think she wants to talk to you.'

Molly tossed her head. 'At least someone wants my company.' She flounced off, swishing her skirts.

'She's getting to be a real handful,' Sam said, watching her with a frown creasing his brow.

'She misses having a mother's guidance. She just needs a firm hand.'

Sam chuckled, his eyes straying to Honoria who had Robert by the hand and was leading him towards the rapidly filling tables. 'And she'll get more than a firm hand if Miss Honoria Stamp has her way.'

Kate stared at him in horror. 'What do you mean by that?'

'You don't listen to enough gossip, my girl. It's all over the village that Miss Stamp has set her cap at your father. Has been so ever since Shrovetide when we all went to watch the skimmity ride in Melbury, and again at the last 'un, not so long ago.'

'You're making it up to vex me, Sam. You know I don't hold with that barbaric custom.'

'Maybe not, but it's a pity you missed the fun all the same.'

'Don't tell me any more.' Kate covered her ears, walking away from him.

Sam followed her and pulled her hands away, his eyes alight with mischief. 'Oh, but you was fine about watching the Ooser at the May Day celebrations. It was there again at the skimmity ride a month or so ago. Do you want to know what they did to the cuckolded husband and his unfaithful missis?'

'No, I don't. Nor do I want to hear any gossip about my pa.'

'Well, he and Miss Stamp was enjoying themselves to the full, I can tell you. When the poor unfortunate fellow was made to put on the Ooser mask and stand outside his house watching his erring wife being beaten through the streets, your pa and Miss Honoria was shouting and laughing and banging saucepan lids together with the rest of the village folk. Then I saw them sneak away together hand in hand, and I doubt if they was aiming to play pat-a-cake.'

'I don't believe it, Sam. She can't be a day younger than thirty-five. My pa would never be interested in a dried up old prune like Miss Stamp, let alone do anything so improper.'

Sam winked and tapped the side of his nose. 'You see what happens when you're not there to keep an eye on the old man?'

'I was with Josie at the big house, but I thought Pa had stayed at home.' Kate stared across the crowded room to where her father and Miss Stamp were now sitting side by side at one of the long tables. It was not possible. Pa would simply not be interested in someone like Honoria Stamp. She bit her lip as she remembered Squire Westwood's suggestion that her father might one day take himself another wife. It must be a coincidence. Surely she could not be the last person to know that there was something going on between them?

'I was only teasing you, Kate.' Sam slipped his arm around her shoulders. 'Don't get all upset. Your pa is just enjoying a bit of female company. You wouldn't begrudge him that, now would you?'

I would, Kate thought angrily, if that female was a mean old woman like Miss Stamp. Perhaps she put the idea of employing me in the squire's head just to get me out of the way. Visions of Pa and Miss Stamp walking down the aisle together, living in the farmhouse, sleeping in the bed where her mother had given birth to her, was a waking nightmare. She disliked Honoria, and she was certain that the feeling was mutual.

'Come.' Sam held out his hand. 'Wake up, Kate. You were miles away. Cheer up and forget about old sourpuss. Let's dance.'

She knew he was right. She was probably making far too much of a mere dalliance. She went onto the floor with Sam and threw herself heart and soul into the country dance. When the music stopped, Sam went to get her a glass of lemonade, and she was sitting on a bale of hay fanning herself when she saw the squire coming towards her. There was no escape, unless she were to leap over the bales and join the rowdy young children in their game of blind man's buff; she had to sit there and wait for him to claim her for the next dance. Luckily, there was very little time to talk as they executed the set figures, and when he led her back to her seat Sam was there waiting for her with a glass of lemonade.

'Will you honour me with another dance later, Miss Coggins?'

'Thank you, Squire Westwood; that would be very pleasant.' Kate sat down, fanning herself vigorously as she accepted the drink from Sam.

'He has his eye on you, Kate.' Sam folded his arms across his chest, glowering at the squire's back as he walked away.

'Don't be silly. Of course he hasn't.'

Sam turned to her, his eyes blazing. 'A man like him don't make eyes at a farmer's daughter with any good intent. I tell you, Kate, he's up to no good and I've a good mind to go over there now and have it out with him.'

Chapter Five

Kate sipped the cool, sweet drink. She was not going to admit her fears to Sam who was as protective as any elder brother, and might do or say something that would get him into trouble. The squire was a justice of the peace and not the sort of man to cross. She put the glass down and rose to her feet. 'They're playing "Grimstock". Shall we do this one, Sam?'

His scowl dissolved into a smile. 'I suppose I'd better keep you company, if only to keep the squire at bay.'

As they joined the other couples in the dance, Kate saw to her dismay that her father had led Miss Stamp onto the floor. Somehow, she managed to keep smiling, even when the steps brought them face to face. Honoria, she thought, looked horribly smug – and her neckline was much too low for a woman of her age. The saying 'mutton dressed as lamb' came forcibly to mind. That's what Josie would have said anyway. Kate glanced over Sam's shoulder as they whirled around in time to the music. It was unusual for Josie to miss the fun. 'I wonder where she is,' she murmured, speaking her thoughts out loud.

Sam missed a step, staring at her with a puzzled frown. 'Who's that?'

'Josie, of course. I thought she would be here by now.'

He pulled a face. 'I was going to tell you but I forgot. I saw Sir Hector arriving at the Manor earlier today, with a couple of carriages following on behind. It looks as if the Damerells are having a house party. I expect Josie's got to stay at home and try to behave like a lady.' He grinned. 'That won't suit her one bit.'

'Oh, heavens. Why didn't you tell me that before? I've been waiting for her all evening.'

'It's not over yet. Maybe she'll turn up. You know Josie.'

Kate sighed. 'Indeed I do.' Unpredictable, unreliable and totally unrepentant for any upsets that she caused was the way in which Josie whirled through life like a dancing dervish. They were exact opposites in looks, character and upbringing, but there was an invisible silken cord that seemed to bind them together, and Kate had an uneasy feeling in the pit of her stomach that something was wrong.

'Don't look so worried, maidy,' Sam said as the dance ended to a round of vigorous applause. 'She'll turn up like the proverbial bad penny. Let's get a drink; I'm parched.'

'Yes, so am I.' Kate slipped her hand into his and they strolled over to the trestle table laid out with the punchbowl and flagons of cider. She sipped a cooling glass of fruit cup while Sam drained a mug of farm-house cider in several thirsty gulps. The band had struck up again and couples had thrown themselves heart and soul into a lively jig when suddenly the barn doors were flung open. There was a sudden hush as the musicians stopped playing and the dancers froze to the spot. Sir Hector entered with his wife on his arm, followed by a glittering entourage. A gasp of admiration rippled round the barn.

Kate could hardly believe her eyes when Josie, resplendent in shimmering ivory satin with ropes of pearls around her neck and pearl drops hanging from her earlobes, swanned in on the arm of Harry Challenor. If she had arrived hand in hand with a royal prince, Kate could not have been more astonished. Behind them were two more couples who were strangers to her, with Mrs Wardle dressed in her customary widow's weeds bringing up the rear. She had a smug smile on her face which made Kate cringe inwardly. What, she wondered, had they done to Josie to make her comply with her parents' wishes? She could not wait to find out.

Sir Hector paused, holding up his hand. 'Good evening, everyone. Please continue with the festivities.'

Parson Daleymount rushed over to him, followed by his prim little wife. 'How kind of you to grace our harvest supper, Sir Hector. May I offer you some refreshment?'

Sir Hector shook his head. 'Thank you, no. We've just dined, but I'm sure the younger members of our party would like to dance.' He shot a stern look at Josie who smiled up at Harry Challenor and laid her hand on his arm.

'Play "Sir Roger de Coverley",' Josie said with an imperious wave of her hand.

There was a subdued murmur from the band, and

when the fiddler, who was both conductor and leader of the quartet, started off the music the others were quick to join in. Harry led Josie into the centre of the floor and the other couples obligingly followed suit.

'Blow me tight,' Sam muttered. 'Who's that toff, Kate? D'you know him?'

'Yes, as a matter of fact I do. It's Harry Challenor, and I thought she hated him.'

'It don't look like it.' Sam thumped the mug back on the table. 'Come on, Kate. We'll show 'em we ain't got straw growing out of our ears.' He grabbed her by the hand and before she had a chance to argue she found herself next to Josie standing in line opposite their partners.

'What's going on?' Kate whispered.

Josie tossed her head. 'A girl can change her mind.'

'But I thought you couldn't stand the sight of him.'

'None of your business.' Josie launched herself into the dance with a fixed smile on her face.

They had executed several turns before Kate had a chance to speak to her again. 'Why is he here? And why are you flirting with him?'

Josie's smile wavered for a second and her dark eyes flashed angrily. 'Shut up, Kate. Mind your own business.'

The music ended and the couples went their separate ways. The villagers were automatically consigned to the end of the barn where the children sat on the bales of hay keeping as close to the food as possible. The party from the big house clustered together, taking seats vacated by the more elderly of the village folk.

Parson Daleymount took the floor, intoning a prayer of thanks for a bountiful harvest, followed by grace and an invitation to the company to partake of the supper which had been set out on the trestle tables. There was a sudden rush for the food. A small mountain of pork pies, together with plates of brawn, glistening with jelly and garnished with handfuls of parsley sat side by side with harvest loaves, shaped like stooks of corn. A wheel of Cheddar cheese and another of Blue Vinney were soon attacked and consumed with pickled onions and a variety of chutneys. Apple cake, seed cake and bowls of frumenty tempted those with a sweet tooth and all was washed down with cider, ale and fruit cup. Sir Hector had a crate of champagne sent down from the big house, but that was reserved for his guests and sipped from cut-crystal glasses.

Kate saw with some consternation that Josie was imbibing rather too freely; her cheeks were flushed, her eyes over-bright and her laughter a little too loud. The other ladies in the party sat with their hands folded in their laps, eyeing the frolics of the locals as if watching wild animals at the zoo. She turned with a start as Sam nudged her gently. 'Look at Josie. She's making a spectacle of herself. I can see the gossips with their heads together. She'll become a laughing stock if she ain't careful.'

'She's just enjoying herself.' Loyal to the last, Kate could not bring herself to agree with him even if in her heart she knew he was right. 'Why don't you ask the band to strike up another tune, Sam? What about "The Barley Mow"? That always goes down well.'

Somewhat reluctantly, Sam went over to the musicians and after a few words and much nodding of heads they struck up again. Kate was watching Sam warily, half afraid that he would march up to Josie and give her a piece of his mind. She only became aware that someone was standing at her elbow when he cleared his throat.

'Miss Nobody. I thought it was you but I couldn't be sure. You look quite different out of that hideous uniform.'

She turned with a start and felt the blood rushing to her cheeks as she met Harry's smiling gaze. She bobbed a curtsey. 'I didn't see you there, sir.'

'No, your attention was fixed on that angry-looking young man. Is he your intended by any chance?'

She might have laughed if she had not been so embarrassed. 'Sam is like a brother to me. Not that it's any business of yours, Mr Challenor. I suggest you return to your party, sir. They're looking daggers at you.'

He inclined his head. 'So you can speak for yourself. I thought you were too well trained to answer back.'

She was angry now. It was obvious that he was amusing himself at her expense, and everyone was looking at them. She would never live it down. 'Go away, please,' she said in a low voice. 'You shouldn't be seen speaking to me.'

'I was going to ask you for this dance.'

'Are you mad?' The words spilled from her lips before she could stop herself. 'Gentlemen do not associate with village girls.'

'But I'm not a gentleman,' he said, chuckling. 'I am in trade. The landed gentry look down on men like me.'

'Please go away. Everyone is looking at us, and I'm in enough trouble with the Damerells as it is. I don't want to make things worse for Josie.'

'I'm sorry if I embarrassed you, Miss Nobody.'

'Stop calling me that silly name and leave me alone.' Her patience was almost at an end.

Harry inclined his head. 'I didn't mean to offend you.' He strolled off to rejoin his party.

Sam threaded his way through the dancers, arriving at Kate's side with an expression on his face that would have made a thundercloud look benevolent. 'What's he been saying to you?'

She shook her head. 'I really don't know what that was all about. He asked me to dance and I refused. Then he apologised and walked away. That was all.'

Sam fisted his hands. 'Men like him and the squire all think that village girls are there for their own amusement. He'd better not bother you again.'

'Don't be ridiculous. It wasn't like that at all.'

'You'd better tell that to your pa. He's glaring at you with a look on his face that means trouble.'

Kate turned her head and saw her father about to rise to his feet despite Miss Stamp's obvious entreaties for him to remain at her side. Kate slipped her hand through the crook of Sam's arm. 'Let's dance. Perhaps that woman can take his mind off what he thinks he just saw.'

Somewhat reluctantly Sam led her into the midst of

the swirling couples who were performing a lively polka, but when the music stopped it was not Robert who came storming towards Kate, but Josie. She was swaying on her feet and obviously more than a little drunk.

'Keep your hands off Challenor,' she hissed, grabbing Kate by the arm. 'I've changed my mind and I'm going to marry him. It's the only way I'll ever get away from this damned village.'

'Josie. You don't know what you're saying.' Kate pulled free from her grasp, causing Josie to stumble. She would have fallen if Sam had not stepped in and steadied her.

'You're drunk,' he said angrily. 'You're making a show of yourself, Josie.'

Regaining her balance, she drew herself up to her full height and slapped him across the face. 'Don't touch me, you peasant.'

'Josephine.' Sir Hector's stentorian tones rang out amongst the rafters and once again there was silence.

Josie flexed her fingers, eyeing her father with a rebellious tilt of her chin. 'I want to dance.' She signalled to the musicians. 'I want to waltz. Harry, dance with me.'

He stepped forward, proffering his arm. 'Perhaps a breath of fresh air might be more beneficial, Josie. Shall we go for a walk?'

'Yes. Capital idea. Take her home, my boy.' Sir Hector nodded with approval. 'Come, my dear,' he said, taking his wife's hand. 'I think it's time for all of us to go and leave these good people to enjoy the rest of the evening.' He acknowledged Parson Daleymount with a nod of his head. 'Good evening, parson. Splendid effort.' With his wife on his arm he followed Harry and Josie outside, with the rest of the party following at a more leisurely pace.

'I think I'd like to go home too.' Kate made a move to go but Sam caught her by the hand.

'No. Not yet. If you leave now everyone will think you're to blame in some way. We'll stay on and dance. It was them from the big house that caused the ruckus, and not you, Kate.'

Molly had abandoned the young man who partnered her in the polka and she came hurrying towards them. 'Who was that man, Kate? Why didn't you dance with him?'

'It's a long story,' Kate said tiredly. 'I'll tell you all about it on the way home.'

'Your pa's coming,' Sam said urgently. 'He's given the Stamp woman the slip for a moment and he don't look too happy. Dance with me, Kate, and then we'll head for home. It'll all be forgotten in the morning.'

Kate was in the dairy churning butter when she heard a familiar voice calling her name. She looked up, frowning. Whatever Josie had to say it had better start with an apology for her behaviour last evening. Kate had endured a long lecture from her father on the way home from the harvest supper, and Sam had been in a bad mood ever since.

Josie hurried towards her, holding out her hands.

'Sorry, sorry, sorry. I was a vixen from hell last night and I apologise a million times.'

'Well, I'm glad you realise it was none of my doing.' Kate could never be angry with Josie for long and she clasped her hand. 'But I'm sorry that Mr Challenor's behaviour upset you.'

'Let's forget the whole thing.' Josie took the churn handle from Kate. 'It's ages since I did this, but I haven't forgotten how.'

'I thought you were too grand for the likes of us now you've decided to join the smart set.'

'Oh, that! It's amusing to act like one of them, but I'm still the same old Josie.'

'You didn't seem so last night.'

'It's all a charade. They're all pretending to be something they're not. All except Harry, that is.'

'You've changed your mind about him then?'

'Papa invited him and his friends for a shooting party, and much to my surprise I found them quite entertaining and charming, as well as being rich and well connected.' Josie shrugged her shoulders and continued churning. 'I've decided that I'll marry him.'

'Is it official?'

'Not yet. He hasn't proposed, but he will.'

'Are you sure about that?'

Josie's dimples deepened and a mischievous sparkle lit her eyes. 'Papa thinks that Harry wishes to further his position in society by marrying a baronet's daughter and I want to be mistress of Copperstone Castle. It's a fair trade.' She slipped her arm around Kate's shoulders. 'Come now, let's do something together. Harry and his chums have gone out to join the shoot. The girls expressed a desire to see the sea and have gone for a carriage ride, and as I didn't want to accompany them, I've got all day to myself. What better than to spend it with my best friend?'

'I'd love to go with you, but I can't. I must finish making the butter and then I've got to collect the eggs.'

'All right, then. You finish making the butter and I'll see to the eggs.'

'You'll get your hands mucky, my lady.'

'It won't be the first time.' Snatching up a wicker basket, Josie posed with it resting on one hip. 'I'd like to see the Honourable Sophronia de Vere and Miss Gwendoline Mortimer doing something like this.'

'I'm sure the hens will appreciate being waited upon by a baronet's daughter,' Kate said, laughing. She continued churning the butter, and glancing through the open door she could see Josie picking her way across the dried mud in the farmyard as she headed for the hen house. She smiled. Last night it seemed that Josie was simply playing a part. It was a huge relief to have her old friend back.

She was patting the butter into a large block when Josie returned with a basketful of eggs.

'Can't you leave that for now? Surely the girl can finish it off for you?'

'Molly has her work in the house. She's got enough to do without taking on my chores.'

'And Sam? Where is he today?'

'Gone beating for your father's shooting party. And my pa has taken the trap and driven over to the

Grange. He said he had business with the squire, but I'm almost certain he went to see the housekeeper.'

'Not the frightful Miss Stamp? Do you think he's courting her?'

'I'm afraid so, but I couldn't stand to live in the same house as that woman.'

'Maybe it won't come to that. Perhaps he just wants a bit of female company.'

'She's set her cap at him. It sticks out a mile.'

'Well, never mind, dear. I've already decided that when I'm married to Harry Challenor and mistress of Copperstone Castle, you shall come and live with us and be my companion. I mean to find you a suitable husband, my girl. One who will keep you in comfort and treat you like the lady you are, and not a dairymaid.'

'Shall I tell you a secret, Josie?'

'I love secrets. What is it?'

'You must promise not to tell a soul. Cross your heart and hope to die.'

'I do. Don't keep me in suspense.'

'Miss Morton is giving up her position as governess to his daughters and the squire has asked me to move into the Grange as paid companion to the girls.'

'And you answered what exactly?'

'I said no, of course. I couldn't leave my pa, but on the other hand, if he marries Honoria, I might just reconsider.'

'And you don't think that the squire might have other plans in mind for you?'

'I'm not stupid, Josie. At first I did think he might

be suggesting something not quite proper, but he's a gentleman and I realise that I was mistaken. I think he genuinely needs someone to keep an eye on his daughters now that they are too old for a governess.'

'Well then, since you refused his offer, there's no need to dwell on it. Let's leave all this and go for a walk. We could gather some blackberries just as we used to do when we were children.'

'And eat them as we picked, turning our lips purple and getting the juice on our clothes.' Kate's laughter trailed off as she looked at Josie's gown. 'But you would spoil your dress, and it must have cost a fortune.'

'It's already muddied and covered in something unspeakable from the hen house, which is a million times worse than berry juice, and I've plenty more gowns at home. Mama has had her dressmaker hard at work all summer in the hopes that I would change my mind, and now I have. I'm back in favour and I can do no wrong, so come along, Kate. I dare you.'

An hour later they had half filled two baskets with ripe berries and had eaten almost as many. As they worked their way steadily along the hedgerows that formed the boundary between Damerell Manor parkland and the home farm, they could hear the distant sound of the beaters in the wood, flushing out the game birds, and the ensuing blast of the shotguns. The carnage of the shoot seemed a million miles away as they waded through a lush meadow spiked with dandelions and daisies. Placid, brown-black Gloucester cows grazed, swishing their white tails and eyeing them benevolently as they headed for the periphery of the recently ploughed ten-acre field. Kate knew that the biggest berries were to be had there, although she had been worried that they were getting perilously close to the guns. Josie told her not to worry about small details like that, and, anyway, she was not about to turn back now when the best fruit was yet to be had. She was smiling as she reached even higher to get the ripest berries from the top of the bramble bush when a gunshot not too far away made them both jump. Judging by the nearness of the sound, they really had strayed too close to the shoot for comfort. Kate was suddenly aware of the beaters thrashing through the undergrowth at the edge of the wood just yards away from them. 'I think we ought to turn back.'

Josie shook her head. 'We're safe enough here. Let's stay and see if Harry is as good a shot as he claims.'

'No, really, Josie. It's too dangerous. We should leave now.'

'Oh, all right then, but we can cut across the field. At least they'll be able to see us and hold their fire.'

Josie dropped her basket and set off, leaving Kate little alternative but to follow her. Despite the blood pounding in her ears she could hear the shooting party getting closer by the second. They were more than halfway across when a loud shout from the lane made Kate stop. She turned to see her father standing in the well of the trap, waving frantically. 'Come away, girls. Come to me.'

'Do as he says, Josie.' Kate grabbed her by the hand

and they raced towards Robert, but his cry of warning had also alerted Sir Hector, who was the first of the party to emerge from the wood. He ran into the line of fire gesticulating frantically, but at that moment the pheasants were flushed from the undergrowth with a loud flapping of wings.

'Papa, go back,' Josie screamed at the top of her voice, but her warning was drowned by a fusillade of shots as the party broke cover. Sir Hector fell headlong to the ground.

Chapter Six

There was a deathly hush and everyone seemed to freeze to the spot, even the gun dogs stood still. Josie was the first to move. She tore across the field, stumbling and tripping over her skirts in her haste to reach her father. She threw herself down on her knees beside him, sobbing, 'Papa, speak to me.' She tried to rouse him but he was lying face down and motionless. The back of his tweed jacket was shredded by lead shot and he was bleeding profusely. She attempted to lift his head, but someone was speaking to her, although she could not make sense of the words. Tears were running freely down her cheeks but she brushed them away with an impatient hand. 'Papa, it's me, Josie.' Strong arms lifted her off the ground; she struggled, but she could not break free. 'Let me go. I must help Papa.'

'We will see to him, Josie.' Harry's voice was calm, but firm. He set her on her feet next to Kate. 'Will you take care of her, Miss Coggins?'

'I'm perfectly all right.' Josie took a deep breath in an effort to control the bubble of hysteria that was threatening to overwhelm her. Suddenly she was calm. 'My father needs a doctor urgently. Why are you just standing about doing nothing?'

Harry laid his hand on her arm. 'Someone has gone to fetch the doctor, and the farmer is bringing the trap to the gate. I've sent some of the beaters to fetch a hurdle. Allow Kate to take you home, Josie. There's nothing you can do here.'

'I will not go home. I won't leave my father.'

'Mr Challenor is right, Josie,' Kate said gently. 'Everything possible is being done for Sir Hector, and someone must break the news to Lady Damerell.'

'Stop interfering, Kate. You can run away if you want to, but I'm staying.'

'That was uncalled for,' Harry said sharply. 'Stay if you must, but keep your voice down. You're upsetting your father.'

A low moan from Sir Hector seemed to confirm his words, and Josie bit her lip. Harry was right, of course. This terrible accident was all her fault; it would never have happened if she had not insisted on venturing too near the shoot. She had ignored Kate's warning and her father had risked his life in order to save her. He might die and all because she had wanted to pick the biggest and best blackberries. 'I'm sorry, Kate,' she murmured. 'I didn't mean it.'

'It's all right,' Kate said softly. 'I understand.'

Harry's taut features relaxed into a smile. 'That was well said. And now, if Josie doesn't object, I suggest that Charlie takes you both to the far side of the wood, where we left the shooting brake.' He laid his hand on Josie's arm. 'Will you go now? I promise that we'll take the best possible care of your father.'

Josie glanced at the anxious faces of Harry's friends.

96

Dudley was kneeling down beside her father attempting to staunch the flow of blood with his previously pristine stock. Charlie, pale-faced and trembling, hovered nervously as if he could not wait to get away. In the distance she could see Sam and three of the beaters carrying a hurdle. Kate was at her side. Dear, faithful Kate. Once again Josie was overwhelmed with guilt for the way she had treated those closest to her. She took a deep breath, forcing herself to sound calmer than she was feeling. 'All right. I'll go now and warn them to be ready at the house.'

'And I will ride your horse back to the stables after I've done the milking,' Kate said with an attempt at a smile. 'Hold on to me, Josie.'

'We'll have you home in two shakes of a lamb's tail,' Charlie said with the hint of a stammer. 'I mean . . .'

'Just take them to the brake, old man,' Harry said, patting Charlie on the shoulder. He beckoned to Sam. 'Over here, man. Be quick about it.'

'Come on, Josie.' Kate tugged at her arm. 'There's nothing you can do here.'

As they followed Charlie into the wood, Josie looked over her shoulder, and it was a grim tableau that met her eyes. She knew that she would never forget the sight of Harry and Dudley kneeling beside her father, with crows wheeling silently overhead like harbingers of death. She was choked with rage at the unfairness of it all; at her own inability to do anything more useful than to be the bearer of bad tidings, and the series of misjudgements that had led to what might prove to be a fatal accident. She looked down at her gown and saw that the skirts were stained dark red; she could not tell whether it was blackberry juice or her father's blood, and her knees gave way beneath her.

It was late afternoon when Dr Smith finally entered the drawing room where Josie and her mother had been waiting anxiously for several hours. Lady Damerell rose to her feet. Her face was ashen and her lips trembled. 'Doctor?'

Josie clasped her hands to her breast; she could feel her heart beating a tattoo against her ribs and she felt quite sick. The expression on the doctor's face spoke volumes. He shook his head. 'Sir Hector lives, ma'am. But I cannot be optimistic about the prognosis.'

'I must go to him.' Lady Damerell made a move towards the door but she faltered and would have fallen if Josie had not rushed to her side.

'Sit down, Mama. Let's hear what the doctor has to say.' She helped her mother to a chair. 'You can speak freely, Dr Smith. We would rather be told the truth.'

He cleared his throat, glancing nervously at Lady Damerell. 'I have extracted as much of the shot as was possible, but I fear that some of it is lodged in Sir Hector's spine, and it would be too dangerous to remove it.'

'But he will survive his injuries?' Lady Damerell clutched Josie's hand. 'Tell me that he will.'

He shook his head. 'It is too early to tell, my lady. But Sir Hector is a strong man and we can but hope and pray for his recovery.'

Josie eyed him with growing suspicion. She could tell by his downcast eyes and tone of voice that he was prevaricating. 'There is something else. What is it?'

He cleared his throat and a dull flush stained his pale cheeks. 'There is no easy way to put this, so you will have to forgive me for being blunt, but I fear that Sir Hector will never walk again. The injury to his spinal cord is such that he is paralysed from the waist down. I am so sorry.'

Lady Damerell gave a low moan and covered her face with her hands.

Josie gave him a searching look. 'Are you absolutely certain?'

He nodded. 'I've seen many spinal injuries, although not many from gunshot wounds. They are usually due to a fall whilst hunting, but the outcome is invariably the same. You asked me to speak plainly, Miss Damerell.'

'Is he still in danger?'

'I am afraid so. I've done everything I can for now, but I'll return first thing in the morning.' He opened his medical bag and took out a small medicine bottle. 'Laudanum. I think her ladyship will need something to help her sleep, and maybe you might benefit from a couple of drops yourself, Miss Damerell. You've suffered a terrible shock and you might need something later to calm your nerves.'

'Thank you, doctor, but I am quite calm. When may we see my father?'

'He is heavily sedated. Miss Hickson is watching over him, but I suggest you hire an experienced nurse.'

Lady Damerell lifted her head. She was still deathly pale, but appeared to have regained some of her composure. 'That won't be necessary, Dr Smith. I will supervise his care, and we have more than enough servants to cater for all his needs. I won't have one of those drunken, snuff-taking, common women who call themselves nurses in my home.' She rose from her chair. 'I'll go to him now, if you have no objections.'

'As you wish, ma'am.' Dr Smith bowed as Lady Damerell glided past him with a swish of silk taffeta petticoats.

He looked so tired and crestfallen that Josie felt sorry for him. 'My mother is naturally extremely upset. I'm sure that you would not recommend anyone who was unsuitable for the position.'

'You can send a servant for me if I am needed before the morning,' he said with a ghost of a smile. 'And should Lady Damerell change her mind, I know of a respectable woman from the village who is an excellent nurse.' He closed his medical bag with a decisive snap. 'I am truly sorry to see your father laid low, Miss Damerell.'

Left alone in the room Josie walked slowly to the window, not knowing quite what to do next. She was not needed in the sickroom, and sooner or later she must face her guests, but not just yet. As she leaned her forehead against the cool glass windowpane, she saw Kate riding along the tree-lined avenue towards the house, with Sam following behind in the trap. Her spirits lifted a little; at least she could talk openly about her father's condition to Kate: they had never had any secrets from each other. She was about to move away from the window when she saw Harry strolling down the wide stone steps to the carriage sweep. Kate reined in, drawing Sheba to a halt, and Harry helped her dismount. They appeared to be deep in conversation and Josie raised her hand to tap on the window, but she changed her mind and lowered it again with an exasperated sigh. She did not want Harry to think she was spying on him, but Kate was at fault. She should have taken the horse to the stables. It was not her place to ride up to the front entrance, let alone spend time conversing with one of the house guests, and especially not Harry. Sam was obviously waiting to take her home on the farm cart, so why the delay? What would a man like Harry find to talk about to a servant?

Commonsense battled with anger. Harry was a charmer and Kate was not versed in the art of flirtation. She must have a heart to heart talk with her, warning her about wealthy men who took advantage of innocent maidens. Harry might not be as bad as her uncle Joseph who had a shocking reputation with women both above and below stairs, but Kate was an innocent. She needed protecting from herself. Hurrying from the room, Josie ran down the stairs, through the great entrance hall and came to a halt at the top of the stone steps. She was relieved and almost ridiculously pleased to see that Sam had climbed down from the trap and was standing beside Kate. At least he was showing good sense. She took a deep breath and descended more slowly.

Harry turned at the sound of her footsteps. 'How is Sir Hector?'

'As well as can be expected. Isn't that what doctors always say?'

Sam dragged off his billycock hat. 'I'm truly sorry. Is there anything I can do, Josie?'

Harry turned to her with an amused smile. 'Are you this friendly with everyone on the estate?'

'We grew up together, Sam, Kate and myself,' Josie said hastily. 'He meant no disrespect.'

Harry shrugged his shoulders. 'It's none of my business. This is your home and you must do as you please.'

'I'll try to remember my place in future, miss,' Sam said, glowering.

'We should leave now.' Kate looped the reins over Sheba's head. 'I'll take her to the stables, Miss Josephine.' She headed off without giving Josie a chance to respond.

Sam tipped his hat. 'Good evening to you, miss.'

Josie sent him a warning glance. 'Thank you, Loveday. Hadn't you better go after Kate? I assume that you are here to take her home.'

He held her gaze for a moment and then backed away. 'That was the plan, miss.'

Josie clenched her fists at her side. The insolent look on his face made her want to slap him. He was treading on dangerous ground. Social mores had mattered little when they were younger, but things were different now. It was time that Sam Loveday acknowledged the fact that they could no longer treat each other like equals. She turned to Harry, but he was staring up at the darkening sky. 'It looks like rain. Perhaps I ought

102

to take Miss Coggins home in my curricle. The poor girl has had a bad enough time of it today without getting a soaking.'

'Really, Harry.' Josie's frayed nerves were beginning to get the better of her. 'Kate's a country girl; she won't dissolve in a shower of rain. Loveday will see her safely home.'

'Aye, us country folk are used to getting a good soaking every now and then,' Sam muttered as he sprang nimbly onto the driving seat. He gave Josie a last, long look and then flicked the reins. The horse obediently started off in the direction of the stables.

'That fellow should be taught a few manners,' Harry said, frowning. 'He needs putting in his place, Josie.'

'Yes, and I will be the one to do it, but are you sure that you were just being chivalrous? Kate is a pretty girl and innocent as a newborn lamb where men are concerned.'

'Of course I was, my dear.' Good humour restored, Harry met her anxious gaze with a smile. 'You know that I have eyes only for you.'

Josie bit her lip; she knew that he was teasing her, but she was not in the mood. 'Your reputation as a flirt preceded you, but when you took charge after the accident, I thought I saw another side to your character. Obviously, I was mistaken.'

'I'm too much of a gentleman to contradict a lady.' He held out his hand, palm upwards as large spots of rain began to fall. 'There now, didn't I say it was going to rain? I think I might take your protégée home after all. She may not be as robust as you think she is.'

She watched him striding towards the stables with anger roiling in her belly. If he had dishonourable designs on Kate, then he had better beware. She would not stand by and see her friend's reputation ruined. The rain was falling heavily now and Josie retreated into the house. She had intended to go straight to her room, but with her mother fully occupied, the duties of hostess now fell upon her shoulders. She ought to go into the Chinese Room where she knew their guests were assembled waiting to hear news of Sir Hector's condition, but she did not feel up to the task. Besides which, she hardly knew them. They were Harry's friends and without him there to support her she would feel ill at ease. Why he had felt the need to go chasing off after Kate was a mystery. She clenched her hands into fists and stamped her foot, causing the footman to jump to attention. She turned away from him with a dismissive wave of her hand. Her mouth was dry and her pulses raced. For a moment she could not understand the anger that threatened to consume her, and then she caught sight of her reflection in one of the many mirrors that adorned the walls. The face of a jealous woman stared back at her, and she realised with a sense of shock that it was Kate who had roused such a tumult of emotion in her breast. The idea was so ridiculous that she laughed out loud. One had to be in love in order to suffer the poisonous bite of that emotional serpent. She could not possibly have fallen for Harry. She intended to marry him but love had not come into her scheme, and if she succumbed to such a passion she knew that it would eventually destroy them both.

She had a sudden urgent need to see her father. Never mind Harry and his hangers-on. She had little or nothing in common with the languid beauty, Gwendoline Mortimer, who had not an original thought in her head, or the vivacious red-head, the Honourable Sophronia de Vere. They might be people whom she ought to cultivate if she intended to become mistress of Copperstone Castle, but at this moment she could not have cared less. She hurried up the grand staircase to the bedroom her parents had shared for more than twenty-four years.

She found her mother pacing the floor in a state of great agitation. 'Mama, what's the matter? Is he worse? Shall I send for Dr Smith?'

Marguerite came to a halt, gazing at her with tears running down her thin cheeks. 'He's just the same, my darling. Your poor father has been cut down in his prime. I can't bear to see him like this, and if the worst happened and he were to die . . . what would become of us then?'

Josie put her arm around her mother's shoulders and led her to the window seat. 'You mustn't think like that, Mama. Even if what the doctor said was true and he is partially paralysed, that doesn't mean it's the end.'

Marguerite sank down on the cushions and fished in her pocket for a scrap of lace that served as a hanky. She dabbed ineffectually at her eyes. 'I know that,

Josephine. But you don't understand. If your father were to pass away, we would have to leave here. The estate is entailed on the closest male heir.'

'Uncle Joseph.'

'Exactly. Joseph and Hermione Damerell will take up residence here and we will be evicted.'

'Surely not. He wouldn't be so cruel.'

'Joseph is an ambitious man and he would love to get his hands on your papa's estate.'

'But there's the town house, Mama. We could live quite comfortably in Bedford Square.'

Marguerite gave her a despairing look. 'Haven't you understood a word I've said, Josephine? The entire estate will belong to Joseph.' She broke off on a sob. 'You should have been a boy. I asked for a boy.'

Josie stifled the sudden desire to giggle. 'I'm sorry that you prayed for a son and got me instead. Perhaps I was a changeling.'

'Don't say such things. It's not true. It's absolutely not true. You are mine.'

Josie stared at her in dismay. Perhaps the shock of her father's accident had turned her mind. Mama was delicate at the best of times. She laid her hand on her mother's arm. 'I didn't mean to be flippant, Mama. But there's really no need to get yourself in a state. Papa isn't going to die. I won't let him.'

'You always were a stubborn child.'

'I'm my father's daughter. We're made of strong stuff, you'll see. You and I will nurse him back to health, and if he can't walk again we'll get him one of those Bath chair contraptions. We're Damerells,

Mama. We won't allow something like this to beat us.'

A muffled moan from the bed brought Marguerite to her feet and she rushed to her husband's side. 'Hector, my darling. Are you all right?'

Sir Hector opened his eyes for a few seconds and then closed them again, groaning.

'Laudanum,' Josie said, seizing the bottle that the doctor had left. 'Give him a couple of drops in some water, Mama. It will take the pain away and help him to sleep.'

Marguerite snatched the bottle from her. 'I'm not a child, Josephine. I know what to do. I'll stay with your father, and you must go downstairs and entertain our guests.'

'But Mama, they'll understand that I'm needed here.'

'Listen to me for once and think about what I'm about to say. It's even more important for you to cultivate Mr Challenor now. I want to see you married and your future assured before the year is out.'

'I would like to be mistress of Copperstone Castle, but I'm not sure I want the man who goes with it.'

'Don't you dare make a joke of this, Josephine. Our whole future rests on your shoulders.' Marguerite's fingers trembled as she attempted to take the cork out of the small glass bottle. She brushed Josie's hand away as she attempted to help her. 'Ring the bell for Hickson. I need her now.'

Dismissed from her parents' room, Josie made her way slowly downstairs, bracing herself to join the party. It was one thing setting her sights on being the wife of a rich man, but quite another to be coerced into marrying a man she could never truly love. She crossed the marble-tiled floor, oblivious to the heady scent emanating from jardinières filled with bronze and gold chrysanthemums, and the bowls of flamboyant dahlias placed on pier tables, their gaudy hues reflecting in gilt-framed wall mirrors. The footman had just lit the candles in the glittering chandelier and had hoisted it up to the ceiling where the crystal drops trembled and sent prisms of coloured light dancing on the ivory walls. She paused for a few seconds outside the double doors, glancing around with a shiver of apprehension. All this grandeur and her comfortable, pampered way of life might vanish overnight if her father were to die from his injuries. Her privileged upbringing had left her without the necessary skills to earn her own living. She would be a pauper unless she made a good match. She painted a smile on her face and opened the door.

Next morning, Josie's attempts to see her father were foiled by Hickson, who had taken temporary charge of the sickroom. 'Your mama is sleeping,' Hickson said, folding her arms across her flat chest and barring the door as Josie attempted to push past her. 'She was up all night and now she's completely exhausted, but she made it clear that your father is to be left undisturbed.'

'You can't keep me out of the room,' Josie cried angrily. 'You're not a nurse. I want to see my papa.'

'I want doesn't get,' Hickson said primly. 'You know that very well, Miss Josephine. Now be a good girl and go downstairs. I believe your guests are leaving for London this morning. You must see them off. It's what my lady would want.'

Josie knew this was true, but it did not make it any easier to take orders from Hickson whom she heartily loathed. She could make a fuss, but then that might wake her father and she knew in her heart that Hickson was correct in stating that he needed rest and quiet. She turned on her heel and marched off with her head held erect. She would not let the hateful woman think that she had won.

The visitors had gone. Josie stood on the gravel carriage sweep gazing at the cloud of dust sent up by the horses' hooves and the carriage wheels. Harry had been serious for once and had shown concern for her father's state of health, but he had not given any indication that he would like to see her again. The invitation to stay at Copperstone Castle that her mother had eagerly anticipated had not materialised, and Josie could not help comparing Harry's casual treatment of her with the concern he had shown for Kate the previous evening. She was suddenly desperate to find out what had passed between them. In all probability Harry had simply been amusing himself with a naïve country girl. She must see Kate immediately and make certain that she had not misconstrued his actions. She went back indoors and sent for the chaise.

Half an hour later Josie leapt nimbly from the vehicle, handing the reins to Molly who was in the farmyard feeding the hens 'Where is Kate?'

'In the dairy, miss.' Molly shot her a wary glance. 'If you want Sam, he's taken the cows back to ten-acre field.'

'Why would I want to see your brother? I don't associate with farm labourers.' Picking up her skirts Josie strode across the yard in the direction of the dairy, irritation prickling like a burr. Why would the silly girl think that she wanted to see Sam? Their summer frolic had been a mere diversion. He was a yokel compared to the suave, sophisticated people she had mixed with in London. Both the Lovedays needed to be kept in their place, and she had more than a few words to say to Kate. She entered the dairy and found her cleaning the butter churn. Strands of fair hair had escaped from the mobcap she wore and her cheeks were flushed to a delicate pink. Adding to her annoyance, Josie had to admit that she presented a pretty picture with her milk-maid freshness and her air of innocence. She could imagine that such an image would excite and intrigue a sophisticated man liked Harry Challoner. Kate would present a challenge to such as he, but once conquered her artless charms would soon pall and she would be discarded, broken-hearted and dishonoured.

As if sensing her presence, Kate looked up. 'Josie, what's the matter? Is it Sir Hector? He's not . . .'

'He's not dead, if that's what you were going to say.

110

He might never walk again, but he's still alive, if you call being paralysed from the waist downwards living.'

'Oh, Josie. I'm so sorry. No wonder you look so upset. I would be too if it was my pa.'

'Yes, yes. It's dreadful and I'm desolated, but that's not why I'm angry. I'm furious with you, Kate.'

'With me? What have I done?'

'Don't act the innocent with me. I saw you last night, throwing yourself at Harry.'

Kate paled visibly. 'I don't know what you're talking about.'

'Of course you do. You've been flirting with him. And don't put on that innocent face. You must have done something to fix his interest in you. Why else would he have paid so much attention to you at the harvest supper? And why did he go chasing after you last night, offering to take you home in his curricle? Why would a man like Harry bother about a servant girl like you unless you had given him some encouragement?'

Kate stared at her, eyes wide and her lips trembling. 'How can you even think such a thing? I've only met him on a couple of occasions, and I've barely been civil to him.'

'Are you so gullible, Kate? Harry is used to women falling at his feet. I doubt if any female has ever turned up her pretty little nose at him before. It would be enough to pique him and make him even more determined to win you over.'

'I don't want anything to do with Mr Challenor, and that's the honest truth.'

'Well, you won't get the chance, and neither will I. He's gone now. They all left this morning, and I doubt if I shall ever see any of them again, least of all Harry. You've ruined my life, Kate Coggins. I want you to know that.'

Josie stormed out of the dairy, but Kate ran after her. 'If anyone has ruined your life, it's you. You told me that you only wanted to marry him for his money. You don't even love him.'

'And you don't understand.' Josie snatched the reins from Molly. 'If my father dies we'll lose everything. My uncle Joseph will inherit Damerell Manor and the house in London. My mother and I will be paupers unless I marry well, and it looks as though you've just ruined any chance I had with Harry Challenor. That's why I'm angry, Kate. How could you be so selfish as well as stupid?'

Kate's eyes flashed and her cheeks flushed. 'Don't take your temper out on me. I've done nothing wrong.'

Josie climbed up onto the driver's seat, glaring down at her. 'If my uncle inherits the estate he'll almost certainly put a tenant of his choosing into the farm. Then we'll all be out on the street.'

Chapter Seven

A week later, Kate and Molly were in the orchard picking apples. They had already filled several sacks with windfalls which were destined for the cider press, and now they were concentrating on filling baskets with ripe eating apples, some of which would be stored for the winter and the remainder taken to market. Molly had hitched her skirts up around her thighs and climbed high up into the branches, but Kate was concentrating on the fruit lower down. It was a busy time of the year, harvesting fruit and vegetables, making preserves and laying down stores for the winter, and Kate had had little time to brood over Josie's unfair and unfounded accusations.

She had been hurt and angry, but she had long since grown accustomed to Josie's tantrums, and she was confident that commonsense would prevail in the end. Pampered and spoiled from the cradle onwards, Josie had a habit of flying off like a badly put together firecracker, but she was always very sorry afterwards. And, when all was said and done, poor Josie had witnessed the dreadful accident that had almost killed her father. Kate suspected that she blamed herself for what happened, and to discover that Sir Hector was crippled for life must have been a terrible blow. She felt pity for Josie who must have been consumed with guilt and grief when she flew into such a rage, but even so it still rankled.

With all this on her mind, Kate had curbed her inclination to visit the big house and try to make amends, even though she was eager to have news of Sir Hector's progress. She had instead to rely on gleaning bits of information from Molly whose friend Sal Cobb worked in the Damerells' kitchens and was always ready to spread a juicy bit of gossip. It seemed that Sir Hector was out of danger now, but it had been confirmed that he would never walk again. The servants were sorry for the master, but more than relieved to know that Mr Joseph would not come into his inheritance for a while yet. Molly had said that things were getting back to normal now that the house guests had left, but the nurse that Dr Smith had put in charge of the sickroom was an old besom and expected to be waited upon like one of the gentry. She was even worse than Mrs Wardle, who had been dismissed much to the delight of everyone below stairs. The sooner this one was gone, the better.

Kate had filled several baskets with apples and she stopped, stretching her aching muscles. Molly's bare legs dangled above her as she reached to the topmost branches, sending down a shower of leaves. 'Be careful, Molly. We don't want any more accidents.'

Molly threw an apple at her but it missed by several inches, and Kate shook the tree, causing her to screech with fright.

'That looks like fun. Can anyone join in?'

Kate looked round and saw Josie standing a few yards away. 'I didn't hear you coming.'

'No, you were too busy trying to shake the poor girl from the tree.' Josie bent down to pick up a rosy-red windfall and she took a bite. 'Delicious. Can you spare a basketful? Your apples always taste so much sweeter than the ones in our orchards.'

Kate smiled. She knew that this was tantamount to an apology and the most she could expect from her old friend. 'Of course. You can have a sackful if you like.'

'No, a basket will do. Perhaps a nice sweet apple will tempt Papa's appetite.'

'How is he?'

'He is the worst patient that anyone could imagine. Dr Smith is pleased with his progress but Papa refuses to accept the fact that he is crippled. To tell the truth, Kate, I'm glad to be out of the house for a few hours.'

Molly shinned down from the tree, jumping from the last branch and landing on all fours. 'Shall I fetch a trug for the apples, miss?'

'So you were the little monkey up the tree,' Josie said, laughing. 'Yes, Molly, if you please. And only the biggest and the ripest will do.'

Molly scuttled away, barefoot and with her skirts flying. Kate chuckled with sheer relief. The cloud that had hung over her head since Josie's angry tirade seemed to dissipate into thin air. 'You are a spoilt brat, Josie.'

'I know it, but I'm here to make amends. What do you say to a carriage ride?'

'I'd love to, but I'm too busy. Maybe another day.'

Josie's smile faded into a frown. 'No, I want to go now, and so will you when I tell you what I have in mind.'

'I can't, Josie. I have to help Molly pick the rest of the apples before the November gales bring them from the trees.'

'Oh, is that all? I'll send one of our men to do that.' Josie took her by the arm. 'Now, Kate, change into something a bit more respectable, for I won't travel with a girl who looks as though she's been dragged through a hedge backwards. Put on your best bonnet.'

'But where are we going?'

'To Copperstone Castle. I'm determined to see it for myself.'

Kate stopped in her tracks. 'No, I don't want to go there. I can't abide Mr Challenor, and I certainly don't want to visit his home.'

'But he won't be there, dear Kate. Harry and the rest of his party went back to London and he wasn't planning to return to Dorset until Christmas, he told me so himself. So I want to inspect the castle, which will one day be my home.'

'I thought you'd given up that idea.'

'Certainly not. Oh, I was a little put out when Harry went away so suddenly, but I've had plenty of time to think about it, and I decided that he acted out of concern for my feelings and respect for my parents. He'll return when he realises that his true destiny is to marry me. Besides which, he has business

116

dealings with Papa, so I know he will come back sometime soon. Now, do as I say. Go and change your clothes. We must hurry if we're to get there and back before dark.'

Kate knew that it was useless to argue. Once Josie had her mind set on something no power on earth would shake her from her purpose, and, although she was reluctant to admit it even to herself, she was immensely curious to see what sort of home had bred a man like Harry Challenor. Besides which, there could be no harm in such an excursion if he were in London, and she was certain that Pa would not mind if she took a little time off from her chores. He had gone to the Grange, ostensibly to discuss business with the squire, but she was afraid that his real purpose had been to call on Miss Stamp. He seemed to be spending far too much of his spare time with that woman.

She went to find Molly who was scrabbling about in one of the outhouses, looking for a trug, and left her with instructions to tell Pa where she had gone and to assure him that she would be back in time for the evening milking. There was rabbit stew simmering on the kitchen range and Molly would have to keep an eye on it, as there was nothing worse than the taste of burnt meat and potatoes. Satisfied that she had understood and would carry out her instructions to the letter, Kate went upstairs to her bedroom to change her clothes.

It was a glorious afternoon for tooling around the countryside in the chaise with Button, the frisky gelding, between the shafts. Josie was a skilled driver but rather too fond of speed for Kate's peace of mind. She held on for dear life as Josie negotiated sharp bends, flicking the whip so that the horse kept up a brisk pace. Kate prayed that they would not meet a lumbering farm cart head on, but it seemed as though their luck was in and they arrived at the main gates of the Copperstone estate in little less than an hour. The gatekeeper hurried out of his cottage and Josie announced grandly that they were acquainted with the owner, who had invited them to view the castle and its grounds. Kate said nothing, but the man was obviously impressed by Josie's self-assured manner. He let them into the grounds, advising them to seek out Mrs Trench, the housekeeper, who would be pleased to show them round the castle.

In spite of her somewhat ambivalent feelings towards Harry Challenor, Kate could not help being impressed as they drove along a wooded avenue, passing by the stable block and carriage house, and out into open parkland. The castle was a square four-storey building with a turret at each corner, and had, so Josie informed her, been built in the seventeenth century as a hunting lodge. In her imagination Kate had envisioned a forbidding granite fortress with a bloody history dating back to medieval times. In complete contrast, the mellow Purbeck stone walls of Copperstone Castle glowed in the late autumn sunlight, making it appear warm and welcoming. Its tall windows glinted like bright, laughing eyes, and the whole ambience was one of peace and serenity.

Josie was fairly bubbling with excitement as she

drew the horse to a halt at the bottom of the perron. The double doors at the main entrance opened and a footman hurried down the steps to hold the horse's head, while another helped Josie alight from the chaise. Kate was left to fend for herself and she climbed slowly down from the vehicle. She felt suddenly dowdy and out of place amidst all this grandeur as she followed Josie up the wide flight of steps that led to the imposing portico.

'Don't worry, dear,' Josie whispered as they waited in the vestibule for the housekeeper. 'They'll assume that you're my maid, so you mustn't feel at a disadvantage, although if you were employed by me I'd see to it that you had something better to wear.'

It was hardly comforting, and Kate began to wish that she had not come, especially when the housekeeper gave her a condescending glance and then turned to Josie with an ingratiating smile. She found herself largely ignored as they toured the ground floor rooms, which were large, airy and elegantly furnished. She had expected to find the walls hung with trophies of the hunt, sombre oil paintings of highland cattle and stags at bay, and maybe a gun rack or two. It was something of a shock to find that there were embroidered fire screens, smiling family portraits, sparkling crystal chandeliers and urns blazing with fiery crimson chrysanthemums and a purple haze of Michaelmas daisies. From the drawing room and study to the dining and billiard rooms, the castle had the lived-in and comfortable atmosphere of a much-loved family home. It was all so different from her mental picture of Harry Challenor's raffish bachelor apartments; which hovered somewhere between an eastern potentate's harem and a bordello in Marseilles, such as were found between the covers of penny dreadfuls. Kate followed silently as Josie exclaimed in admiration at the furnishings, the size and proportion of the rooms, and the view from the windows; in fact everything she saw seemed to fill her with delight. In the midst of her complimentary remarks, Josie threw in the odd question about Harry's habits when living in the country. Kate felt her cheeks burn with embarrassment, but Josie was unrepentant, even when Mrs Trench made it quite clear that she did not gossip about her master.

When the tour finally came to an end, Josie angled her head, smiling. 'You have been so obliging, Mrs Trench. I don't want to trespass on your goodwill, but I would dearly love to see the view from one of the towers.'

Mrs Trench folded her arms across her chest and her thin lips disappeared into a straight line. 'I'm afraid that is not possible, Miss Damerell. My rheumaticky knees will not allow me to climb the steps to the top of the turrets.'

'I understand perfectly,' Josie cooed. 'But I'm sure Harry would not mind if we went up unaccompanied. I do so long to admire the view from the top.'

'Very well, miss. But do take care. The spiral steps are worn in places and there have been accidents in the past.' Mrs Trench sniffed and walked away with an irritated twitch of her shoulders.

Josie seized Kate by the hand, dragging her across the billiard room and into the southeast tower. A steep spiral staircase rose up in front of them. 'Race you to the top,' Josie said, chuckling.

Kate drew back. 'I don't know, Josie. It doesn't seem right to be intruding into Mr Challenor's private life like this.'

'Don't be a silly goose. Harry wouldn't mind and we're only going to look at the view.'

'It's getting late. I have to be home in time for evening milking.'

Josie picked up her skirts and started up the staircase. 'You can be so boring at times, Kate. The cows can wait, but I can't.'

There was little that Kate could do, except to follow her. It seemed that the stairs went on forever, and she had to stop several times to catch her breath, but Josie bounded on ahead. By the time Kate caught up with her Josie had recovered from the long climb and was staring out of the window with a rapt expression on her face. 'Isn't this just marvellous, Kate. Come here and look at the view.'

Her legs were trembling and Kate fought to catch her breath as she peered out of the window. Above the treetops, she could see the gap in the cliffs where the land sloped down to the cove and beyond it a thin stripe of ultramarine sea. Josie left her side and ran to the far window, pointing excitedly. 'The estate must be vast. Just think, Kate. One day I will be mistress of all this.'

Kate crossed the floor to look at the view of the

park and the woodland that stretched as far as the eye could see. In the distance, visible in a gap between the trees, she could see the spire of a church and the dazzling white stucco frontage of a large Georgian house. 'It's very fine, Josie. But I wouldn't get my hopes up too high, if I were you.'

'Nonsense. I've made up my mind that I will have Harry and his castle. When I decide on something, nothing can stop me. You ought to know that by now.'

Kate shook her head but she refrained from making a comment. Josie usually did get her own way once she had set her heart on something. As she glanced across the green velvet carpet of grassland, Kate realised that the shadows were lengthening. 'We must go, Josie. It's getting late.'

Reluctantly, Josie turned away from the window. 'I know, and the wretched cows need milking. The sooner I get you away from that beastly farm, the better. Don't look so worried, dear. I've seen all I wanted to see. We'll go now.'

A groom brought the chaise to the front entrance and Josie took her seat, glancing at Kate with a mischievous grin. 'You wanted to get home quickly, so hold tight.' She flicked the reins and the vehicle lurched forward. Kate had to hold on as Josie encouraged Button to a dangerously fast pace along the narrow country lanes. 'Don't look so scared, Kate. You are the one who wanted to hurry.' She flicked the whip above the horse's left ear.

'It will be dark soon,' Kate said anxiously. 'Oughtn't you to stop and light the lamps?'

'It's only dusk and we'll be home before long. Anyway, there are not likely to be many other vehicles on the road at this hour.'

Kate lapsed into silence. They were driving along a lane through dense woodland, and the trees formed a tunnel overhead, cutting out what little daylight was left in the darkening sky. Dry leaves fluttered gently down, carpeting the road and deadening the sound of the horse's hooves and the carriage wheels. As they emerged at the edge of Puddlecombe village the road widened slightly and the steep banks gave way to grass verges, but at that moment a farm wagon came round the corner, approaching them at a speed that matched their own. The driver stood up in the well of the cart, shouting at Josie as he reined in his sturdy carthorse. Josie tugged on Button's reins, but the frightened animal reared in the shafts. The horses' terrified whinnies, the crunch of splintering wood and screams filled the air, and suddenly the world was upside down.

Dazed, bruised and momentarily winded, Kate stared up at the sky through the spokes of a spinning wheel. She dimly heard male voices shouting and the sound of running footsteps. Her first thought was for Josie, but the chaise was on its side and the driving seat was empty. Someone was speaking to her and at first she could not make out the words.

'Are you all right, miss?'

'I – think so.' Kate raised her head and found herself looking into the face of a middle-aged woman wearing a starched and goffered white mobcap. A hand came towards her and she clasped it, allowing the woman to pull her gently upright.

'Can you climb out now, miss?'

Kate was trembling with shock and her head was throbbing; she felt battered and bruised, but somehow she managed to clamber out of the upturned vehicle. A young boy had rescued Button from the shafts and was intent on calming the terrified animal, and the farmer was cursing volubly as he surveyed the damage to his wagon. Even in her distressed state, Kate was relieved to see that neither horse had been injured in the collision.

She leaned against the woman for support as her knees threatened to give way beneath her. 'Josie, my friend. Is she hurt?'

'Don't fret, miss. Your friend is being cared for by the master. Let me help you into the house.'

Kate limped round the back of the chaise and saw Josie lying on the roadside with a clerical gentleman kneeling at her side. She stifled a cry of dismay as she saw the livid bruise on Josie's forehead and a trickle of blood running down the side of her face. She was deathly pale and her eyes were closed. 'Oh, my goodness!' Kate exclaimed, covering her mouth with her hands. 'Is she . . .'

The man, who Kate vaguely supposed must be the vicar of the parish, looked up with a reassuring smile in his grey eyes. 'She is very much alive, but she's had a nasty bang on the head. We must get her into the house immediately.' He rose to his feet, lifting Josie gently in his arms, and he turned to the woman who had helped Kate from the wreckage. 'Mrs Trevett, be so good as to send Ethan for Dr Drage.'

'Certainly, Reverend. I'll do it right away.' She turned to the boy. 'You heard what the master said. Take the animal to the stables and then run for the doctor.' She beckoned to Kate. 'If you would care to come this way, miss?'

She hurried up the path which led to the front entrance, but Kate did not follow immediately. 'Josie will be all right, won't she, vicar?'

'As far as I can tell there are no bones broken, but the doctor will give her a thorough examination.' He pushed the wicket gate open with the toe of his boot. 'Come inside, my dear. You've had a nasty shock, but thank goodness nothing worse.'

Kate walked slowly, her bruised limbs moving reluctantly as if she were wading in deep water, and she paused in the doorway, looking over her shoulder as she heard a commotion in the lane. Several men had come running from the neighbouring cottages, and were attempting to right their vehicle. She could hear the angry voice of the farmer ranting about the damage to his cart, and it was a relief to leave it all behind as she entered the candlelit hallway. She stood there, dazed and disorientated after the shock of the accident. 'Where are we, ma'am? What place is this?'

'Why, it's Puddlecombe of course, and you came to grief outside the home of the Reverend John Hardy. I am his housekeeper, Mary Trevett, Mrs Mary Trevett, widow.'

'I – I'm sorry to put you to so much bother, ma'am,'

Kate said, wondering vaguely if she should follow Mr Hardy up the stairs. She really ought to be with Josie even if there was little she could do to help. 'Will the doctor be long, Mrs Trevett?'

'Lord, no, miss. He only lives a hundred yards or so up the lane. Come with me to the parlour and I'll send the girl in with a tray of tea.'

'But I really should be with Josie.'

Mrs Trevett shook her head. 'She's in good hands, Miss – er – I didn't catch your name.'

'Coggins, Kate Coggins and my friend is Miss Josie Damerell of Damerell Manor near Dorchester. We must get word to her family, and to my father who'll be out of his mind with worry.'

Mrs Trevett opened the door to a small, cosy room with a log fire burning brightly in the grate. She bustled about lighting candles. 'Take a seat, Miss Coggins. We'll have to wait until Dr Drage has been, and then we can see about sending messages home. I doubt if you'll be able to travel on tonight, so I'll have a room made up for you.'

'Thank you,' Kate said wearily, suddenly feeling tired and tearful. She sat down on the nearest chair. 'You're very kind, ma'am.'

Mrs Trevett stood in the doorway, staring at her in a way that made Kate feel uncomfortable.

'Is there anything wrong?' Kate's hand flew to her forehead, where she could feel a bump that was the size of a pullet's egg.

'No, miss. You sit there and rest, while I see to everything.'

Kate settled down, relieved to have a few minutes' respite before the maidservant brought her a tray of tea and placed it on a small rosewood table by the window. 'Mrs Trevett says that the doctor is with the young lady now. The Reverend will be down in a moment.' She bobbed a curtsey and was gone before Kate had a chance to question her further. She would have liked to know more about the damage to the chaise, and how long it might take to do the necessary repairs. She drank a cup of tea and nibbled a biscuit, but she was too concerned about Josie to have much of an appetite. At last, the door opened and the Reverend John Hardy entered the room. Kate rose to her feet. 'How is she, sir?'

He pressed her gently back onto her chair. 'The doctor is with her now. She's in good hands.'

'Is there any way that I can get a message to my home, sir? My father will be worried sick.'

'Not tonight, I'm afraid, Miss Coggins. Mrs Trevett tells me that you have come from Kingston Damerell and I'd hesitate to send the stable boy out after dark. You yourself have seen how dangerous the roads can be at nightfall, but first thing in the morning I'll send Ethan with a message informing them that you are both safe.'

'Thank you, sir.' Kate bit her lip as tears burned the backs of her eyes. She would be in terrible trouble when she finally arrived home. She should never have agreed to Josie's harebrained scheme, and now her friend was injured and lying in a strange bed far away from home.

'Things will look better in the morning, Miss

Coggins.' John Hardy looked up as Mrs Trevett entered the room. 'Has the doctor finished his examination?'

'Yes, sir. He's waiting for you in the study.' Mrs Trevett turned to Kate. 'When you're ready, I'll show you your room.'

Kate bowed to the inevitable. She must accept the fact that there was no possibility of returning home that evening. She was tired, bruised and aching in every joint, but she could not rest until she knew the extent of Josie's injuries. 'If you don't mind, I'd like to hear what the doctor has to say first.'

Mrs Trevett pursed her lips but John Hardy held his hand out to Kate. 'Of course you would. Come with me, Kate. We'll see the doctor together.'

A badly sprained ankle was the doctor's verdict. The young person had suffered a few minor abrasions and a possible slight concussion, but nothing more serious. She should be fit to travel in a day or two.

Kate received the news with a sinking heart, but there was nothing she could do other than to follow Mrs Trevett upstairs to the first floor, where she was shown into a room at the back of the house. 'I think you'll be quite comfortable in here, miss,' Mrs Trevett said, holding the candle higher so that its flickering light slid round the bedroom creating monstrous shadows on the walls. 'This was the room that Lady Hardy, his reverence's mother, liked best in the house. She always slept in here when she came to stay.'

'It's very pretty,' Kate said, glancing round appreciatively. Even in the dim light, she could see that the floral wallpaper matched the curtain material, and the frilled bedcover was of a similar pattern. Bowls of dried lavender and rose petals filled the air with their fragrance, and a fire crackled merrily in the grate.

Mrs Trevett paused with her hand on the porcelain door knob. 'If you need anything, just ring the bell.'

As she placed her candle on the washstand, Kate looked up into the wistful blue eyes of a young woman, barely more than a girl, whose portrait hung on the wall. It was so lifelike that it made the hairs on the back of her neck prickle. 'Mrs Trevett, before you go. Who is the lady in the picture?'

'She is lovely, isn't she? She was the Reverend's sister, who died young. I never knew her, but I believe it is a good likeness. Will there be anything else, miss?'

'No. No, thank you.'

A thin smile flitted over Mrs Trevett's severe features as she left the room. Kate dragged her gaze from the portrait and began to unbutton her blouse, but she had the uncomfortable feeling that those haunting blue eyes were watching her and following her round the room. She knew she was being ridiculous; it was just a painting, and she was probably over-tired. She took off her clothes and laid them neatly on a chair. Mrs Trevett had left a white, cotton-lawn nightgown on the bed, but as she picked it up Kate realised that the material was yellowed with age and smelled strongly of mothballs. She couldn't help wondering if it had belonged to the young woman in the portrait, and she put it aside, preferring to sleep in her shift. She was about to climb into bed when she was startled by a loud scream which seemed to be coming from the adjoining bedroom. She snatched up the candlestick, but as she opened the bedroom door a strong breeze extinguished the flame and she found herself in darkness. Another scream shattered the silence.

Chapter Eight

Kate burst into the room and found Josie lying in bed with the sheet pulled up to her chin. Illuminated by a shaft of moonlight filtering through the diamond windowpanes, Josie's face was ghostly white and her open mouth a dark hollow. 'Shush,' Kate said, holding her finger to her lips. 'You'll have everyone rushing upstairs thinking you're being murdered. What is it, Josie? Are you in pain?'

'Of course I'm in paid, stupid.' Sounding more like her old self, Josie made an attempt to sit up and groaned, falling back on the pillows with tears trickling from her eyes. 'Where am I? What happened? I'm sore all over and my head aches.'

'We had an accident. The chaise overturned and you hit your head. The doctor didn't think you'd broken any bones but you've got to rest.'

'I want Hickson. Tell her to run my bath for me, and . . .' Josie's eyes focused on Kate as if seeing her for the first time. 'Where are your clothes? Oh, my head aches so badly and I think I'm going to be sick.'

Kate made a grab for the washbowl and held Josie's head while she vomited. When the spasm had passed she dipped a piece of cloth in the jug from the washstand and bathed Josie's face and hands, whispering soothing words as if she were dealing with a small child. She sat with her until Josie drifted off to sleep and then, overcome by sheer exhaustion, Kate went to her own room leaving the door ajar in case Josie awakened and called out to her. She climbed stiffly into bed, curled up and, almost instantly, fell into a deep sleep.

When she opened her eyes next morning she could not at first remember where she was. Sunlight poured in through the open curtains and a young housemaid had just placed a ewer filled with hot water on the washstand. She bobbed a curtsey. 'Good morning, miss. Mrs Trevett's compliments and she said to tell you that breakfast is at half past seven. The vicar likes to start the day early.'

Kate pulled the coverlet up to her chin, hoping that the girl had not seen the discarded nightgown on the floor. She did not want Mrs Trevett to think that she was ungrateful. 'Thank you, er – what is your name?'

'Hester, miss.'

'Thank you, Hester. Please tell Mrs Trevett that I'll be down directly.'

She nodded and scuttled from the room, putting Kate forcibly in mind of a small, brown field mouse. However, having a maid bring hot water to her room was an unheard of luxury. It was a far cry from her days as housemaid in Bedford Square when it was she who had to wait hand and foot on the family. Even now, at home on the farm, she would have been up at least an hour earlier, and if Molly had not fetched a bucket of water from the pump in the yard she would have had to do it herself.

Kate stretched her bruised limbs and climbed stiffly out of bed. As she washed her hands and face in the rose-patterned bowl, she found herself glancing up at the portrait. In daylight, she could see clearly that the young woman was about her own age, and the artist had captured a hint of mischief as well as sadness in those expressive eyes. A faint tapping on the wall made her jump, almost spilling the water. 'All right. I won't be a moment.' Two more taps on the wall expressed Josie's customary impatience. She was obviously on the road to recovery. 'Hold on, Josie. I'm coming.' She slipped her gown over her head and hurried into Josie's room, struggling with the buttons and laces. 'What's the matter?'

'I'm unwell, Kate,' Josie said plaintively. 'My head aches, and I'm sure I have a fever. I hardly slept a wink last night.'

Kate knew this was untrue. She was a very light sleeper and she would have heard Josie had she been tossing and turning. She laid her hand on her forehead. 'You are a bit hot.'

'I'm burning up, I tell you. I want to go home and be looked after properly. I'm sure these sheets are damp. I shall die of lung fever if I have to stay here any longer.'

'Nonsense. You've probably just caught a cold.'

'You must send someone to Damerell Manor. Hickson may be an old witch, but she'll know what to do. She'll send the carriage for me.'

Kate could see that there was no point arguing with her in this mood, and she patted Josie's hand. 'I'll go downstairs right away and speak to the Reverend.'

'Yes, do that. And send the maid up with some hot chocolate and toasted muffins. I'm starving.'

Kate eyed her speculatively. There could not be much wrong with Josie if she was hungry. She bit back a sharp rebuke, realising that it would be wasted on her imperious friend.

She found John Hardy already at breakfast in the morning parlour. He stood up as she entered the room. 'Good morning, Miss Coggins. I trust you slept well?'

'I did, thank you, vicar. But I am afraid Miss Damerell is rather poorly, and she wondered if a message could be sent to Damerell Manor asking them to send the carriage for her.'

'Perhaps we'd better wait until the doctor has examined her again, in case she is not well enough to make the journey. I'll send Ethan to fetch him, but in the meantime won't you take a seat and join me for breakfast?'

'Thank you.' Kate sat down, feeling slightly unnerved. She was more used to waiting on other people than being treated as a house guest. The vicarage might be small when compared to Damerell Manor or the house in Bedford Square, but it was furnished with taste and elegance.

He rang the bell. 'Mrs Trevett will bring fresh tea and toast, but if you would prefer a boiled egg or . . .'

'Thank you, but toast will be sufficient, and I should take something up to Josie as she cannot come downstairs.'

'Don't worry about that. My housekeeper will look after Miss Damerell.' He looked up as Mrs Trevett came in answer to the bell. 'Would you be kind enough to send Hester upstairs with a breakfast tray for our guest, please, Mary?'

Mrs Trevett sniffed and folded her arms across her flat bosom. 'I've already done that, sir. What can I get you?'

'More toast, please, and a fresh pot of tea.'

'Yes, sir.' Mrs Trevett picked up the silver teapot.

'And Mary, would you be kind enough to send Ethan for Dr Drage? I understand that Miss Damerell is not too well this morning.'

'Yes, sir. Of course.' Mrs Trevett's tone was neutral, but her tight-lipped expression and disapproving sniff spoke volumes. She left the room, muttering beneath her breath.

'I'm afraid we are putting you to a great deal of trouble, Mr Hardy,' Kate said, frowning.

'Nonsense. It's no trouble at all.'

'I could drive the chaise if there is a delay in sending the carriage.'

'I'm afraid it suffered a broken axle amongst other things, and it will be some days before it's roadworthy again.'

'That is bad news. But I'm sure that Lady Damerell will send their carriage for Josie, if she's well enough to travel.'

'We'll just have to wait and see what the doctor says. In the meantime you must feel free to treat this house as you would your own home. It's very nice to have young company for a change. I sometimes feel that I am sliding fast into middle age and becoming a crusty old bachelor.'

Kate shot him a sideways glance. His smile was infectious and made him look years younger. Last night she had thought him to be quite old but she could see now that he was probably in his early forties, although it was hard to be exact. Perhaps it was the greying of his hair at the temples that had given her the false impression of advancing years, or the lines of worry etched on his aquiline features, as if he had taken the cares of his parishioners on his own shoulders. Above all, he had a kind face, and a sympathetic manner. It would be easy, she thought, to tell him anything without fear of being judged. 'You're very kind, but I have to get back to the farm as soon as possible. My father is a widower and he relies on me.'

'He's a very lucky man to have such a caring daughter. I, alas, was never married and am never likely to be now that I am set in my ways.' He folded his napkin into a precise square. 'I don't know if you like to read, but I have a library filled with books.' He hesitated and his long, thin fingers drummed nervously on the table top. 'And there is a pianoforte in the drawing room. Do you play at all, Miss Coggins?'

'Not very well, I'm afraid. I did have lessons with Josie, but Miss Brooks rather gave up on me. She said I had two left hands and was tone deaf.'

'How unkind of her. I'm sure that you were a very good pupil, and if you would like to play the instrument while you are waiting to hear from home, then you are most welcome.'

'Thank you, but I hope we won't have to trespass on your hospitality any longer than necessary.'

He rose to his feet. 'And now, if you'll excuse me, I have a sermon to write.' He was about to open the door when Mrs Trevett entered carrying a rack of toast and the teapot.

'I've sent the boy for the doctor, sir. And Miss Damerell has cleared her tray, so I don't think there is very much wrong with that young person.'

John's eyes twinkled, but his expression was grave. 'We can't have our guest fading away, Mary. I'll be in my study. Let me know when Dr Drage has seen Miss Damerell.'

Mrs Trevett set the teapot down on the table and put the toast in front of Kate. 'In my opinion, it's just a bump on the head, but I can see that the young lady is used to being waited on hand and foot. I'm afraid she won't get any of that here, Miss Coggins. And perhaps you could tell her so.'

'Yes, Mrs Trevett, I certainly will, and I hope we will be able to go home later today.'

'I don't hold out too much hope of that, miss. Dr Drage has only two remedies that I can see – bleeding and bed rest. I shouldn't be surprised if the young lady gets both.'

Ethan returned to say that the doctor was attending a particularly difficult confinement and he would be unable to visit until mid-morning at the earliest. When he finally arrived it was closer to midday and Kate had been sitting with Josie, trying to keep her entertained, but she was in pain from her contusions, feverish and irritable; in fact, a difficult patient. Dr Drage examined her head, listened to her chest, took her pulse and temperature and diagnosed a feverish chill, although the concussion was not as bad as he had feared at first. 'You must stay in bed for a week at least, young lady.'

'But I want to go home,' Josie wailed.

'I would not advise going out in this damp weather.' Dr Drage pointed to raindrops running down the windowpanes. What had begun as a bright sunny day had rapidly deteriorated into thick cloud and heavy showers. 'You must stay in an even temperature, Miss Damerell. Drink plenty of fluids and sweat out the fever. I will call again tomorrow, when I will bleed you.'

'Oh no you won't,' Josie said firmly. 'You can forget that, doctor. I'm not having leeches anywhere near me.'

He snapped his bag shut. 'We'll see about that, Miss Damerell.' He was about to leave the room but he paused in the doorway, beckoning to Kate. 'May I have a word?'

She hesitated, gazing anxiously at Josie. 'I'm sure your mama will insist on your being brought home as soon as possible.'

'Go downstairs and tell him that I shall die if I am forced to stay here,' Josie said, scowling. 'I'll die of boredom, never mind the fever. Why, I feel better already.' She sat upright, clutched her forehead with her hand and fell back against the pillows. 'Well, maybe not completely better.'

'You heard what the doctor said. You must rest.'

138

'I want to go home. Go and speak to him, Kate.'

Kate hurried downstairs and was about to enter the parlour when she overhead Dr Drage, speaking earnestly. 'For the young lady to go outside in this inclement weather would be to court disaster, John.'

'I understand, and she is most welcome to stay for as long as she likes.'

'I recommend a light diet only. Broth, calves' foot jelly, milk puddings. I'm sure that Mrs Trevett will know exactly the sort of thing.'

'I'm sure she will, David.'

Kate hesitated. She knew that Josie desperately wanted to go home, but it did sound as though staying here until she was well enough to travel was in her best interests. She was about to tell them so when she was distracted by a loud rapping on the front door. Mrs Trevett came scurrying down the hall, wiping her hands on her apron.

'All right, all right. There's no call to break the door down.' She wrenched it open. 'Tradesmen round the back, if you please.'

'I ain't a tradesman, ma'am. I come to enquire after Miss Coggins.'

'Sam.' Kate ran to greet him.

Mrs Trevett turned on her, frowning. 'Do you know this person, Miss Coggins?'

'Yes, I do. May he come in, please, Mrs Trevett. Sam is from home.'

Reluctantly, Mrs Trevett stood aside. 'It's most irregular. Servants and tradesmen go round the back.' She stomped off in the direction of the kitchen.

139

Kate flung her arms around Sam's neck. 'I was never so pleased to see anyone in my whole life.'

He hugged her so tightly that she could scarcely breathe. 'And a proper fright you gave us all, and no mistake, Kate. What was you thinking of, going off like that and without a word to anyone?'

'Molly knew I'd gone with Josie.'

'Yes, she told us that you'd gone off on some hare-brained scheme of Josie's. Your pa was out of his mind with worry when you hadn't returned by dark.'

'Is he very angry?'

'He was scared to death. We all was, Kate. We've been out most of the night scouring the countryside looking for you. And Lady Damerell's had all the men on the estate out too.'

'We had an accident. There was nothing we could do until morning.'

Sam's face paled beneath his tan. 'Are you hurt? You look all right.'

'I'm fine, but Josie's suffered a mild concussion and now she's down with a fever. The doctor says she mustn't be moved.'

'Well, serves her right if you ask me. I daresay it was her idea for you two to go gallivanting off like that.'

'I know, it was a mad venture, but Josie wanted to see Copperstone Castle. We would have been home last night but for meeting a farm cart in the lane outside.'

'And her driving like the devil was after you, I suppose.'

'We were going too fast, and it was a sharp bend.'

'Then it's just as well that I've come to take you

home, Kate. The squire lent me his dog cart, which is faster than the old farm wagon.' He caught her by the hand. 'Come on.'

She shook her head. 'I can't leave without saying goodbye to Josie. It wouldn't be right.'

Sam's dark brows knotted together over the bridge of his nose in an ominous scowl. 'I doubt she would give you so much consideration, but all right then, if you insist. Just tell her that you've got a home to go to and a father who's been worried to death and all because of her wayward behaviour.'

She realised that Sam's anger had been caused by fear both for her and also for Josie and she withdrew her hand gently. 'Give me five minutes, Sam,' she said with an apologetic smile. 'Wait for me on the cart and I'll be out as soon as I've said my piece.'

Muttering, he went outside and strode down the path towards the lane. Kate sighed. She was not looking forward to facing her father when she arrived home. She had only seen him lose his temper on a few occasions when he had been very drunk, but now his anger would have been fuelled by concern for her safety as well as her lack of consideration. She would just have to face up to it, admit her guilt and take the consequences. She ran up the stairs to break the news to Josie.

'You can't leave me here all on my own.' Josie's eyes were bright with fever and her fingers plucked at the sheet. 'I won't let you go. You are a bad friend. I hate you, Kate Coggins.'

'Hush, now.' Kate laid her hand on Josie's forehead and she was shocked to feel the heat radiating from her body. 'You must keep calm. You'll only make yourself worse.'

'I am worse. I'm very, very sick. And you want to run off home and leave me here with strangers.' Josie began to wail and thrash about on the pillows.

Kate perched on the edge of the bed and caught her flailing hands. 'Stop this at once, Josie. Stop it, I say.'

'Not unless you promise to stay here with me until I get better.'

Kate could hear footsteps on the stairs, and she knew that Josie was quite capable of making herself physically sick if she did not get her way. 'I'll promise, but only if you stop this hysterical nonsense.'

Josie gave her a beatific smile. 'Cross your heart?'

'And hope to die, you wretch.'

The door opened and Dr Drage hurried into the room followed by John and Mrs Trevett. 'As I feared,' he said, shaking his head. 'She is delirious. She must on no account leave this room, John. That is my professional opinion.'

'Of course, David. But her parents might insist on having Miss Damerell brought home.'

Mrs Trevett edged past them and stood with arms akimbo, eyeing Josie with a set look on her face. 'Miss Damerell will do as the doctor orders, won't you, miss?'

Josie opened her mouth, but Kate frowned at her, shaking her head. 'You will be good now, won't you, Josie?'

'Only if you promise to remain here.' Josie's bottom lip trembled and her eyes filled with tears.

'I'll let your man know that you'll be staying here

142

to nurse your friend, Miss Coggins.' Mrs Trevett eyed her severely, as if daring her to disagree. 'You will be in charge of the sickroom, and I'll see that your orders are obeyed.'

Caught between two very different but equally determined females, Kate knew that she had no choice. 'All right. I'll remain here until Josie is fit to travel.' She waited until they were alone before turning on Josie, and this time she was not amused. 'You little madam. You may be a bit poorly, but you're not that sick.'

Josie's lips curved in a triumphant smile. 'You'll find a way to get me home, Kate. I simply couldn't manage if you left me here to the mercy of that old harridan. I do love you, you know. We may not be related by blood, but we were born on the same day, so that makes us sisters.'

Kate plumped up the pillows and smoothed a lock of dark hair back from Josie's brow. 'Yes, you minx. We do share the same birthday, but you were born to the gentry and I'm a stableman's daughter. Of course that makes us twins.'

Josie closed her eyes. 'Now you are laughing at me. I want to sleep now, so go away, Kate. But not too far.'

Downstairs in the entrance hall, Kate could hear raised voices, and one of them was Sam's. She ran down the stairs, coming to a halt at the bottom as she saw Sam and Mrs Trevett in the middle of what appeared to be a fierce argument.

'And I'm telling you to go about your business, my good man.' Mrs Trevett squared up to him. 'If you don't leave this house now I shall send for the constable.'

'I'm not going nowhere until I've spoken to Miss Coggins.' Sam looked up and saw her. He pushed past Mrs Trevett. 'This woman tells me that you're not coming home after all. Is it true?'

She laid her hand on his arm. 'Stop shouting, Sam. It is true. I was going to come with you, but Josie has a fever and I've promised to stay with her until she is well enough to travel.'

Sam's eyes widened with concern. 'You said it was just a bump on the head.'

'I'll be in the kitchen if you need me, miss. And you, young man, had best leave now and take the message to Damerell Manor.' Mrs Trevett stalked off, bristling with affront.

'The old battleaxe!' Sam said, eyeing her retreating figure with a hostile look. 'I couldn't stand a day in the company of that woman.'

Kate smiled wearily. She felt wrung out and drained of all emotion. 'She's not so bad really. She just likes things to be done properly.'

'And you're really going to stay here? Tell me the truth now, Kate. Is it serious with Josie, or are you afraid to go home to face your pa? If you are, don't be. I'll stand by you.'

'I know you would, Sam. I'm not afraid of Pa. As to Josie, I think it's just a feverish chill, but you know what she's like. She was working herself up into a tantrum so I promised her that I'd stay. I can't break my word.'

'What am I to tell them at the big house then? And what do I say to the gaffer?'

'For a start you can ask them to send a change of clothes for Josie, some fresh undergarments and some slippers. And then tell them whatever it was that Mrs Trevett told you to say. As for Pa, please try and explain to him why I have to remain here. Tell him that I'm sorry that I caused so much upset. And you might ask Molly to pack a bag for me too. The Damerells' groom could collect it on his way here.'

'I'll do all that gladly, but I blame Josie for this mess. She may be a lady, but she's a wild thing at heart. It would be easier to tame the wind than to keep her in order.'

Kate squeezed his hand. 'Go home, Sam. Tell Pa I'm very, very sorry, and I'll come as soon as I can. Will you do that for me – and for Josie?'

'I'll go, but only because you say so.'

She reached up and kissed his cheek. 'I'm relying on you, Sam. And don't let Pa put too many of my chores on to Molly. He can always hire a dairymaid from the village for the short while I'm away.'

A dark flush stained Sam's weathered cheeks and he stared down at his boots, shuffling his feet. 'There's something else, Kate. Something I think you ought to know.'

'What is it?'

He shook his head. 'It may be nothing, but I seen it coming for weeks.'

'You're frightening me, Sam. Tell me now.'

Chapter Nine

'It's probably just gossip, Kate,' Josie said impatiently. 'Why can't you forget what Sam said and stop worrying?'

Kate stared out of the drawing room window, her whole body rigid and visibly trembling. She sighed, shaking her head. 'Because Sam wouldn't have told me that Pa was engaged to Miss Stamp if it hadn't been true. I can't believe that my father would do something so foolish. It's obvious what sort of woman she is.'

'He's a man,' Josie said, thumping her hands down on the piano keys. 'They don't think. He wants someone to run round after him and warm his bed.'

'Don't.' Kate turned to her with a worried frown. 'She'll do anything to trap him into marriage and then she'll make his life a misery.'

'You don't know that. Do stop going on about it.'

Kate snatched up her shawl. 'I'm going out for a walk. I can't talk to you when you're in this mood.' She opened one of the French doors and stepped out into the garden, shutting it again with unnecessary force. A gust of cool air turned the page of sheet music in front of Josie. She slammed the piano lid with an exasperated sigh.

'My poor piano must have offended you today.'

She turned her head to see John standing in the doorway, and she was instantly ashamed of her fit of pique. 'I'm sorry. I didn't mean to take it out on the instrument. My playing was diabolical today.'

'It was no such thing. I've been sitting in my study listening to Mozart, when I should have been writing my sermon. Perhaps your head injury is causing you more pain?'

His smile was sympathetic but that only served to make things worse. She would have felt better had he scolded her for her bad behaviour, and she was not in a mood to be forgiven. 'No, in fact my head is much better and the bruises are fading, but I ache all over and it makes me hobble about like an old woman. I can't say that I enjoy looking and feeling like an old hag of ninety.'

'I hear that convalescent invalids are often bad-tempered.'

'Now you are laughing at me, and I think it is very mean of you, vicar.'

'You only call me that when I've upset you.' He held up his hands in a gesture of submission, but there was laughter in his eyes. 'No, don't worry. I won't apologise, Josie. I know that annoys you more than anything. You see, I have grown to know you well during your brief stay in this house.'

'Too well, John. You've seen through me. I'm spoilt, shallow and wayward – in fact, not a very nice person at all.' It amused her to tease him, and this dull house did not offer much in the way of entertainment. If she

147

were to tell the truth, she was bored to death, and could not wait to go home.

His smile faded and he crossed the floor to sit on the chair nearest to her. 'That's not what I meant at all. I see someone quite different beneath the façade that you present to the world.'

'Do you, vicar? I wonder if that knowledge is divine, or if in fact it comes from the other place?' She leaned forward, smiling into his eyes and lowering her voice. 'You know where I mean, of course.'

'You love to tease me, I know that. I also know that you are loyal to your friends and can command their deep affection, as evidenced by Kate. Now, if you were the bad person who you claim to be, I don't think a charming young lady like Miss Coggins would be so fond of you.'

His earnest expression and the heartfelt tone of his voice were oddly disturbing. Even though she had not had an official coming out season, Josie had attended private parties both at her parents' London home and in the country. She was well versed in the art of flirting, but she could also recognise the signs when it had gone too far and a young man was in danger of falling in love with her. At that point in the past, when things were getting serious, she had always put a stop to the game, even if it meant breaking a few hearts along the way. In her experi-ence, her would-be suitors recovered extremely quickly and lived to flirt another day – but she was not so sure about John Hardy. She sensed that his feelings ran deep and his love, once given, would never be withdrawn. She did not want him to fall in love with her; such deep devotion was frightening in its intensity, and she still had plans for Harry Challenor. His apparent indifference made him all the more of a challenge.

She managed a tight little laugh, which sounded false even to her own ears. 'Oh, heavens, vicar. You'll have me in tears in a moment.' She peered out of the window, hoping that Kate would return and put an end to this tête-à-tête, but she was nowhere in sight. She stood up a little too quickly and a spell of dizziness almost caused her to lose her balance. She clutched at the piano for support.

John leapt to his feet, slipping his arm around her waist in order to steady her. 'You must take things slowly, my dear. Allow me to help you to a more comfortable seat.'

She could feel his breath warm against her cheek and the touch of his hand on hers was not unpleasant. She had a ridiculous impulse to lay her head against his shoulder, which only went to prove that she had been away from the real world for far too long. It was definitely time to go home.

'Josie. Oh, my goodness, are you all right?' Kate stood in the doorway, gazing at them in consternation. 'Are you ill?'

'There's nothing wrong with me,' Josie said irritably. 'I stood up too quickly, that's all. Thank you, John. I'm fine now, really.'

He released her and moved away to stand by the fireplace. 'Good. I mean, I'm glad you are all right.'

'And I've got some splendid news for you,' Kate said, smiling. 'I've just seen Ethan and he told me that the axle has been repaired. If you feel up to it I could drive us home this afternoon.'

'So soon?' John's brow creased into a frown. 'Shouldn't Josie consult the doctor before undertaking such a journey?'

'That man is dying to bleed me and I won't have any of it.' Josie tempered her words with a smile. 'Kate, go upstairs and pack our bags. And John, be a dear and ring for Mrs Trevett. We need to give her the good news. I'm sure she will be delighted to have her household back to normal.'

He tugged at the bell pull. 'I can't speak for Mary, but I shall miss your company. The old house won't seem the same without you and Kate.'

Josie met Kate's disapproving glance with a toss of her dark curls. 'I daresay you'll find plenty to keep you occupied in the parish, vicar. I'm afraid we've kept you from some of your duties during the past week.' She regretted the words the moment they left her lips. His pained expression only made things worse. 'But I'm truly grateful for all your kindness.' She turned her head away. Guilt was not an emotion she felt very often and it was as unwelcome as it was unusual. Why did people have to be so sensitive? For the first time, she almost welcomed Mrs Trevett's arrival on the scene.

An hour later, Josie was perched on the driving seat wrapped in a travelling rug borrowed from the vicarage. Kate held the reins while Button moved

150

restlessly in the shafts, as if eager to be off after a week of enforced idleness. John stood by the garden gate with Mrs Trevett at his side. Despite his smiles, Josie sensed his genuine sadness at their departure. It flattered her vanity, but it was also disturbing – she had not deliberately set out to charm the Reverend John Hardy, he had just taken a harmless bit of flirting much too seriously. Smiling, she waved. 'Goodbye John, and thank you once again for everything.' At least old Ma Trevett was not bothering to hide her relief that they were leaving. She would, no doubt, be delighted to rule her small empire once again.

John raised his hand, acknowledging her thanks with a faint smile. 'You will be most welcome to come and visit us at any time, won't they, Mary?'

'Yes, sir. Of course.' Mrs Trevett's tone was meek but Josie was quick to note the look of satisfaction in her steely eyes.

'Perhaps one day you might venture as far as Kingston Damerell,' Kate said softly. 'I'm sure my pa would be glad of the opportunity to thank you for taking care of us.'

'I'll do that, Kate. I know my good friend, Harry Challenor, speaks very highly of your part of the county.'

Josie stared at him in disbelief. 'You know Harry?'

'Copperstone is within my parish, Josie. I visit the castle at least once a month and take a service in the chapel. Had you been able to stay longer you would have been able to accompany me there next Sunday. It's certainly worth a visit.'

At a loss for words, Josie nudged Kate in the ribs.

'Drive on.' She bared her teeth in a smile, waving automatically as Button obeyed a single command and surged forward. 'Why didn't the silly man tell us that in the first place,' she said angrily. 'A whole week wasted. If I'd known he was Harry's friend I would have stayed on longer and might have met Harry in his home surroundings. I would have had a chance to charm him and show myself off to my best advantage.'

'Then it's just as well you didn't find out until too late.' Kate flicked the reins and Button obligingly broke into a trot. 'I've got eyes, Josie. You were flirting outrageously with poor John. You had him quite bemused and I'm sure that he is head over heels in love with you.'

'Poppycock! He is a crusty old bachelor who isn't the slightest bit interested in women except to save their souls.'

'If you say so, Miss Delilah Damerell.'

'I do say so, and you were extremely accommodating yourself. I think you have a soft spot for our clerical gentleman.'

'I admit that I like him immensely. I think John is one of the nicest men I have ever met – too nice for you, Josie. You would tear his poor heart to shreds.'

Kate was smiling but Josie sensed an underlying seriousness in her words and an inescapable truth. She turned her head away. 'I am not that cruel, Kate. And we are not likely to meet again, so your holy man is safe from my evil clutches.'

'It was just a pity that you chose to overturn the trap outside the vicarage. Now if you'd been really clever, you would have had the accident in the grounds of Copperstone Castle. We could have spent a week in Mr Challenor's magnificent home.'

'That would have been my idea of heaven.' Josie wrapped her mantle a little more tightly about her as a spiteful wind brought showers of dead leaves down around them and ominous clouds rolled across the sky.

It was late afternoon by the time they reached the home farm. Sam was crossing the farmyard, heading towards the milking parlour, but he stopped and his face split in a grin of delight when he saw them. He helped Kate down to the ground, hugging her and planting a smacking kiss on her cheek. 'Well I'm blowed. This is a turn-up for the books. We wasn't expecting you until next week at the earliest. Welcome home, Kate.' He lifted her small case from beneath the seat. 'I'm glad to see you're fully recovered, Miss Josie.'

Josie eyed him warily. She felt the air charged about them as though a thunderstorm were about to break. His words were bland enough but there was a fire in his eyes that sent her pulses racing. She curved her lips in what she hoped was a casual smile. 'I've brought Kate home to you, safe and sound. Although I hear you blamed me entirely for the accident.' Try as she might to remain aloof, she could not resist goading him. She had always enjoyed provoking Sam until his eyes flashed with anger. She would keep on and on until he forgot his subservient position and fought with her on equal terms.

Sam's smile was replaced by a frown. 'You could both have been killed.'

'And you would have been proved right,' Josie shot

back at him. 'That would have made you very happy, wouldn't it?'

'You've no idea of the fuss and bother you caused, have you?'

'I'll thank you to remember your place, Sam Loveday.'

Kate threw up her hands. 'Stop it, the pair of you. We're home now, and that's all that matters. I must find Pa and make my peace with him. Where is he, Sam?'

His expression softened. 'I think you'll find he's visiting the Grange, Kate. But I'm not in his confidence, so I can't say for certain.'

'You mean he's calling on Miss Stamp?'

Josie seized the horse whip and flicked it at Sam. 'Hold your tongue, you stupid fellow. If you don't know for sure, then keep silent. Farmer Coggins could have gone to see the squire.'

Sam reached out and snatched it from her. 'Don't never do that again, Josie Damerell, or I'll forget that you're supposed to be a lady and put you over my knee.'

'Touch me and I'll show you what a good whipping feels like, you country bumpkin.'

Kate moved between them, grabbing Sam by the hand. 'You're acting like a pair of spoilt children.'

His angry expression melted into a smile. 'Don't take no notice of me, Kate. Go indoors out of the cold.'

'I will, but only if you promise to stop fighting with Josie and see her safely home.'

'Don't be silly,' Josie said, slithering across the seat to take the reins. 'I can drive myself. Let Loveday get back to his cows.'

154

'No, I won't hear of it.' Kate stood her ground. 'I want to be certain that you've arrived home in one piece, and he doesn't mind a bit, do you, Sam?'

He pushed his cap to the back of his head. 'But the milking, Kate. It has to be done.'

'And I'll be glad to get back to work. I've missed my dear old cows, and I expect they've missed me too.' She gave him a gentle shove towards the chaise. 'Go on, Sam. I'll be fine, really I will.'

Reluctantly, Josie moved over and allowed him to take the reins. Her heart was pounding inside her breast and her pulses raced. She stifled the urge to claw her fingers and attack Sam like a tigress, if only to feel his strong arms holding her to him so that their bodies fused into one. She struggled to push such dark thoughts from her mind as Sam urged Button from a steady trot to a canter. 'Steady, Sam. Thoroughbreds only need the lightest hand on the reins.'

He shot her a sideways glance. 'Are you talking about yourself or the horse, Josie?'

Responding to the mischievous gleam in his eyes, she moved a little closer. 'You are an impertinent rogue, and you forget your place.'

'I'm very well aware of my lowly position, but I recall a time when we played together as equals.'

'That was long ago.' She reached up and touched the blue jay's feather stuck in his hatband. 'Do you remember when we found the poor dead bird?'

'And you cried as though your heart would break.'

'I did not.'

'You did too.'

'We buried it by the lake, all but one feather; I gave it to you as a token of our everlasting friendship.'

'And I've worn it ever since. It will go to the grave with me.'

She laid her head on his shoulder. 'Do you remember how we used to climb the great oaks in the park, daring each other to reach the highest branch?'

'I do, for I always won.'

A gurgle of laughter escaped from her lips. 'Kate always said you were half monkey.'

'I might have been half monkey but you were no mermaid. I remember pulling you from the lake, very nearly drowned and wearing nothing but a cotton shift.'

'I was ten years old and you'd dared me to swim the length of the lake in the dark.' She shivered as she remembered the cold water closing over her head and the finger-like fronds of the pond weed clutching at her bare legs. 'We were just children then.'

'Aye, I know. Now we're grown up and you're the fine lady and I'm the farm labourer. I do know my place, Josie, but I sometimes wonder if you know yours.'

She glanced up at his strong profile and the determined set of his jaw. Sam was right, of course, they were no longer carefree children, and he was her social inferior, but something remained of their old unquestioning devotion to each other, even though it had recently undergone a subtle change. She had seen the way he looked at her when she and her friends had joined in the dancing at the harvest supper. She had pretended to ignore him, for he was just a clumsy yokel, especially when compared to the elegant Harry Challenor, but she had been only too aware of Sam's strong physique and handsome, suntanned face. Her society friends were pale and insignificant in comparison. She felt his muscles tauten as she huddled closer to him, and she was even more conscious of the strange stirring inside her that had nothing to do with courtly love or genteel flirtation. She had been kissed by ardent young gentlemen who had somehow managed to extricate her from the clutches of her chaperones, but their embraces had been exciting only in the fact that they were illicit. Her heart had never been touched by any man, not even Harry Challenor. It was slightly alarming, but being this close to Sam she found herself longing to feel his mouth on hers and to taste his lips. She nestled closer. 'I'm sorry, Sam. I didn't mean all those things I said before.'

He laid his work-roughened hand over hers as it rested on his sleeve. 'I know, maidy. You and I are one and the same. It were always so.'

They continued on in silence until they reached the avenue of trees leading up to the manor house. It was almost dark now and the windows were illuminated by the soft glow of candlelight. Above their heads, the naked branches of the copper beech trees were interlaced and Sam drew the horse to a halt in their shadow. Josie held her breath; she knew what was going to happen even before he took her in his arms. Closing her eyes she inhaled the intoxicating male scent of him as she clasped her hands behind his head, drawing him closer until their lips were almost touching. His kiss was everything that she had imagined it might be

157

and more. It was tender and yet savage in its intensity, sending fireworks exploding in her breast and eliciting her passionate response. She ran her fingers through his thick dark hair, parting her lips and tasting the sweetness of his tongue as it explored her mouth. She nipped his top lip with her teeth and he cupped her breasts with his hands, causing her nipples to form hard peaks of desire. She moved beneath him, pressing her body against his, half fainting with the need for him to take her here, in the open air like the beasts of the field, but he drew away from her suddenly, leaving her shivering with frustration. 'How dare you,' she hissed, but it was disappointment rather than outrage that fuelled her anger. She should never have allowed this to happen, and her cheeks burned with shame.

He said nothing. Taking the reins, he urged the horse into movement. He did not look at her and she slapped at him with the flat of her hands. 'You are an uncouth brute, Loveday. You shan't take liberties with me and then just drive on as if nothing has happened.'

He turned his head to meet her furious look, but his eyes were in shadow. 'I am everything you say I am, and it won't happen again.'

'Set me down now. I won't travel another inch with you.'

'I'll take you to the door and see you safe inside.'

'You've insulted me. I could have you horsewhipped for that.'

'It weren't no insult, and you know it. You kissed me back, Josie, and you can't deny it. You wanted me as much as I wanted you.'

'If you don't stop, I shall jump out.'

'And break your neck in the process. We're nearly there, so sit tight.'

Her heart was hammering so hard against her ribs that she was sure he must be able to hear it. The blood was pounding in her ears and she could still feel the heat of his mouth on hers; the taste of him and the scent of him filled her senses until she felt her head would explode. She moved as far away from him as she could without falling off the seat and clenched her hands in her lap, staring straight ahead until he drew the horse to a halt. Before she had a chance to alight, Sam had leapt from the seat and he was at her side holding up his arms. She would have refused his help but for her sprained ankle, which still ached miserably, and reluctantly she allowed him to lift her down from the chaise. The clouds had parted and a shaft of moonlight turned the gravel carriage sweep from grey to silver. Sam held her for a long moment, looking deeply into her eyes with an unfathomable gaze that sent a frisson of excitement travelling down her spine. For a moment she thought he was going to kiss her again, and worse still, she wanted his embrace with a ferocity that both thrilled and frightened her. But at that moment, the doors were flung open and a footman hurried down the stone steps towards them. In the gold spillage of light from the entrance hall, she saw the silhouette of her mother standing in the doorway.

'Josie, my darling.' Lady Damerell opened her arms. 'My dear girl, you're home. Your father and I have been out of our minds with worry about you. Mason, you may carry Miss Josie into the house.'

Josie could walk very well by now, but she allowed the footman to pick her up as it was easier than arguing. Even so she could not resist the temptation to take a last look at Sam. He was standing by the trap staring after her and their eyes met and locked in a fierce tussle of wills. It must stop here, she thought, choking back tears. We must pretend that none of it has happened. But it had, and she knew her feelings for Sam Loveday had undergone a sea change. He had awakened passions and emotions that she had not known she possessed, and he was right, they were two sides of the same coin. She knew she must fight this terrible obsession that had the power to destroy them both.

'Hurry up, Mason,' Lady Damerell cried, fluttering about them like a white moth in her long floating dinner gown. 'Take Miss Josie to the drawing room.'

'Yes, my lady.'

Mason bounded up the steps two at a time, even though Josie knew she was no lightweight. He carried her to the drawing room where they found Sir Hector seated by a roaring log fire with a blanket wrapped around his knees. He looked up and his face crumpled, halfway between tears and laughter. 'Josie, my dear girl.' He held out his arms.

'Set me down,' Josie commanded. 'You may leave us, Mason.'

He bowed and left the room.

She limped to her father's side, taking off her bonnet and tossing it onto one of the brocade sofas. She threw

160

herself down on her knees beside him. 'Papa, I'm so sorry I caused you so much distress.'

He dropped a kiss on top of her dark head. 'You're home now and that's all that matters, my dear.'

She took his hand and raised it to her cheek. She was shocked to see how pale and drawn he looked. It might only be a week since she had seen him but his physical condition seemed to have deteriorated enormously in that short space of time. 'How are you, Papa? Are you in pain?'

He squeezed her fingers. 'The gunshot wounds are healing, I believe, but I cannot feel anything below the waist. I suppose I should be thankful for small mercies.'

'Oh, Papa, it is so unfair. And I caused you so much worry, too. I am a bad daughter.'

'You are my little Josephine, and you are the best daughter a man could have. Now, don't look so tragic. I want to hear about your stay in Puddlecombe with the Reverend John Hardy. I knew his father well. Sir Esmond was a fine man, and it was a tragedy that he lost his only daughter to consumption. But how did you find his son? I haven't seen him for years.'

Lady Damerell swept into the room. 'You mustn't tire yourself, Hector. And there will be plenty of time for questions later, when Josie has had time to settle in.' She glanced at her daughter's travel-stained clothes with a pained expression on her face. 'You'd better go and change for dinner, Josie. I'll ring for Hickson to help you dress.'

Chapter Ten

The next few weeks were difficult for Josie. She had been shocked to see the deterioration in her father's condition, and, despite his brave words, his health did not seem to be improving. Dr Smith was noncommittal, insisting that it would take time for Sir Hector to adjust to his disability. Some of the wounds had become infected, but that was only to be expected, and they would eventually heal. Lady Damerell hovered in between states of wild optimism and deep depression, during which Josie was unable to comfort her. She missed Kate, and her time at the vicarage seemed almost like a holiday compared to the dullness of the daily routine at home. She tried to spend as much time as she could with her father, reading to him, or playing chess or backgammon, but he tired easily, and in spite of her eagerness to please him, Josie found herself growing more and more restive.

She went out riding every day, but she avoided the home farm. She longed to see Kate, but she did not feel equal to facing Sam. Her feelings and emotions were in total turmoil whenever his darkly handsome face trespassed on her thoughts, which was almost every waking moment. He invaded her dreams, causing her to awaken in the early hours of the morning, sick with longing for an impossible love that rendered going back to sleep impossible. She would get up then and pace her room, coming to a halt at the window and staring at the sweep of lawn that led down to the lake.

In her mind's eye she could see them as children, chasing each other, laughing and rolling down the grassy slope to the water's edge. They had been a happy trio, during those long hot summers spent in the country, but inevitably it had come to an end after the incident in the lake. Sam had carried her back to the house and been caught by Hickson as he tried to get her back to her room unnoticed. He had been banned from the house and beaten soundly. In the ensuing years she had tried to ignore her deepening feelings for Sam, concentrating on her ambition to marry money, but when he kissed her she had known that her life would never be the same again. She struggled daily with her desire to see him just once more; to feel his arms around her and his lips caressing hers. She knew it was never to be, but that did not take away the longing or her desperate need for her wild boy.

After being kept indoors by the November rain and gales, she could stand it no longer and one morning she donned her riding habit and boots, having sent to the stables to have her horse saddled. She had volunteered to go into Dorchester to collect her father's medicine from the chemist's shop, despite her mother's protests that a servant ought to go in her stead. It was market day, and Josie knew that she ran the risk of bumping into Sam, but she was past caring. In fact she was desperate to see him, if only to prove to herself that she was strong enough to resist temptation. Prompted by her mother she had written to Harry, explaining that her father would enjoy a visit from him and inviting him to call when he was next in the vicinity. She kept telling herself that Sam was attractive simply because he was forbidden fruit. Nothing could ever come of what was a purely physical attraction.

With a list of small items that her mother required from town, Josie was about to leave the house when Hickson came hurrying towards her.

'You should not go alone into town, Miss Josie. It isn't proper. If you'll wait until I get my cloak and bonnet, I'll come with you.'

'Thank you, Hickson, but there's no need. I am perfectly capable of performing a few errands on my own.'

'Young ladies should not go out unaccompanied, Miss Josie. You know that.'

'Come now, Hickson. What could possibly befall me on the road to Dorchester, or in the town itself where everybody knows me?'

'That's just it, they all know you, and they expect Miss Damerell of Damerell Manor to be more circum-spect in her behaviour.'

'My behaviour is my business, Hickson.'

'I saw you,' Hickson said in a low voice. 'I saw you and him on the evening when you arrived home from Puddlecombe. It won't do, it just won't do, and you know it.'

Josie tossed her head. 'I'm sure I don't know what you're talking about.'

'Don't act the innocent with me. I've known you all your life and you can't fool me with your innocent face.'

'You're talking in riddles, Hickson. I'm going into town.'

'Bad blood will out,' Hickson muttered.

'What did you say?'

Hickson blinked and shook her head. 'It was nothing, Miss Josephine.' She stalked off in the direction of the servants' quarters.

Josie shrugged her shoulders. Hickson was just being difficult and deliberately mysterious to goad her. She checked her appearance in one of the wall mirrors before setting off. It would be a coincidence if she happened to come across Sam in the market place.

In the town, she accomplished her shopping, filling a small basket with the bottles of medicine for her father and skeins of embroidery silk and a packet of needles for her mother. It was a bleak sunless day and bitterly cold. She walked briskly back to the market place where she had left her horse tethered to a post, and she arrived just as the squire drove up in a smart new gig with Kate sitting at his side. Kate's face lit up with a delighted smile when she saw her and she leapt down from the vehicle, barely giving it time to stop. She threw her arms around Josie in an affectionate hug. 'Josie, how are you? Why haven't you been to see us?'

165

'I've had a million things to do, but I see that you're encouraging your admirer.'

Kate pulled a face. 'Hush, he'll hear you.' She slipped her hand through Josie's arm. 'Thank goodness you're here. It gives me a good excuse to escape from Squire Westwood.' She pulled a face as he strolled over to join them. 'Oh, dear. Too late.'

'Good morning, Miss Damerell.' Edmund Westwood doffed his hat with a courtly bow. 'How is your father getting along? I'd like to call and see him, if he's well enough to receive visitors.'

'He's as well as can be expected, but I'm sure he would be most pleased to see you, Mr Westwood.'

'Then I'll be certain to visit him very soon.' He hesitated, looking from one to the other. 'I expect you young ladies have a great deal to chat about. But I hope you will allow me to drive you home when you've finished your business in town, Miss Coggins. It looks like rain.'

'Thank you, but I don't want to put you to any trouble. I can quite easily find my own way home.'

'I wouldn't hear of it, my dear.' He glanced up at the lowering sky. 'I'll wait for you in the Antelope Hotel. Take your time, I'm in no hurry.'

'He definitely has his eye on you, Kate,' Josie said, chuckling as he strode off towards the town centre. 'Do you fancy being the second Mrs Westwood?'

'Don't say such things. He's just being kind. Or at least I hope that's all it is. I wouldn't marry an old man like Squire Westwood if he was the last person left on earth. But I must talk to you, Josie.'

166

'What's wrong? Is someone ill?' Josie immediately thought of Sam and she held her breath.

'No, nothing like that.' Kate quickened her pace.

'Well, what is it? Are you going to tell me or not?'

'It's my father. He's going to marry Miss Stamp next week.'

'He doesn't believe in long engagements then.' Josie suppressed a chuckle with difficulty. Poor Kate, she must have known that this was inevitable.

'It's not funny, Josie. Pa told me that he wanted female companionship and someone to look after him in his dotage. He spoke as if I were about to desert him, and I would never do that.'

'But you will get married one day, and then you'll have a husband and children of your own. You can see his point.'

'That's just what Squire Westwood said, and he's repeated his offer of a position at the Grange. I don't know what to do. All I know is that I can't stand the thought of living in the same house as that woman.'

Josie was at a loss as to how to comfort her. She dragged Kate to a halt outside a milliner's shop. 'Just look at that adorable bonnet. Now that would suit you to perfection, Kate. Why don't we go inside and you can try it on?'

'I can't afford to buy a new bonnet, and even if I could, it wouldn't solve anything. And don't offer to purchase it for me, Josie. I still have the one you bought me in Soho, and I only wear that on Sundays. I know you mean well, but it's not the answer.'

'If you wore that you would outshine the bride on her wedding day,' Josie said hopefully. 'And the squire would fall on his knees begging you to accept all his worldly goods.'

Kate shot her a reproachful glance. 'You are the biggest tease in the county.'

'And you, my dear friend, are taking all this much too seriously. So what if your father marries the ghastly Miss Stamp? From the little I've seen of that person I doubt if she will interfere in the running of the house or the farm. She will probably lie in bed all day reading penny dreadfuls and eating chocolate. She is already as fat as a pig in farrow.'

'And she'll expect me to wait on her.'

'You've a maidservant to do that, haven't you? I'm sure that young Molly will be happy to oblige a new mistress, or you could promote Sam from farm labourer to butler. Now there's a thought.'

'Molly isn't a servant.' Kate turned to her, frowning. 'Have you and Sam fallen out? Is that why you haven't been near the farm for so long?'

'What a ridiculous notion.' In an attempt to steer the conversation to safer ground, Josie opened the door and stepped into the shop. 'Come along, Kate. That lovely bonnet is calling out to me. I must try it on even though I know that it would look much better on you.'

An hour later they left the shop with Kate wearing the sapphire-blue velvet creation trimmed with fur, and Josie having bought three new confections of straw, satin, feathers and flowers. Her extravagance would get her into trouble when her father received the bill, but she had learned long ago that a show of repentance and a few tears would make him end up by apologising to her for his parsimony. She would smile again and all would be well.

'There,' she said, eyeing Kate with genuine pleasure. 'See how that bonnet has transformed your sad expression. You look quite enchanting in it, so admit that I was right.'

Kate stole a look at her reflection in the shop window. 'It is very becoming. Thank you, Josie, although I know I should not have accepted such a generous gift.'

'Nonsense. That's what friends are for, and my papa can well afford such luxuries. Anyway, your bonnet cost nothing in comparison with mine, and Papa is not in the least bit stingy.' She held up the bandbox containing her purchases as a demonstration of her extravagance. 'I'm sure that he's well aware that if I'm to be sold to the highest bidder in the marriage mart, I must always look my best.'

'How can you even think such a dreadful thing? You make marriage sound like a cattle market.'

'Well, isn't it? My parents expect me to marry well. There is no room for love or sentiment when money and position are involved.'

'You don't mean that, do you, Josie?'

'Of course I do. Why do you think I was so eager to see Copperstone Castle? I'm expected to make a good match and I think that Harry Challenor would suit me well enough.'

169

'But you don't love him.'

'I love his castle and his wealth; that will have to be sufficient. Besides which, I'm not such a mercenary creature; I do like him and he's a handsome rogue. I'm sure we'll muddle along somehow.' The conversation was becoming too personal and Josie walked on. In the past she had been able to convince herself that she was thoroughly selfish, but now everything had changed. She could no longer deny her feelings for Sam, but they must be crushed out of existence. It was the only way.

'But have you never had a fondness for anyone? What happens if you meet someone and fall in love with him?'

'I shall take a lover, of course. That's what wealthy women do, isn't it?'

'I don't believe you're that shallow.'

Josie stopped outside the Antelope Hotel. 'I am me, Kate. You know me better than anyone else and I will survive no matter what befalls me. But you're the one in need of sympathy at this moment. Do we go inside and meet the squire? Or have you any other business in town today?'

'No. I mean, I was going to change my book at the library after I'd taken the eggs to Biddy Madge's stall, but the squire arrived just as we were leaving and invited me to ride in his new gig. I could hardly refuse without giving offence, and Sam promised to take the eggs to market. I was in such a state that I left my book on the kitchen table. Why, what's the matter?'

Josie tugged playfully at the ribbons on Kate's

bonnet. 'Nothing's wrong with me. You're the one who's in a state.'

'I was, but I'm calm now. I just feel rather silly for allowing myself to get upset when I should be happy that Pa has found someone to his liking.'

'Come, then. I want to see the expression on the squire's face when he sees you looking so ravishing in that new bonnet.'

'Wait,' Kate said, catching her by the elbow as Josie was about to enter the hotel. 'This one is far too fine for everyday wear. I'll put on my old bonnet.'

Josie twisted her round and gave her a gentle push. 'Don't be silly. Walk in as though you own the place.'

'He's only offered me a position in his household,' Kate said in a low voice. 'There has been no hint of anything else.'

'He's quite a catch, my dear. And it would be a slap in the face for Miss Stamp.'

As Josie followed Kate into the hotel lobby, she wrinkled her nose at the smell of stale beer, tobacco smoke and sweat emanating from the public bar. The sound of deep male voices and gusts of raucous laughter echoed round the wainscoted entrance hall.

Kate hesitated on the threshold. 'This wasn't a good idea. I'd rather walk home in a thunderstorm than do this.'

'Too late,' Josie whispered. 'There's the squire now. Give him your best smile, my dear.'

Edmund Westwood was advancing on them, his craggy features creased into a welcoming smile. 'Miss Coggins, how charming you look in your new bonnet.

I think that must have been chosen under your guidance, Miss Damerell.'

Josie shook her head. 'No, Squire. It was entirely Kate's choice. She has excellent taste.'

'So I see. I count myself a fortunate man to have the company of two such elegant young ladies. It would give me great pleasure if you were to join me for a light luncheon.'

'Thank you, but I really ought to be going now.' Kate shot a warning glance at Josie. 'I came to tell you that Sam will take me home in the trap.'

In spite of herself, Josie could not resist the temptation to tease her. 'But, Kate, you don't know where to find him. I daresay he returned to the farm ages ago.'

'And you would be wrong there.' Sam strolled out of the public bar. 'The trap is in the stable yard, Kate. If you're ready to come with me now.'

He was addressing himself to Kate, but Josie was acutely aware that his gaze was fixed on her. She looked away, for once in her life lost for words.

'It's all right, Loveday. I'll bring Miss Coggins home; you may go on your way.' Edmund held his hand out to Kate. 'I've booked a private parlour, away from the riffraff.'

Josie clenched her hands at her sides. She would have liked to slap the squire's smug face for the implied insult to Sam. She sent him a warning glance, but she could see that he was ready for a fight. She forced herself to sound calm. 'You heard the squire, Kate. Let's go where we can enjoy our luncheon in private away from the common herd.' It almost broke her heart to see the look on Sam's face, but it was better that he turned his anger on her than on an important man like the squire. If he lost his temper with a magistrate he might well end the day in court, incurring a jail sentence, but try as she might she could not keep up the pretence for more than a few seconds. She turned to Kate, hoping that she at least had understood, but judging by her angry expression she had taken offence on Sam's behalf.

'I don't see good, honest country folk in that way,' Kate cried angrily. 'I am one of the common herd as you put it, Josie. And I daresay I belong with the riffraff, Squire. So you'll forgive me if I go home with Sam. Good day to you.'

'Well said, girl. I didn't know you had it in you.' Sam glowered at Josie as he offered Kate his arm. 'Good day to you, Miss Damerell, and to you, Squire.'

Josie could bear it no longer. Ignoring the squire's protests she snatched up her packages and hurried from the room. She caught up with Kate and Sam in the stable yard. 'I didn't mean it, Sam.'

His eyes burned into hers with blind fury. 'You said what you truly feel, Miss Damerell. You put me in my place.'

'Yes, Josie,' Kate said, shaking her head. 'You've made it clear where we stand. I'm sorry if I allowed myself to think that we could ever be true friends.' She allowed Sam to hand her up into the trap, and sat down, staring straight ahead.

'No. You really don't understand,' Josie cried in

desperation. 'You mistook my motives, both of you.' She stood back as Sam leapt onto the driver's seat and took the reins, urging the old carthorse through the archway that led to the London road.

Josie blinked away angry tears. Why would neither of them listen to her? She had acted in Sam's best interests. She loved him. Why would she do anything that would cause him pain? She walked slowly as her ankle had begun to ache miserably. In her confused state she only narrowly missed being run down by a cabriolet as it pulled into the stable yard. The horse between the shafts reared and whinnied in fright. 'Look out there.' The driver drew the startled animal to a halt before leaping to the ground. 'Josie? By God, it is you.'

She gazed at him blindly. The voice was familiar but he was muffled in a caped greatcoat and had a felt hat pulled down low to protect him from the rain that had begun to fall in earnest. 'Harry?'

He tossed the reins to a stable boy. 'See to him and there's a silver sixpence in it for you.' Harry pulled off his hat, staring at Josie with a puzzled frown. 'Why may I ask are you wandering about an inn yard unattended?'

'It was all a mistake.' She stared at him dazedly. 'Why are you here, if it comes to that?'

'You invited me to call on your father. Have you forgotten?'

'No. I mean, I didn't expect you to come.'

'I've been attending to business matters in Weymouth and I came here for something to eat and drink before travelling on to Damerell Manor.' He took her by the arm. 'You're obviously upset. Perhaps you'd better tell me about it over a cup of hot coffee or something stronger.'

'No, thank you. I must go home.'

'And I'll take you in my carriage, but you'll have to wait until my horse has been fed and watered. I can't allow the poor animal to travel on again until he's rested.'

'My horse is nearby. It won't take me long to walk to the market place.'

'It's pouring with rain. I'll take you home and we'll collect your horse on the way.'

Josie remained unconvinced. The thought of facing the squire again so soon was enough to make a walk in the rain seem a much more attractive alternative, but Harry refused to listen to her arguments and eventually she agreed to accompany him into the hotel where he requested a private parlour. He might not be as well known as the squire, but she had to admit that he had a commanding presence, and was obviously used to getting his own way. They were immediately ushered into one of the best rooms, where there was a roaring log fire. She realised then that she was chilled to the marrow and she was glad to sit in a comfortable chair, warming herself and sipping a glass of hot toddy.

Harry took a seat opposite her. 'Now then, perhaps you feel able to tell me what it was that upset you so much?'

She met his anxious gaze with a straight look.

175

She was seeing a completely different side to Harry. There was no suggestion of the flirtatious man about town image that he liked to portray; he seemed genuinely concerned as to her welfare and was being almost unbearably kind. It did not sit with her earlier impression of him. She chose her words carefully. 'It was something and nothing.'

'A very large nothing then.' He smiled but there was no hint of mockery in his eyes.

'It's complicated, but Squire Westwood wanted to be alone with Kate, and then Sam intervened and it all became very confused and I said some things I shouldn't. I was upset, but I'm fine now.'

'I'm glad, and I won't ask any awkward questions.' He rose to his feet as a maidservant entered carrying a tray of food. He gave her what appeared to be a generous tip, as the girl's face creased into a huge grin. She bobbed a curtsey and scurried from the room.

'What will you have?' Harry asked, picking up a fork and surveying the spread. 'There's cold ham, meat pie, cheese, celery, pickles. It all looks splendid and I must admit that I'm ravenous. You will join me, won't you, Josie?'

She was beginning to feel more like her old self and the food smelt good enough to tempt any jaded appetite. She accepted a plate of ham and a slice of pie with a generous helping of mustard pickle.

He watched her with a smile of approval. 'I like to see a woman with a good appetite.' He took a seat at the table opposite her. 'So how did Kate come to be with Westwood and who is Sam?'

'Sam Loveday. He and his sister were abandoned by their father and raised by Kate's grandfather as his own children.' Josie swallowed a mouthful of pie, and once she started to tell him what had happened she found that she could not stop. The only thing she omitted was her involvement with Sam, which was far too private to share with anyone, least of all the man she intended to marry.

Harry listened intently. 'I remember Loveday. He's the ferocious-looking young man who guards Kate like a faithful hound.'

'We all grew up together. We were childhood friends.'

'In that case you have no need to worry. They might have taken offence at something you said, but when they calm down it will all be forgotten.' He cut himself a slice of cheese. 'Can I tempt you to a piece of this excellent Cheddar?'

She shook her head, watching him curiously. 'Were you really on your way to Damerell Manor?'

'I received your note, but I would have come anyway. I was waiting until your father had recovered sufficiently to receive visitors.'

Josie was suddenly curious. 'What is it you do exactly? I know you're in trade, but no one talks about it. Why is it such a deep dark secret?'

'It isn't as far as I'm concerned. I'm proud that my family made their money honestly as merchants and ship owners, and I've carried on the tradition. It's looked down upon by some, but I suspect that it doesn't matter much to you.'

She met his quizzical gaze with a gurgle of laughter. 'Not at all. I have to marry a rich man and you're on the top of my list.'

His laughter echoed round the wainscoted parlour. 'And you could overlook the fact that my fortune was made in such a vulgar manner?'

'Possibly, if the rewards were sufficient.'

He almost choked on a mouthful of coffee. 'Do you know, Josie Damerell, if I were in the marriage market, I think I would be hard pressed to find a woman who amused me as much as you do.'

'So you're not looking for a wife?'

'When the right woman comes along I will hope to prove myself worthy of her.'

'But you do want to marry someone from a good family?'

'Birth and breeding don't come into it.'

'Mama will be so disappointed.'

He rose to his feet. 'I think it's high time I took you home, Josie, and I genuinely want to pay my respects to your father. He's a good man and it was a terrible injury he sustained.'

She stood up, reaching for the bandbox containing her purchases and her basket. 'Yes, I've been away too long as it is. They'll be starting to worry about me.'

It had stopped raining by the time they reached Damerell Manor and the sun had forced its way through a bank of clouds to send fitful rays onto the wet grass. Harry helped Josie down from the cabriolet and she stood for a moment staring up at the house, which seemed oddly silent. Someone should have noticed their approach. On a normal day the front door would be flung open with a footman standing to attention, and a groom would come running in order to take the equipage to the stables.

She had a sick feeling in her stomach as she raced up the steps to hammer on the door. Something was terribly wrong. She pounded the solid oak with her fists until she heard the sound of footsteps and it was Toop himself who opened the door. His set expression seemed to wilt before her eyes and his bottom lip trembled.

'Toop, what's happened? What's wrong?'

Chapter Eleven

News of Sir Hector's stroke had travelled round the village long before it was announced during matins on the following Sunday, and therefore it came as no surprise to the concerned villagers. Kate had called at the manor house as soon as she heard about the squire's condition, but Hickson had sent her away with the proverbial flea in her ear. She had written a note to Josie but had no way of knowing whether or not it had been received. This, together with the fact that plans for her father's wedding were already in hand, had made her feel extremely low. Sam and Molly had sympathised and tried to comfort her, but the end result was inevitable.

Robert and Honoria were married by Parson Daleymount in the parish church of Kingston Damerell at the beginning of December. The squire gave the bride away as she had no living relatives, and he had also generously provided the wedding breakfast which was laid out in one of the barns at the home farm. Kate had had little to do with the arrangements, except for hanging the rafters with swags of evergreen. The squire had sent everything else, including the crockery and cutlery from the Grange, and his servants had set the tables and laid out the food.

Sir Hector was not well enough to attend the service, and Lady Damerell declined to come without him, but Josie was there, sitting in the family pew, and to Kate's surprise Harry Challenor was at her side. As Kate walked up the aisle behind Honoria and the squire, Josie looked up and winked at her, and the coolness that had existed between them was dispelled in a moment. Kate sighed with relief. She stole a sideways glance at Harry, but he was giving his full attention to Josie, who was whispering something in his ear that made him smile. They seemed to be such an established couple that Kate felt her heart sink down to her satin slippers. So Josie had caught her man after all. She ought to have been happy for her, but the sight of them together left a bitter taste in her mouth which she could not explain. As if it were not bad enough to witness her father exchanging marriage vows with Honoria, she had to watch her lifelong friend entering a loveless marriage which would almost inevitably bring unhappiness to both parties.

Outside the church in the fitful December sunshine, Robert threw a handful of copper coins at the feet of the village children, who scrambled and fought over the pennies, halfpennies and farthings. Sam had decked the farm cart with ribbons and laurel, and was waiting to drive them the short distance to the barn. Robert was about to hand Honoria onto the driver's seat when Harry stepped forward. 'My dear sir, might I offer you and your bride the use of my carriage for the journey to the wedding breakfast?'

Robert's cheeks flushed dark red above his starched shirt collar. 'Thank you, sir. I wouldn't want to put you to so much trouble.'

'It is no trouble at all.' Harry signalled to his coachman.

Honoria beamed at him. 'How very kind of you, sir.'

'Thank you, Mr Challenor,' Robert said stiffly. 'But my cart is good enough for me and for my wife too.'

Kate recognised the martial spark in her father's eyes and she could see that he was mortally offended, but before she could say anything Honoria had turned on her new husband, bristling like a turkeycock. 'This behaviour won't do, Robert. You must not turn down such a generous offer.' With her foot already on the step and her hand on the coachman's arm, she flashed a smile at Harry. 'You're very kind, sir. We will be delighted to accept your offer.'

'There you are, Coggins. Your lady wife has made the decision for you.' Harry's lips twitched as though he wanted to laugh, and mischievous glints danced in his eyes even though his tone was serious.

Kate saw her father's shoulders stiffen and he gave Harry a curt nod. Poor Pa, she thought, as she watched him climb up into the carriage. He's been married barely half an hour and Honoria is already showing her true colours. She knew then for certain that life at home would never be the same again. She looked up and met Harry's amused gaze. So he was just entertaining himself at the expense of the peasants, was he? She would have liked to give him a piece of her mind, but she did not want to make a scene.

'What's wrong, Miss Coggins? Have I managed to offend you yet again?'

'Why would you think that, Mr Challenor? Why should I mind if you use your wealth to undermine my father's standing in the eyes of his bride? I'm sure he is honoured to be humiliated by a man such as you.'

'You humble me, Miss Coggins.'

'I didn't think that would be possible.'

Josie had stopped in the church porch and was speaking to Parson Daleymount, but she broke off and came hurrying to Harry's side. 'What's this? You two look very serious and it is supposed to be a happy day.'

'Miss Coggins is cross with me, Josie. I'm afraid my good intentions have gone awry.'

Josie slipped her hand through his arm, but the smile froze on her face as Sam brought the farm cart to a halt in front of them. She eyed him with a stony stare. 'It's very easy to bruise the pride of stiff-necked country folk.'

'Then perhaps you should not have lowered yourself to come among us, miss.' Sam's expression was hostile as he leapt from the driver's seat.

Josie clenched her gloved hands into fists, and Kate felt the tension between them crackle and spit like green wood on a fire. She laid her hand on Sam's arm. 'Pa and Honoria will be halfway there by now. We should follow them.'

'Go on then,' Josie said, tossing her head. 'I'm not sure that I want to attend a bucolic romp, and I'm afraid that you will find it utterly boring, Harry.'

'On the contrary, my dear. I'm looking forward to it enormously.'

Sam thrust the reins into Harry's hands. 'There you are then, sir. Since you gave your carriage to the happy couple, perhaps you would like to ride country style.'

Kate held her breath, waiting for Harry's response. She thought he was about to cut Sam down to size, but he turned to Josie with a lazy smile. 'What do you say, Josie? Shall we accept the fellow's offer?'

'Why not? And I shall take the reins. I'm a competent whip, Harry. As you will soon discover.' She eyed Sam with a contemptuous curl of her lips. 'You may help me up, fellow.'

Without saying a word, Sam lifted her in his arms and tossed her onto the driver's seat. The startled horse whinnied and reared in the shafts. Harry caught hold of his bridle and stroked the frightened animal's muzzle. 'That was a damn fool thing to do, Loveday.'

Sam touched his forelock. 'What do you expect from a simple country lad, sir?'

Kate stepped in between them. 'Enough of this. Josie, if you run my dear old horse into the ground I'll never speak to you again. And you, Sam! For shame on you speaking to Mr Challenor like that. It makes you almost as bad as he is.' She marched off with her head held high, but she was struggling to control a maelstrom of emotions from anger to humiliation and perhaps a tinge of jealousy. Josie held men's hearts in the palm of her hand, and yet it did not seem to occur to her that she was creating havoc in their lives. Kate could not be certain but she guessed that Josie had given Sam some encouragement, and now he was tormented by a hopeless passion. By her own admission, Josie had set out to make Harry fall in love with her. Had she succeeded? Kate felt tears stinging her eyes as she walked on as fast as her long skirts would allow. Harry Challenor was not her concern – he could take care of himself. He had no doubt left a string of broken hearts in his wake. It would serve him right if he did fall in love with Josie.

She turned her head as the trap drew up beside her. Josie leaned down and held out her hand. Her eyes sparkled with mischief. 'Jump up beside me, Kate. I've left the silly men to take shanks's pony.'

Kate hesitated, but she could not resist Josie's wicked grin. She hitched up her skirts and climbed up beside her.

Josie flicked the whip. 'Giddy-up, old chap. Let's show them you're not yet ready for the knacker's yard.'

'Don't drive him too hard,' Kate said, holding onto the sides of the trap.

'Look at him go. I'm sure the poor nag is dying to get the wind under his tail and show you what he can do.' Josie flicked the whip above the horse's ears and he responded by breaking into a canter. They arrived shortly after the happy couple, and were just in time to see Robert help his new wife alight from the carriage. They took their place in front of the barn doors to greet their guests. Honoria gave Kate a triumphant smile as she walked past her, but Robert caught her in his arms and gave her a smacking kiss on both cheeks. 'You are still my best girl, Kate. And I hope that you will grow to love Honoria as I do.'

He could not have said anything worse, and although she knew it was well meant, Kate's eyes brimmed with tears.

'There, now. I've made you cry, my dear. I never meant to.'

He looked so crestfallen that she swallowed hard and forced her lips into a semblance of a smile. 'I just want you to be happy, Pa.' She turned to Honoria. 'And I wish you well too, ma'am. I'm sure I'll try to be a dutiful daughter to you.'

Honoria bared her teeth, but her eyes were cold. 'You'd better,' she whispered. 'There isn't room for two mistresses in the house, if you get my meaning.'

Biting back an angry retort, Kate moved away quickly.

'What on earth did she say to you?' Josie demanded anxiously. 'You look as though you've seen a ghost.'

'She's just declared war. Well, if that's the way she wants it – that is what she will get.'

'Oh, Lord,' Josie said with feeling. 'The sooner I hook Harry the better, then I can get you away from all this, and we can both live happily ever after in Copperstone Castle.'

Kate saw her gaze wander to the doorway where Harry had entered, followed closely by Sam. Josie's expression was guarded, but Kate saw a haunting sadness in her eyes as she watched Sam walk across the barn to speak to Molly. Josie might pretend to be

186

hard, but Kate sensed that it was not only Sam's heart that was breaking.

'Miss Coggins.'

Kate turned with a start. 'Mr Challenor?'

'I apologise for any offence that I may have caused you.'

'Really? You don't look very sorry to me.'

'Come now, Kate,' Josie said with a forced laugh. 'Harry doesn't very often apologise for his behaviour. Let's not spoil your father's special day.'

Kate frowned. She was not going to let Josie get off so lightly. 'I think you should tell Sam you're sorry for the way you treated him.'

'If it will make you happy, I'll go down on my bended knees and beg his forgiveness.' Josie cast an arch glance in Harry's direction.

'Go on then,' Kate said, unimpressed. 'I want to see it.'

Josie took Harry's hand and linked it with Kate's. 'I will make my peace with Loveday, if you two will shake hands and agree to be friends.' She reached up to kiss his cheek. 'Be a good boy, Harry. And I will reward you.' Without waiting for his answer, Josie danced across the barn towards Sam.

Kate tried to pull her hand away but Harry held it in a warm grasp. 'Am I forgiven?'

'I'm sure that what I think matters very little to a man like you.'

'You're quite wrong. I make it a firm rule that everyone I meet has to like me.'

'Now you are laughing at me.'

187

'Not at all. I'm laughing at our ridiculous social customs that make us say what we do not think or mean. And I respect you for speaking the truth even though it is not always palatable.'

If she was not careful, she might actually begin to like him. Kate attempted to withdraw her hand, but he raised it to his lips and brushed it with a whisper of a kiss. 'As you haven't slapped my face, I take it I am forgiven. So will you do me the honour of dancing with me, Miss Coggins?'

It was impossible to refuse when he put it so charmingly, and inexplicably she wanted nothing more than to be held in his arms, although she was uncomfortably aware that there were many curious eyes watching them. It would be all round the village by teatime that Kate Coggins had danced with the owner of Copperstone Castle, and that he had chosen her to partner him rather than Miss Damerell. The fiddlers struck up a lively polka and before she had a chance to refuse, Harry had whirled her into the dance. Breathless and wishing that she had not made Molly tighten her corsets so that her waist was little more than a hand's span, Kate had to concentrate hard in order to keep up with Harry. It would be so humiliating if she were to tread on his feet or to miss a step that she forgot all about remaining aloof, and found herself actually enjoying the feeling of being twirled round in strong arms so that it was almost like flying. Her hooped skirts swung like a bell and her satin slippers barely touched the packed earth floor. When the dance finally came to an end, Harry still held her. 'There, that wasn't so bad, was it?'

She was breathless from the exertion and exhilaration had made her pulses race. She shook her head. 'No, not at all.'

'Admit it, Miss Coggins, you enjoyed dancing with me.'

His smile would have melted a stone. Kate struggled to recall why she disliked him so much, and failed. 'You are a good dancer, Mr Challenor,' she murmured reluctantly.

'What an admission. You had better be careful or you might even begin to like me, Kate. May I call you that?'

Before Kate could respond, Josie pounced on them seemingly from nowhere. 'Harry Challenor, are you flirting with poor Kate?' There was an edge in her voice even though she was smiling. 'You are a brute, you know. Leave the poor girl alone and dance with me.'

Harry kissed Kate's hand, and for a moment his eyes held hers. 'Kate and I have called a truce.'

'Is that so?' Josie tucked her hand in his arm. 'Kate, I've just been talking to the squire and I think he wants this next dance with you.'

'What have you been saying?' Kate knew by the look on her face that Josie had been up to some devilish mischief, which only she would find hilariously funny. 'What have you done?'

Josie tossed her head and her ruby earrings flashed like tiny balls of fire. 'I said that you had something important to tell him. You have, haven't you?'

'Really, Josie. You should know better than to meddle with other people's lives,' Harry said, frowning.

'This has nothing to do with you, Harry. Kate knows very well what she should say to the lovelorn squire.'

Kate glanced over Josie's shoulder and her heart sank as she saw Squire Westwood waving to her from the far side of the barn. He was beaming at her in such a delighted way that she felt quite sick, and he was coming towards them, threading his way through the dancers. She could only guess at the extent of Josie's meddling. 'What exactly did you say to him, Josie?'

'I told him that you wanted to speak to him about his proposal. You do, don't you?'

'It was not that sort of proposal and you know it. Anyway, you were supposed to be making your peace with Sam, not putting false notions in the squire's head.'

'I thought I was doing you a favour by encouraging the squire to make you a more appealing offer.'

'You know that is the last thing I ever wanted, Josie. How could you put me in this position?'

Josie shrugged her shoulders. 'Dear me, I must have misunderstood. Anyway, he's coming to speak to you, so I suggest you put the poor man out of his misery.'

'It seems to me that you started this, Josie,' Harry said severely. 'And it is up to you to put things straight. Kate has made her feelings quite clear.'

'It's well known that the squire is hopelessly infatuated with her and she will never get another chance to equal this. She would be a fool to turn down a man with wealth and position, especially when she is about to be ousted from her own home by that dreadful woman.'

'How could you, Josie?' Kate stared at her aghast. 'He has never spoken to me of anything other than being a companion to his daughters.'

'I think you'll find that he will now, my dear.' Josie smiled up at Harry. 'Don't look so cross. I meant it all for the best.'

'I should go and see if my father needs me,' Kate said, backing away.

'He has Honoria to look after him now.' Josie caught her by the hand. 'You can't keep running away, Kate. Stay here and speak to the squire. If you do not wish to encourage his suit then you must make it plain.'

Edmund was just a few feet away, and his face with wreathed in smiles. Kate snatched her hand free from Josie's grasp. 'I don't know what you said to him, but I'll never forgive you for this. Never!'

'Josie, it was very wrong of you to interfere,' Harry said angrily.

Kate did not wait to hear Josie's reply; she turned and ran. Outside the barn, she stopped to catch her breath. It was quite dark now and a cold sleety rain had begun to fall. She shivered, wrapping her arms around her body in an effort to keep warm. Her hands and feet were cold as ice but her cheeks were burning with anger and humiliation. How could Josie do this to her? And how would she ever face the squire again?

'Kate. What's the matter?' Sam hurried to her side. 'What are you doing out here in the cold and wet?'

He took his jacket off and wrapped it round her shoulders. 'For heaven's sake, maidy, what made you run off like that?'

'I didn't run off. I just needed some fresh air.'

'I saw you dancing with that man of Josie's. Did he say something to upset you? If he did, he'll have to answer to me.'

'No, Sam. It was nothing like that. I had an argument with Josie, that's all.'

'That young lady needs to be put in her place.'

'And you're not the one to do it. You have to forget her, Sam. She's not for you and if you let her, she'll break your heart.'

'Never mind me, Kate. It's you I'm worried about.'

'I can take care of myself.'

'That may be so, but I'm not letting you out of my sight for the rest of the evening.'

She forced a smile. 'That won't be necessary, but perhaps we'd better go back inside. You can dance with me, and that will keep us both out of harm's way.'

As they walked slowly back into the barn, arm in arm, they were met in the doorway by a worried Robert. 'Are you ill, my dear? I saw you go outside and I would have followed but for Honoria, who wanted me to dance with her.'

'I'm all right, Pa. I was just a bit hot and needed some air.' Kate shrugged off Sam's jacket and returned it to him with a grateful smile.

Robert eyed her suspiciously. 'You look flushed to me. Are you sure you aren't coming down with something?'

192

'Quite sure, Pa. This is your party, go and enjoy yourself with your new wife.'

'Wife? It sounds strange, but I daresay I'll get used to it again in time. But I wish she weren't quite so energetic. I'm not cut out for this prancing about.'

'Robert.' Honoria's voice was shrill enough to shatter glass.

'Coming, my love.' He patted Kate on the shoulder and hurried off to where Honoria was waiting for him, tapping her toe impatiently.

'He's under the thumb already,' Sam said, chuckling. 'I never thought I'd see the day when the gaffer was ruled by a woman. You'd best look out for that one, Kate. She'll have you living in the stable afore she's done.'

He was joking, of course, but Kate felt as though a heavy weight was pressing down on her shoulders. She could see Josie dancing the waltz with Harry: his dark head was angled as if he was hanging on every word she said, and Josie in her turn was smiling up at him – they looked every inch a perfect couple. Her father had led Honoria onto the floor and was making a clumsy attempt to keep in time with the music. Everyone was happy, it seemed, except her.

Sam held out his hand. 'I can't promise not to tread on your toes, Kate, but I'll have a go at this here waltz thing.'

She eyed him doubtfully, but the squire had spotted her and she had yet to decide on the best course of action. She took Sam's hand and allowed him to lead her into the dance.

* * *

It was later, at the supper table that Edmund managed to corner her. 'Have you been avoiding me, Miss Kate?'

'Yes, Squire Westwood. I'm afraid I have.'

His bushy eyebrows shot up his forehead, almost disappearing into his hairline. 'At least that's honest. But why? Have I done something to upset you?'

'No, sir. But I think Josie might have spoken out of turn.'

'She said that you wished to speak to me, that was all.'

'She was mistaken. I have nothing to say to you that I have not said before.'

'I won't press you then, but my offer still stands. Now that Miss Morton has left us my daughters are in great need of a suitable companion. I've managed to replace Miss Stamp as housekeeper, but my girls are running wild and would greatly benefit from your gentle guidance. If you come to feel differently, for any reason, just let me know.'

'I will, sir,' Kate murmured, looking round desperately for a change of subject. 'Have you tried the apple pie, Squire Westwood? The fruit came from our orchard.'

'It looks delicious.' He picked up a knife and cut a large slice. 'Did you make the pastry yourself?'

She nodded. 'Yes, sir.'

'What an accomplished young lady you are, and extremely pretty into the bargain. I shall savour every mouthful.'

Kate left him piling his plate with pie as if he had not eaten for a week, and went to join Sam who was sitting alone at one of the trestle tables. He looked up and grinned. 'So you put the old fellow straight, did you?'

'I think he was just being kind, Sam. It's Josie who has been making too much of his offer. He only wants someone to look after his girls. I suppose I should be flattered that he wants me.'

'You turned him down, that's all that matters. And if anyone bothers you, Kate, you just let me know and I'll set them to rights.' Sam shot a darkling glance at Harry who was sitting at the top table with Josie. 'There are some men who think they can behave exactly as they please, especially where a girl like you is concerned.'

Kate followed his brooding gaze and she laughed. 'Don't be absurd, Sam. Mr Challenor only has eyes for Josie. You of all people should have noticed that.'

'I have and more. He'd make free with you too, given the opportunity. You keep clear of him and his like.'

Kate squeezed his hand. 'There's no need to worry on that score, Sam. I've never liked Harry Challenor. I think he is arrogant and a good deal too pleased with himself for his own good, and the feeling I am sure is mutual, since he never loses the opportunity to annoy me. Josie is welcome to him and his castle.'

'She's only playing with him.' Sam stabbed his knife into a piece of cheese. 'Josie and I were meant to be together, and she knows it too.'

'Don't, Sam. You know it's impossible.'

He rose abruptly to his feet. 'I'm going to get a

tankard of ale. Would you like some of the cider cup?'

Glancing over his shoulder, Kate caught sight of Josie whispering something in Harry's ear. She was flirting quite outrageously. Kate suspected that she was being deliberately provocative in order to tease Sam, in the same way that the farm cats caught a mouse and tormented it before the final kill. 'Yes,' she murmured, praying silently that he would not turn round and witness the spectacle. 'That would be lovely.' She breathed a sigh of relief when he walked off in the opposite direction. This was turning out to be the worst evening of her life so far, and she could not wait to return to the sanctuary of her room at home. The sooner Harry Challenor went back to his friends in London or to Copperstone Castle, the better for all concerned. She could see her father making ready to leave, although Honoria did not seem to be eager to abandon the party, which was becoming rowdier with every passing minute. Some of the older children had obviously been imbibing something stronger than fruit cup and their shrieks echoed off the rafters as they cavorted and chased each other round the hay bales. Molly was standing in their midst making an attempt to calm them down, but she might as well have been King Canute attempting to stop the incoming tide.

Kate rose to her feet, thinking that this would be an appropriate moment to slip away unnoticed. Sam was deep in conversation with one of the grooms from the big house and seemed to have forgotten about her.

She was about to make her way towards the door when it opened and a gust of cold air sent dust devils spinning across the floor. Miss Hickson flew into the barn, her black cloak streaming about her like the wings on a bird of ill omen.

'Stop the music,' she screamed, holding up her hand. 'This isn't the time for revelry. The master is dying.' She hurled herself at Josie, grasping her by the shoulders and shaking her. 'Your father is at death's door. You must come now, before it's too late.'

Chapter Twelve

Josie was first down to breakfast. She had made a point of rising early since the arrival of her uncle who had travelled from London the moment he received news of his brother's sudden collapse. She had decided that eating on her own was preferable to suffering Joseph Damerell's sly looks and constant innuendoes. Avoiding him had become a way of life; or rather it was a case of keeping out of reach of his wandering hands. He seemed to be impervious to both insults and her dire warnings that she would tell his wife if he attempted to touch her inappropriately. His memory was lamentably short, and his profuse apologies soon forgotten, as he continued to offend. It seemed that his hands and his brain were somehow unconnected. Josie's nerves were frayed and her temper was close to breaking point. The events of the past few days had taken their toll on her, and the safe world that she had always known seemed to be crumbling about her head. Papa was hovering between this world and the next. Dr Smith said that it was only a matter of time now, and Josie had to watch her mother growing paler and more drawn with each passing hour as she kept a vigil at her husband's bedside. Uncle Joseph might put on an outward show of concern, but it was obvious to Josie that he could not wait to claim his inheritance. His wife, Hermione, seemed to be genuinely upset and sympathetic. She did her best to comfort Marguerite, but tact was not her strong point and she usually ended up making matters worse.

Then there were practical matters to address. When the worst happened, how would they manage to exist on a small annuity, and where they would live? Joseph had made it clear from the outset that both Marguerite and Josie would be welcome to stay on at Damerell Manor, but Josie was determined that this was not going to happen. Her mother might not resent the fact that she was being treated like a poor relation, but Josie had other plans. As each day passed, she became even more determined to bring Harry up to scratch. She must marry, and marry well, even though her heart belonged to another. Loving Sam was like a fever in her blood; she only had to think of him and her whole body was consumed in a firestorm of desire. Try as she might, she could not forget their passionate embrace or the look in his eyes when he had admitted his feelings for her. But she must put all that behind her. There was no future for them. She could not see herself living in a farm labourer's cottage, and if she were to marry Sam it would break her mother's heart. Selfish and self-centred she might be, but she could not do that to the woman who had brought her into the world.

Seated alone at the vast mahogany dining table, she dragged her thoughts back to the present, toying with a plate of devilled kidneys, but she had little appetite for food. Harry's brief visit had been frustrating, and she had a sneaking suspicion that Kate had been his main reason for visiting Kingston Damerell. She had seen the way he looked at her and had been quick to note the subtle change in his tone when he was speaking to her. She pushed her plate away; she was not proud of herself. She had put a stop to his romantic notions concerning Kate. She had lied to him. She had told him that Kate was engaged to Sam, and she could still recall the stark expression in his eyes as he had received the news. It had been a spiteful and foolish thing to do, but she had drunk too much wine and she had been jealous of the fact that he preferred a person of low birth to herself. She had seen her means of escape slipping from her grasp, and now with Papa at death's door she was even more determined to become Harry's wife. They would deal famously together for neither of them had a heart to break, and they would be impervious to future pain.

She sipped her coffee; it was cold. She rang the bell to summon a servant, and it was Toop who answered the call.

'This coffee is undrinkable, Toop.'

He cleared his throat, standing to attention by the door. 'You have a visitor, Miss Josie. I've shown him into the morning parlour.'

'Who is it?'

'Mr Challenor, miss.'

She leapt to her feet. 'Why didn't you say so in the first place?' She rushed past him and ran across the entrance hall to the small room next to the library. She hesitated, glancing at her reflection in the gilt wall mirror. She patted her hair in place and bit her lips in order to redden them. She pinched her cheeks until they bloomed pink, and she took a deep breath. She must not appear too eager. She entered the room, pausing on the threshold and greeting him with an attempt at a smile. 'Harry, how good of you to come. I thought you might have returned to London.'

He crossed the room in two strides and took her hands in his. 'I couldn't leave without seeing you. I gather there is no change in Sir Hector's condition?'

'None, I'm afraid. He seems to be lingering between life and death. It's too awful.' She dropped her gaze. 'I am very glad you came, Harry. Your presence gives me such comfort.'

'I'm flattered that you put so much trust in me, my dear Josie. Is there anything that I can do?'

She thought of Sam and the ready tears sprang to her eyes. She allowed them to roll unchecked down her cheeks. 'Just having you here is enough, Harry. I'm in desperate need of a friend just now. Will you stay until . . .'

He took a clean white handkerchief from his coat pocket and pressed it into her hand. 'Of course I'll stay, if you think it will help.'

She blew her nose in the soft folds and smiled up at him. 'You are too kind, Harry.'

'Is there no one else who could be with you, Josie? What about Kate? Surely she is a comfort to you?'

Josie's heart lurched against her ribs and serpents of jealousy writhed in her stomach. She closed her fingers around the handkerchief, crushing it into a ball. 'I don't see her any more. She has deserted me in my hour of need.'

'How so? I find that hard to believe.'

She narrowed her eyes. She was fighting for her survival. Kate was her rival. 'I told you at that dreadful wedding supper that she was engaged to be married. Well, her father didn't approve and she ran away with Loveday.'

Harry was very still and his expression gave away nothing. 'This doesn't sound like the Kate I know.'

'That's just the point, Harry. You don't know her as I do. I, for one, am not at all surprised.'

'Where did they go? Didn't her father try to bring her home?'

'I believe they are lodging somewhere in Weymouth. She has broken her father's heart, Harry. And mine too.' Josie buried her face in his handkerchief and sobbed. She might have told a dreadful lie, but her grief was for the loss of the one man she could ever truly love, and it was genuine. There was no future for her and Sam; she must not weaken now.

'She wouldn't do a thing like that. Not Kate.'

Harry's voice was harsh and when she took a peep at him through her parted fingers, Josie was shocked to the core by his stricken expression. She knew now that his feelings for Kate ran deep. Driven by fear and desperation, she let the hanky fall to the floor and she clutched his arm. 'She has deceived us all, Harry. I loved her like a sister and yet she did not trust me enough to tell me what she planned.' She stared up into his stony face. 'I am so sorry, my dear.

It seems that you were also deceived by her innocent face.'

'When did they leave?' Harry fixed her with a hard stare. 'I must go after them and bring her back. She is too fine a person to be allowed to throw herself away on a scoundrel.'

She felt his muscles tense into bands of steel. 'It won't do any good, Harry. I – I don't know how to tell you this . . .' She paused, eyeing him warily.

'What? What is it that you must tell me?' His eyes were hard and his voice as cold as steel.

'They were caught in a compromising situation. It is too horrible to talk about.' She lowered her gaze. 'It is not something that a lady can discuss with a gentleman.'

'Are you trying to tell me that they were lovers?' Harry gripped both her hands in his. 'Is that what you are saying, Josie?'

'Yes, I'm afraid so, Harry. It is just too sordid. He could not even wait to make an honest woman of her before . . . I can't bring myself to put it into words.'

He relaxed his grip, dropping his hands to his sides. 'You've said enough.'

'And you will not attempt to follow them? It will do no good; I can assure you of that. Kate is very strong-willed.'

'No, I won't follow them, but I must leave at once.'

'You've only just arrived. You can't go so soon.'

'I can see that my presence here is only making matters worse. I think it best if I leave right away.'

'But what about me? I thought you were going to stay and be a comfort to me?'

'Tell me honestly, Josie. Is Sir Hector in imminent danger, or not?'

She could not look him in the eye. She turned away, biting her lip. 'His condition is the same as it was, but that doesn't mean that I don't need you here, Harry.'

'You don't need me, my dear. You never did. There is not a pennyworth of tenderness in your feeling for me. I've known that all along.'

He made a move to leave the room but Josie barred his way. 'That is just not so, Harry. I – I love you.'

He looked deeply into her eyes, and a wry smile curved his lips. 'I don't think so.'

'How can you say that to me?'

'Because I know it's true.' He picked up his handkerchief from where it lay on the floor and he wiped the tears from her cheeks. 'I've led an entirely selfish life up to now, Josie, but the ladies with whom I dallied were always worldly-wise. They were not in love with me, nor I with them.'

'I don't want to know about your past exploits,' Josie said angrily. 'I'm telling you that I love you and I need you here, by my side.'

'When a woman tries to convince a man that she has tender feelings for him, she should look at him with love in her eyes.'

Josie grasped his hand and held it to her cheek. 'But I do love you. I do.'

He shook his head. 'I've seen more emotion in the eyes of a hardened card sharp than in yours, my dear. You fell in love with Copperstone, not with me. I'm truly sorry about your father, he's a good man, but I can do nothing more here.' He turned on his heel and left the room.

Josie stared after him in disbelief. In a flash of rage, she seized a porcelain figurine from a side table and hurled it at the door as it closed behind him.

Almost immediately, the door opened. Josie held her breath, thinking that it was Harry returning to tell her that he was sorry for the cruel way in which he had just spoken to her, but it was her uncle who entered the room. His patent leather shoes crunched through the shards of broken china. 'My, my,' he said, smiling. 'What a little virago you are to be sure, Josie. I take it that all is not well in paradise.'

She backed away from him. 'Shut up.'

'That's not the way to talk to your future protector, my pet.' Joseph advanced on her with a lascivious look in his dark eyes. 'I passed young Challenor in the hall. He did not look very happy, so I take it that he has resisted your abundant charms.'

'Think what you like, you hateful man,' Josie snapped. 'Leave me alone.'

'Now that wouldn't be very kind of me, would it, my angel?'

Josie slipped past him and ran to the door, but just as she reached out to grab the doorknob Joseph spun her round to face him, pinning her to the wooden panels with his corpulent body. He placed his hands either side of her head so that she could not turn away from him and kissed her on the lips. She kicked out with her feet, but it was hard to breathe with his considerable weight pressing her to the door. She opened her mouth to cry out but he forced his tongue between her lips, and she could feel his warm saliva running down her chin. The more she struggled, the harder he pushed himself against her. She knew very well what he was doing, and as he moaned with pleasure she bit his tongue as hard as she could. He pulled away from her with a yelp of pain. 'You little bitch.'

'You dirty old dog,' Josie hissed, kicking him hard on the shin. 'If I were a man I'd kill you for that. As it is I'll just have to tell Aunt Hermione.'

She tried to push him away but he caught her by the hair. 'Breathe a word of this to anyone, and the moment my dear brother expires you and your mother will be out on the street.'

Josie spat in his face. 'You are a disgusting pig. My father is not yet dead. Until that time, he is the master here and not you.' She gave him a mighty shove, catching him off balance and made her escape. She fled from the room, tearing across the hall and up the staircase to her bedchamber. She locked herself in and paced the floor, too angry and distraught for tears. She could hardly believe what had just happened. It was like a bad dream – no, a terrible nightmare. She had been convinced that she could wrap Harry round her little finger, and that he would marry her once Kate was safely out of the way. Now it seemed that she had totally misread the situation. He really had fallen in love with Kate, and her attempts to blacken her friend's name had backfired. Now she was the loser in the complicated game of love.

Josie paced over to the window and rested her forehead against the cool glass. What had she done?

She had told a dreadful lie about her dearest friend, and she had alienated the man she wanted to marry. Her knees gave way beneath her and she slipped to the floor, covering her face with her hands as great rending sobs convulsed her whole body.

How long she stayed there, huddled against the wall with her knees drawn up to her chest and her head resting on her arms, she did not know. She must have cried herself to sleep, as time seemed to slip away from her. She came to her senses at the sound of someone hammering on her door. She raised her head, staring blearily round the room. 'Go away.'

'It's Hickson. Open the door at once, Miss Josie.'

Slowly, she rose to her feet. Pins and needles shot up her legs and she hobbled slowly across the floor. She unlocked the door and opened it just a crack. 'What is it? What's wrong?'

Hickson thrust the door wide open. 'You must come immediately.'

There was a note in her voice that brought Josie back to reality with a jerk. 'Is it Papa?'

'Best hurry or you'll be too late.' Hickson hurried off with Josie following close behind.

As she entered her father's room, Josie knew that it was already too late. Her mother had collapsed across Sir Hector's inert body and she was weeping. Hermione was standing at the foot of the bed, holding a lace handkerchief to her lips, and her blue eyes were swimming with tears.

Dr Smith laid a hand on Josie's shoulder. 'I'm sorry, Miss Damerell. There was nothing that I or anyone else could have done to save him. Please accept my sincere condolences.'

'He felt no pain, Josie dear,' Hermione whispered. 'It was so sudden. We were sitting with him, your mama and I, and Dr Smith had just come into the room, when Hector opened his eyes and he looked up at Marguerite. I swear that his lips moved and then he closed his eyes with a deep sigh, and he was gone.'

'Mama.' Josie tried to raise her mother, but Marguerite clung to her dead husband as if she would never let him go. 'Mama, please.'

Dr Smith cleared his throat. 'Perhaps we ought to leave Lady Damerell and allow her time to grieve.'

'He's gone, Mama,' Josie insisted. 'Papa is at peace now. Come away, please.'

Hermione hurried to her side, placing her arm around Josie's shoulders. 'The doctor is right, Josie. Come with me, my dear. You must be strong for your poor mama's sake.'

Josie hesitated, staring down at her mother's prostrate figure as she wept over her husband's body. Looking at the dead man's face, Josie saw, not her adored father, but a stranger lying on the bed. His pale features might have been carved from Carrara marble. The spirit of the man whom she had loved and respected was gone. A shiver ran down her spine, but no tears came. She had spent her grief and she felt wrung out; withered and dry as a dead leaf. Hermione was murmuring something in her ear, but the words were all jumbled up and meant nothing. Someone was holding her hand. Josie raised her head and found herself looking into Hickson's slate-grey eyes. 'Come with me, Miss Josie. A lie-down is what you need.'

'But, Hickson, I can't leave Mama.'

'Mrs Damerell will stay with her until I get back.' Hickson led her out of the room. She lowered her voice. 'Everything belongs to you now, and you must not let the servants see you weaken, even though you are grieving for Sir Hector. He would want you to be strong.'

Josie said nothing as she went slowly back to her own room. Hickson and all the servants would discover the truth soon enough.

The whole household was plunged into deep mourning. The clocks were stopped, curtains drawn and mirrors covered. Sir Hector's body lay in a satin-lined oak coffin in the candlelit Blue Room on the ground floor. Everyone in the house, from the hall boy to the new master, wore unrelieved black.

The day of the funeral dawned fine and dry, with a touch of hoar frost sparkling on the bare branches of the trees. A hearse drawn by four black horses took the coffin to the village church, followed by a procession of mourners. Heavily veiled, Marguerite leaned on Joseph's arm with Josie and Hermione walking slowly behind them. Josie held her head high in a gesture of pride and defiance. The news that she was not the heiress to her father's lands and fortune had spread rapidly. She was no longer a person of consequence, although she knew that the villagers still held her in respect, if only for the sake of her dead father. Sir Hector had been a good landlord in his lifetime, and she knew that he would be sorely missed. She wondered whether Joseph would turn out to be half the man, although to be fair to him, he had behaved himself well since her father's death. No mention had been made of the episode in the morning parlour, and he had not laid a finger on her since.

The villagers lined the route, the men standing cap in hand with their heads bowed, and some of the women were crying. Even the children were silent as they watched the plumed horses drawing the glass-sided hearse through the lanes to the church. As the pall-bearers carried the coffin through the lychgate, Josie was suddenly aware of Kate, who was standing at the edge of the path with Molly by her side. There was no sign of Sam and that sent a barb of pain into her heart. He could have come, if only to give her a modicum of comfort. She could hardly bear to look at Kate as she drew level with her. The lies that she had told Harry lay heavily on her conscience, but Kate's pretty face was as innocent of ill feeling as an angel's, and as their eyes met Josie's reserve broke. She threw her arms around Kate's neck and gave way to a storm of weeping.

'Don't take on so, Josie,' Kate whispered. 'Sir Hector wouldn't want you to be unhappy. He loved you very much.'

With a supreme effort, Josie drew away and fumbled for her handkerchief, but she seemed to have lost it. Kate produced a piece of ragged cotton and gave it to her. 'Dry your eyes. It's quite clean.'

Hickson hurried up to Josie, taking her arm in a tight grip that made her wince. 'You're making a show of yourself, Miss Josie. Think of your poor mama.'

Josie mopped her eyes. 'I'm sorry for everything, Kate.'

'Come along, Miss Josie,' Hickson hissed, tugging at her sleeve. 'You're holding everyone up.'

Josie shook her hand off with an impatient frown. 'I'll come when I'm ready, Hickson.' She turned back to Kate. 'Can you ever forgive me?'

'What is there to forgive? I don't understand.'

'Nothing really. I don't know what I'm saying.' Josie reached out to touch Kate's hand briefly before moving on into the cool, echoing interior of the church. The scent of hothouse lilies would, she thought vaguely, forever remind her of her father's funeral. Parson Daleymount conducted the service and the church was crammed with mourners. Those who could not get inside had to stand in the churchyard, shivering with cold, but they joined in the hymn singing with more enthusiasm than musical expertise.

Afterwards, Joseph magnanimously invited the whole village to the manor house where, he informed them grandly, tables had been set out with refreshments in the entrance hall, and several of the ground floor rooms had been opened up to the public. There was an undignified stampede as the villagers, most of whom had never set foot inside Damerell Manor, competed to get there first and sample their new lord's hospitality.

'Are you all right, Mama?' Josie asked anxiously, as she helped her mother into the barouche. Showing an unusual degree of thoughtfulness, Joseph had ordered the carriage to be brought to the church so that the ladies did not have to make the journey back to the house on foot.

Marguerite was pale, but remarkably composed. She even managed a ghost of a smile. 'I will be when this is all over, my dear.'

'I'm sorry that I made a complete fool of myself outside the church, Mama.'

'Don't be silly, Josie. You've been so brave and strong during the last few awful days. I don't know what I would have done without you.' Marguerite climbed into the carriage and sat down beside Hermione.

Joseph had stayed behind to speak to Parson Daleymount, but he joined them just as Josie was about to follow her mother into the carriage. 'Allow me, my dear,' he said, placing one hand round her waist while he fondled her buttocks with the other. 'Get in, my dear niece. We need to get back to the house before the hoi polloi get there and start wrecking the place.'

She gave him a withering look. 'You invited them to the house, Uncle.'

'So I did. Well, we need to keep the tenants sweet if I am to raise their rents.' Joseph clambered into the barouche and sat down beside her.

She moved as far away from him as she could. 'What do you mean, raise their rents? You can't do that.'

'My dear girl, I am the landowner now and I can do as I please. Poor old Hector wasn't a very good businessman. The estate isn't paying its way and that trend must be reversed pretty damn quickly.'

'Joseph,' Hermione said in a shocked voice. 'Language, please.'

'Sorry, my dear, but it's true. Something must be done soon, or we'll end up in Queer Street. You wouldn't like that, now would you, Marguerite? I mean, good old Hector didn't exactly leave you a rich widow, did he?'

Marguerite's face crumpled and she buried her face in her hands.

'Oh, Joseph, how could you be so unfeeling?' Hermione demanded, and her bottom lip trembled.

'You really are a pig, aren't you?' Josie hissed. Not that either her mother or Hermione could have heard her words, as they were clinging to each other, weeping loudly.

'Women.' Joseph groaned. 'One word out of place and they turn on the tears just to make a man feel bad.'

'There was no need to rub it in,' Josie said angrily. 'Mama and I know that we are dependent on your charity.'

His eyes narrowed to slits, almost disappearing into his fat cheeks. 'Yes, just bear that fact in mind, my dear Josie. You and she depend on me to keep a roof over your heads. But you are a bright girl and I'm sure we can work out a way for you to repay me for my generosity.'

'I would sooner die than allow you to lay your filthy paws on me, Uncle.'

Hermione looked up at that moment, peering at them through her tears. 'Joseph. What have you said to upset dear Josie?'

He placed his arm around Josie's shoulders, hugging her to him with his fingers digging into her flesh. 'I'm just comforting the poor little thing, Hermione. After all, I am going to be her surrogate father from now on.'

Josie gritted her teeth.

'Oh, my dear husband, you are such a kind-hearted man,' Hermione said, with a watery smile. 'Marguerite, see how Joseph comforts your daughter. We will be a happy little family together, I am sure. And you, dear Josie, will be the daughter that I never had. Marguerite is already like a sister to me. We will be so happy in our lovely new home.'

'Yes, indeed. I couldn't have put it better myself,' Joseph said, chuckling.

Josie had to choke back a bitter retort. For her mother's sake, and until she had thought of a better plan, she would have to pretend that all was well. For all his bluff geniality, she knew that Joseph would be a dangerous man to cross. She could barely wait for the carriage to come to a halt before she scrambled to the ground and ran up the steps into the house, leaving Hermione to look after her mama. At least Hermione was kind; she couldn't help being stupid.

Inside the house, Josie was surrounded by tenants and villagers, all wanting to offer her their condolences. Eventually, she made her way to the Chinese Room where she found Kate and Molly. Until this moment, Josie had never given a thought to young Molly, but now she saw her as Sam's sister and suddenly she was looking at her in a new light. 'Kate, I'm so glad you came. And you too, Molly.'

Molly's dark eyes opened wide and she bobbed a

curtsey. 'I was sorry to hear of your sad loss, Miss Damerell.'

'Thank you.' Josie stared hard at her, attempting to see a likeness to Sam. If there was one, it was very subtle. Perhaps there was a similar look about the eyes, but Molly's youthful prettiness was in sharp contrast to Sam's rugged good looks.

'Are you all right, Josie?' Kate asked. 'This must be so difficult for you.'

Josie managed a smile. 'I'm all the better for seeing you again. I was unkind to you when we parted and for that I am truly sorry.'

'It's all forgotten.'

'Shall I fetch you a glass of wine, miss?' Molly asked shyly.

'Yes, thank you, and I'm sure that Kate would like something too.'

Kate smiled and nodded her head. 'A glass of cordial would be nice. Would you like me to help you, Molly?'

'I can manage.' Molly made her way towards the entrance hall and was soon lost in the crowd.

A feeling of deep sadness threatened to overwhelm Josie, and it was not simply the loss of her father. She realised suddenly that Kate was staring at her with a question in her eyes. 'I'm all right, Kate. At least our friends from the village seem to be enjoying themselves.'

'I'm afraid it's the drink that makes them forget that this is a sad occasion.'

'My father would not have wanted anyone to grieve for him. He liked to see people happy. Papa was a kind and generous man and I will miss him terribly.'

'He loved you very much, Josie.'

'Yes, I think perhaps he was the only person in the world, apart from Mama, who really loved me.'

Kate laid her hand on Josie's arm and her eyes were filled with sympathy. 'Sam loves you desperately. The only reason he didn't come today was because he thought you didn't want him here.'

'That's not true. I wish he had come. I didn't mean to hurt him.'

'But you made it quite clear that it was Harry you wanted.'

'I know I did, and I've hated myself for it ever since, but I couldn't marry Sam. It wasn't to be. My future doesn't lie in the muck and mud of a farmyard.'

'And you are going to wed Harry Challenor?' Kate's voice trembled.

The memory of her last meeting with Harry came flooding back. Josie had pushed it to the back of her mind, but meeting Kate's candid, trusting gaze she felt bitterly ashamed of herself. She, who called herself Kate's friend, had sent him away thinking that the woman he loved had given herself to another man. Even though her conscience was plaguing her, Josie could not bring herself to tell Kate the truth. She tossed her head, forcing her cold lips into a smile. 'Yes, of course. We just have to set the date.'

Chapter Thirteen

Sir Hector's sudden death sent the whole village into mourning, and with it came a sense of disbelief and uncertainty. Everyone from the smallest child to the oldest inhabitant was now painfully aware that the estate would go to his younger brother. When he had proved his right to succeed to the title, and as soon as his name was entered on the Official Roll, he would become Sir Joseph Damerell, Baronet.

Robert admitted to being worried about the future of the home farm under the new owner, who was known to be a spendthrift and a gambler, unused to country ways. Rumours were circulating that Sir Joseph intended to put up rents, which would affect everyone from the humblest cottager to the better-off tenant farmers. Robert was thrown into a fit of despondency, which did not go down well with his bride, who demanded to be first in his attentions at all times.

Kate was distressed for her father's sake but even more anxious about Josie. She had attempted to see her several times after the funeral but had been turned away. She wrote a note to Josie expressing her sympathy and Sam gave it to one of the under grooms, bribing him to give it to Miss Damerell at the earliest opportunity. Kate had no way of knowing whether Josie received the message, and her heart ached for her friend's loss. She knew how she would feel if it had been her own father who lay in his grave. He had been a changed man since he gave up strong liquor, but she could not help noticing as the days went on that he was once again resorting to a glass or two of brandy after supper. Honoria made it plain that she disapproved, although she was obviously keeping a guard on her tongue in front of her husband; but not so with Kate who bore the brunt of her stepmother's ill temper only a little less than Molly.

Honoria did not lie in bed all day as Josie had predicted; she rose early every morning and Kate would find her downstairs in the kitchen ordering Molly about as if she were a slave. The poor girl always ended up in tears, and although Kate tried to intervene, Honoria was not to be gainsaid. At the end of her first month as mistress of the house she demanded the set of keys that hung from Kate's waist, and the household accounts book.

'But, Honoria,' Kate protested, 'I've kept the books faithfully since we moved here from London, and Pa has never once complained about my housekeeping. As to the keys, well, they are only to the dairy, the cider press and the cellar. I'm sure you don't want to be bothered with the likes of that.'

Honoria held her hand out. 'I am mistress of the house now, not you. I will run my own household and I want you to keep a daily record of the number of eggs laid, the amount sold and the same for the milk, butter and cheese. On market day you will hand the money taken to me and I will check it against the list of produce. There will be no taking the odd sixpence to spend on ribbons or fancy bonnets, like the one you wore to our wedding. That must have cost a pretty penny.'

'It did, but it was a gift from Josie.' Kate forced herself to sound calm, although inwardly she was seething. 'And I do not take money without first asking Pa. You have no right to say that I do, Honoria.'

'I have every right, miss. You will do as I say now, and you will not run to your father every time you disagree with me, for I assure you he will take my side and not yours.'

Molly had been riddling the cinders in the range, but she leapt to her feet and ran to Kate's side. 'You can't talk to Kate like that.'

Honoria raised her hand and slapped Molly's face so hard that the sound reverberated round the room. 'Don't be insolent. Get on with your work or I'll find another little drudge to take your place.'

Kate hooked her arm around Molly's shoulders. 'That was very wrong of you, Honoria. There was no need for that.'

Molly wept silently, holding her hand to her cheek.

'Stop blubbering and get on with your work, girl.' Honoria dragged her away from Kate's protective arm and pushed her down on her knees in front of the range. She spun round to face Kate with her eyes flashing. 'You will be the next one to receive a slap, or worse. I'll speak to Robert about you, and he'll put a stop to that surly manner you adopt with me. Now give me the keys and the account books and then you can get on with your work in the dairy. I don't want to see your face until noon when you come in for your meal.'

'I'll have breakfast first,' Kate said, taking the keys from her belt and handing them over. 'Sam will be here as soon as he's taken the cows to the milking parlour and we will eat with Pa, as usual. No one can work on an empty stomach.'

Honoria glared at her as if she were about to argue, but at that moment Robert breezed into the kitchen looking very pleased with himself. His smile faded as he looked from one to the other. Molly was snivelling quietly as she raked the embers of the fire into life and Kate stood with her hands clenched at her sides. She was about to tell Pa what had just happened, but Honoria rushed over to him and flung her arms around his neck. 'Robert, I want you to speak to your girl. She resents my presence and will not do as I say.'

'Well, now. Harrumph.' Robert cleared his throat noisily. 'Come, come, ladies, this is no way to start the day.'

Honoria clung to him, pressing his hand to her ample breasts as she gazed up into his face. 'Please, dear. You know I have your best interests at heart. I want to be a good wife to you and learn to run the household, but I cannot do it if I meet with resistance at every turn.'

'That's not true, Pa,' Kate said angrily. 'Honoria is being unfair and she slapped Molly.'

'Well, I – er – perhaps she deserved it.' Robert loosened the stock at his neck. 'You must just get used to living together, my dears. I've enough to worry about with the old master dead and gone. I can't have a war going on in my own home.'

Honoria stood on tiptoe to nibble his earlobe. 'I am prepared to be generous, Robert, dear. But your girl has made it plain from the outset that she doesn't like me, and that creature is just as bad.' She jerked her head in Molly's direction. 'I think you should put her to work on the farm and I will have a maidservant of my own choosing.'

A flicker of impatience crossed Robert's florid features, and he gently disentangled her arms from round his neck. 'Suit yourself, Honoria. I'm sure there's plenty of work for young Molly outside. She can help Kate with the chickens and in the dairy.' He turned to Kate, frowning. 'As to you, daughter, I know it's hard having another woman take your mother's place even if my poor Bertha did depart from this earth many years ago, but I want you to try to get on with Honoria. I don't want to hear a lot of tittle-tattle about who said what and who's to blame for this and that. All I want is peace in my house and food on the table at the right time. Speaking of which, why don't I smell bacon frying and bread baking? What is the world coming to?'

'Yes, get to work, you lazy slattern,' Honoria said, scowling at Molly. 'Didn't I tell you to have breakfast ready on time?'

'I thought you said we were not to have anything

to eat until midday,' Kate muttered through clenched teeth. She was aching to tell Pa exactly what Honoria had said and done, but it could wait.

'How's this, wife?' Robert sat down at the table. 'Breakfast is the most important meal of the day on the farm. Can't get a good day's work out of hungry folk.'

Honoria cast a withering glance at Kate, but she turned to Robert with a smile. 'I am sorry, my love. I am so new at being a wife with all that entails.' She ran her fingers through his hair, making it stand up like a cock's comb. She bent down and whispered something in his ear, making him chuckle. He patted her hand as it lay on his shoulder. 'Well, well, no harm done. I daresay young Molly can fry up some bacon and eggs. Kate will show you how to make bread when she's seen to the milking.'

Honoria folded her arms across her expanding stomach. 'I don't think so, my dear. I was a much respected housekeeper to the squire, not his cook. I will not bake bread, nor will I soil my hands in the kitchen, but I will keep the household and farm accounts, and I will supervise the servants. I will raise you to the status of gentleman farmer before I am done, and I'll start by inviting the parson's wife to tea and perhaps the mayor's lady as well. We will take our rightful place in society, you and I, Robert.'

His cheeks flushed wine-red above his white shirt collar. 'I'm a plain man, Honoria. I never pretended to be anything else. I've come up all I want to in the world, from groom to tenant farmer, and the sooner you get that into your head the better.'

Kate had to turn away to hide a smile. She could have kissed Pa for putting Honoria in her place, but she knew better than to say anything at this precise moment. She went over to Molly, who had stopped crying and had at last managed to coax the fire into life. 'You fetch the bacon and eggs from the larder, Molly. I'll make the tea.'

'I can see you're all against me,' Honoria said, sniffing. 'Robert, am I your wife and mistress of this house, or not?'

'Of course you are, my dove. You'll soon get used to our ways, won't she, Kate?'

She nodded, unable to withstand the pleading look in his eyes. 'Yes, Pa. I'm sure we will all do very well once we get to know each other properly.'

'I wouldn't count on it,' Molly muttered as she scuttled into the larder.

'What did she say?' Honoria demanded, bristling. 'I won't stand for insolence from servants, Robert.'

He rose to his feet, thumping his hand down on the table. 'I've had enough of this. Can't a man get any peace in his own house? I'm going outside but I want my breakfast ready in ten minutes, or I'll need to know the reason why.' He strode out of the kitchen into the farmyard, slamming the door behind him.

'Don't cross me, Kate,' Honoria hissed. 'I come first in your father's affections now, and I will have my own way. You can send the girl to light a fire in the parlour and I will have my breakfast in there. Ladies do not eat in the kitchen with the servants. You may bring me tea and toast, and I will have the account books too. Molly is not the only one who will have to learn her place.' She turned on her heel and stalked out of the room.

When Sam came in for breakfast, and before Kate could stop her, Molly blurted out everything. White-lipped with anger, and despite Kate's protests, he stormed out of the kitchen heading for the parlour. She followed him, begging him to stop, but he shook off her restraining hand. 'No, Kate. I won't have it. From what Molly told me, that woman was just as bad to you. I'm not letting her get away with such behaviour.'

'Pa won't like it, Sam. You'll only get yourself into trouble.'

'The gaffer is a fair man, and he's always listened to reason in the past.' Sam pushed the parlour door open and strode inside with Kate close on his heels.

Honoria jumped to her feet. 'How dare you burst in here without knocking?'

Sam dragged off his hat. 'I've been a part of this household a lot longer than you, Mrs Coggins. My sister and me was brought up like family by the old gaffer and his good lady, God rest her soul. Now, I don't know what you've been used to at the Grange, but I won't have you put my little sister out to work like a farm labourer. She ain't strong, missis, and a winter out working in the cold could prove fatal.'

'You impertinent dog.' Honoria raised her hand as if to slap his face, but Sam caught her by the wrist.

'No, missis. You may get away with slapping little

girls, but I'm a man and I don't stand for such treatment.'

'Get out of here!' Honoria screeched. 'Kate, fetch Mr Coggins. Fetch him now. I won't be spoken to this way in my own home.'

Kate stood her ground. 'No, Honoria. Listen to Sam, I beg you. I know we must all try to get along together, but he's right about Molly's health. She has a weak chest and is often taken poorly in the winter. You can't condemn her to work out of doors; it might well be the death of her. She's a good girl and will try hard to please you.'

Honoria sank down in her chair. 'I feel faint. I won't be spoken to in this way. Just wait until Mr Coggins hears about this, Loveday. I'll have you and your sister thrown out. Let's see how a winter living on the streets affects her delicate constitution.'

Sam took a step towards her, but Kate grabbed him by the arm. 'Don't, Sam. We'll speak to my father. You're only making matters worse.'

'Get out of here.' Honoria picked up the nearest object, which happened to be a china teapot, and she flung it at Sam, narrowly missing him. It shattered against the wall and cold tea trickled down between the black beams, staining the whitewash.

Reluctantly, Sam allowed Kate to lead him from the room. She closed the door but Honoria's hysterical cries could still be heard. 'That was not a good idea, Sam. She'll tell Pa anything to get him on her side.'

He shrugged his shoulders. 'I don't care what she says. I'm going to find the gaffer and have it out with him man to man. I won't allow Molly to be bullied by the likes of her, and I don't like the way she treats you either, Kate.' He strode off along the narrow passage and she heard his boots clattering on the flagstone floor of the kitchen; a door slammed and then it was quiet. Kate sighed. Once this was a happy home, but Honoria had changed all that. She made her way to the kitchen and found Molly hovering by the scullery door, wringing her hands.

'What shall I do, Kate? Sam was so angry.'

'He's gone to find Pa. Let the men sort it out, Molly. It will be all right, don't you worry.'

But everything was far from all right, as Kate realised when her father burst into the kitchen minutes later. His high colour and his beetling brows were not an encouraging sign. He flung his hat on the kitchen table, knocking over the milk jug. 'Can't I leave you women for a few minutes without you fighting and scratching each other's eyes out like wildcats?'

'It wasn't like that, Pa.'

'No? That's not the way I heard it from Sam. It seems to me that you two are ganging up against my poor Honoria. Well, I won't have it, do you hear me?'

'I hear you, Pa. But it really wasn't our fault. Honoria is set on making Molly work in the fields. Sam was angry, and it's only natural—'

'Natural, my eye. Now you listen to me, Kate. Whether you likes it or not, Honoria is my wife, and she is the mistress here now. She's got a lot to learn, I'll grant you, but I need you to help her and not go

226

against her every which way; especially at a time like this.'

'I don't understand,' Kate said slowly. 'At a time like what?'

Robert's cheeks flushed a darker shade of red and he ran his finger round the inside of his collar. 'You must expect her to be a bit high-strung these days. Honoria is in the family way, so to speak.'

'You mean . . . ?' Kate stared at him in disbelief. She had thought that Honoria was long past childbearing, and this news had come as a total shock. It was true that Honoria seemed to be putting on weight by the day, but she had put that down to simple greed and idleness. 'She can't be, Pa.'

'A baby.' Molly leaned against Kate for support. 'Heavens above.'

Robert cleared his throat loudly. 'It happens amongst married folks. You ought to be pleased for us, not looking at me like a pair of silly dumbledores.'

'I – er – it's a surprise, Pa. I mean, at her age. I didn't think . . .' Kate's voice trailed off as she struggled to find the right words.

'Honoria is only thirty-seven,' Robert said with an aggrieved look on his face. 'Not young, I'll grant you, but not old neither. I want you to do everything you can to keep her calm and content.'

'Like a cow in the field,' Molly whispered, grinning.

'I don't want none of that talk, young Molly.' Robert frowned at her. 'And if I hears as how you've been upsetting her, then you will be severely chastised for it. As for you working in the fields, that won't happen.

227

You can help Kate in the dairy and the hen house. You can do the cleaning indoors so long as you keeps out of Honoria's way, and I'll hire a maid to wait on her while she's in a delicate condition. You, Kate, can do the cooking. You've done it well enough all these years and I don't fancy being poisoned by some wretch from the village. Do you both understand me?'

'Yes, Pa,' Kate murmured. She nudged Molly.

'Yes, master.'

'Good. Now I'll go and speak to Honoria and you girls set out the breakfast. I'm famished.'

As the door closed on him, Molly began to giggle. 'That were quick work, considering they've only been married such a short while. I didn't know the master had it in him.'

'That's enough of that talk,' Kate said severely, but she was shocked nonetheless. So what Sam had said about her pa and Honoria going off together after the last skimmity ride must have been true. Although it was a long time since her mother had died, she had never thought of her father as being a man with physical needs. He was just her dear pa, kindly when sober, hard-working and growing old, more likely to end up a grandfather than father to another child. Having a baby in the house would change things even more.

Molly nudged her in the ribs. 'Don't look so worried, Kate. I won't breathe a word of it in the village.'

'We must try and be a bit more patient with Honoria. Maybe her megrims are all due to her condition. I expect things will get a lot better when she gets over the first difficult months.'

'Aye,' Molly said, nodding wisely. 'I've heard that women can be real bitches at the beginning, and then they cheer up and become almost normal. That's what Sal says anyway, and she ought to know for don't her ma drop a new baby every year regular as clockwork?'

But matters did not improve. Now that her secret was out, Honoria became more difficult and demanding. Robert was terrified of upsetting her in case she miscarried, which he told Kate had happened several times to Kate's own mother before she arrived as a gift from God, and everyone had to tiptoe around Honoria, giving in to her slightest whim.

The weeks went by without further incident but Kate's nerves were stretched to breaking point. She was beginning to hate Honoria with a slow-burning passion, and she knew very well that her stepmother wanted her out of the house and out of their lives. Although Honoria was always sweetness itself to her when Robert was near, her claws came out when they were alone together. Molly and Sam knew what was going on, but they had been banished to a small one-up, one-down cottage that had once housed the pig man and the lingering smell of swine persisted despite Kate and Molly's best efforts to scrub the place clean. The Lovedays were allowed to eat in the kitchen with Kate, but Honoria insisted that she and Robert took their meals in the parlour, which hitherto had only been used for special occasions. Kate's position in the house was reduced to that of a servant, and worse was to come when Robert grudgingly allowed Honoria to hire a lady's maid.

Tilda Harvey had worked as a chambermaid at the Grange, and Kate suspected that Honoria had been planning to employ her all along. Tilda turned up at the farmhouse one morning at the beginning of February with her belongings packed in a carpet bag. She was allowed to have the bedroom that Molly and Sam had shared when they were children, and she ate her meals in the parlour with Honoria if Robert was out working in the fields, or in her room if the master chose to dine with his wife. This treatment immediately placed her above Kate, and although Tilda did not say so to her face, she made it plain that she considered herself to be Honoria's favourite. When Kate complained to her father he simply said that she was imagining things and that keeping Honoria happy and contented was the most important thing at this critical time. Kate was left to fume inwardly, unable to do anything other than to put a brave face on things, but she was beginning to think that her days as a servant in Bedford Square had been a bed of roses compared to the life she was forced to lead now.

She was in the dairy one morning, making butter, when Josie appeared in the doorway. She was smartly dressed in a sapphire-blue velvet mantle trimmed with sable with a matching bonnet and muff, but she looked far from happy.

'Josie. This is a pleasant surprise.'

'I can't stand it any longer,' Josie cried passionately. 'I've left home and I'm never setting foot in that house again while that disgusting creature is there.'

Kate stared at her in dismay. She was used to Josie's volatile moods but she could tell that this was something more serious than a childish tantrum. 'What's happened?'

Josie dropped a leather valise on the flagstones, holding her hands out to Kate. 'I need you to come to London with me. I'm going to the house in Bedford Square, and I can't travel unaccompanied.'

'I don't understand. You're talking in riddles.'

'That beast who calls himself my uncle has been making improper advances to me ever since he first came to Damerell Manor. It stopped for a while after Papa died, but now he's made it clear that the only way I can stay on in my home is if I warm his bed.'

'That's terrible, Josie. Are you certain he wasn't just teasing you?'

'Of course I'm sure. His hands were all over me and it wasn't the first time. I just packed a bag and walked out. I didn't even tell Mama, although she'll find out soon enough. That sneak Joseph will make her think it was all my doing.'

'But running away isn't going to solve anything. You should tell your mother what he's been doing. Get it all out in the open and shame the hateful man.'

'Don't you think I've thought of that?' Josie paced the floor, wringing her hands in an obvious state of agitation. 'I've spent sleepless nights trying to work out a plan of action, and I've been playing for time in the hope that Harry would come up to scratch and propose.'

'But he hasn't?' Kate held her breath, waiting for Josie's response.

'No, and I suppose that makes you happy. I know you wanted him for yourself.' Josie rounded on her, eyes blazing. 'I know that you have feelings for him, Kate, but he's not for you, any more than Sam is for me. We've both fallen in love with the wrong men, but we've got to accept the fact that it can never be. I can't marry a farm labourer and you have no hope of hooking a man of Challenor's standing. It's hard and it's cruel, but it's the way things are.'

Kate bowed her head. She knew that Josie was only stating a fact, but the truth hurt. She had hoped that she had conquered her feelings for Harry, but she had been deluding herself. She raised her head, forcing herself to look Josie in the eye. 'What you say is true, but at least I know that my case is hopeless. Are you so certain that you can ignore the bond between you and Sam? And doesn't he have any say in the matter?'

Josie tossed her head. 'Of course not. I can't tie myself to a clodhopper with no prospects. I'm going to London to set myself up in my own establishment and I intend to pursue Harry until he catches me. Now are you with me, or do I go to London on my own?'

Chapter Fourteen

Kate sat opposite Josie in the first class railway compartment, and as she watched the fields and hedgerows flash past the window she wondered if she had done the right thing. Josie had made it almost impossible to refuse her plea to accompany her to London. Kate had had serious misgivings at first, but her life on the farm was proving to be intolerable, and she could see that when the baby arrived things would get progressively worse. It was Honoria who had tipped the scales in Josie's favour, and when Kate had asked for permission to accompany Josie to London, Robert was obviously too afraid of upsetting his wife to raise any objections.

'It's a fair offer, maidy,' he had said with an attempt at a smile. 'Miss Josephine will look after you, and you will have some standing in the household. It will be like old times.'

Kate had thought she heard a note of envy in his voice, and she had seen a hint of wistfulness in his smile. He might not have been a Londoner born and bred, but she realised then that he missed his old life. He had taken on the role of farmer, but she suspected that in his heart he yearned for the companionship of the stable yard, and the ordered simplicity of his old job as head groom.

Kate leaned her forehead against the cool glass pane of the carriage window. She had been sad to leave her pa, and she had not had the opportunity to explain her sudden departure to Sam, who had taken Molly to market to sell the butter and cheese to Biddy Madge. She glanced at Josie who was huddled in the corner and appeared to be asleep. For the first time Kate noticed the dark circles underlining her eyes and the telltale droop at the corners of the mouth. Josie might put a brave face on what had happened in the manor house, but Kate knew her well enough to realise that Sir Joseph's unforgivable conduct had shocked her to the core. Coming so soon after her father's death, Josie must have been desperate to walk away from the place where she had been born and raised, and which but for the rights of succession should have been her home for life.

Kate settled back against the padded squabs. She could not help wondering if they were doing the right thing. It was all very well for Josie to state that she would set herself up on her own in the London house, but even with her limited knowledge of society, Kate knew that life was not going to be easy for a young, unmarried woman living without the protection of her family. She suspected that her main objective would be to save Josie from herself, and that was a challenge she had yet to meet. As for herself, she knew that she must face the prospect of seeing Harry again. Josie had her sights set on marrying him and it was inevitable that he would be invited to the house in Bedford Square. She was painfully aware that her feelings counted for nothing. She would have to melt into the background. She really was Miss Nobody. She closed her eyes, blotting out all thoughts and fears and drifting into a dreamless sleep.

They arrived at Waterloo on time and took a hansom cab to Bedford Square. It was late afternoon and rain was falling from a pewter sky as they trudged up the steps to the front door. Josie rang the bell several times, cursing the weather and the idleness of the servants who were taking their time to answer her summons. When the door finally opened she was about to step inside, but her way was barred by the footman.

'May I be of assistance, ma'am?'

'Yes, you can stop being ridiculous and let me in. Do you know who I am?'

He remained impassive and unmoving. 'I regret to say that I do not, ma'am.'

'I'm the owner of this establishment, Miss Josephine Damerell,' Josie said angrily. 'Now stand aside, my man, and let me in.'

'I think there is some mistake, ma'am. The owner of this house is Mr Geoffrey Keaton, QC, but if you wish to leave your calling card I will put it before him on his return.'

'No, you are mistaken. This house has belonged to the Damerell family for generations. I don't know who Mr Keaton is, but this is not his home.'

The footman was ousted by a grim-looking butler. 'What appears to be the problem, Jones?'

'This young lady seems to think that she owns this residence, Mr Brown.'

Brown drew himself up to his full height. 'I think you are labouring under a misapprehension, ma'am. This house was purchased recently by my master, I believe from the former owner, Sir Joseph Damerell.'

Josie staggered backwards and would have missed her footing if Kate had not stepped forward to save her. 'That's impossible. This house belongs to my family.'

'Not any more, ma'am. I suggest you leave now and take the matter up with Sir Joseph if you are in any doubt.' Brown closed the door firmly, leaving Josie and Kate standing on the doorstep.

'He can't have sold it so quickly,' Josie said, shaking her head in disbelief. 'Even Joseph would not do such a thing without consulting Mama.'

'It appears that he did, Josie.' Kate shivered. 'We'd best find shelter because the rain is running down my neck and soon I'll be soaked to the skin, as will you.'

'This can't be happening. Where will we go?'

'We could try the stables in the mews. Perhaps some of the old grooms have been kept on. We could shelter there until we've decided what to do next.'

Josie glanced up at the building, blinking the rain-water from her eyes. The fur on her bonnet was sticking up in wet tufts and dark patches stained her velvet mantle, but she held her head high. 'I'm not going there to be humiliated by mere servants.'

'Well, what do you suggest?'

'Be quiet. I'm thinking.' Josie stomped down the

steps, allowing her long skirt to trail on the wet paving stones.

Kate followed her, picking up Josie's valise and her own, much smaller, carpet bag into which she had thrown a few necessities. She waited patiently, stamping her feet in an attempt to keep warm while Josie paced up and down in front of the house.

'We could take a chance and call on Harry,' she said at last, and then shook her head. 'No, I won't go cap in hand to him. We must meet again, but on equal terms. I won't turn up on his doorstep looking like a drowned rat.'

'Perhaps we should return to Dorset,' Kate suggested tentatively.

'Never. I'd rather die than go back and live with that beast.'

'Maybe we could find lodgings somewhere? We can't stay here and it will be dark in a couple of hours.'

'Don't go on so. I have an idea.' Josie moved swiftly to the edge of the kerb and hailed a passing cab. 'There's only one person I can think of who would willingly take us in. I just hope and pray that she's still in the land of the living.' She climbed into the cab. 'Hackney Terrace, my man.'

'It's a fair way, miss. I'll take you there but it will cost you.'

'I'm aware of that,' Josie snapped. 'Get in, Kate. Don't stand there gawping. Hand me my valise.'

Kate lifted the cases into the cab and clambered in with difficulty, hampered by her damp skirts. She sat next to Josie, closing the folding doors as the cab lurched forward. 'Where are we going?'

'Hackney. I've no idea where it is exactly, but my old nanny retired there some years ago. I know that because I send her a present every Christmas. Toop used to let one of the under footmen take it to her. I suppose she's still in the land of the living, although I must confess I forgot all about her last year.' She broke off on a sob and Kate put her arm around her shoulders.

'At least it will be a roof over our heads for tonight. You're worn out, Josie. You'll feel better after a rest and something to eat.'

Josie managed a grim smile. 'You always look on the bright side, Kate. Sometimes I wish I were more like you.' She stared gloomily at the road ahead. 'I've got to think of a plan. I can't allow Harry to find me living like a pauper in the East End.'

'Have you got any money left? I mean, it was quite extravagant to travel first class, and the cab fare is going to be expensive.'

'We don't talk about things like that. It's vulgar.'

'It's only vulgar if you're rich. If you're poor it's vital to know how much you have to spend, or how little.'

Josie fished in her velvet reticule and pulled out a leather purse. She thrust it into Kate's hand. 'Here you are. Count it. I don't know how much there is in it. I didn't think we'd need more than our fare to London.'

Kate stared at her in amazement. 'So how do you think the household runs itself?'

'I've never given it a thought. I suppose Papa paid all the bills, but either Toop or the housekeeper saw to the day to day running of the house. Anyway, how should I know about sordid things like that? I was brought up to be a lady, not a housemaid like you.'

Kate subsided into silence. Josie might pretend that they were equals when it suited her, but at other times she made the difference in their status painfully clear. After a moment, Josie nudged her in the ribs. 'Are you sulking? Have I said the wrong thing again?'

'You speak without thinking, but it's no use pretending. You've got to choose one way or the other. I'm either your friend or your servant. I can't be both.'

Josie screwed her face up against the rain and the foul smells emanating from the dung-covered city streets and overflowing gutters. 'We're friends, of course. I wish you wouldn't be so sensitive, Kate.' She kissed her on the cheek. 'But when we're with Harry you will pretend to be my maid, won't you? It's even more important for me to impress him now. I must marry him, Kate. I really must.'

'And where does that leave Sam?'

'On the farm where he belongs. One day I hope he'll marry a nice cheerful country girl who'll never utter a cross word and will bear him lots of chubby-cheeked children.'

'You're lying.'

'Yes. I am, but don't you dare tell him what I said. I'm going to marry money and that's that.'

Kate stole a sideways glance at Josie and stifled a sigh. She knew by the stubborn set of Josie's jaw that she had made her mind up and nothing would shift her from her purpose. There was little that she could do at this moment other than to go along with whatever her capricious friend decided. She settled back to endure the cold, bumpy ride to the wilds of Hackney. The streets grew narrower and poorer the further east the hansom cab travelled. Beggars and half-feral children crowded the pavements, beseeching passers-by for money. Skeletally thin cats and dogs roamed the narrow courts and alleyways, sniffing out morsels of barely edible detritus in the gutters. It was scene after scene of poverty and deprivation, and even though the rain had ceased a sulphurous gloom wrapped itself around the stark outlines of the manu-factories and the streets lined with back to back dwellings.

The lamplighter was just finishing his rounds as they reached Hackney Terrace which overlooked the wide expanse of Hackney Common, Josie awakened with a start, staring round wide-eyed and dazed with sleep. Kate climbed down from the cab, after paying the cabby what seemed like an exorbitant amount. She lifted their luggage to the ground and Josie alighted to stand on the pavement, smoothing out the creases in her clothes, seemingly oblivious to the dangers of being in a rough part of the city. The cab drove off at a spanking pace and they were alone. Kate had seen enough of the raw underbelly of London life to be aware of the perils lurking in the darkness. The common and surrounding market gardens would be the ideal haunt for thieves and robbers. She could see tiny

240

pinpricks of light from fires lit by the homeless who huddled together for warmth, hoping to live through yet another bitterly cold winter night exposed to the elements.

They had been left outside a row of near derelict artisans' cottages with front doors that opened out directly onto the pavement. Kate's heart sank as she took in their surroundings. 'Which house is it, Josie? Where does this woman live?'

'Number ten, I think. I don't remember.' Josie gazed longingly at the far side of the street where a crescent of once elegant Georgian houses was set back from a tree-covered green. Even in the soft glow of the gas lamps they appeared to be sadly run down and the gardens a neglected tangle of brambles and ivy, but lights shone invitingly from the tall windows and their slightly tarnished opulence was in sharp contrast to the dwellings on their side of the road. 'Why couldn't she have lived in one of those?'

'I expect it's because she earned so little as your nanny that she couldn't save a penny towards her old age.'

'Don't take that tone with me, Kate.' Josie tossed her head. 'At least she's got a roof over her head. It's just that I'm not entirely sure which one it is.' She marched up to the door of number ten and rapped on the knocker.

Kate glanced over her shoulder. She was certain that she saw dark figures skulking in the shadows. She crossed her fingers, hoping that Josie had picked the right house. When no one answered, Josie knocked again and eventually the door opened a crack.

241

'Who's there?' The voice quavered nervously and an eye peered out at them.

'Nanny Barnes.' Josie's voice shook with relief. 'Thank goodness, it is you.'

The door opened wide. 'Miss Josephine?'

Josie flung her arms around the tiny woman, lifting her off her feet. 'It is I, Nanny. I'm so glad to see you.'

'Put me down, child. Come in and shut the door.' Nanny Barnes squinted short-sightedly at Kate. 'And bring your friend. I'm afraid I haven't any seed cake or muffins for tea. The delivery from Fortnum's is late once again, but you're welcome anyway.'

Kate followed them into the small space that served as both kitchen and living room. In the dim light of a single candle it was patently obvious that Josie's old nanny was not living in the height of luxury. A fire had been lit in the grate but the tiny nuggets of coal glowed fitfully amongst a pile of damp twigs spitting sap and creating more smoke than heat. The packed earth floor was covered in straw and the air felt damp, a feature made worse by the kettle hanging on a hook over the fire sending puffs of steam into the room.

'Sit down, both of you.' Nanny Barnes pointed to two wooden chairs tucked beneath a deal table. 'I was just going to make a pot of tea.' She frowned at Josie. 'You look perished, my dear. Take off those damp things before you catch your death of cold. You too, young lady.' She took in Kate's appearance with a nod of her head. 'You must be Miss Josephine's maid. Well, we don't stand on ceremony in my house. You're welcome to stay to tea.' She hobbled over to the fireplace and lifted the kettle with both hands.

Noting Nanny Barnes' gnarled fingers, twisted by rheumatism into grotesque shapes, Kate took a step forward intending to help her but Josie frowned and shook her head. 'Thank you, Nanny. A cup of tea will be lovely.' She took off her bonnet and mantle and hung them over the back of her chair. 'Sit down, Kate,' she whispered. 'She won't thank you for interfering.'

Kate did as she was told, taking off her damp cloak and sitting down at the table which was laid with an embroidered cloth, stained by many years of spilt tea and lacy with moth holes. She glanced round at the roughly plastered walls with large bare patches revealing the bare brickwork. She could feel the cold and damp rising from the floor. No wonder the poor woman was crippled with rheumatism.

Nanny Barnes placed the teapot on the table and took two teacups from a shelf on the far side of the chimney breast. 'I don't often have company,' she said, beaming. 'Did I tell you that there isn't any seed cake? Anyway, there's plenty of bread and butter.'

Kate's stomach rumbled at the mention of food. She had not eaten since breakfast that morning, but despite Nanny Barnes' boast there seemed to be only the end of a loaf and a tiny pat of butter on the table. There was little enough for one person, let alone three. She could see that Josie was thinking along similar lines.

'We don't want to take your supper, Nanny,' Josie said hastily. 'In fact, I was going to treat you to something from the – er . . .' She sent a mute appeal for help to Kate. 'I suppose Fortnum's is out of the question.'

Taking her cue, Kate rose to her feet. 'I'll go out and find a pie shop.' Used as Josie was to relying on servants for every mouthful of food she ate, she would have no idea that there were shops selling such things as meat pies, stewed eels and pease pudding. She would never have eaten fish and chips wrapped in yesterday's newspapers. In fact, Kate realised, Josie had not the foggiest notion how ordinary people lived. She slipped her damp cloak around her shoulders and picked up the purse. There would be enough for a meal for three. How they would manage tomorrow was another matter.

Despite Nanny Barnes' protests that it was unfitting for a young woman to go out alone at night in this part of the East End, Kate was driven by hunger, and she slipped out of the house leaving Josie to calm Nanny's fear. She had seen a pie and eel shop next to the Baptist chapel in Grove Street and it was not far to walk. The tasty aroma of hot meat pies kept her going and she left the shop with the comforting heat of the parcel clutched to her bosom. She had almost reached the end of Terrace Road when she was accosted by a man who leapt out of a doorway, grabbing her by the arm.

'Hand it over, girl.'

She clutched the parcel of food even tighter. 'Let me go.'

'Me wife and nippers is starving. Give us it.'

Kate made a vain attempt to struggle free but the man was obviously desperate and in no mood to be gentle. He pushed her roughly to the ground and was attempting to wrest the package from her when someone grabbed him by the collar and flung him aside. Her assailant scrambled to his feet and ran off.

'Are you all right, miss?'

Still clutching her precious parcel, Kate allowed her saviour to help her up. 'I'm fine, thank you.'

He tipped his cap. 'You shouldn't be out alone, miss.' He started to walk off towards the common but Kate hurried after him and caught him by the sleeve.

'Thank you for what you just did.'

'It were nothing, miss.'

'It was very brave of you.' Kate fumbled in her pocket for her purse. 'I should like to thank you properly. That man would have taken everything.'

He pushed her hand away. 'Like I said, it were nothing. Go home, miss. I don't want your money.'

In the light of a street lamp she could see his features clearly. His dark curly hair was streaked with silver, and he had the swarthy look of a Romany. It was odd that as a child she had always been warned to avoid gypsies, but this was the man who had saved her. 'Are you camped near here?'

He grinned. 'Aye, miss. We're on the far side of the common. Should you want your fortune told, you know where to come.'

'Could you tell me your name? I'd like to know.'

'Marko, miss.'

She held out her hand. 'Kate. Thank you, Marko.'

He shook hands, bowed and walked off into the night. Kate hurried the last few yards to the house and let herself in.

'You took your time,' Josie said crossly. 'We've been waiting for ages.'

'You would have had to wait even longer for your food if it hadn't been for a gypsy who saved me from a mugger.'

Nanny Barnes threw up her hands. 'Oh, dearie me. I told you not to go out alone, my girl. It's not safe with all those desperate men loitering around. I suppose you can't blame the poor things who can't find work and have families to feed.'

Josie took the food from Kate's hands and peeled off the newspaper. 'Never mind, you're here now and I'm absolutely famished. Pass your plate, Nanny. This smells all right, but frankly I could eat a horse.'

'You always were a greedy girl,' Nanny Barnes said, shaking her head.

Later, when Nanny Barnes had gone upstairs to her room, Kate and Josie were left to make themselves as comfortable as possible with one blanket each and a rag rug laid out in front of the fire. They huddled together in front of the dying embers.

'It's awful to see her living like this,' Josie murmured sleepily. 'I wish Toop had told me more of her circumstances.'

Kate tugged at the thin blanket in an attempt to cover herself and keep out the draughts that whistled

246

under the front door. 'I doubt if you would have believed him if you had not seen it for yourself.'

'You're right, of course. I never gave the poor old soul a thought.'

'Perhaps you'll have a chance to make it up to her.'

'You mean when I marry Challenor?'

'I suppose so. But you might decide to return home. Your mother must be out of her mind with worry.'

'She'll recover soon enough. She's thick as thieves with Hermione, and Joseph isn't stupid enough to pick on Mama. He likes to keep his wife happy so that he can do what he pleases with girls from the village, or willing chambermaids. I'm just disgusted to think that he puts me in that class.'

In spite of everything this wrought a chuckle from Kate. 'So says the girl who is sleeping on the floor in a hovel. This is what they call finding out the hard way how the other half live, Josie. I hope you remember it when your fortunes are restored.'

'And they will be.' Josie snapped into a sitting position. 'How much money is there in my purse?'

'Fifteen and sixpence three farthings. See how far that gets you.'

Josie subsided onto the rug, curling up against Kate's back. 'I'll think about that in the morning, but right now I'm really sleepy . . .' Her voice tailed off as she settled down with a hearty sigh.

Next morning the full extent of Nanny Barnes' poverty became clear to both Kate and Josie. The small terrace of houses had been built at the beginning of the century to house factory workers and artisans, but it appeared that the landlord had neglected to do the necessary repairs and the row was fit only for demolition. All the occupants were forced to share a block of privies in the service lane which abutted the common, and the tiny back yards were too small to allow the tenants to grow their own vegetables. On questioning, Kate discovered that Nanny Barnes had no family to support her and that she had existed on the small pension that Sir Hector had given her, but even that had ceased since Joseph had inherited the family fortune. She was all but destitute and facing the worst horror of all – the workhouse.

This last piece of information had the power to shock Josie out of her despondent state and had galvanised her into action. She washed in ice cold water drawn from the communal pump and donned her gown, grumbling that it was creased but having to wear it anyway as Nanny did not possess a flat iron. Kate put her hair up for her and helped her into her travel-stained bonnet and mantle.

Josie stared down at damp patches on the once perfect blue velvet and frowned. 'This won't do at all if I'm to impress Harry. I don't want him to think I'm desperate.'

'You look a treat, my dear,' Nanny Barnes said, peering at her through the thick lenses of her spectacles. 'I never thought that my little scamp would grow up to be such a lovely young woman.'

Josie preened herself in front of the fly-blown mirror

above the mantelshelf. 'I suppose I'll pass muster. At least, I hope so for all our sakes.'

Kate tucked her hair into a snood and put on her bonnet, which was still soggy from last night's rain. 'You do know where Mr Challenor lives, don't you, Josie? Have you ever been to his London house?'

'No, but I'm not stupid. I took care to find out everything I needed to know about him, including the town house in Finsbury Circus and his office in Wapping.'

Kate was still not convinced. 'But supposing he's not at home?'

'I'll sit on the doorstep and wait until he returns,' Josie said firmly. 'Don't forget, Kate. This is just a social call. He's not to know that we haven't come from Bedford House, so don't you say a word. Keep in the background and let me do all the talking. If we don't get an invitation to Copperstone Castle my name is not Josephine Marguerite Damerell.'

'Well, good luck, dear,' Nanny Barnes said gently. 'You will be coming back tonight, I hope.'

Josie gave her a hug. 'Of course we will, Nanny. I'm going to look after you properly from now on. There'll be no talk of the workhouse. When I am mistress of Copperstone I will make sure that you are well cared for, and that's a promise. Come, Kate.' She swept out of the house with Kate following in her wake.

In order to save money they walked as far as they could before hailing a passing hansom cab. Even so, the cost of travelling in relative comfort to Finsbury Circus took an alarmingly large proportion of the remaining money in Josie's purse.

249

'He'd better be at home after all this expense,' Josie muttered as she mounted the steps of the Georgian town house. A liveried footman opened the door to them. 'Please inform Mr Challenor that Miss Damerell wishes to see him,' Josie said with an imperious toss of her head.

'I'm afraid you've just missed him, miss. Mr Challenor left for the country an hour ago, and is not expected to return to London for some weeks.'

Josie stared at him in disbelief. 'That can't be true. There must be some mistake.'

Bristling with affront, the footman shook his head. 'There is no mistake. Good day, miss.' He closed the door firmly in her face and Josie stood for a moment before turning to Kate, pale-faced and visibly shocked. 'What on earth will we do now?'

Chapter Fifteen

There was no alternative other than to return to Hackney Terrace, but with dwindling resources they had to resort to public transport and a series of horse-drawn omnibus rides. Tired, hungry and emotionally drained, Kate settled Josie in a chair by the fire in Nanny Barnes' living room.

'This is so exciting,' Nanny Barnes said, clapping her hands. 'To have both of you staying here is more than I could have wished for. I do hope the order from Fortnum's arrives in time for tea. I'm so looking forward to cucumber sandwiches and walnut cake.'

Josie frowned. 'Nanny, you know that's just wishful thinking, don't you?'

'No, dear. They will come. I wait for them every day, but sometimes I'm afraid they must deliver to the wrong house.' Her bottom lip trembled and she sank down on the nearest chair. 'I do so love walnut cake.'

Kate patted her on the shoulder. 'Perhaps I'd better go out and see if I can find the delivery van, Miss Barnes. Then we can have tea by the fire.'

'That would be nice, dear. Ring for the tweeny, Josie. We need more coal, and tell her to fetch another candle. It will be dark soon.'

Josie met Kate's worried glance with a wry smile. 'Yes, Nanny. I'll do that in a minute.'

Nanny Barnes shook her finger at her. 'What have I told you about procrastination, Josephine?'

'It's the thief of time, Nanny.'

'Quite so. Now where was I?'

Kate picked up Josie's purse. She knew to the last farthing how much was left and it would not stretch to walnut cake and cucumber sandwiches. A quick glance out of the window made her reluctant to go out again. The wind was whipping up eddies of straw, dead leaves and bits of detritus that had drifted into the gutters. Raindrops trickled down the window-panes, leaving sooty marks like tearstains on the grimy glass. With a sigh of resignation, she slipped her cloak around her shoulders and reached for her bonnet. 'I'll go out and get something for supper, Josie.'

'Yes, please do; I'm starving. And fetch a bag of coal too.'

'Yes, miss.' Kate pulled a face, receiving an apologetic smile from Josie.

'It's Miss Josephine to you, Kate,' Nanny said severely. 'We mustn't forget our place, must we?'

'No, Miss Barnes.' Kate made her escape. Outside it was bitterly cold and the rain had turned to sleet. They were in desperate need of coal and kindling, and a foray into Nanny's cupboard had revealed a distinct lack of candles and vestas. Quite how the old lady had managed to survive all this time on her own was beyond Kate, but now the responsibility of looking after Nanny Barnes and Josie had fallen on her shoulders. She quickened her pace. It would be dark in an hour or so and she did not want to risk another mugging. They were in enough trouble without losing the small sum of money in her purse, and with Josie's plan of enlisting Harry's help dashed they were in a pretty pickle, as Pa would say. A wave of homesickness washed over her as she walked along the street lined with pawnshops, pubs and bawdy houses. Slatterns loitered in doorways and their ragged, barefoot children clung to their skirts or hung about waiting to dip into pockets of unwary passers-by. Kate was up to their tricks and she clutched the purse beneath her cloak, glaring at the urchins if they came too close. Dealing with youngsters under the age of ten was one thing, but she knew enough to avoid confrontation with the older boys and the grown men who leered at her and made suggestive remarks.

She stopped outside a pawnshop and on an impulse went inside. She came out minutes later, half a crown richer but bareheaded. The bonnet that Josie had bought her in Dorchester had seen better days but it was still finer than anything displayed in the pop-shop window. She spent the money on a few necessities, tipping the shop boy a penny for delivering the small bag of coal to the house together with bundles of kindling. The rest of her purchases she carried in a battered rush basket, found at the bottom of a pile of junk in the pop-shop for which she paid only a farthing. On the way back to the house she bought three baked potatoes and a bunch of watercress from a street vendor, which they ate for supper washed down with hot sweet tea.

Kate was still hungry when she lay down on the floor beside Josie that night. 'What are we going to do now?'

Josie raised herself on one elbow, staring into the fire. 'I'm not going home, that's for certain. I suppose I could throw myself on the mercy of John Hardy, that nice vicar who took us in after the accident.'

'You don't mean that?'

'Why not? He was rather taken with me, as I recall.'

'Josie, you're shameless.'

'I'm desperate, Kate. I can't go on living like this with poor old Nanny, whose mind is wandering. Another few days in this place and I might go mad myself.'

'You're not serious about renewing your acquaintance with the Reverend, are you?'

'It's the only solution that comes to mind. I can hardly turn up at Copperstone on the pretext that I was passing and decided to drop in.'

'Why not? You were prepared to do that in London.'

'That's quite different. I would have been paying a social call on an equal footing if I'd been living in Bedford Square, or pretending to. I would have to receive an invitation to Copperstone, and that's out of the question now.' Josie threw herself down on the rag rug, groaning. 'What a ghastly muddle. I'm afraid it's the vicar or dying of starvation in this hovel.'

'Aren't you forgetting something?' Kate sat up, wrapping her arms around her knees. 'We haven't got the money for the train fare. We've just about sufficient to buy a loaf of bread for breakfast and not a penny more.'

Josie opened her eyes, staring up at Kate. 'Really?

I thought you sold your bonnet. That cost a guinea when new.'

'And it fetched half a crown in the pawnshop. I was lucky to get that.'

'I wish I'd packed one of my ball gowns. As it is I suppose I could get some money for some of my clothes. We could sell them and then we'd have enough money to get to Dorset. Maybe even enough to hire a carriage and pair.'

'And what would you wear? You could hardly arrive looking like me, for instance.'

'Heavens no. What a thought.' Josie turned on her side. 'I'm exhausted. I'll think of something in the morning.'

Kate lay down, but sleep evaded her. She could hear Josie's rhythmic breathing and she marvelled at her friend's ability to ignore what to most people would be pressing problems. She herself was only too well aware of their desperate situation. The sensible solution for both of them would be to return home. Josie might not relish living under the same roof as her profligate uncle, but she had very little choice. As to her own situation, Kate knew she must face the inevitable. She would have to suffer her father's wrath and live with Honoria's whims and tempers, or she could accept Squire Westwood's offer of a position as companion to his daughters. Neither prospect filled her with enthusiasm, but at least she had come to terms with the fact that Harry was not for her – almost. She huddled down, pulling the blanket up to her chin. At least she had a proper bed at home. The hard floor beneath her was a constant reminder of their sorry plight. The chill penetrated her bones, making sleep seem like a welcome escape, but it eluded her until she was finally overcome by mental and physical exhaustion.

Next morning she awoke early, determined to make Josie see sense. She stretched her cramped limbs, stifling a groan as every muscle in her body ached. Josie was still sleeping soundly. Kate scrambled to her feet and set about the business of clearing the grate and lighting a fire. She went out into the yard and filled the kettle at the pump, returning to hang it on a hook over the flames. Whilst waiting for it to boil she took stock of their supplies, which were meagre enough for one person let alone three. A heel of cheese, half a loaf of bread and a tiny pat of butter were all the food they had, and perhaps enough tea to last until evening, so long as the leaves were dried and reused. She checked Josie's purse and tipped out the copper coins – tuppence three farthings would not go far. She glanced at Josie's sleeping form and sighed. Josie was noted for her stubbornness, but surely even she must see that their situation was hopeless.

Kate looked up as the door to the narrow staircase opened and Nanny Barnes appeared, still wearing her nightgown with her hair tied up in rags. 'Today is the day I have luncheon with Miss Spalding who lives in a big house in Cassland Crescent,' she announced with a triumphant smile. 'She was lady's maid to a very important personage, and they look after her extremely well.'

Kate slipped the coins back in the purse. 'Why

don't you sit down, Miss Barnes? I've made a pot of tea.'

'That would be lovely, dear. But as soon as breakfast is over I'd like you to help me dress. I have to look my very best when I visit Miss Spalding.'

'Of course,' Kate said, pouring tea into two cups. 'Would you like some bread and butter?'

'Oh, no, dear. I don't want to spoil my appetite. Miss Spalding's luncheons are always quite substantial. She has her own personal maid, you know.'

Thinking that this was one of Nanny's flights of fancy, like having Fortnum's deliver cucumber sandwiches and walnut cake, Kate nodded and smiled. Let the old lady keep her dreams; they were far nicer than the reality the poor soul must face every day of her life.

Josie yawned and sat up, her dark hair cascading around her shoulders like a lustrous velvet cape. 'Tea, please, with two spoonfuls of sugar. I'm famished. Is there any toast?'

Nanny Barnes shook her finger at her. 'Get up, you lazy girl. I see you haven't mended your ways, Miss Josephine. You were always hard to rouse, even as a small child.'

Josie rose to her feet, stretching her arms above her head and smiling as though she had just risen from a feather bed. 'I haven't slept so well for months. Now what will we do today?' She turned to Kate with an eager smile. 'Have you thought of a plan?'

'Plan? What plan?' Nanny Barnes put her cup down on the saucer, staring at Josie in apparent amazement. 'It's my day for lunch with Miss Spalding. Naturally you

257

will be included in the invitation. I'll have living proof that I was nanny to a baronet's daughter. Sometimes I think that Millicent doesn't believe me when I tell her about Bedford House and Damerell Manor.'

Kate dared not look at Josie. She knew if their eyes met they would both dissolve in a fit of giggles. It was small wonder that Miss Spalding did not believe Nanny's tall tales, if she existed at all. Perhaps Millicent was also a figment of Nanny's imagination.

'Yes, Nanny,' Josie said, helping herself to a cup of tea. 'I would love to meet your friend.' She winked at Kate. 'But I expect you have better things to do today. We need to increase our funds. Have you thought of anything, Kate?'

'We must find work. We can't exist on air.'

'Perhaps Miss Spalding might be able to help,' Nanny Barnes said thoughtfully. 'There are several retired gentlefolk living in the neighbouring houses; maybe one of them is in need of a maidservant.'

Humouring her, Kate and Josie went along with Nanny's determination to put on her one and only best gown, and yellowed lace cap. At midday precisely they walked the short distance to the crescent where Nanny insisted that her friend had rooms in one of the large houses. Still in a state of disbelief, Kate and Josie followed her into the building and up a flight of stairs to the first floor. Nanny Barnes led the way down a long landing and was about to knock on a door at the far end when it opened and a young girl carrying a bundle wrapped in brown paper flew

258

out. She paused, glaring at Nanny Barnes. 'You're welcome to the old bitch,' she cried angrily. 'That's the last she'll see of me. I'd rather starve in the gutter than work for her.' She raced off, disappearing down the stairs with a clatter of booted feet on the bare treads.

'Dearie me. Whatever next?' Nanny Barnes marched into the room, with Kate and Josie following her. 'Millicent, are you all right?'

A tall, lean woman in her mid-sixties rose from a chair by the fire. Her gaunt features were set in what appeared to be a permanent frown. 'You're two minutes late, Dora.'

'I – I'm so sorry. I know how you value punctuality, Millicent.'

Josie stepped forward. 'You must blame me, Miss Spalding. I'm afraid it was my fault that Miss Barnes kept you waiting.'

'And who may you be?' Millicent glanced at Josie and allowed her gaze to travel to Kate. 'And who is this? I didn't extend my invitation to luncheon to half the town, Dora.'

Nanny Barnes squared her shoulders. 'Allow me to introduce my one-time charge, Miss Josephine Damerell, daughter of the late Sir Hector Damerell, Baronet.'

Josie inclined her head graciously. 'Good afternoon, ma'am. It's a pleasure to meet any friend of Nanny Barnes.'

Miss Spalding twitched visibly, her arrogant demeanour momentarily shaken, but she made a quick recovery. 'Welcome to my home, Miss Damerell.'

Josie smiled graciously. 'And this is Coggins, my maidservant. We're staying with Nanny for a while.'

'Yes, Millicent. They're staying with me.' Nanny Barnes nodded emphatically.

Miss Spalding raised an eyebrow. 'You must be very cramped in that tiny house.' She waved her hand towards a small sofa and two rather uncomfortable-looking chairs upholstered in faded damask. 'Do take a seat, although I'm afraid luncheon is out of the question. That stupid girl has just left without so much as giving a week's notice. I don't know what young people are coming to these days.' She resumed her seat by the fire.

'My maid will be happy to take over in the kitchen. She is perfectly capable of preparing food, aren't you, Coggins?' Josie nudged Kate in the ribs. 'We can't turn down the offer of a free meal,' she added in a whisper.

'Of course,' Kate said, taking her cue. 'I'd be glad to help out.'

'She's a dear girl.' Nanny Barnes smiled and nodded. 'They've been such a comfort to me, Millicent, and I am rather peckish.'

'The kitchen is below stairs.' Miss Spalding's tone implied that it might as well be in a foreign country. 'I've no doubt that silly girl will have left everything in a dreadful mess, but there should be someone there to tell you what's what. You may go, but remember I want luncheon on the table at half past twelve on the dot. I hate unpunctuality.'

Josie flashed a smile at Kate. 'Hurry up then, Coggins. Don't keep us waiting.'

Ignoring the fact that Josie was making the most of the situation, Kate made her way down two flights of stairs. Even if she had not seen the green baize door at the rear of the entrance hall when they came in, she would only have had to follow her nose in order to find the kitchen. A variety of smells filled the air, rancid cooking fat being the most powerful, run a close second by sour milk and rotting cabbage. She wrinkled her nose and held her breath as she entered the dimly lit room. A large range occupied most of the far wall and various soot blackened pots and pans hung from a beam above the fireplace. A rectangular pine table occupied the centre of the room, its surface smothered in dirty crockery, half-eaten meals and vegetable peelings which spilt over onto the flagstone floor.

A small misshapen creature emerged from the shadows brandishing a ladle. 'Get out of my kitchen.'

Kate leapt backwards uttering a cry of alarm.

'Get out.' The voice was high-pitched but the face scowling at her was wizened like that of an old man. 'You got no right to be here.'

As he shambled towards her Kate could see that the creature she had mistaken for a malignant dwarf was little more than a child. Beneath the dirt the youth's face was lined with suffering and his eyes were clouded with pain. His clothes were ragged and he had a wary look as if expecting nothing other than kicks and blows. Kate felt a sudden surge of pity for the odd looking creature and she smiled, holding out her hand. 'I'm sorry. I didn't mean to startle you. May I come in?'

He stared at her open-mouthed. 'Who are you?'

'My name is Kate. What's yours?'

'Boy.'

'I can see that you're a boy, but what do they call you?'

'Boy. That's all.' He backed away from her. 'What d'you want? Where's the daft girl?'

Taking him to mean the unfortunate female who had worked for Miss Spalding, Kate shook her head. 'She ran away. Perhaps she didn't like working here.'

'No one lasts long, except me, and I got nowhere to go.' He limped over to the range and picked up a wooden spoon. He stirred the pan bubbling away on the hob. 'I live here.' He pointed to a pile of rags in one corner of the room. 'That's where I sleeps. This is my kitchen.'

'Then perhaps you can help me. I have to take Miss Spalding's luncheon up to her room.' Kate stared at the mess on the table. 'But I don't know what to do. Can you help me, please, Boy?'

'Why should I?'

He turned his back on her and she stifled a gasp of dismay as she saw the full extent of his deformity. His crooked spine formed a huge hump, which gave him the lop-sided gait and accounted for his stunted growth. Kate had seen plenty of crippled children begging on the streets, but there was something about the boy that touched her heart. She knew instinctively that any show of sympathy would be met with hostility and she made her tone brisk. 'I'd help someone if they asked me nicely. I'm sorry if I'm in your way but I was sent down here to do a job.'

He lifted the spoon to his lips and tasted. A slow smile spread across his face. 'That's good. I may be a cripple but I'm a good cook.' He stared at her for a moment and then held out the spoon. 'Try some?'

It was a challenge as much as an offer and Kate realised that to refuse would only confirm his suspicions that she was just another person who either condemned or ridiculed him because he was different. She crossed the floor and took the spoon from him, dipping it in the pot and tasting. She did not have to pretend. 'That is delicious. You are a very good cook.'

'Yes,' he said, grinning. 'I know.'

She licked her lips, savouring the tasty dish. She could have eaten a bowlful of the stew with ease. 'I can cook, but not like that.'

He thrust a ladle into her hand. 'Have some more.'

'You don't know how tempting that is, but I must take Miss Spalding's food up to her.'

'There ain't none. That girl couldn't butter a slice of bread without making a mess of it.' He put his head on one side, giving her a calculating look. 'You can give the old besom some of mine. The master won't be home until this evening. He don't eat much and there's plenty in the pot.'

'I can't take his food. It wouldn't be right.'

'You ain't taking – I'm giving. It's me who'll get the whipping if he finds out, which he won't. I'm too fly to be caught out by the likes of him. I learned the hard way in the workhouse. There's nothing that frightens me now. Help yourself.' Boy shuffled off leaving Kate standing by the range with a ladle in her hand. She struggled with her conscience but hunger won.

*　*　*

'This is excellent, Coggins,' Miss Spalding said, wiping her lips on a damask napkin. 'I don't know what you did to make this palatable but you've worked wonders.'

'It is very good.' Nanny Barnes scraped her plate, licking the spoon and receiving a withering look from Miss Spalding. 'I know it's not done, Millicent, but I haven't had a meal like this for years.'

Josie beckoned to Kate, who had eaten her food at a separate table. 'You may clear now, Coggins.' She lowered her voice as Kate was about to take her plate. 'How did you do that?'

Kate smiled. 'Magic.'

Miss Spalding nodded as Kate picked up her plate. 'Very well done, Coggins.' She leaned back in her chair, eyeing Nanny Barnes keenly. 'Now are you going to tell me the real reason why these young people are staying with you, Dora?'

Josie held up her hand. 'I'll tell you the truth, Miss Spalding. I'm sure it will go no further since you were a trusted employee in a great house.'

Miss Spalding's sallow skin flushed delicately. 'You can rely on my discretion, Miss Damerell.'

'I'm escaping from an arranged marriage. My uncle has chosen my future husband, whom I cannot abide. I was on my way to stay with a wealthy aunt but my purse was stolen and I am temporarily without funds. It's necessary for Coggins to find work to enable us to live until my aunt sends money for our fare to – er – Scotland.'

Kate almost dropped the pile of plates she was

holding. She glared at Josie but Josie merely smiled, turning her lambent gaze on their hostess.

Nanny Barnes frowned. 'That doesn't sound quite right, Miss Josephine.'

Josie patted her hand. 'You get a bit confused sometimes, Nanny dear. I'm sure Miss Spalding understands, and maybe she could help. Perhaps someone in the house is in need of a maidservant, or a cook.'

Miss Spalding pursed her lips. 'I can see that you are in need of food and shelter, Miss Damerell, but to be perfectly frank, I don't believe a word of your cock and bull tale.'

Josie rose to her feet. 'How dare you, ma'am?'

'I'm too old to fall for every tale of woe I hear, Miss Damerell. Moreover, I don't believe that you are who you say you are. I have a nose for quality and you don't fit in.'

'That's outrageous. Tell her, Nanny. Tell her who I am.'

Nanny Barnes covered her face with her hands. 'I do get confused at times. Don't tell me that I'm losing my mind.'

Kate put the plates down with a thud and wrapped her arms around Nanny's heaving shoulders. 'Of course you're not, Nanny. Miss Spalding is mistaken.' She shot an angry glance at her. 'I grew up with Miss Josephine. She is Sir Hector's daughter and you ought to know better than to question a lady.'

'Hoity toity.' Miss Spalding's face cracked into a semblance of a smile. 'Whatever the truth of the matter, I know that my good friend Dora has brought you both here because you need my help. I may be getting on in years, but I'm not stupid and I've seen a great deal more of the world than either of you young things. Now, do you need my help or don't you?'

Nanny Barnes sniffed and raised her head. 'They do, Millicent. Money is a problem . . .'

'All right, then I'll tell you what I'll do.' Miss Spalding looked from one to the other, obviously enjoying her moment of power. 'Miss Josephine can stay here with me as my maidservant. She'll get her bed and board, that's all. Coggins can come in daily and see to my meals. I will pay her four shillings a week, which I consider to be very generous in the circumstances. It will come out of my meagre pension and the small annuity which I received on the death of my father, but if Coggins continues to provide meals like that it will be worth the expense.'

Josephine leapt to her feet. 'That's a preposterous suggestion. How dare you ask me to be lady's maid to someone who spent their life in service?'

Miss Spalding eyed her with contempt. 'I've spent my entire life being looked down on by my so-called betters. I've seen them behave like trollops and libertines and get away with such behaviour because they are the landed gentry. Now it's my turn.'

'That is very hard, Millicent,' Nanny Barnes said softly. 'These girls are not responsible for the actions of others.'

'They can take my offer or leave it. But I suspect that there is much more to this case than either you or I know, Dora.'

'Well, you can go to hell as far as I'm concerned,' Josie cried angrily. 'I've never been so insulted.'

Kate took her by the arm and led her to the far side of the room. 'Think about it, Josie. Why not humour the woman and do as she asks? After all, it's only until we can save up enough money to return to Dorset, and I'll put every penny of my wages by.'

'What? Do you really expect me to wait hand and foot on her? And who said that I was prepared to go home?'

Kate bit back a sharp retort, forcing herself to remain calm and objective. 'When you've a better idea, let me know, because I can't see any other way out of this predicament.'

'I can't stay here with that old harpy and I won't live under the same roof as my uncle.' Josie shot a sideways glance at Miss Spalding. 'Look at her. She's enjoying every minute of this. I won't give her the satisfaction of agreeing to her plan.'

'At least give it some consideration, and if you feel hard done by you want to go downstairs to the kitchen and see the poor boy who's living like an animal for the simple reason that he's crippled. Perhaps we should think ourselves lucky and return to our families and our comfortable way of living.'

Josie stared at her in amazement. 'Is your brain addled? Have we come all this way and slept on a dirt floor, eating food fit only for pigswill, for nothing?'

Miss Spalding cleared her throat. 'It's very rude to whisper, ladies. You've heard what I have to say. I want an answer now or I'll withdraw my offer.'

Chapter Sixteen

In some ways it seemed to Kate that she had the best of the bargain, and this was largely due to Boy. Spending much of her time in the kitchen gave her a chance to get to know him better and within a few days he had become her staunch ally. She cleaned the kitchen, sweeping, scrubbing and throwing out all the rubbish to be collected by the dustcart. She discovered mouldering food, dead mice and an intrusion of cockroaches in the larder, which she attacked with vigour. Boy was at first suspicious of this war on dirt and grime, but eventually even he had to admit that the kitchen smelt a lot better and it was easier to prepare food when there was space on the table. In return for her hard work, Boy did all the cooking. Kate soon realised that he was happiest when he was creating a meal even from the most meagre ingredients, and she encouraged him with praise and genuine admiration.

The other occupants of the house rarely used the kitchen. They were mostly single gentlemen who went out to business every day and ate their meals elsewhere. Occasionally one of them might wander into the kitchen with a request for hot water for shaving or to make themselves a cup of tea, but for the most part they were quiet, sober and rarely seen. The exception was Timpson, the manager of the India Rubber Works, who spent more time in the local pub than in his attic room and often returned late at night singing loudly as he stumbled up the stairs. Miss Spalding regularly complained to their landlord, but her remarks were largely ignored as Timpson paid his rent regularly and none of the other tenants seemed disturbed by his behaviour.

Boy's employer was one of the invisible businessmen who came and went as quietly as ghosts in the night, until one day when Kate was on her hands and knees scrubbing the kitchen floor. Boy had been unusually taciturn and she had not been able to get a civil word out of him, but when the door burst open and a thickset man strode into the kitchen she knew by the expression on Boy's face that this must be Mr Wharton, the former workhouse master who was now employed as a rent collector.

Wharton kicked the pail of water so that it tipped over, spilling its contents on the floor and soaking Kate's skirts. Without so much as an apology he made a grab for Boy, catching him by the collar and lifting him off his feet so that his thin legs dangled pathetically and his face turned purple as he struggled to catch his breath. Wharton caught him a savage blow round the head and then dropped him onto the floor. 'I'll teach you to steal money from my pockets, you thieving little bugger.' Boy lay on the ground yelping with pain as blows rained down on him.

Unable to bear it any longer, Kate leapt to her feet

and caught Wharton by the arm. 'Stop that. You're hurting him.'

Wharton threw her off so that she fell against the table, momentarily winding herself. 'Keep out of this, slut. I don't take orders from the likes of you.' He aimed a savage kick at Boy, catching him in the stomach. 'Next time I'll kill you and be done with it, crookback.' He stomped out of the kitchen, slamming the door behind him.

Gasping for breath, Kate went down on her knees and lifted Boy gently so that his head rested on her lap. 'Are you all right?'

His lips twisted into a grimace. 'Not so you'd notice.'

She helped him to his feet, wiping his tears away with the corner of her apron. 'He's a brute. He should be reported to the police.'

Boy twisted away from her. 'They won't do nothing. He's still a respected man, even though he's the meanest brute this side of the River Lea. I never took his bleeding money. He's out of his head on opium most nights, that's his trouble. He don't know where he's at or what he's doing, but one day I'll do for the brute. When I'm a man I'll sort him out good and proper.'

Kate eyed him doubtfully. Boy's spirit might be strong but his body was frail, and Wharton was a hefty brute. Any more beatings like that might prove fatal. 'You should get away from here. Have you any relations you could go to, Boy?'

He shook his head. 'I dunno who my parents were. I was born in the workhouse, that's all I knows. He took me with him when he left but only because I could earn him money. He used to make me beg on the streets when he was short of the reddy. People like to give to a cripple; it makes them feel good about themselves. Then they walk away.'

Kate blinked away tears that threatened to spill from her eyes. She would not let him see her pity. She knew him well enough to understand his fierce pride and independent spirit. She jumped as Miss Spalding's bell jangled on its spring. 'Oh, dear, is it that time already? She wants her food, I suppose.'

Boy opened the oven door and protecting his hands with a scrap of cloth he took out a pie, placing it carefully on the table. 'This should keep her highness happy, and there's enough for the devil upstairs when he comes home from robbing poor folk of their hard-earned money.'

'I did well at market yesterday,' Kate said, changing the subject. 'But it's you who've turned scrag end of mutton and some vegetables into a feast.'

'You and me work well together,' Boy said with a rueful grin. 'I'll miss you when you leave us, and she will too. The greedy bitch.'

'Who says I'm leaving?'

'You will. You ain't no kitchen maid. I seen a few come and go since I been here and they ain't like you. One day you'll up and leave and I'll be all on me own again with nothing but him between me and the work-house. Sometimes I think I'd be better off back inside.'

Kate cut into the pie, putting a generous helping on two plates; one for Miss Spalding and the other for Josie, who might moan constantly about her lot, but at least

271

she had a warm bed at night and one square meal a day. 'I'll just take this upstairs and then I'll come down and we'll eat together, Boy.' She put the plates on a tray and headed for the doorway. She paused, turning her head to give him an encouraging smile. 'Perhaps you'd like to go for a walk with me this afternoon. Miss Spalding has given me a list of things she needs from the shops, and I could do with some company.'

Boy's eyes widened. 'Me? You don't mind being seen out with me?'

'Of course not. Anyway, it's bad for a boy of your age to be cooped up in this airless basement day in and day out.' She glanced out of the window set high in the wall. She could just see a hint of blue sky. 'It's stopped raining for once. We could go across the common.'

'Green grass,' Boy said softly. 'I often dream of green fields and trees. Sometimes in the summer I goes out in the crescent for a bit of fresh air, but then kids throw stones at me and people call me names and I comes back indoors out of sight.'

'They won't call you names today,' Kate said firmly. 'And if anyone throws a stone we'll pick it up and toss it straight back at them.' She had the satisfaction of hearing Boy's laughter as she walked up the stairs.

With her rush basket over her arm and two shopping lists in her purse, one from Miss Spalding and the other from Nanny Barnes, Kate set off with Boy to visit the local shops and make the necessary purchases. The sun was shining from a peerless blue sky. Although it was still quite chilly it felt as though the savage bite had gone from winter and that spring might be on its way at last. Kate felt her spirits soar as they made their way back across the common. The ground was slightly soggy underfoot but that was a small price to pay for the scent of crushed grass and the gentle breeze blowing off the marshes. The noxious fumes from the chemical works, dye factories and tanneries on the other side of the River Lea seemed less noticeable on a day like this, but she felt a sudden longing for the rolling countryside of Dorset and the smell of the sea. She had held Boy's hand while they walked the city streets, glaring at anyone who dared to poke fun at his deformity and murmuring words of comfort to him when she felt him falter. He turned to her, smiling for the first time since they had left the house, and loosened his hold on her hand. He gambolled forwards, running with a rolling gait through the tufts of grass like a young animal let loose for the first time.

Kate quickened her pace in an attempt to keep up with him, but she stopped suddenly as a crowd of gypsy children appeared from behind a clump of gorse bushes to surround Boy. She broke into a run, arriving at his side breathless and ready to defend him, but the children were silently appraising Boy, and he was staring back at them with his head held high.

Kate tugged at his sleeve. 'Come, Boy. We'd best get home.'

He glanced up at her, his eyes filled with pain. 'I have no home.'

'What is this?' The sound of a stern male voice made the children snap to attention.

Kate spun round, putting a protective arm around Boy's thin shoulders, but she relaxed a little as she recognised the man who had saved her from the muggers. 'Marko?'

He nodded his head. 'You are the young lady who almost lost her purse to those cowards who attack defenceless women.'

'And you saved me, for which I'm truly grateful. You disappeared before I had a chance to thank you properly.'

His stern features melted into a smile. 'No thanks needed, miss.' He turned to the children, waving his hands. 'Shoo. Go to your mothers and see if they have any jobs for you.' They scampered off towards a group of colourful caravans on the far side of the common. Spirals of blue smoke wafted skywards from camp fires and Kate could see the Romany women gathered together in small groups. She suffered an intense feeling of sadness as she saw the children run up to their mothers and were welcomed with hugs. That was something she would never experience again. She wondered if they realised how lucky they were to be part of a caring family and a close community. She looked down as she felt Boy tug at her hand.

'We'd best get back,' he muttered, eyeing Marko warily.

'You need not fear me,' Marko said as if reading his thoughts. 'You will come to no harm from any of us.'

'I ain't afraid,' Boy said stoutly. 'I been beaten by a bigger chap than you, mister.'

'That is not our way.' Marko gave Kate a searching

look. 'You have fallen amongst bad people, miss. I can't foretell the future like my wife and her mother, but I know that you are in the wrong place, as is this child.' He tipped his cap and was about to walk away, but hesitated, glancing over his shoulder. 'If you wish to consult my wife, Dena, you will find her in the red and gold painted vardo.' He pointed to a caravan in the middle of the group. 'We will be leaving soon, so don't delay.' He strolled off towards the encampment.

'I told you,' Boy said mysteriously. 'You shouldn't be waiting on that old woman. It ain't right.'

Kate took him by the hand. 'Life isn't fair, Boy. That's something I've learned the hard way. Let's get back to the house. It's going to rain unless I'm very much mistaken.'

That night, as she settled down to sleep on the floor in Nanny Barnes' living room, with the dying embers of the fire giving up the last of their feeble warmth, the gypsy's words came back to Kate. She had given them little thought during the afternoon as Miss Spalding had been more demanding than usual and Josie had gone off in a sulk and had not returned until supper time. She had refused to say where she had been even though Miss Spalding had scolded her severely, complaining that she had taken her in as a companion and that did not mean being left alone for hours on end. If Miss Damerell thought she was too high and mighty for the position, perhaps she ought to return to the family home where her megrims and tantrums would be tolerated. This diatribe had merely served to aggravate Josie's ill humour and she had

275

vented her feelings on Kate at the first opportunity. She closed her eyes recalling the angry scene.

'It's all your fault,' Josie hissed, pinching Kate's arm. 'If you hadn't taken that creature out for a walk this afternoon, she would have had her cucumber sandwiches on time and her wretched madeleines, or whatever they call those cake things, and I would have been able to escape for a few hours without incurring her anger.'

'Ouch, that hurt.' Kate rubbed her arm, glaring angrily at Josie. 'You undertook to act as her companion in return for food and shelter. I'm the one who's working hard to keep us and saving every penny I can towards our fare back to Dorset.'

'Well, you needn't bother much longer. I'm sick of being independent and I'll never catch a husband while I'm stuck in this dreadful mausoleum with her. I've sent a telegram to my uncle, asking for funds so that I may return home. I've given in, Kate. I never thought I'd say that, but it's done.'

Kate stared at her in dismay. She knew what it must have cost Josie to beg her uncle for money, and how it would hurt her pride to return home like a wayward schoolgirl who had chosen to play truant. 'I'm sorry,' she murmured. 'I really am, Josie.'

'And you will come too. I'm not suffering the humili-ation on my own.'

Kate opened her eyes, smiling to herself as she recalled Josie's words. How typical of her that she rode roughshod over everyone and everything in her path in order to get her own way. It was understood that they must return to Dorset, but now there were others to consider. She could not bear the thought of leaving Boy to Wharton's not so tender mercies, and then there was kindly, but slightly dotty, Nanny Barnes. What would happen to the old lady if she were left to fend for herself?

Several days later Kate had just arrived home, having been to market to purchase bread, vegetables and a bullock's head, which Boy would make into a tasty stew. She was about to enter Cassland Crescent when she had to step back onto the pavement as a hansom cab drove past her, drawing to a halt outside the house. She quickened her pace, her curiosity aroused, but she stopped dead when she saw Harry Challenor alight from the carriage. She froze to the spot, wondering whether she could make it to the servants' entrance without him seeing her, but it was a vain hope. Harry turned, as if sensing her presence and he smiled. 'Good morning, Miss Coggins. At least I know that I've come to the right address.'

Her limbs felt leaden as she walked slowly towards him. 'How did you know we were here?'

'I paid a call on Sir Joseph at Damerell Manor. He had just received a telegram from Josie asking for his help. I was travelling to London anyway and I volunteered my services.'

'And so you came to rescue her.' Kate could not quite keep the note of disappointment from her voice. He must genuinely care for Josie or he would not have taken the trouble to seek her out.

277

'I came to ensure that you both arrived home safely.'

'How did you know that I was here? Did Josie mention me?'

'On the contrary, she had convinced me that you had run away with your lover and were living with him in Weymouth.' He held up his hand as she opened her mouth to protest. 'I was a fool to believe it, but the man you were supposed to have eloped with was Loveday, and I happened to pass him in the lane close to the home farm. It was he who told me that you had gone to London with Josie, and that is why I went to see Sir Joseph.'

Kate stared at him nonplussed. 'I don't understand any of this. Why would Josie make up such a terrible lie?'

'I suspect that it appealed to her sense of mischief and she was amusing herself at your expense. Anyway, it was all a misunderstanding, and now I'm here to take both of you home.'

She did not know whom she blamed the most: Josie for her childish and cruel attempt at ridding herself of a supposed rival, or Harry for believing her. Suddenly both of them seemed equally at fault. She drew herself up to her full height. 'You don't have to concern yourself with me, sir,' she said with as much dignity as she could muster. 'I have almost enough saved for the return train fare.' It was a lie, but at this moment she did not want to have anything to do with either of them.

'I wouldn't hear of it, Kate. You are more than welcome to travel with us. I wouldn't think of leaving you all alone in London, particularly here in the East End.'

She opened the front door and ushered him into the building. 'I'll show you upstairs to Miss Spalding's rooms, sir.'

He caught her by the hand as she was about to move away. 'Must we be so formal? Can't we be friends?'

She stared down at his fingers intertwined with her own and she felt her heart miss a beat. His touch warmed her chilled body but she dared not look him in the eye for fear of betraying her emotions. Until now she had managed to keep her feelings to herself, but in the confined space of the hallway his proximity was disturbing and her resolve weakening. She knew she could not hate him no matter how hard she tried. She pulled her hand away and headed for the stairs. 'Follow me, sir.'

He moved swiftly to her side. 'What on earth brought you both to Hackney of all places? Why did you allow Josie to involve you in this harebrained scheme?'

'It's not up to me to explain, sir.' Kate ascended the stairs as quickly as was possible when hampered by a heavy basket and long skirts.

He stopped, taking the basket from her. 'Can't you speak for yourself, Kate Coggins? Are you always going to run away from me?'

She raised her eyes to meet his. She could see that he was in deadly earnest and his sincerity both shocked and surprised her. She needed time to think, but he was barring her way and she realised that he would not give up until she had given him an answer.

'Yes,' she said simply. 'A gentleman like you only wants one thing from a girl in my position.'

She wished the words unsaid the moment they left her lips. She knew it was not true but she had wanted to lash out at him for the hurt and humiliation she had just suffered. His shocked expression might have been amusing to an onlooker but it only added to Kate's embarrassment. She had obviously misunderstood his intentions and made a fool of herself. She hurried on ahead without giving him a chance to respond. Her cheeks felt as though they were on fire and her heart was hammering against her stays so that she could barely catch her breath, but somehow she managed to reach Miss Spalding's door. She knocked and entered without waiting for permission. 'You have a visitor, Miss Josephine,' she said, standing aside to allow Harry to enter the room. She did not wait to see Josie's reaction. She snatched the basket from him and ran.

Less than half an hour later Josie burst into the kitchen. She stopped short, her triumphant smile fading as she looked round the dingy room. 'My God, how have you put up with this? I'd no idea the kitchen was like this. Anyway, it doesn't matter now. We're going home, Kate.'

A groan from Boy was followed by a sound resembling a growl as he shuffled towards Josie, brandishing a knife. 'Get out of me kitchen. You ain't taking Kate nowhere.'

She stared at him in disgust. 'What is this monstrosity, Kate? Have you stolen him from a freak show?'

'That's a cruel thing to say.' Kate put her arm around Boy's shoulders, gently relieving him of the knife.

'This child has been preparing all the delicious meals that you and Miss Spalding have eaten. He's a brilliant cook and he's my friend.'

'Well said.'

Kate had not seen Harry enter the room, and, judging by her reaction, neither had Josie. She turned to him, smiling. 'I was joking, of course. The boy is a very good cook, I'll give him that.'

Harry regarded Boy with a friendly smile. 'A rare talent in one so young.'

Visibly unimpressed, Boy glared at him. 'You ain't taking Kate away from me. She's me one and only friend in the whole world.'

'I won't leave you,' Kate said, giving him a reassuring hug.

'I'm going back to Dorset with Harry. You can do what you like, Kate.' Josie made a move towards the door. 'Are you coming or staying? Make up your mind because we're leaving immediately.'

'You told dreadful lies about me and Sam. Why, Josie?'

A momentary flicker of something akin to embarrassment flickered across Josie's features and then she laughed. 'It was a joke. I never meant Harry to take it seriously. Come on, Kate, where's your sense of humour?'

'It was a terrible thing to do.'

'All right, it was. You know me, Kate. I say things without thinking. Forgive me, please, and let's get away from here.'

Kate stood her ground. 'But what about Nanny Barnes? You can't abandon her now.'

281

'I'll send her some money or a food hamper as soon as I get home. She'll be all right.'

'Don't go, Kate.' Boy's small features crumpled and tears ran down his cheeks. 'Don't leave me.'

Undecided, Kate looked from his stricken face to Josie's set expression, and she knew she must choose. She longed to go home, but she knew that Honoria would not welcome her return, and Josie would forget her promises the moment she became engaged to Harry. As to Challenor himself, she shot a glance at him as he stood in the doorway and her heart felt like a lead weight inside her breast – he would marry Josie. She did not need the gypsy's crystal ball to foretell the future.

'I'm not leaving Boy or Nanny Barnes,' she said slowly. 'You don't know what it's been like down here, Josie. That brute Wharton will kill Boy one day and no one will lift a finger to stop him.'

'In that case, he should accompany us to Dorset.' Harry beckoned to Boy. 'How would you like to work in the kitchens of a big house? You would have to start at the bottom, but my chef would teach you all he knows.'

Boy stared at him in amazement. 'You ain't serious.'

A muscle twitched at the corner of Harry's mouth but he kept a straight face. 'I meant every word I said.'

'For goodness' sake stop all this chitchat and let's go.' Josie caught Kate by the arm. 'Are you satisfied now?'

'I'm more than happy for Boy, but there's still Nanny Barnes. She's not capable of looking after herself and you know it.'

'Then we'll take her too.' Harry consulted a half-hunter watch he had taken from his waistcoat pocket.

'It's getting late. Where does Miss Barnes live? If we're to take her with us you need to make her ready for the train journey.'

'Not far from here,' Josie muttered. 'But I don't think that Hickson will be very pleased to have Nanny Barnes back in the servants' hall.'

'And who is Hickson?' Harry raised his eyebrows.

'It doesn't matter,' Josie said impatiently. 'I'll sort it out when we get home. Just get everything and everyone together, Kate. I'll wait upstairs until Harry has organised our transport to the station.' She flounced out of the kitchen.

Harry turned to Kate. 'May I leave the arrangements to you?' He smiled. 'I'm not the libertine you take me for, and I'm sorry I allowed myself to be taken in by Josie's silly games. Can we at least call a truce for the journey home?'

'She's got me to protect her,' Boy said, taking Kate by the hand. 'I won't let no one take advantage of her.'

'Then I am happy to leave her in your care.' Harry hesitated, frowning. 'What is your real name? I can't keep calling you Boy.'

'I dunno, sir. It's what Wharton calls me.'

'Well, Boy will have to do for now. Go with Kate and I'll leave a note for Wharton. I don't think he'll bother you again.' He held the door open for them. 'Don't worry, Kate. This disreputable fellow might prove to be a gentleman after all.'

The journey back to Dorset was uneventful. Harry had bought first class tickets for them all, and Nanny Barnes fell into a deep sleep almost as soon as the train pulled out of Waterloo. Boy sat on the edge of his seat, staring out of the window, seemingly in a trance. He hardly spoke two words throughout the whole journey, although Josie kept up a constant stream of mainly one-sided conversation, telling Harry in detail of the hardships she had suffered during their time in Hackney. Kate said little, simply nodding in agreement when Josie asked for confirmation of one trivial fact or another. She had mixed feelings about returning home. She longed to see her father, Sam and Molly, but she was painfully aware that life under Honoria's rule would still be difficult. Then there was the hateful Tilda to contend with. Kate sat back in her seat and closed her eyes, in an attempt to pretend that Harry was not sitting opposite her, but she could not shut him out no matter how hard she tried. It was heaven and hell at the same time. The journey could not end soon enough for her.

It was almost a relief to say goodbye to the rest of the party when the cab that Harry had hired at Dorchester station dropped Kate off at the home farm. It was dark and the lighted windows sent a welcoming glow onto the muddy farmyard. She stood for a moment, watching the cab disappear down the lane with a sudden feeling of loss. Josie would no longer need her and she might never see Harry again. She felt unaccountably nervous of returning home unannounced. Acting on impulse she made her way down the lane to the tiny cottage where Sam and Molly now lived. She knocked on the door.

Sam's face was a picture when he saw her. 'Kate. I don't believe it.' He stepped over the threshold and wrapped his arms around her in a bear hug. 'Come inside, maidy, and get warm.' He closed the door. 'Sit by the fire, and I'll make a pot of tea, or are you too grand a lady now to drink tea with a farm labourer?'

She slipped off her cloak and laid it on a ladder-back chair. 'I'd love a cup of tea, Sam. And I'll never be a grand lady.'

'So how was it?' Sam took the steaming kettle from the trivet. 'How did you fare amongst the gentry?'

'It's a long story.'

'And did Josie get her rich gentleman to propose marriage?'

Kate studied Sam's profile. His jaw was clenched in a hard line and her heart ached for him; she could feel his pain that was so similar to her own. 'Not yet, Sam.'

'But you think he will?'

'I don't know.' Kate rose to her feet. 'Don't bother about the tea. I think I'd better hurry home or I might find myself locked out.'

'You've got time for a cup of tea. I've got to go for Molly soon; we can walk together.'

Kate eyed him over the rim of the teacup. There was something in his manner that was disturbing. 'What is it, Sam? What aren't you telling me?'

Chapter Seventeen

Sam threw a bundle of furze onto the fire. 'You always could read me like a book, Kate.'

'What is it? Is Pa ill? Has he had an accident?'

He had been staring into the blaze, but he turned his head to look at her and his lips twisted into a wry grin. 'In a manner of speaking I suppose it was an accident of sorts.'

'What are you talking about?'

'You've got a baby brother, Kate. He come all of a sudden a few days ago.'

'But that's impossible. Honoria's baby wasn't due yet.'

'She might act all goody-goody and high-nosed, but it's obvious that she and the gaffer was at it like rabbits, if you'll excuse the expression, long before they were wed. She ain't the first and I daresay she won't be the last woman to catch a man by fair means or foul.'

'I thought she was getting large, but I put it down to the fact that she was eating for two. I suppose it's all round the village by now?'

'You know what they are for gossiping in Kingston Damerell, but there'll be something else to talk about afore too long. And the gaffer's as proud as Punch.'

'He always wanted a son,' Kate said, sighing. 'Honoria will be even more unbearable now.'

'Your pa loves you, Kate. Having a son won't alter that.'

'No,' she said with an attempt at a smile. 'Of course not.'

'Then let's get you home safe and sound. I want to make sure that the hens is all locked up safe for the night. What with the gaffer wrapped up in fatherhood and poor Molly being run ragged by Honoria, things has got a bit slack while you've been away.'

Kate rose to her feet. 'Well, I'm back now. I won't allow Molly to be bullied, I promise you that.'

'I know you won't.' Sam picked up her cloak and wrapped it around her shoulders. He hesitated for a moment as if struggling with a knotty problem, and when he spoke the words came out in a rush. 'Tell me truthfully, Kate. What went on between Josie and Challenor? Will she marry him?'

She patted his hand as it rested on her shoulder. 'Forget her, Sam. She's not for you and you know it.'

'Aye, I know it. But it ain't that easy.' He moved away to shrug on his jacket, and he plucked his billycock hat from its peg, fingering the jay's feather for a second before ramming the hat on his head. He turned to her, holding out his arm. 'Shall we, my lady?'

She managed a smile, but she felt sick with apprehension. If Honoria had succeeded in making her feel like a stranger in her own home before the child was born, what was it going to be like now that she was the proud mother of a son?

As she entered the farmhouse kitchen, Kate's nostrils were assailed by the familiar scent of burning apple wood and freshly baked bread. Her father was asleep in the rocking chair by the range with his chin resting on his chest and soft snoring sounds emanating from his lips. She tiptoed across the flagstone floor to drop a kiss on his forehead. He gave a startled snort and opened his eyes. He blinked hard and his mouth curved in a smile. 'Kate, it really is you. I thought I was dreaming.'

She flung her arms around his neck and kissed his whiskery cheek. 'You're not dreaming. I've come home.'

Sam shuffled his feet. 'I'll just go and check on the hens, gaffer. And then I'll come back for Molly.'

'She can't be far away,' Robert said, rising stiffly to his feet. 'I expect she's upstairs with Honoria. Did he tell you, Kate? I'm a father for the first time.'

She stared at him, frowning. 'For the second time, Pa.'

'To be sure. I meant to say that it's the first time I've been father to a son. He's a fine boy, Kate. And he looks just like me.'

'I'll be back in two shakes of a lamb's tail. Tell Molly to wrap up warm.' Sam went outside, closing the door behind him.

'What did you name him, Pa?' Kate took off her cloak, gazing round the old familiar farmhouse kitchen with a mixture of relief and sadness. Suddenly this did not feel like home.

'Robert, of course, after me. He's got a fine pair of

lungs on him, Kate. No doubt you'll hear him when he wakes up for his feed. Do you want to go up now and see him?'

She shook her head. 'I don't want to disturb Honoria. I expect she needs her rest. I'm really tired after the journey from London. If you don't mind, Pa, I think I'll go straight to bed.'

He cleared his throat, staring down at his socked feet. 'Er, Kate, my dear. I'm afraid we had to move your things into the attic room.'

'What?' She stared at him in disbelief. 'Why would you do a thing like that?'

'Honoria thought that your bedroom would make a good nursery. It makes sense, maidy. Tilda's room is too small to take a cradle as well as her bed, and your old room is closer to ours.'

'You've taken my bedroom without asking me? And why the attic? If it was going to be done, then why wasn't I put in Molly's room, the one that Honoria gave to Tilda?'

'Come now, maidy, you know that's little more than a box room. There's plenty of space for all your pretty things in the attic.'

'Amongst the spiders and mice! No one has slept up there since Sam moved to the cottage. I'd rather be cramped and warm in the small room than freeze to death under the eaves.'

'It's out of the question, maidy. Honoria wanted a dressing room. She said that is what proper ladies have and who was I to deny it to her, especially in her delicate condition.'

289

Kate flung up her hands. 'She's changed everything. I simply can't believe you've let her get away with it, Pa.'

'Don't start putting on airs and graces, Kate. Honoria warned me that it might be like this. She said that no good would come of your having spent time with the gentry, and now I can see that she was right.'

'But, Pa . . .'

He held up his hand. 'That's enough of that, daughter. I don't want to hear another word on the subject.'

'This is all her doing,' Kate said angrily. 'She's been trying to push me out ever since you married her.'

'Now you're talking nonsense. Honoria is my wife and naturally I have to put her wishes first. You'll sleep in the attic room and you won't mention a word of this to her. She needs rest and quiet, and I won't have women spitting at each other like farm cats, so you bear that in mind, maidy.' He stomped out of the room, narrowly missing Molly who had just come through the door. She uttered a cry of delight.

'Kate, you've come home. I was never so glad to see no one in my whole life.' She ran to Kate, flinging her arms around her. 'It's been dreadful here since you went away.'

'I'm home now, Molly,' Kate said, holding her close. 'Things will be better, I promise.'

Molly sniffed and wiped her eyes on her sleeve. 'I wish I could believe that. You can't imagine what it's been like. What with Honoria going on and on at me all the time, and that hateful Tilda creature behaving like she was the queen, there's been times when I've felt like running away.'

'I won't let Tilda bully you, dear. And you can be sure that I'll have a few words to say to Honoria in the morning.'

Molly pulled a face. 'She's a bitch and I don't care who hears me say so. I spoke up for you when she told me to shift your things to the attic room, and I got a clout round the ear for me pains.'

'It really doesn't matter. I'm sure I'll do very well under the eaves,' Kate said with more confidence than she was feeling. 'Best wrap up warm, Molly. Sam will be back for you in a moment or two.'

Molly eyed the dirty crockery in the stone sink. 'I daren't leave that lot till morning, Kate, or I'll be in dire trouble.'

'I'll take care of it. Go home and get a good night's rest. I'll see you first thing and we'll have a long chat. I'll tell you all about my adventures in London.'

In the attic room, Kate put the candlestick down on the deal washstand and stood for a moment, gazing round with a tight knot of despair in her stomach. It was a large space under the eaves, with headroom in the apex only, and a small dormer window cut through the thick covering of thatch. A draught whistled through the cracks between the floorboards and she could hear the scrabbling sound of tiny feet in the rafters. She shuddered at the thought of rats and mice running around overhead. In her old room there would have been a fire blazing away in the grate, gaily patterned rugs on the polished floorboards and the comfortable bed in which she had slept when she was a child. Sleeping here was reminiscent of the bad old days in the mews, but perhaps a little better than lying on the dirt floor in Nanny Barnes' house.

After a quick inspection, Kate found that her clothes had been put away neatly in a roughly constructed beech-wood chest, but there was neither a dressing table nor a mirror. She sat down on the edge of the truckle bed, grimacing at the hardness of the flock-filled mattress and the coarseness of the cotton sheets. She lay down, fully clothed, and wrapped herself in the coverlet. Cobwebs hung like grey lace from the rafters above her head and she closed her eyes, trying hard not to cry, but hot tears forced their way between her eyelids, cooling rapidly as they ran down her cheeks. She tried to force the memory of the precious hours seated opposite Harry in the first class compartment to the back of her mind, but she could still see the way his eyes crinkled at the corners when he smiled, and hear the deep tones of his voice. Try as she might, she could not conjure up the louche, arrogant Harry Challenor she had met in the Soho Bazaar. That person might have existed in London society, but he was quite different from the man she had come to know.

She curled up in a ball beneath the thin coverlet. Allowing him to invade her thoughts would lead to misery and maybe even madness. He had taken Josie back to Damerell Manor, and Sir Joseph would almost inevitably see his actions as a declaration of his intent to marry her. This was the stark reality and she would have to deal with it as best she could.

She awakened early next morning. It was bitterly cold in her room even though winter was gradually giving way to a reluctant spring. She slipped off her crumpled gown and put on her old, serviceable working clothes. She tucked her hair into a cotton mobcap and pulled on her boots before making her way downstairs to the kitchen. The fire in the range was not quite out, and she riddled the ashes, adding some dry kindling and using the bellows to coax the embers into flame. When she had a good blaze going, she took a bucket from the scullery and went out into the yard to fetch water from the pump. She could hear the cows lowing in the barn and she guessed that Sam must have arrived to begin milking. At least that was one chore she would be able to take off his shoulders now that she was home.

Trudging back across the yard, Kate glanced up at her father's bedroom window. The curtains were drawn and there was no telltale chink of light to suggest that he was up and about. She had been awakened in the night by the strange sound of a baby crying, and it had taken her a few moments to realise that it was her tiny half-brother who was making all that noise. She knew she ought to feel something for a child who was related to her by blood, but somehow she could not summon up any enthusiasm for Honoria's baby. Perhaps she would grow to love him. She turned her head as she heard the muffled sound of approaching footsteps, and she saw Molly hurrying towards her, red-cheeked from exertion and panting. 'I'm late. I overslept and Sam didn't wake me.'

'Don't worry. I seem to be the only one who is up, and I've seen to the fire. Come inside, Molly. We'll have a nice hot cup of tea.' Kate picked up the bucket of water and hooked her free arm around Molly's shoulders.

'Don't never go away again, Kate,' Molly said, shivering. 'Promise you won't leave us.'

'I won't leave you, Molly.'

'And you'll tell that old hag a few home truths?'

'That too.'

Later that morning, when Kate entered her father's bedroom, she found Honoria sitting up in bed with a shawl wrapped around her shoulders and the baby suckling at her breast. Her expression was not welcoming. 'So you've deigned to return home.'

'Good morning, Honoria. How are you this morning?'

'Don't use that saucy tone with me, young lady. And don't put on airs just because you've been mixing with people above your station. You're home now and you'll have to learn your place.'

'I'm still my father's daughter, Honoria.'

'And this is my son, your baby brother. Aren't you happy to see him?' Honoria's eyes issued a challenge even as her lips twisted into a semblance of a smile. She stroked the baby's downy head. 'He is a fine boy. See how he feeds on my milk. Soon he will be big and strong and he will inherit the farm.'

'The farm belongs to the Damerell estate. Your son will never own it.'

Honoria's lips tightened into a pencil-thin line. 'And you will remain a poor spinster for the rest of your days. You should have taken up Squire Westwood's offer. At least you would have had a roof over your head, and I'm sure he would have been very generous, providing you kept a civil tongue in your head.'

'Why don't you say what you really mean, Honoria? You want me out of this house, don't you?'

'Yes, between you and me, that is exactly what I want. There is not room enough here for both of us.'

'My father would have something to say about that.'

'Don't try to come between a man and his wife, my dear. I have weapons that you do not possess.'

'I don't doubt it, and I have too much respect for my father to want to make him unhappy. But you had no right to turn me out of my room.'

Honoria shifted the baby to the other breast. 'I've every right. As an unmarried daughter you have no say in anything. You are a nobody.'

'My father doesn't think so.'

'Robert agrees with everything I say. I can do no wrong, and I must not be upset or my milk will dry up. Don't try and fight me, my girl, for it is you who will come off the worst. Now stop bothering me and go about your business on the farm. Send Molly up with my breakfast. I want tea and toast, butter and honey too.'

'You can treat me as you please, Honoria. But I

won't allow you to bully Molly. She has been like a sister to me and she deserves better.'

Honoria curled her lip. 'Well, you two sisters might find yourselves living together in the poorhouse if you continue to cross me. Now do as I say, and send Tilda to me as well. Baby needs changing and putting down for his nap.'

Biting back a sharp retort, Kate made a hurried exit. She went to knock on Tilda's door, and without waiting for a reply she opened it and walked into the room – her room. Tilda was standing in front of the dressing table admiring her reflection in the mirror. She turned with a guilty start and her hand flew to the string of beads at her throat.

'You little thief,' Kate cried in horror. 'That's my necklace. Take it off this instant.'

Tilda's eyes widened in fear as Kate advanced towards her. She fumbled with the clasp at the back of her neck. 'I found it. I didn't know it was yours.'

'You're lying. My mother gave me that string of beads, and it was in my dressing table drawer. Molly must have missed it when she took my things up to the attic, unless you had found it first and intended to keep it for yourself.'

'No, miss. Honestly, I found it in the back of the drawer. I was just trying it on.' Tilda's fingers trembled as she handed the necklace to Kate. 'Take it. What do I want with glass beads, anyway?'

Kate snatched it from her. 'You have no right to be in this room in the first place, and if you ever touch any of my things again I'll see that you are dismissed.'

She had not meant to blurt that out. None of this was Tilda's fault, but seeing her with Ma's necklace, even if it was only made out of cheap glass beads, had made something snap inside her.

'The mistress put me in here. It weren't my fault.' Tilda's small eyes glittered with cunning. 'I'll tell her that you want your room back, shall I, miss?'

'You'll do nothing of the sort.' Kate made a move towards the door. 'She wants you. Go to her. That's what I came to say.'

'Now you know how it feels,' Tilda said, sidling past Kate. 'Being treated like a servant ain't no fun, is it, miss?' She shot out of the room and ran along the landing, turning her head and poking out her tongue as she reached Honoria's door.

Kate ignored the gesture, slipping the beads into her pocket with a sigh as she went downstairs to the kitchen to pass Honoria's order for breakfast onto Molly.

'I'll give her tea and toast,' Molly said, hacking at the loaf. 'And I'd like to stick her head in the hive and let the dumbledores sting her to pieces.'

An involuntary chuckle escaped from Kate's lips, relieving the hard knot of anger that had stuck in her throat. Molly, who was normally so quiet and gentle, was attacking the bread like an avenging angel. She looked up at Kate and frowned. 'Have I said something funny?'

Kate shook her head. 'No, Molly dear. It's just that I've never seen you so angry, but it's not at all funny. If I didn't laugh, I'd cry.'

'That's what makes me so mad,' Molly said, brandishing the knife. 'She can say what she likes to me, but the old cow is treating you worse than a slave. I can't stand by and watch it, Kate.'

'Don't upset yourself, Molly. I have broad shoulders and I'll deal with Honoria in my own way. In the meantime, I suggest you toast that bread and take up her breakfast tray. I'm going out to collect the eggs.'

Molly muttered something unintelligible as she jabbed the toasting fork into the bread. Kate took her workaday fustian jacket from its peg and shrugged it on. She slipped her booted feet into her pattens before venturing out into the muddy farmyard. As she made her way to the hen house she knew that life was going to be difficult from here on. She was tempted to seek out her father and put her case to him, but she knew in her heart that Honoria was right in her assumption that he would take her side. Pa was no longer a grieving widower dependent on his daughter for everything. He was a middle-aged man who was besotted with a younger woman, and she had given him a son. No longer a mere housekeeper, Honoria was now revelling in her position as wife and mother, and she had made it clear that she did not want a rival for her husband's affection.

As Kate moved about the hen house collecting the eggs, she realised that her options were limited. If she stayed at home she would have to put up with Honoria's machinations and snubs, in the hope that her stepmother would eventually tire and call a truce. She had considered applying for the teacher's job at the village school but Miss Winter was relatively young and likely to remain there for years. The only other alternative would be to accept the squire's offer of a position at Westwood Grange. As her fingers explored the straw, feeling for the warm oval of a newly laid egg, Kate felt as though her world was splintering around her like shards of broken glass. She really was, as Harry had said, Miss Nobody. Even remembering the way he had teased her at their first meeting was enough to shoot an arrow of pain through her heart. She had tried hard to dislike him, but she had failed miserably. She put the last egg in the basket and straightened up.

'I thought I'd find you in here.' Sam stood in the doorway grinning at her.

She smiled. Dear Sam; so solid and dependable. She was suddenly overcome with emotion. 'Oh, Sam. What would I do without you?'

'There, there, maidy. What brought this on?'

She shook her head, unable to speak.

His dark eyes flashed with anger. 'Don't tell me. It's that old besom, Honoria. I knowed she was going to cause trouble the moment I set eyes on her. 'Tis a great pity she didn't go off with that big burly army sergeant who was sweet on her afore she got her claws into your pa.'

Momentarily diverted, Kate blinked and swallowed hard. 'What army sergeant? I didn't know about that, Sam.'

'Well, it might just have been tittle-tattle, but as I heard it she thought he was going to pop the question, but his regiment was sent away somewhere. I reckon he had a lucky escape meself.'

She shrugged her shoulders. 'It's probably just gossip, Sam. Anyway, I don't care about her. At least I've got you and Molly on my side. Honoria has Pa exactly where she wants him for now, but he'll come round eventually. I'm sure he will.'

'Eventually won't do, maidy. I'll not stand by and see you treated worse than a servant in your own home.' He grabbed her by the hand. 'Come with me. We'll go and find the gaffer. Last time I saw him he was in the hay barn. At least we can talk to him there without her eavesdropping, or that stuck-up Tilda spying on us.'

'But the eggs,' Kate protested.

'Leave them for now. They won't come to no harm, and this is more important than a few eggs.' Taking her firmly by the hand, he led her out of the hen house and across the yard. A pale, watery sun had filtered through the clouds and there were brush strokes of blue in the sky.

They were nearing the barn when a shout from the lane made Sam stop and turn his head. Above the hedge Kate could just see the crown of a coachman's hat and the ruddy cheeks of Smith, the Damerells' coachman. He waved his hand as he drew the sturdy horse to a halt outside the farm gates. 'Miss Kate. I've got a message from the big house.'

Kate clutched her jacket tightly around her body as a spiteful wind plucked at her clothing and dragged tendrils of hair from beneath her mobcap. 'What is it, Mr Smith?'

'Miss Josie wants to see you, miss. She said I was to bring you to the manor house right away, and no nonsense.'

That sounded so like Josie that Kate smiled. 'I'm busy, Mr Smith. It can't be that urgent. Please tell her that I'll come later. Sam will bring me in the trap.'

Smith shook his head. 'She won't like it, miss. You know what Miss Josie's like when she gets an idea into her head.'

Sam tapped Kate on the shoulder and when she turned to him she saw something akin to desperation in his eyes. 'Let me take you there. We can be back before the gaffer misses us.'

Kate looked from one to the other, undecided. Surely nothing much could have changed since yesterday? And then Harry's words came back to her. Josie had told him that she had eloped with Sam. When challenged, Josie had passed the whole thing off as a joke, and Kate had accepted her explanation at face value. Now Josie was commanding her to attend, as if she were royalty. Kate turned to Sam. 'Fetch the pony and trap. I've got a few choice words to say to Miss Damerell.'

Chapter Eighteen

Josie paced the floor, pausing at each of the four tall windows in the drawing room to gaze out at the carriage sweep and the tree-lined avenue. Despite the wild March winds, there was a faint haze of copper-coloured buds on the beech trees, and beneath them a sea of golden daffodils swayed and bowed like courtiers anticipating the arrival of a monarch.

Where was Kate? Smith had returned with the barouche but he had not stopped outside the house as she had expected, and had driven on towards the coach house. Surely he would send word if Kate had refused to accompany him? She bit her lip, drumming her fingers on the windowsill. She wondered if Kate was angry with her after Harry's revelation yesterday. But she had seemed to accept that it was all a joke, and not meant to be taken seriously. Josie could not bear to admit, even to herself, that she had uttered the lies in a fit of pique. Even so, Kate would forgive her. She always had in the past and there was no reason to suppose that she had changed.

Wrapping her arms around her body, Josie began to pace the floor between the windows. If Kate brought the matter up she would have to apologise again, and say that it had all been a silly misunderstanding. It was all in the past, and today she longed to share her good news with her friend. She also wanted to let Sam know of her engagement before the servants had a chance to spread the glad tidings around the village. She felt a cold shiver run down her spine. Lies were like a spider's web; they had a habit of entangling the perpetrator in their silken threads.

Come what may, she had sealed her own fate last night when Harry had finally proposed. She sighed, rubbing her hand across her temples. If she were to be honest he had not exactly asked her to marry him, but the result was the same. The cigar band on the ring finger of her left hand was proof that they were engaged, but it was she herself who had put it there. Did that count? She tugged it off and tossed it into the fire, watching the tiny paper band curl up and turn to ashes as she recalled the scene at dinner the previous evening.

Joseph had invited Harry to dine with them and Squire Westwood was also one of the guests at dinner. Tired, nervous and desperate, Josie had drunk rather too much wine during the meal. It had gone to her head, making her reckless enough to refuse to leave when her mother and Hermione retired to the drawing room. She had been flirting with Harry all evening, making it perfectly plain to all those present that she encouraged his attentions, and when Toop brought in the box of Havana cigars she had insisted on choosing one for Harry. Sir Joseph had laughed at her antics, telling her how much he had missed her lively company, but Squire Westwood had remained poker-faced and disapproving. Harry had been amused by her unconventional behaviour, but had done his best to turn the conversation to matters of business which would have excluded her completely. The prospect of living under her uncle's roof once again and dwindling into an unwanted and unloved spinster was too awful to contemplate. She had moved closer to Harry, sitting on the edge of his chair. She had slipped the cigar band onto her finger and held it up for him to see. 'Does this mean that we are engaged, Harry?'

She felt a blush rise to her cheeks as she recalled the startled look on his face. He had attempted to laugh it off, but she had leapt to her feet, holding her hand high. 'Look, everyone. Harry and I are engaged to be married. Isn't that splendid?'

He had been too much of a gentleman to embarrass her by a denial, and Sir Joseph had sent for champagne to celebrate the good news. Squire Westwood had offered his congratulations, although she had seen the look of disapproval in his eyes. He knew that she had tricked Harry, but Sir Joseph was too drunk to have seen through her ruse, and was patently delighted. He might have inherited the title, but Harry had the business connections and the money. Even in her tipsy state, Josie had seen her uncle's eyes gleaming with avarice.

Now, in the cold light of day she struggled with feelings of remorse. She knew very well that Harry was still pining after Kate, but a match like that would spell ruin for an ambitious man. She needed a rich husband and he needed a well-bred wife to assure his position in society and to bear him a son and heir. It was a business contract, and both parties would benefit. She smiled. She had lied and cheated, but these were just ploys that anyone with ambition might use to further their own advantage. If she were a cat she would be purring. Her abominable uncle was delighted and Mama was smiling for the first time since the death of her beloved husband. Even Hickson had managed a tight little grimace that passed for satisfaction on hearing the good news. Now all she had to do was to tell Kate and Sam.

She came to a halt by the middle window as she spotted the familiar pony and trap at the far end of the avenue. As it came closer she could see two people on the driver's seat and she knew instinctively that it was Sam who held the reins. Her heartbeats quickened and her pulses raced at the sight of him. She made a valiant attempt to replace his earthy image with that of Harry Challoner, but she was painfully aware that there was no magic in Harry's touch. There was no fire in his eyes when they met hers. There was no heat in her blood when he was close to her. She controlled her erratic breathing with difficulty and forced herself to walk sedately as she left the room and made her way down the wide flight of marble stairs to the entrance hall.

The footman opened the double doors at her command and she descended the steps slowly, hoping that no one but herself could hear her heart thudding against her ribs. She waited until Sam helped Kate alight before moving forward and holding out her hands. 'You've come. What kept you so long, Kate? You must have known that I needed you.' She addressed her words to Kate, but she intended them for Sam and she shot him a sideways glance to see if he had understood. The bond between them was so strong that she could feel him silently embracing her, even though they were not physically touching. She knew in that moment that he had forgiven her for running away without telling him. Despite her intention to appear aloof, she could not tear her gaze from his face, but she forced herself to speak harshly to him. If she weakened now she would fling herself into his arms and never let him go. 'Go round to the servants' entrance, Loveday.'

Sam tipped his hat. 'Yes, my lady.' He turned on his heel and strode off without a backward glance.

'Why did you speak to him like that?' Kate demanded as she followed Josie into the house. 'That was so cruel. You know how fond he is of you.'

Josie tossed her head. 'Sam has to learn his place. We aren't children now, Kate. Anyway, forget him. Come up to the drawing room. I need to talk to you.'

'What is it that couldn't wait? What has changed since yesterday?'

'Wait until we're alone.' Josie shot a meaningful glance at the stone-faced footman. '*Pas devant les domestiques*, Kate.'

Kate followed her up the stairs and into the drawing room. 'I'm sure they already know whatever it is that you are dying to tell me.'

Josie closed the doors, leaning against them. The thrill of keeping Kate in suspense faded a little as she met her earnest gaze. She would have to be cruel to be kind. 'I think you'd better sit down, Kate . . .' She broke off abruptly as Hickson entered the room without knocking. 'Yes? What is it, Hickson?'

'Lady Damerell wants to speak to you about the guest list,' Hickson said, eyeing Kate's working clothes with a disdainful sniff. 'In my day no one would visit the big house looking like that, Coggins.'

Josie turned on her in a sudden fury. 'Don't speak to Kate like that, Hickson. She came at my request.'

'She should be in the servants' quarters.' Hickson appeared unabashed.

'Mind your own business, Hickson. And tell Mama that I'll come as soon as I can.'

'Her ladyship doesn't like to be kept waiting, Miss Josephine.'

'She'll understand. Now go away and leave us alone.'

Hickson left the room with a disapproving twitch of her shoulders, closing the door firmly behind her.

'Abominable woman,' Josie said with a wry smile. 'I don't know why Mama puts up with her. Anyway, she's not important. Sit down, Kate. I've something to tell you.'

Kate perched on the edge of the nearest chair. 'What list was Hickson referring to? Are you having a party?'

Josie clasped her hands tightly in front of her. Suddenly it was not so easy to tell Kate something which would break her heart. 'It's for my wedding.

That's what I wanted to tell you before you heard it from someone else.'

'He proposed?' Kate's eyes were wide with shock and disbelief. 'Harry actually asked you to marry him?'

'He did, and I accepted. I'm going to be mistress of Copperstone Castle before the year is out.'

'But you don't love him.'

'This isn't about love, and you know it.'

Kate leapt to her feet. 'How can you stand there so calmly, admitting that you're marrying for money and position?'

'Because that's what we do. Women in my position have little choice. I can stay here and suffer the insults and degradation handed out by my dear uncle, or I can marry a man who will give me everything.'

'Everything but love.'

'Oh, he loves me, Kate. Make no mistake about that. I can twist men round my little finger if I choose.'

'As you have done with Sam. You cut your teeth on his poor heart and he's devoted to you. Do you want to destroy him as well as yourself? You told Harry dreadful lies about me and Sam, and then pretended it was a joke. I hate you for what you're doing to us, Josie.'

The pain was excruciating. Josie gasped, clasping her hands to her breast. She had not been prepared to face her own feelings head on, but Kate's words cut deep. A red mist hazed her vision and she was suddenly furious, but her anger was directed at herself.

She alone had created this situation, and she must be the one to make it right again. 'Why are you so upset, Kate?' she cried angrily. 'Is it because I'm going to marry the man you wanted for yourself, or do you resent the fact that I love Sam?'

Kate's hands flew to cover her mouth and her eyes filled with tears but she did not answer.

'Why do you look at me like that, Kate Coggins? You've always known that Sam and I love each other.'

'I – I didn't know. I mean, I know you care for Sam, but I've never heard you speak of him in such a passionate way. I know he loves you, but you treat him so badly . . .'

'Yes, I do. And why do you think that is? Because if I allow my true feelings to show, if he ever knew how much I want him, it would destroy us both. Our situations in life are too different – we can never be together. But Sam and I are one and the same being. I'm afraid that parting from him forever will kill me.'

'And yet you are prepared to marry a man whom you don't love, just for the sake of position and wealth? How could you, Josie? How could you even think of deceiving a man like Harry into thinking that you love him and want to be his wife?'

'Don't be such a little hypocrite. You'd fall at his feet if he looked twice at you.'

'Yes, you're right, but more than anything I want him to be happy. If you really loved him I would wish you well.'

Josie stared at her in amazement. 'I didn't know you felt so strongly, Kate,' she said slowly. 'Maybe I would have acted differently if I'd realised how much you care for him.'

Tears spilled unchecked down Kate's cheeks. 'I know that he's not for me and never could be. We're worlds apart, and even if he had any feelings at all for me, he wouldn't sully the Challenor name by marrying so far beneath him.'

'Merciful heaven! What have we come to?' Josie laid a tentative hand on Kate's shoulder. 'What have we become?'

'We've grown up, Josie. We aren't children any longer and we have to face what life has in store for us.'

Josie absorbed this in silence. She was seeing herself in a new and unfavourable light and she was truly shocked. She knew that she had been spoilt from birth by doting parents, who had given her everything she desired. She had gone her own merry way, taking love and friendship for granted. She could not mend Kate's broken heart, but Sam was different. He was and always would be a part of her – the better part. She met Kate's sad gaze with a determined lift of her chin. 'I must see him, Kate. It will be for the last time, I promise you, but I have to talk to Sam, setting things straight between us.'

'You must not let him hope.'

'I need to speak to him while I have enough resolve to end it.'

'Shall I send him to you?'

'No. We mustn't be seen together. Go now, please.

Tell him to meet me in the summerhouse by the lake. I'll be waiting for him.'

Kate hugged her. 'Be kind to him, Josie. He's a good man and I love him like a brother.'

Ten minutes later, Josie was in the summerhouse, waiting anxiously. How long could it take for Kate to find Sam and pass on her message? Perhaps he had taken umbrage at the way in which she had treated him earlier? He might be punishing her by refusing to come. She spun round as she heard a muffled footfall on the lichen-covered steps outside, and breathed a sigh of relief when she saw his outline through the dusty windowpanes. The door opened and he entered on a gust of cool air. He held out his arms and she walked into his embrace without stopping to consider whether it was right or wrong. He brushed her forehead with the softest of butterfly kisses, whispering her name over and over again. His lips caressed her eyelids and the tip of her nose, and when her knees were threatening to give way beneath her he claimed her mouth in a passionate kiss. She wound her arms around his neck, running her fingers through his hair and returning his embrace with an almost savage intensity.

When at last they drew apart, Sam's eyes were dark with desire. 'Josie, my love. My little love.'

Her eyelashes were wet with tears but she smiled up at him, losing herself in the depths of his gaze. 'Oh, Sam. Don't make this harder for me.'

He answered her with another kiss, blotting out time and reason. The musky scent of him filled her nostrils and the taste of him only made her hungry for more. The smell of the farmyard was still on him, but now it was sweeter to Josie than all the perfumes of Araby. She could feel his hard muscular body pressed against hers and her treacherous limbs gave way beneath her. They sank to the floor and the cold, bare boards were as soft to Josie as the finest feather bed. She lay beneath him and her blood roiled with passion. Until this moment, she had never experienced the physical need for a man, but now her desire matched his and it ran like fire through her veins. He was undoing the buttons of her bodice. His lips caressed the slim column of her neck, travelling down to the hollow at the base of her throat. She did not feel the cold as his hands found and cupped her breasts. She uttered a soft moan of pleasure as his tongue teased her nipples and his gentle fingers sought the seat of his desire. He stopped, quite suddenly, raising his head and staring at her with dark, unfocused eyes. 'I want you, but it cannot be. You are my beautiful maidy and always will be, but I cannot take you here, like a common serving girl.'

'I don't care,' Josie cried in a hoarse whisper. 'I want to be that common serving girl. I don't care if the world ends here, this minute, Sam.' She pulled his head down until their lips met, tongue caressed tongue and she arched her body against him.

'You know that I would never do anything to hurt you, maidy.'

'I know that and I love you, Sam. I always have and always will, God help me.' She closed her eyes, giving herself up to the powerful sensations that set her whole body aflame.

He kissed her tenderly on the lips, but the sound of the door opening and a screech of horror made them pull apart. Hickson stood in the doorway, her black shape silhouetted against the cold morning light. She stared at them with contempt. 'You little whore. I might have known you'd end up like this. Get off her, Loveday, you swine. Have you any idea what you've done?'

Sam scrambled to his feet. 'We love each other, Miss Hickson. I want to make her my wife.'

Hickson's shout of laughter echoed off the rafters and rattled the window glass. 'You're a common farm labourer and you want to marry a baronet's daughter. You're dreaming, boy. She's not for you and you know it.'

Josie's heart was thudding against her ribs and the blood was drumming in her ears, almost deafening her. She buttoned her dress with trembling fingers, getting up slowly and with as much dignity as she could muster. 'It's not how it appears, Hickson. Go away and leave us alone.'

'Not how it appears? You were whoring in the summerhouse and your father barely cold in his grave. What would he think if he could see you now?'

'Don't speak to her like that,' Sam cried angrily. 'Leave Josie alone. This was all my fault.'

Hickson regarded him with a curled lip. 'I know that, you gypsy bastard. You haven't heard the last of this. I've a good mind to report you to Sir Joseph.'

Josie clutched her arm. 'No. I forbid you to do any such thing, Hickson. Think how it would upset my mother if this were to become servants' gossip.'

'Maybe you should have thought of that before you arranged an assignation, Miss Josephine.' Hickson folded her arms across her flat chest. 'Get yourself back to the house this instant and we'll keep this between ourselves.' She moved swiftly to open the door. 'And go straight to your room. You're all dusty and dirty from lying on the floor. Dirty inside and out, that's you, my girl.'

'That's enough, Hickson.' Josie reached for Sam's hand, clutching it and taking comfort from its warmth. 'I won't allow you to talk to me like that.'

'Nor I neither,' Sam said, scowling. 'Who do you think you are to speak to Miss Damerell in that tone of voice?'

'Keep out of this, Sam Loveday, or it will be the worse for you. You mustn't be seen together, so you'd best leave now.'

Josie squeezed his hand. 'Hickson's right. You should leave here at once. Don't go anywhere near the house.'

'I'm sorry, maidy. I never meant this to happen.'

'It's too late for that,' Hickson said angrily. 'A horse-whipping is too good for you, Loveday.'

Sam turned his back on her. Taking Josie's hands in his, he looked deeply into her eyes. 'I'll never desert you, Josie. Marry me and I'll take care of you for the rest of my life.'

Hickson uttered a derisive snort. 'And have her

living in a hovel on twelve shillings a week, with a new mouth to feed every year. Is that the bright future you plan for Miss Josephine Damerell?'

'It wouldn't be like that.' Sam's fingers tightened their grip on Josie's hands until she winced. 'I'll make something of myself so that I am worthy of you, Josie. Life is nothing to me without you. You belong to me, body and soul.'

The moment of madness had passed and Hickson's harsh words had brought Josie back to stark reality. 'It's no use, Sam,' she said softly. 'What she says is true.'

'I love you, Josie. And I know you love me. Nothing else matters.'

'No, Sam. You're wrong. I've been brought up to be a lady. You can't expect me to give up everything I've always known and live in poverty. We would end up hating each other.'

'It wouldn't be like that.'

'Yes, it would. And that was what I came here to say. We have to end it here and now.'

The stricken look in Sam's eyes went straight to the core of her being, and Josie had to steel herself not to throw her arms around him. She wrenched her hands free from his grasp. 'Go now, Sam.'

He stared at her with a dazed look in his dark eyes. 'But you want me just as much as I want you.'

'How dare you speak to a lady in that way?' Hickson's shrill voice made them move apart. 'Do as Miss Josie says and leave here at once, or I'll have you thrown out.'

'Look at me, Josie,' Sam said urgently. 'Look me in the eyes and tell me that you don't love me.'

He reached out to her, but she drew away from him. Summoning all her willpower, she eyed him coldly. Kate had been right. She must not allow him to hope. 'I don't love you. I was just amusing myself, pretending to be in love with you. It's the done thing in London society. Ladies of quality take common men as their lovers so that they can boast about their conquests.'

'No.' His expression was bleak and his eyes filled with pain. 'I don't believe you.'

'I came here this morning to tell you that I'm going to marry Harry Challenor, the master of Copperstone Castle.'

If she had slapped his face, Sam could not have looked more shocked. He stared at her in disbelief. 'Why are you doing this, Josie? It isn't true.'

She tossed her head. 'I can assure you that it is. Our engagement will be announced in *The Times*. Oh, I forgot. You don't take it, do you, Sam? It's not exactly the reading material of a country bumpkin.' Turning on her heel, Josie ignored the smirk on Hickson's face and she marched out of the summerhouse with her head held high. She dared not look back as she crossed the dew-covered grass, heading towards the house. She wanted to run, but she was determined not to show the smallest sign of weakness or distress. Sam must believe her cruel words. He must never know how much it had hurt her to utter them, or that her heart had shattered into shards inside her breast. She entered the house and made her way slowly to her room, intent on changing out of her soiled and crumpled gown. She would never wear that dress again as long as she lived. As she mounted the staircase, she came face to face with Kate.

'Josie, you look awful. What's wrong?'

'Leave me alone. I don't want to talk about it.'

Kate caught her by the sleeve. 'You look as though you've seen a ghost. Did Sam say something to upset you?'

'I don't want to hear his name mentioned ever again. Do you understand me, Kate? He is dead to me. Dead and gone.' Picking up her skirts, Josie raced up the stairs to lock herself in her room, where she collapsed on her bed in a storm of grief that racked her whole body.

Chapter Nineteen

After a disturbed night's sleep when dreams of Harry had turned into nightmares, Kate rose from her uncomfortable bed before dawn. The rest of the house was in silence as she made her way downstairs to the kitchen. She was home, but it was no longer the happy place it had once been. Honoria's presence had soured the atmosphere in the farmhouse. The shadows seemed darker and the whole building seemed to be sighing. Chiding herself for her silly notions, she picked up the hod and was about to go outside to fetch coal for the fire when Molly burst into the kitchen. Kate opened her mouth to greet her but the words stilled on her lips. 'Molly, my dear, what's wrong?'

'It's Sam,' Molly sobbed. 'He's going away. He's leaving us, Kate.'

'I don't believe it. Sam wouldn't abandon you.'

Molly's dark eyes swam with tears. 'He says he can't stay any longer. He's going to sea, Kate. He says he wants to get as far away from here as he can.'

Kate's worst fears were suddenly realised. If Sam was leaving she knew who was to blame. She made an effort to sound positive. 'He won't do it. He's just saying that because he's upset.'

'He's going away forever. He said so last night.'

'We'll see about that.' Kate gave her a reassuring hug. 'I'll go and speak to him. You'd better make breakfast. You know how Pa creates if he hasn't got a cup of tea waiting for him when he comes downstairs.' She took her shawl from its peg near the door. 'I won't be long, Molly.'

A cool green light in the sky was rapidly giving way to an orange glow as the sun rose in the east. Birds were singing their spring song and Kate could hear the soft lowing of the cows as she picked her way across the muddy farmyard towards a beam of light emanating from the open barn door. She found Sam inside, and to her relief he was on his own. He was sitting on a three-legged stool, leaning against the haunches of the cow that he was milking. The rhythmic sound of the warm, sweet-smelling milk hissing against the side of the wooden bucket seemed to have a soothing effect on him, and, for once, he appeared to be calm and relaxed. He looked up and grinned.

Encouraged, Kate returned his smile. 'You've begun early, Sam.'

'I have much to do today.'

'Molly says that you are going away.'

He nodded his head. 'Aye, it's true.'

'But why, Sam? Why must you leave us? What will Molly do without you?'

'I have to go, maidy. I can't bear to stay in this place another day.'

'But running away to sea isn't the answer.'

He turned his head away. 'I have to go, and I know that you will look after Molly for me.'

'Of course I will, but you don't have to leave the farm. Pa relies on you and so do I. Why must you do this to us?'

'Don't question me, Kate. My mind's made up.'

'It's to do with Josie, isn't it?'

'She's set on marrying that Challenor fellow. She told me so herself.'

'You've always known that she would marry within her own class, Sam.'

He leapt to his feet, knocking over the bucket in his haste. 'Leave me be, Kate.' He backed away from her, and there was a wild gleam in his eyes that sent cold shivers down her spine.

'What happened? You can tell me.'

'I can't.' Sam ran his hand through his thick mop of dark hair. 'You would hate me if you knew that I'd almost dishonoured the girl I love with all me heart and soul.'

'I could never hate you, Sam.'

'I was going to take her on the floor of the summer-house like a common whore, and would have if Hickson hadn't come upon us at that moment. Is that plain enough for you? Do you still love me like a brother? The miserable wretch that I am.'

Kate caught her breath. She had guessed that something had happened between them, but Sam's crude admission shocked her to the core. 'I – I don't know what to say.'

'No, of course you don't. It's not the sort of thing that you would expect a high-born lady like Josie to do with a rough fellow like me, is it? Well, I'm not proud of myself, but I really love her, Kate. I love that girl with all my heart and soul, and without her there is nothing here for me. I'm not going to stand by and see her married to someone else. I can't stand it any longer and I have to get away, don't you see that?'

She stared at him in dismay. His words were shocking, but she felt his pain as deeply as she felt her own. They had both loved deeply and were having to face the loss of the one person in the world for them. She wrapped her arms around him. 'Oh, my poor Sam.' She felt his hot tears on her cheek as he pulled away from her, dashing his arm across his eyes.

'Leave me be, Kate. I'm not worthy of your sympathy. I know how bad I've behaved and I also know that she despises me for it. She told me so herself. She don't never want to see me again.'

'She said that?'

'Aye. That's what she said all right. And I don't rightly blame her. How could she wed a fellow like me? What have I got to offer her?'

'You love her,' Kate said softly. 'What more could a woman ask than to hold the key to a man's heart and soul?'

'It's not enough for Miss Damerell of Damerell Manor. I thought she might have second thoughts and come to see me, but she hasn't. She wants more than I can ever give her.' He wiped his eyes on his sleeve and sniffed. 'Leaving you and Molly is the hardest thing I've ever had to do, but I've got to go. I'm going to tell the gaffer now, and I'll be off by mid-morning.'

'Please, Sam. I'm begging you not to do this.' Kate choked on a sob, unable to hold back tears. 'Let me speak to Josie. Let me tell her how you really feel.'

'It won't do no good, maidy. She's engaged to that toff Challenor. She told me so herself.'

'I know, Sam. She told me yesterday. I know it's hard for you, but won't you reconsider, please?'

'My mind's made up,' Sam said firmly. 'I've got to go and tell the gaffer I'm leaving. I can't run off without a word. He's been good to me and Molly and I won't never forget it.' He marched out of the barn, walking purposefully towards the house.

Kate followed him slowly, but even as she approached the open doorway she knew that her father had received the news badly. She hesitated, not wanting to go inside and make matters worse. She could hear Pa shouting at Sam and calling him an ingrate. Hadn't he always treated him like a son? And now he was going away, leaving the farm just as the fields were ready for spring sowing. If he must go, why could he not wait until after the hiring fair, giving his master time to find a replacement for his best worker?

Kate could bear it no longer and she entered the kitchen as Honoria joined in, shrieking insults at Sam and uttering veiled threats to evict Molly from the cottage. Robert hastily denied this, but Kate could see that Sam was in an agony of indecision. He hugged Molly and over the top of her head his eyes pleaded with Kate for help.

'I'll move in with Molly,' she said hastily. 'I'm sure that Honoria will be glad to get me out of the house.'

'That's nonsensical talk,' Robert protested. He shook his finger at Sam. 'See what you've done? You've upset everyone with your selfish talk of going to sea. Change your mind, boy. Stay on in the cottage and work for me as you've always done.'

'I can't, gaffer. You've always been good to me, but I have to find my way in the world. When I make enough money, I'll send for Molly and set her up in a home of her own, but until then I'd be more than grateful if you would let her live on in the cottage.'

'I can do some of Sam's chores,' Kate said stoutly. 'I can milk the cows. The other men can share his work between them until the hiring fair in Dorchester.'

'And who are you to tell your father what to do, I'd like to ask?' Honoria spat the words like an angry cat. 'Tell her to mind her own business, Robert.'

He had the look of a man defeated. 'I'm tired of all this bickering and fighting. If Kate can cope with the extra chores, I've no objection to her moving in with young Molly, but it'll only be until I find a replacement for Sam. Is that understood?'

Kate nodded her head. 'Yes, Father.'

'Thank you, Kate. I'll never forget this.' Sam gave her a grateful smile. He turned to his sister who was sobbing uncontrollably. 'Be a good girl, Molly. Send me on me way with a smile and not a tear.'

She grasped the lapels of his jacket, holding on as if she would never let him go. 'I c-can't. I'll never smile again. Don't leave me, Sam.'

Kate moved to her side. 'You still have me, Molly.

I'll look after you, and Sam won't be gone forever. He'll come home as often as he can. He'll bring you presents from foreign places, you'll see.'

'I've got to go.' Sam hurried from the kitchen, leaving the door swinging on its hinges.

'Stop that caterwauling, you stupid girl,' Honoria said, covering her ears with her hands. 'And think yourself lucky that we don't throw you out on the street. Heaven knows, you're not much use as a cook or a housemaid.'

'I've had enough of this.' Robert made a move towards the doorway. 'I'm going to gather the men together and divide Sam's work up between them. They won't like it one bit, but it's him they'll blame, not I.' He stomped out of the kitchen.

Honoria glared at Kate with narrowed eyes. 'Take her outside and hold her head under the pump until she stops wailing. And as for you, miss, once you've left this house, don't expect to come back.'

'Don't worry, Honoria,' Kate said calmly. 'Wild horses wouldn't drag me back to that beastly attic room.'

Later that day, while Honoria took her customary afternoon nap, Molly helped Kate to move her things into the cottage. A steady drizzle had begun to fall from a desultory sky and the lane was thick with mud and cow dung, but Kate was so relieved to be moving out of the farmhouse that she cared little for wet feet and damp skirts clinging to her legs. The tiny cottage with its thatched roof and whitewashed cob walls looked welcoming, even as the rain dripped off the thatch like teardrops. It had a garden, which, although small, was big enough for the occupants to grow vegetables at the back and a few flowers in the front. Surrounded by a picket fence, it was to Kate like a small fortress and her spirits lifted a little as she trudged up the garden path. Sam had left the wood store stacked with logs and bundles of dried furze, and they soon had a fire blazing merrily in the hearth.

Kate took stock of her new home. There was just the one room downstairs, which served as a kitchen and a living room. It was simply furnished with a pine table and two fruitwood chairs, a pine dresser and a beech-wood rocking chair by the fire. It was spartan but clean and it felt like home. She slipped off her wet jacket and hung it on a peg behind the door. 'We'll do very nicely here, Molly. Where do I sleep?'

Molly filled the kettle from a battered enamel jug and set it on a hook over the fire. 'You can have Sam's room. He won't be needing it now.' Her voice hitched on a sob, and Kate went to her and gave her a hug.

'He'll be home again before you know it.'

Molly managed a watery smile. 'Yes, you're right. Come upstairs and I'll show you where you'll sleep.' She led the way up a narrow staircase to the first floor, where there were two small bedrooms. 'This one is yours,' she said, flinging the door open. 'Mine is across the landing.'

Sam's room was uncompromisingly masculine with a narrow wooden bed covered with a patchwork quilt and a small chest of drawers beneath the window. The bare walls were whitewashed and in its unadorned simplicity it could have been a monk's cell. Kate put the carpet bag containing her clothes down on the bed and turned to Molly, who was standing in the doorway, watching her anxiously. 'This is splendid. I'm sure I will be a lot cosier in here than I was in that draughty attic room.'

'Really? I mean, I know you're used to a much grander way of living at the farm.'

'I'll be perfectly comfortable here, and the best part of it is that I no longer have to put up with hateful Honoria.'

'Oh, heavens!' Molly clapped her hand over her mouth. 'I must get back before she wakes from her nap and demands a cup of tea, and then I have to start preparing supper. I'll leave you to settle in, Kate.'

'I would love that, but you're forgetting that I have to do some of Sam's work now, and that means the late milking, or there will be no cream to skim off in the morning, and neither butter nor cheese.'

'Can you really manage all those extra chores?'

'I don't know, Molly. But I'm certainly going to try.' Kate managed a cheery smile, but inwardly she was worried. She was painfully aware that one slip, one false move on her part would give Honoria the ammunition she needed to have them both turned out of the cottage. She knew that her father would take her back in the house, but returning to the attic room was unthinkable, and now she was responsible for Molly as well as herself. She would have to step warily.

The living conditions in the cottage were basic; the privy was a little hut set over a stream that eventually filtered into the River Frome, and water had to be drawn from a well in the back garden, but Kate was happier now than she had been since her father's wedding. She had achieved an uneasy truce with him, although she sensed that he still blamed her for upsetting Honoria, but she had little time to brood over what had happened in the past. She rose at four o'clock every morning and trudged the half-mile or so to the farm. There was the milking to be done, cream to be skimmed, butter to be made, hens to be fed and eggs to be collected. When she finished scouring the butter churn and scrubbing the dairy floor it was late in the evening, and she waited outside the scullery for Molly so that they could walk home together. There was hardly any respite from the daily grind, even on a Sunday, but Robert still insisted that everyone must attend matins. He drove to church every Sunday morning, with Honoria sitting beside him decked out in her best clothes and Tilda hunched in the back of the farm cart clutching the baby in her arms. Kate watched them drive past the cottage, but she never received as much as a nod from Honoria, and Robert kept his gaze fixed on the road ahead. Tilda was the only one to acknowledge her presence, and she would either stick her tongue out or cock a snook. Kate and Molly were left to walk to the village, whatever the weather. Kate's boots were in desperate need of mending: rainwater seeped through the worn soles, so that she often had to sit and shiver through the service with wet feet. Perhaps even more disconcerting were the curious looks that she and Molly received from the rest of the congregation. The whole village knew that Sam had left in rather a hurry, although the true reason for this had not yet been identified. Rumours abounded. Some said that he had been making up to Kate and that Farmer Coggins had discovered them in a compromising situation. Others said that he had fallen foul of the new Mrs Coggins and she had sent him packing, but to Kate's intense relief no one had linked his name with Josie's.

As she sat at the back of the church on the third Sunday in April, Kate could see Josie sitting in the Damerell family pew with her mother, Hermione and Sir Joseph. Kate could only guess that Josie was present to hear the final reading of the banns, and she bowed her head. Once the wedding date was set there would be no going back. She longed to see Josie, but she had not had a spare moment since Sam left, and Josie had not attempted to make contact. She was obviously preparing for her life in a quite different world.

As the congregation stood to sing a hymn, Josie turned her head and looked at Kate. Their eyes met for an instant, and the blank expression on Josie's face shocked Kate to the core. They might be complete strangers. She had not expected to be greeted with open arms but she could not imagine what she had done to deserve such a look. The page of the hymnal blurred before her eyes as she stared down at the print, which seemed to have turned into dozens of wriggling black tadpoles. Molly's clear soprano voice rang out beside her, but Kate's mouth was dry and she could not utter a single note. As the hymn ended and everyone sat down, she looked up and caught Squire Westwood's eye. He smiled at her, and, feeling suddenly lost and quite alone, Kate smiled back at him. He was waiting for her outside the church when the service ended. He doffed his top hat. 'Miss Coggins, how delightful it is to see you looking so well.'

'Thank you, Squire.' Kate could think of nothing else to say to him. His two precocious daughters were standing behind him, giggling behind their hands.

'I really must call at the farm and pay my respects to your father and his wife.' He inclined his head in the direction of Robert, who was assisting Honoria to climb onto the cart. 'And I suppose there will be a christening soon.'

'I don't know, sir.'

He raised his eyebrows. 'I heard that you had moved out of the farmhouse and into the cottage with young Molly.'

'She is too young to live alone, and I'm very fond of her. She's like a sister to me.'

'You have a sweet nature, Kate, and I lived with Honoria under my roof for long enough to know that she is, or can be, a difficult woman.'

'I really must be going, sir. Molly will be waiting for me.' Kate looked round for Molly and saw her standing by one of the yew trees with her friend Sal. They were chattering like a pair of excited starlings, totally oblivious to their surroundings.

'I think young Molly is enjoying herself with Farmer Cobb's daughter,' Squire Westwood said, smiling. 'Why don't you come back to the Grange with us, Kate? You would be a most welcome guest at luncheon, and I have something particular to say to you.'

She glanced over his shoulder at the mean little faces of Amy and Letitia. 'Thank you, sir. But I'm sure your daughters would prefer to have you to themselves.'

'My daughters are thoroughly displeased with me, Kate. They say that I do not understand them, and complain bitterly because I don't entertain enough. To which I reply that it is difficult for a widower to invite people to his home when there is no lady of the house to act as hostess. I'm sure they would enjoy your company.' He turned to his scowling daughters. 'You would like Miss Coggins to come to luncheon today, wouldn't you, my dears?'

'Yes, Papa,' they chorused, but the expression on their faces was as sour as yesterday's milk.

'Young girls,' Edmund said with an indulgent smile. 'They are as flighty as a pair of silly sparrows, but they are mine and I love them. You will come, won't you, Kate?'

'Thank you, no, sir. I'm sorry, but I still have work to do on the farm. The livestock don't care how holy the day, they still have their needs.'

He shook his head, and his bright blue eyes clouded

to a dull grey. 'It's not right, Kate. You are a well-educated young lady. You should not be doing the work of a farm labourer. I feel that I ought to speak to your father and tell him that it will not do. In fact, I shall tell him just that when I call at the farm tomorrow. Perhaps a few judicious words in Honoria's ear . . .'

'Please don't even think of doing such a thing.' Kate cast an anxious glance at the farm cart, smothering a sigh of relief as she saw Pa flick the whip over the horse's ears and the vehicle lurched off in the opposite direction. 'I mean, it is very kind of you to be concerned, but I am quite happy with the way things are. And it is only until the hiring fair; then my father will find a man to replace Sam.'

'Papa, do come along. We're getting cold and we're hungry.' Amy prodded her father in the back with her leather-bound hymnal, and Letitia sniggered.

'Girls, please.' Edmund turned on them, frowning.

'I really must go, Squire,' Kate said, seizing the chance to wave frantically at Molly while his back was turned. 'Good day to you all.'

He turned to face her. 'But I will see you tomorrow when I call at the farm? I need to speak to you in private, Kate.'

She nodded her head, unable to think of a valid excuse, and then, out of the corner of her eye, she saw Molly hurrying towards them.

Squire Westwood tipped his hat. 'Until tomorrow, Kate. Come, girls.'

'We don't want a drab like that as a companion, Papa,' Amy protested as they walked away.

'We want someone who knows how to keep herself clean and tidy,' Letitia added in a stage whisper, casting a malicious look over her shoulder in Kate's direction. 'She smells like the farmyard.'

Kate could hear the squire scolding his daughters for their lack of manners, but that did not help. She glanced down at her mud-spattered grey dress with a damp patch seeping upwards from a wet hem. Her boots had seen better days and her shawl had moth holes the size of pennies. She knew that what they said was spiteful, but true. She forced herself to smile as Molly came bounding up to her like an excited puppy. 'What did the squire want with you, Kate?'

'Nothing much. Let's go home. I need to change back into my working clothes and so do you.'

Molly tucked her hand through the crook of Kate's arm. 'Are you going to see him again? I think he's sweet on you.'

'Nonsense.'

'But he wanted something from you. Sal and me could tell that by the way he was bending over you, all friendly like and looking as though he wanted to gobble you up for his dinner.'

'That's just your over-active imaginations, Molly.'

'We think he wants to marry you, Kate. He may be an old man, but he's very rich.'

'And I'm the Queen of Sheba,' Kate said, chuckling. 'Come on, don't dawdle. I'm looking forward to a bowl of that vegetable soup you made for us.'

Molly did a little hop and a skip. 'At least I don't have to go back to the farmhouse today, and I have the gaffer to thank for that. Her ladyship wouldn't think twice about making me work all day Sunday without any time off. It's just a pity that you have to see to the cows.'

'Well, they can't milk themselves, poor things. We'd best hurry, Moll. It's starting to rain.'

Molly quickened her pace in order to keep up with her. 'And what do you think about Miss Josephine marrying the toff from London? Sal says that he's too good for the likes of her. What do you say to that?'

Next morning, Kate was in the barn keeping out of the squire's way. She had seen him arrive more than an hour ago, and Pa had come out of the house to greet him. Molly had continued to tease her about her would-be suitor's intentions, and Kate had given up trying to dissuade her from her romantic notions. If he had a proposition to make, she was certain that it was a repeat of his offer of a position as companion to his wayward daughters. There had been times when working at Westwood Grange had seemed like a perfect way out of an almost impossible situation, but that had been before Sam had left Molly in her care. She jumped as a voice from the doorway dragged her back to the present.

'Your father told me that I might find you here, Kate.' Edmund Westwood took off his silk top hat as he stepped over the threshold. 'Good morning, my dear.'

She bobbed a curtsey. 'Good morning, Squire.'

He stood with his back to the door, clutching his

hat in his hands. 'I – er . . .' He cleared his throat. 'I have something to ask you, Kate.'

'Yes, sir?'

'I – I don't quite know how to put this.'

'If it's about being a companion to your daughters, Squire, then I'm –'

'No, my dear.' He seized her hand and held it to his breast. 'It's not about my girls, although of course they will be delighted if you accept my offer.'

'Please let me go, sir.'

'I know that I'm doing this very badly,' he said, clasping her hand even tighter. 'Kate, I'll come to the point. There is no easy way to say this. I'm not a romantic man, and I know I'm many years your senior, but –'

She snatched her hand away. 'Please don't say any more.'

'I must. I've gone too far to retreat. I've admired you for a very long time. I'm asking you to marry me, Kate. I need a wife and my daughters need a mother. My dear Kate, will you do me the honour of becoming my wife?'

Chapter Twenty

The squire had taken Kate's refusal with good grace, but she had seen disappointment in his eyes and heard a note of regret in his voice even as he wished her well. She had not told anyone about his proposal, not even Molly, who would have taken great delight in saying 'I told you so'. Sometimes, in the dead of night when sleep evaded her, Kate wondered if she had done the right thing, but in the cool light of dawn commonsense reasserted itself, and she knew that marriage to the squire would make them both miserable. She would rather die an old maid than marry a man she did not love.

As the days went on, rumours abounded in the village. Most people seemed to think that Josie's wedding would take place in June. Sal Cobb kept Molly up to date with gossip from the manor house. She told her that the servants' hall was abuzz with excitement at the prospect of a big party. Miss Josie's engagement had not, she said, sweetened her temper, and Mr Challenor's visits to the house were infrequent and short. Some hinted that he was reluctant to come up to scratch, but Miss Hickson quickly put a stop to such gossip. It also transpired that Nanny Barnes was proving to be quite a handful. Lady Damerell, it seemed, was losing patience with the old woman who kept wandering about the house searching for the nursery. Being back at Damerell Manor seemed to have made her condition worse and quite often she was found lost and bewildered somewhere on the estate, and brought home by one of the gardeners or farm labourers. Kate felt somewhat responsible for her as it was she who had insisted on bringing Nanny Barnes back with them, but her attempts to see Josie and plead Nanny's case were foiled by Hickson. Sometimes she saw Josie out riding, but they were now living in two completely different worlds. Their childhood friendship seemed to have ended and when Josie was married their separation would be permanent. Kate resigned herself to the fact and made a brave attempt to get on with the unrelenting day to day work on the farm.

The morning sun filtered through the windowpanes in the dairy, and a warm breeze wafted in through the open door, bringing with it the smells of the farmyard and the welcome scent of apple blossom from the orchard. Kate was humming as she used the Scotch hands to form the butter into shape. She looked up as a shadow momentarily blotted out the sun and she turned with a start to see the squire standing in the doorway.

He doffed his top hat. 'Good morning, Kate. I was hoping to find you here.'

'Where else would I be, Squire?'

'I'm going to the hiring fair in Dorchester. I wondered if you would care to accompany me?'

There was no hint of embarrassment in his manner. He might have been speaking to an old friend rather than the woman who had rejected him so firmly just a few weeks previously. Kate glanced down at her soiled skirts and dusty boots. 'As you see, I am not dressed for going into town, sir. And I have work to do. I don't think that my father would allow me to go.'

'That's easily settled, my dear. I've already had a word with Robert and he gave his permission for you to have the rest of the day off. He's going to the hiring fair to look for a strong fellow to replace young Loveday, as well as extra men to help in the fields.'

Kate hesitated. She could see her stepmother's hand in this. She was well aware that Honoria's attempts at matchmaking were motivated by a desire to rid herself of a stepdaughter who, even though she was banished from the house, was a constant thorn in her side. Kate also knew that her father felt guilty about the way in which she had been treated. He had taken to calling in at the cottage on his way home from market or business in Dorchester, bringing gifts of tea, sugar or other small luxuries which she and Molly could ill afford. A string of sausages or a hock of ham would find their way to the porch outside the cottage, sometimes even a truckle of cheese, which should have been taken to market but was left outside wrapped in butter muslin. There was, however, no question of Kate returning to the family home. Her father might have forgiven her for speaking out against her stepmother, but Honoria ruled the household with a rod of iron.

'Come, Kate,' Squire Westwood said with a jovial

smile. 'I promise that I won't embarrass you by repeating my offer of marriage. Let us put the past well and truly behind us. I would simply enjoy the company of a pretty young woman on this fine day. What do you say?'

An involuntary smile curved her lips at the thought of shedding her working clothes for something tidier. It would be wonderful to get away from the hard physical work of the farm, even if only for one day. 'Thank you, sir. I think I would enjoy it very much.'

'There is one condition, Kate.'

She eyed him warily. 'What is that, Squire Westwood?'

'That you stop calling me sir, or Squire Westwood, and call me Edmund.'

She felt a blush rise to her cheeks. 'I'll try, sir. I mean, Edmund.'

'That's better. Come with me. I'll drive you to the cottage, where you can change out of those disgusting rags and put on something more suitable.'

After an initial period of awkwardness, Kate found herself relaxing in the squire's company. She had changed out of her working clothes into her only decent gown, which she had washed and ironed, so that at least it looked respectable if not exactly elegant. She tied the blue ribbons of her straw bonnet at a jaunty angle beneath her chin and slipped a shawl around her shoulders. Glancing in the small, fly-spotted mirror that Molly had smuggled out of the farmhouse, Kate was satisfied that at least she looked clean and tidy. She might have chosen a different person with whom to spend her free time, but she felt a frisson of excitement running through her veins at the thought of a day out and a rest from the back-breaking chores that had been heaped upon her slender shoulders.

Edmund Westwood proved to be a considerate, if slightly dull, companion. Even when he was doing business, hiring men to work on his land, he saw to it that Kate did not feel neglected. He asked for her opinion on the suitability of each candidate, listening to her views as though they really mattered to him. He was solicitous as to her comfort. If there was a chair handy, he made certain that Kate was seated. He introduced her to his friends and acquaintances, and when he thought she might be tiring, he took her to the dining room at the Antelope Hotel where they enjoyed a pleasant midday meal. He was obviously trying his hardest to please her, and, in spite of everything, she found that she was enjoying herself.

When the business of hiring was done, there was a fair held in the fields just outside the town. Jugglers, acrobats, fire-eaters and pedlars crowded between the tents and gypsy caravans. Kate wondered if Marko and his family were present at the gathering, but the milling crowds made it difficult to pick anyone out. She caught a glimpse of her father with Honoria on his arm as they strolled amongst the stalls selling everything from meat pies to china fairings. The afternoon stretched into evening and the sun was setting in the west, creating deep chasms of amethyst shadow. Naphtha flares were lit on the stalls, making bright pools of light in the gathering gloom, and music from a barrel organ filled with air. Sporting a red velvet jacket the organ grinder's monkey jumped onto Edmund's shoulder and shook a tin can in his face. He laughed heartily and dropped a couple of pennies into it. The animal chattered excitedly and leapt back to its place on the gaudily painted instrument.

In the distance, Kate could see a merry-go-round, and the strains of a Dutch organ were competing with the tuneful barrel organ and the sounds of merry-making from the milling crowd.

'Are you enjoying yourself, my dear?' Edmund had to bend his head close to hers in order to make himself heard above the din.

'Yes, thank you, Edmund. It's quite magical.'

He smiled indulgently. 'See, over there, the gypsy caravan painted red and gold. The fortune-teller seems to be attracting quite a lot of interest. Why don't you cross her palm with silver, or whatever they demand nowadays?' He put his hand in his pocket and took out some coins.

'Why not?' Kate was feeling reckless, or perhaps it was the plate of frumenty which she had just shared with Edmund in the refreshment tent that had made her feel quite light-headed. The addition of rum had made it extra tasty, and Edmund had assured her that it was good for keeping out the chill of evening.

As they made their way towards the circle of people gathered around the caravan, Kate saw Josie, looking every inch the grand lady in her elegant silk gown, with a ridiculous confection of flowers and feathers perched on her coronet of silky dark curls. She was walking just ahead of Sir Joseph and Lady Damerell, but Kate could tell by the expression on her face that she was not particularly happy.

'Look, Edmund. There's Josie. I'd like to have a word with her.'

'Of course, my dear. Make way there.' He led her through the throng, which parted respectfully as people recognised the squire.

Kate tapped Josie on the shoulder. 'May I speak to you for a moment?'

Josie turned to stare at her. 'What do you want?'

Kate recoiled slightly at her brusque tone, but she knew Josie well enough to realise that all was not well with her. 'You look absolutely splendid.'

Josie smiled reluctantly. 'I'm sorry, Kate. I was being horrid, but I just can't help it. I hate Joseph and I can't wait to get away from the place that was once my home.'

'Have you named the day yet?'

'It was to be at the beginning of June but Harry keeps finding excuses to postpone it. Anyone would think that he didn't want to marry me.' She tossed her head, and her bottom lip trembled. 'I don't suppose you've heard from Sam?'

Kate shook her head. 'No. Not a word. I'm so sorry, Josie.'

'Hush, the old gypsy woman is going to speak.' Josie pointed to an old Romany woman seated in front of a crudely made wooden table on which rested a crystal ball. 'Perhaps she's going to tell us that we'll be blessed with health, wealth and happiness, and all that rot.'

The Romany woman rose to her feet, casting her eyes round the assembled crowd. 'I see that there are many amongst you who would like to know what the future holds for them. Who will be the next one brave enough to hear what Madame Zolfina has to foretell?'

'Hold on to your purses, my good people,' Sir Joseph said in a loud, clear voice. 'The old crone is out to fleece the unwary.'

Zolfina turned her head to stare at him with narrowed eyes. 'You are a fine gentleman, or so you think, master. But others know you better.'

'What impertinence is this?' Sir Joseph flushed scarlet to the roots of his hair. 'Do you know who I am, woman?'

'Aye, master. I know who you are and what you are.'

'Come away, my dear,' Hermione said, clutching at his arm. 'Please don't make a scene.'

'He makes more than that, lady,' Zolfina said, chuckling. 'Your man may have a fine title but he's like a rutting stag when it comes to innocent young girls.'

There was a moment of shocked silence and then a ripple of laughter went round the crowd. Someone started clapping and it was taken up in a welter of applause and a few muffled boos.

Hermione uttered a faint scream and closed her eyes. 'Take me home, Joseph.'

Ignoring his wife's plea, he took a step towards Zolfina with his fists clenched at his sides. 'Shut up, you foul-mouthed old hag.'

'And you ain't too particular about who you choose

to fondle, are you, Sir Joseph Damerell?' Zolfina turned to Josie who had been standing silently, wide-eyed with horror. 'I'm sure that you can vouch for what I just said, little maid.'

Kate hooked her arm around Josie's shoulders. 'Please stop this, madam. You don't know what you're saying.'

'Leave the old girl be,' someone in the crowd called out. 'Let her tell what she knows.'

'Tell, tell, tell.' The crowd took up the chant.

Sir Joseph held up his hands, a sickly smile painted on his face. 'Come now, good people. This has gone far beyond a joke. I don't want to have to call a constable, but I will if you threaten to become disorderly.'

Someone threw a half-eaten bun at him and it struck him on the nose.

'Be silent, Uncle,' Josie said in a low voice. 'You're only making matters worse.'

'Why are you protecting him, maid?' Zolfina demanded, moving close to Josie. 'You are not a bad girl at heart and yet you allow this man to take liberties with you.'

'You don't know what you're talking about,' Josie muttered, blushing. 'You're making it all up.'

'You may choose to deny it, but the truth is in your eyes.' Zolfina pointed a finger at Sir Joseph. 'I can see him touching you and caressing you, even though you tell him to stop. He cannot help himself where women are concerned and he does not know that you are his own flesh and blood.'

Josie raised her hand and slapped Zolfina across the cheek. The sound ricocheted off the surrounding gypsy caravans. There was a horrified intake of breath from the onlookers.

'Well done, my dear.' Sir Joseph puffed out his chest, smirking triumphantly. 'That'll teach the bitch to respect her betters. I'd have done it myself, except that I am too much of a gentleman.'

Zolfina glared at him, clutching her cheek. 'You, a gentleman!' She spat on the ground at his feet. 'She is your daughter, Joseph Damerell. You have been abusing your own child.'

Kate stared at Josie in horror. 'This can't be true.'

Josie drew away from her. 'Of course it isn't. He's my uncle. My father was Sir Hector Damerell, old woman. You are addled in the head.'

Hermione had fainted quietly away, but no one seemed to have noticed. Kate knelt down on the damp grass beside her. She cast a pleading look at Squire Westwood who had been standing close by. 'Please put a stop to this, Edmund. This must not go on.'

He laid his hand on Sir Joseph's shoulder. 'Come away, Joseph. This spectacle is unworthy of your family name.'

'You are a troublemaker, old woman,' Josie cried, taking Zolfina by the shoulders and giving her a shake. 'What you say is untrue. Admit that you lied. My father was Sir Hector Damerell.'

'Stop this.' A younger gypsy woman emerged from the shadows, pale-faced and trembling. She held her hands out to Zolfina. 'Mother, please. Say no more.'

Zolfina was also shaking, but her face was contorted with rage. She seized her daughter by the shoulders and thrust her towards Sir Joseph. 'This is my child, Dena, the Romany girl you took to your bed more than twenty years ago, Joseph Damerell. You fathered her bastard, and now you are trying to have your way with your own daughter. For shame on you.'

'Shame, shame, shame.' The cry was taken up by the delighted crowd.

Kate could bear it no longer. She leapt into the middle of the circle holding up her hands. 'Please don't do this. Some of you may know Josie, but there is not one amongst you who did not know Sir Hector. For his sake, please stop this now.'

'Come away, Kate. Don't get involved in this.' Robert stepped out from the shadows. 'You're making a spectacle of yourself.'

'Father, how can you say such a thing to me? I must stand up for what is fair and right.'

'Let the little bitch make a fool of herself, Robert,' Honoria cried. 'Leave her. She is nothing but trouble to us.'

Squire Westwood helped Hermione to her feet, thrusting her into Sir Joseph's unwilling arms. 'Take your good lady home, sir.'

'It is all a pack of lies,' Sir Joseph spluttered. He gave Hermione a shake. 'Pull yourself together, woman.'

Someone booed him and it was taken up in a low growling murmur.

'Send for the constable,' Joseph shouted. 'Fetch the police.'

Dena moved to her mother's side. 'Say no more, I beg you, Mother.'

'It isn't true.' Josie stared at Dena. 'You can't be my mother.'

'Ask the woman in black,' Zolfina sneered. 'Ask the maidservant who placed you in the bed of the barren lady. Ask your widowed mother to tell you how she tricked Sir Hector into thinking that you were his child.'

'Stop it,' Kate cried. 'These are wicked lies, old woman.'

Zolfina turned on her. 'And you, my lady. You were born on the same day on that ancient mound, a monument to heathen gods. You are the child of a young gentlewoman whose man had died fighting for his country. The person you call father will tell you the truth.' She pointed at Robert, as he comforted Honoria who had chosen this moment to have hysterics. 'Ask him how he put you in place of his wife's stillborn babe.'

'Father, say it isn't true.' Kate held her hand out to him, but he shook his head.

'Don't listen to her, maidy.'

Honoria's hysterics ceased immediately. She pulled away from Robert's arms and advanced on Kate with narrowed eyes. 'I knew it. You are a changeling, but it wasn't the fairies who left you in the cradle. You are a little bastard, just like her.' She pointed a shaking finger at Josie. 'Two little bastards. You both deserve everything you get. As for you, gypsy woman . . .' Honoria took a purse from her muff and tossed it on the ground at Zolfina's feet, 'you were worth every penny. Come, Robert. We're going home.'

'Father . . .' Kate tried to follow them, but Honoria barred her way.

'You have no home. You are not wanted on the farm, and you will move your things from the cottage. We have found a replacement for Loveday, and his sister. You can go together, and good riddance.' She seized Robert by the arm and marched him off through the hissing, booing onlookers.

Kate raised her hand in a mute appeal as she watched them walk away. She was too stunned to comprehend the enormity of what had just occurred. This time it was Josie who put her arm around Kate. 'Let them go. You can come home with me. That is, if I still have a home to go to.' She glanced over her shoulder, but Sir Joseph had also left followed by a sobbing Hermione, and the crowd was melting away.

'It can't be true,' Kate said, rubbing her hand across her eyes. 'You don't believe what they said about Sir Joseph, do you, Josie?'

'Of course not,' Josie cast a scornful look at Zolfina. 'The old witch was just making trouble. Joseph isn't my father. He couldn't be.'

'Are you satisfied, Mother?' Dena demanded. 'Why did you do it?'

Zolfina tipped the contents of Honoria's purse into her palm. 'Mean bitch. There's barely three shillings here.'

Dena pushed past her with an exclamation of annoyance. 'Miss Damerell . . . Josie. I don't know what to say to you.'

Josie eyed her with a blank stare. 'I don't believe that you are my mother.'

Dena's eyes brimmed with tears. 'I was young, just like you. He was so handsome then, and charming. I was headstrong and I thought I was in love. I never wanted to give you away, child. But I had no say in the matter.'

Josie backed away from her. 'If it's money you want, then you are out of luck for I have none, and if this gets around you'll ruin my chances of a good marriage.'

'I want nothing from you.'

'Then you won't be disappointed,' Josie snapped, tossing her head. 'You've made a spectacle of my family, gypsy woman. I ought to have you arrested.'

'Why should you believe me? Sometimes the truth is too painful to bear.' Dena bowed her head. 'I have lived with my shame for many years. I cannot blame you for not wanting to know your true identity.'

'But I do,' Kate said, clutching Zolfina's arm. 'Who am I? If half of what you say is true, then you must have known my real mother. Who was she?'

Zolfina tipped the money back into the purse and slipped it into her pocket. She eyed Kate with her head on one side. 'You are the lady, child. Your poor mother was a gentlewoman and your father a serving army officer, killed in action in the Crimea.'

Josie uttered a derisive snort. 'So, you are the lady and I am part gypsy. Isn't that too funny for words? What do you think Harry would make of that, Kate?'

Ignoring this barb, Kate reached out to take Zolfina's

348

gnarled hand in hers. 'My mother, do you know her name?'

'Clara. That's all I know. She did not live long enough to tell me more.'

'Clara,' Kate whispered. 'I shall never know her by any other name than Clara.'

'Come home with me, Kate,' Josie said, linking her hand through her arm. 'I don't believe a word of all this. As far as I am concerned it's all a pack of lies.'

'I am sorry,' Dena said, bowing her head. 'I am sorry that you have had to suffer on my account. But just believe that I did love you, and parting with my baby was the hardest thing I have ever had to do.'

Josie eyed her coldly 'I don't doubt that you gave your baby away, but that child was not me. I am going home, and I don't expect that I will ever see you again.'

Dena turned and ran, disappearing into the darkness. Zolfina hobbled after her, muttering beneath her breath.

'Josie, that was unkind,' Kate said angrily. 'Whatever you think, she obviously believes that you are her lost child.'

'She gave me up, if it's true, which I sincerely doubt. None of this is my fault, any more than the way in which you were born, and we don't know if that is just a tissue of lies.' Josie shivered, wrapping her mantle more closely around her. 'At least it entertained the masses, but now the show is over and I suppose my dear uncle Joseph has left me to find my own way home.'

Edmund cleared his throat. 'Kate, I can't tell you

how sorry I am for bringing you here. If I had not persuaded you to come today, none of this would have happened.'

She had forgotten that he was standing quietly behind them, and she turned to him with a grateful smile. He could have walked away, but he had stayed. 'It wasn't your fault, Edmund.'

'I still feel responsible, my dear. I'll send a boy to fetch the dog cart and then I'll take both you young ladies home.' He disappeared into the dusk.

Josie angled her head, giving Kate a searching look. 'What's going on between you two?'

'Nothing. He's just being kind.'

'If you believe that then you are a complete noodle, Kate. The man is obviously besotted with you. Has he asked you to marry him?'

'As a matter of fact . . .'

'I knew it. Well then, you are made for life. Accept him and become the lady of the manor.'

Kate lowered her gaze. 'I can't marry a man I don't love.'

'I hope you aren't still pining for Harry.'

'No, of course not. He loves you and soon you will be his wife.'

'Yes, of course. I'll make certain that I hold him to his promise, and when I'm mistress of Copperstone Castle no one will dare speak ill of me. All this nonsense will be forgotten by the end of the week anyway, Kate. Let the peasants gossip if they will; it can't hurt either of us.'

Edmund came striding back to them. 'Come. The

dog cart is over there on the other side of the caravans. I'll have you both safely home in no time at all. Josie first, I think.'

As they walked behind him, Josie nudged Kate in the ribs. 'He is eager to get rid of me so that he can have you all to himself, Kate. I told you so.'

'You're just being silly,' Kate said automatically, but she took a seat in the back of the vehicle, allowing Josie to sit up front with Edmund. In spite of everything, Josie managed to keep up a cheerful conversation, but during the drive to Damerell Manor Zolfina's words kept going round and round inside Kate's head. Until this morning, she had been Kate Coggins. Now she was not certain who she was. But if it was all a pack of lies, why had her father remained silent? Why had he said nothing when Honoria threatened to have her thrown out on the street? The questions buzzed around inside her head like wasps around an overripe apple. She jumped as Josie called her name.

'Kate. Are you asleep? We're here.'

The lights of the big house blazed from the windows. Edmund drew the cob to a halt on the carriage sweep. 'Will you be all right now, Josie? Would you like me to come in with you?'

She tossed her head. 'Thank you, but this is still my home, Squire. My uncle is the one who was embarrassed by the old gypsy woman, but I still think that she was lying. My mother will confirm it, I'm certain.'

Edmund handed Josie down from the cart and he walked with her to the foot of the perron. Kate looked up at the starry sky and watched her breath curling up into the atmosphere. She wondered where Harry was at this moment, but she knew for certain now that he was well and truly lost to her. A short time ago she had been a farmer's daughter, respectable enough, although below him in social class; now she was the illegitimate child of a runaway lady and a soldier, both of them long dead. Although she did not want to believe it, deep down she knew that it was true. Her father's silence had been more convincing than an admission of the truth.

She looked down and saw Edmund standing at the side of the dog cart, holding his hands out to her. 'Won't you come and sit beside me, Kate?'

It seemed churlish to refuse, and she allowed him to help her onto the driver's seat. He climbed up beside her. 'I'll have you home in no time, my dear,' he said, wrapping a fur rug around her knees. 'You must be worn out.'

She leaned against him as he urged the cob into a trot. He was solid and dependable, and old enough to be her father. 'Yes, Edmund. I am rather tired.'

'You must not take to heart what the old gypsy woman said, Kate. They do that sort of thing to drum up a crowd.'

'I don't know what to believe. Honoria obviously thought it was true.'

'My dear girl, I know Honoria all too well. She is a jealous woman and she wants Robert to herself. I am sure that he will see things differently in the cold light of day. After all, no man in his right mind would abandon his daughter.'

She yawned, resting her head against his shoulder, only to awaken what seemed like seconds later to find that they had stopped outside the cottage. 'I'm sorry, Edmund. I must have fallen asleep.'

'Kate, my dear. I'm not the sort of man who would take advantage of your present situation, but I want you to know that my offer of marriage still stands. I don't expect an answer right away. You need time to think it over, but you would make me the happiest man in the world if you were to accept.'

'I am truly honoured, but . . .'

'I am old enough to be your father, but with age comes experience and tolerance. You would not find me as demanding or impatient as a young man. I would love and cherish you for the rest of my life, if you would let me.'

'Please, don't say any more.'

'I won't press you now, my dear. Take all the time you need to consider my offer. I'll come back in the morning to make certain that your father has seen sense, and that he has not carried out Honoria's wish to have you evicted from the cottage.'

'I am grateful to you for everything,' Kate said with feeling. 'But I'll have it out with my father first thing. I must know if what the gypsy woman said was true.'

'And if it is?'

'I don't know, Edmund. I just don't know.'

Chapter Twenty-one

Josie took off her mantle and handed it to the waiting footman. She shivered. It might be early summer but the night air was cool. Log fires burned in the two great stone fireplaces on opposite walls of the imposing entrance hall, spitting out sparks as if in competition with each other. The firelight flickered off the gilded cornices, making patterns on the intricate moulded plasterwork of the high ceiling. Josie stood in the middle of the floor, looking around her with a lump in her throat. She had always assumed that this magnificent house would be hers some day, but it now belonged to her uncle. The old Romany woman's words came flooding back to her and she began to tremble as their full import dawned on her. She could hardly bring herself to think about the consequences if what she had said were true.

The footman cleared his throat. 'Will there be anything else, Miss Josie?'

She dragged herself back to the present with an effort, hoping that her voice was steadier than her nerves. 'Where will I find Sir Joseph?'

'He is in the drawing room, ma'am.'

'Thank you, Mason. That will be all.' Josie headed for the drawing room. She would face Joseph and demand to be told the truth. She entered without knocking. Sir Joseph was standing with his back to the fire, and Marguerite was seated on the sofa next to Hermione. The conversation halted and three pairs of eyes turned to stare at her: Josie's nervousness gave way to anger. It was obvious that they had been discussing the events of that evening, and yet no one seemed to have noticed that she was missing. Ignoring Sir Joseph, she went straight to her mother. 'Well, Mama? Is it true?'

Marguerite bowed her head. 'Don't shout at me, Josie. Can't you see I'm upset?'

'Your mama has had a shock. Joseph told her what that wicked woman said.' Hermione's plump white hands fluttered around Marguerite's shoulders like a pair of agitated doves. 'It is too ridiculous for words. I've never heard anything sillier.'

'Is it?' Josie turned to Sir Joseph, eyeing him coldly. 'Well, sir? Since you have obviously been discussing the subject, am I or am I not your daughter?'

He puffed his cheeks out, shaking his head. 'Of course it's nonsense,' he blustered. 'Damn woman was off her head. As if I would have anything to do with a didicoi.'

'Of course, he wouldn't,' Hermione said, placing her arms around Marguerite who had begun to sob. 'Don't take on so, my dear. We know that you would not have done anything so wicked as to pass off another woman's baby as your own. Why, the whole idea is totally preposterous. And as to my Joseph consorting with a gypsy – I never heard the like in my whole life.'

Josie stared at her in surprise. This was the longest sentence she had ever heard coming from Hermione's lips. What was even more astonishing was the fact that she could love a toad like Uncle Joseph, and be so blind to his obvious faults. She turned her attention back to her mother. 'Mama, you haven't said anything.'

Marguerite raised a tear-stained face and her lips trembled. 'I am so dreadfully distressed. Everyone will believe the worst, whether or not there is a grain of truth in it, which there isn't, of course.'

'Will you swear to that, Mama?'

'You are my daughter, Josie. You are a Damerell through and through.' Marguerite unsteadily rose to her feet. 'This has all been too much for me. Hermione, will you see me to my room? I feel quite faint and I need to lie down.'

Hermione stood up, taking her by the arm. 'Shall I ring for Hickson?'

'Yes, but only when I am in my room. I don't want to give the servants any more cause for gossip or speculation. This dreadful rumour will be all round the village as well as Dorchester, and might even get as far as Bedford Square. I don't know how I will hold my head up in public from now on.'

'Take her to her room, for God's sake,' Sir Joseph said, pouring a large tot of brandy from a decanter on a side table. He took a mouthful and his cheeks flushed wine-red, matching the tip of his bulbous nose. 'And don't mention any of this in front of that wretched servant, Hermione. I don't trust her an inch.'

Marguerite muffled a sob in her handkerchief as Hermione led her from the room.

Josie turned on him in a fury. 'Do you have to make things worse, Uncle?'

He gulped his drink, glaring at her with narrowed eyes. 'You'll keep a civil tongue in your head if you know what's good for you, Josie. Just remember that you and the Dowager Lady Damerell are my dependants now. You are living off my charity and if I so choose I could turn you out of this house.' He moved closer to her and his lips parted in a leering smile. 'But if you are nice to me you will have everything that your heart desires.'

She drew away from him, sickened by the smell of drink on his breath and the rancid odour of his sweating body. 'You are disgusting. You would not dare to speak to me like that if Harry were here.'

'But Harry isn't here, is he, my love? And I don't believe that he ever will be.'

'You're wrong. The banns have been read. We'll be married very soon.'

'Then why does he keep putting off the evil day? Is it that he can see you for what you are: a scheming little trollop masquerading as a lady?'

Josie lifted her hand to strike him, but he caught her by the wrist, squeezing her flesh until she winced with pain. 'Let me go, you brute.'

He twisted her arm so that it was bent behind her back. 'I don't admit anything, but if what the old hag said were true it would mean that you are part Damerell, part gypsy. If you are the result of my coupling with that harlot, then you have my blood coursing through your veins, and you are no better than I.' He pushed her away so that she stumbled and had to catch hold of a chair to prevent herself from falling. He threw back his head and laughed. 'That would be the final irony, wouldn't it, my sweet? What would Mr Challenor think if he knew that you had encouraged the advances of your own father? And don't think I wouldn't tell him, because I would. Just you bear that thought in mind before you attempt to cross me.'

'I've never encouraged you.' Josie's heart was racing and a red mist clouded her eyes. 'You forced yourself on me. You are an unspeakable cad.'

Shrugging his shoulders, Sir Joseph topped up his drink. 'I've been called worse.' He poured brandy into a second glass and thrust it into her hands. 'Here, drink this and stop play-acting. Face the truth, Josie Damerell. You are a hard-hearted little bitch hell-bent on marrying for money and position. Don't think for a moment that I don't know what is going on under my roof. I applaud your single-mindedness, but you have backed the wrong horse, so to speak, with Harry Challenor. I know him, and for all his reputation as a man about town, I suspect that deep down he has the heart and soul of a puritan. One word out of place, my love, and I will reveal all.'

'You black-hearted bastard!' Josie threw the brandy in his face. Hurling the empty glass into the hearth, she stormed out of the room. His mocking laughter followed her as she ran towards the staircase, heading for the relative safety of her own room.

She could not sleep. She tossed and turned as the events of the past evening were replayed over and over again in her mind's eye. The safe and secure world that she had always known had crumbled about her head. She did not even know who she was. The idea that Joseph could be her father was making her feel physically sick. She would rather die than allow him to be intimate with her; the very thought of it was utterly disgusting. She rose from her bed and put on her robe, pacing the floor and wringing her hands. Rain was lashing at her bedroom windows and she could hear the wind soughing around the outside of the house like a wailing banshee intent on driving the occupants out of their minds. The fire had gone out and to ring for a servant at this hour in the morning would only spark off further tittle-tattle below stairs. She knew that everyone would be talking about what had happened at the hiring fair, but her main worry was that the gossip might reach as far as Copperstone Castle. Shivering and with tears running down her cheeks, she walked up and down until she was weak with exhaustion. Why did Harry keep postponing their wedding day? Something must have come between them and she knew who was to blame. She did not know how she had done it, but Kate had managed to wheedle her way into his affections, and Harry could not put her out of his mind.

Josie stopped pacing and leaned over the fireplace

in the vain hope that there might be a little warmth left in the pile of grey ash. Thinking of Kate, she sighed and shook her head at her own folly; she knew in her heart that her friend was innocent and guileless. It was she, Josie Damerell, who had ruined Kate's chances of happiness with Harry. When she had fabricated the story of Kate eloping with Sam it had been done out of jealousy. Sam. His name was forced from her lips in a cry of pain that was almost too much to bear. He was gone and she might never see him again. She crumpled to her knees, wrapping her arms around herself and rocking backwards and forwards. How long she remained in that position she did not know, but a spasm of cramp in her leg brought her back to the present. Her limbs were rigid with cold but somehow she managed to crawl back into bed, and she huddled down beneath the covers. If what the Romany woman had said was true, then both she and Kate stood to lose everything they held dear. Josie closed her eyes. She could not do anything to bring Sam back to her, but she might be able to make reparation to Kate for the wrong she had done her. She drifted into a troubled sleep.

It was light when she awakened and she reached out for her father's old pocket watch, which her mother had given her soon after his death. It was a little after six o'clock, and suddenly she knew what she must do. She rose from her bed and dressed herself without the assistance of a maid, donning her riding habit and boots. Throwing a cape over her arm she left her room, treading softly so as not to draw attention to herself. A sleepy hall boy opened the door to let her out of the house and she went to the stables.

Lawson emerged from one of the loose boxes, touching his cap. 'Good morning, Miss Josie. You're up bright and early.'

'Yes, good morning, Lawson. I fancied an early morning canter. Will you have Sheba saddled up for me, please?'

'Do you want one of the grooms to accompany you, miss?'

'That won't be necessary.' Josie eyed him warily as he went off to carry out her instructions. She couldn't help wondering how much the servants already knew, but Lawson was too well trained to show any emotion. It was only a matter of minutes, but it seemed like longer as she waited for her horse to be brought to the mounting block. One of the under grooms held the mare while Josie settled herself on the side saddle. Sheba pawed the cobblestones, eager to be off, and once they were clear of the stables, Josie rode her at a gallop across the parkland. The sun was struggling to come out from behind a bank of clouds and a brisk wind whipped her cheeks, tugging strands of hair from beneath her veiled top hat, but it was exhilarating and Josie's spirits rose.

As she approached the cottage, she was aware of an unusual amount of activity. Blocking the lane, two vehicles were drawn up side by side. The cottage door was wide open and she could hear raised voices. Dismounting, Josie tethered her mount to the fence. As she hurried up the path she could see Squire

Westwood and Farmer Coggins standing in the middle of the room. They appeared to be having a heated discussion. Molly was huddled in a chair by the empty grate and Kate was obviously trying to calm the situation.

Josie stepped inside. 'What's going on?'

Robert turned an angry face to her, scowling. 'With all due respect, Miss Josie, this has nothing to do with you.'

'You can't speak to Josie like that, Father,' Kate said angrily. 'This isn't her fault.'

'Yes, Coggins,' Squire Westwood said sternly. 'Show a little respect.'

Robert shook his head. 'Keep out of this, Squire, and you too, Miss Damerell. This matter is between me and this young woman.'

'I'm still your daughter, Pa. I'm the same as I ever was.'

Robert shook his head and his expression softened as he looked at Kate. 'I've done you an injustice, maidy. You are no kin to me and now the whole world knows it.'

'No. I don't believe you. The Romany woman must have made a mistake. I am your daughter. You loved me until Honoria came into the house. That woman has turned you against me.'

'Have a heart, Coggins,' Squire Westwood said, frowning. 'You can't expect me to believe this absurd tale.'

'I should have known that the truth would out in the end.' Robert's face crumpled into lines of distress. 'I am

362

sorry, maidy. But it is true. My poor Bertha lost three babes soon after birth, and the last one was stillborn. Dr Smith said then that she would never bear another child, and, as if by a miracle, the Romany woman turned up at my door with an infant in her arms. She told me that the mother had died in childbirth and there was no one to care for the poor little mite.' His lips trembled. 'That baby was you, Kate. I laid you in my dead child's crib and I never let on to Bertha. She believed you was her baby, and she loved you dearly.'

Josie made a move towards Kate, longing to comfort her, but Edmund edged her out of the way, placing his arm around Kate who burst into tears. 'I l-loved her too. Now I have no one,' she sobbed, leaning against his shoulder.

Molly covered her face with her apron and began to rock backwards and forwards in her chair, moaning softly.

Josie laid her hand on Kate's arm. 'You still have me, Kate.'

'And I am here.' Squire Westwood glared at Robert over the top of Kate's head. 'That was cruel, Coggins. I have known you for many years, but I always thought you to be a fair man.'

'And I am, Squire. I do my best to be a good Christian, and I am still fond of the little maid, but I am married to a strong-willed woman, and she has pointed out the error of my ways. I have to atone for bringing a cuckoo into our nest. Kate has to leave and she must take young Molly with her, or I will never have peace in my home.'

Kate raised her head and her expression was bleak. 'And you have a son now. You don't need me.'

'I have a son, and maybe another on the way, so my Honoria thinks, although I'd say it was too soon to be certain, but she assures me it is so. I have married a fertile woman and I have a new family to raise, Squire. You've offered for my girl, and I trust you to keep your word. I know if she goes with you that she will be well looked after.'

'I will take her, Coggins. But you must understand that I cannot marry her now. I've given it a lot of thought since last night, and I realise that I can't give the name of Westwood to someone whose origins are unknown. Even so, both Kate and Molly are welcome in my home. I'll keep them in my employ and treat them well. You have my word on that.'

Kate drew away from him, dashing her tears away with the back of her hand. 'And you said you loved me.'

'I do care for you, Kate. But you must see my dilemma.'

'Take his offer, maidy,' Robert urged. 'You won't get a better one.'

Josie went to stand beside Kate. 'Don't listen to them. Men are all the same. They use us and then they discard us. I have no time for you, Farmer Coggins, nor you, Squire Westwood. If you really cared for this girl, nothing on earth would prevent you from honouring your proposal of marriage.'

Edmund's bushy eyebrows drew together in a frown. 'You are also involved in this scandal, Miss

Damerell. I would be careful what I said if I were you. Your own position may be in doubt now.'

'Aye, you'd best set your house in order, Miss Josie, afore you start acting high and mighty with honest working folk.' Robert jammed his cap on his head. 'I must be going. I've work to do.'

'Don't worry about me, Josie,' Kate said, managing a smile. 'I understand the squire's concern, and even if he renewed his offer I wouldn't accept.'

'Come home with me, Kate. Whatever happens, I am still Miss Damerell of Damerell Manor. You will never be homeless while I have a roof over my head.'

'If only Sam was here,' Molly sobbed. 'He wouldn't let you men bully us poor girls. He'd stand up to you both.'

Robert shook his head. 'I've said what I came to say. I'm sorry, Kate. I honestly wish there was something I could do for you, but my hands are tied. You and Molly must be out of the cottage by noon.' He tossed a small leather pouch onto the table. 'There's enough there to keep you both in food and lodging for a week or two, until you find work. I can do no more.' He went outside, closing the door behind him.

Squire Westwood turned to Kate. 'I beg you to reconsider, my dear. Come and work for me, as I suggested originally. You can be a companion to my wayward girls, and you will be treated like one of the family.'

'And he'll be creeping to your room in the middle of the night, no doubt,' Josie said, curling her lip. 'Come home with me.'

Kate shook her head. 'I can't do that, not now, Josie.

You will soon be married and then I would have to find somewhere else to live.'

'I would take you with me.' Josie knew in her heart that this was a lie. Even when she had a wedding ring on her finger she would never allow Kate near her husband. But she could not abandon her old friend, and her main aim at this moment was to save Kate from the clutches of Squire Westwood. It was obvious that he still wanted her, and for all his fine words, he was just a man.

'I couldn't impose on you.' Kate turned her head away and her voice broke on a sob.

'Harry won't mind,' Josie said stoutly. 'He is as fond of you as I am, my dear.'

'I couldn't bear it, Josie. You know very well why.'

Molly jumped to her feet. 'What about me? You two are so bound up in your own problems that you don't give a tinker's cuss about me.'

Josie stared at her and her heart gave an uncomfortable jolt as she saw a passing likeness to Sam. It might have been the tilt of Molly's head, or the stubborn set of her jaw, or perhaps it was the sudden flash of anger in eyes that were so painfully like Sam's that it cut her to the quick. She dug her fingernails into her palms to prevent herself from crying out with pain and longing. A bitter taste flooded her mouth as she remembered their parting words, but she had sent him away, and now she must pay for her cruelty and ambition. 'I care about you, Molly. I want you to come with me as well as Kate.'

'I will look after Molly.' Kate drew herself up to her

full height. She was deathly pale, but composed. 'We will find lodgings in the village and I'll look for farm work. It will be no hardship to me.'

'Kate, I beg of you, don't do this.' Squire Westwood took a step towards her, holding out his hands. 'Miss Damerell is wrong, and she does me a great injustice. I wouldn't dream of dishonouring you with unwanted attentions. I really do care about you, my dear, and I can't bear to think of you working like a common peasant.'

'Whatever the accident of my birth, Squire, I've lived in a squalid mews in London working my fingers to the bone as a housemaid, and I've laboured on the farm like a man. I'm not afraid of hard work. Molly and I will do well enough on our own.'

'Is there nothing that I can say to make you change your mind?'

She shook her head. 'Nothing, sir.'

'Then come with me, Kate,' Josie pleaded. 'Let me help you and Molly.'

'You have your own problems to solve, Josie.'

'You are a stubborn girl,' Josie cried, losing her patience. 'I'd wash my hands of you if I didn't love you so much, Kate Coggins.'

Kate gave her a watery smile. 'I am not Kate Coggins now, Josie. I don't know what my name is. I don't know who I am. Harry was right – I am Miss Nobody.'

Josie enveloped her in a hug. 'You are my dear Kate. Nothing else matters. I regret every nasty word I ever said to you. I didn't mean any of them.'

'I know you didn't, Josie. I love you too.' Kate

hugged her back, and then she pushed her gently away. 'You have much to do also. If you are having difficulties at home, then you should go straight to Harry and tell him everything. He will understand.'

Josie nodded wordlessly. She wished that she was so certain of her fiancé's love and understanding. She moved towards the doorway, desperate to escape. 'Goodbye then, Kate.' She let herself out of the cottage, stepping into the early morning sunshine. It was a relief to be away from the turmoil of emotions inside the small cottage, and she could think more clearly now that she was alone. Farmer Coggins had confirmed her suspicions that there was truth in the Romany woman's words. Her family might be in denial, but there was one person who would not lie to her. She knew exactly what she must do.

Sheba whinnied at the sight of her and Josie led the horse to a tree stump, which she used as a mounting block. She dug her heels into the mare's flanks and clicked her tongue against her teeth. 'Walk on, old girl. Let's go home.'

Although it was too early for those above stairs to have risen, the servants were already busy with their morning duties. Having left her mount in the stables, Josie entered the house through the trademen's entrance. She found Hickson in the linen room.

'Miss Josie, what are you doing down here?' Hickson's eyes were round with surprise and a hint of suspicion flickered in their cold depths.

This was just what Josie had planned; she needed to catch Hickson off her guard. She closed the door and leaned against it, folding her arms across her chest. 'I want the truth from you, Hickson. You are the one person who knows what happened all those years ago, and you are going to tell me.'

Hickson's sallow skin paled to the colour of whey, but she met Josie's gaze with a defiant toss of her head. 'Why don't you ask your mother?'

'You know very well that she's terrified of losing everything, and you should be too. If my uncle Joseph throws us out, you will lose your position in this house, and my mother won't be able to keep you on. I want the truth and I want it now. I'm not going anywhere until you tell me what you know.'

'As I hear tell, the gypsy woman has already told you what happened.'

'I want to hear it from your own lips, Hickson.'

'Very well, since you force it out of me – it's all true. Your mother could not conceive, and your father was desperate for an heir. Joseph was a wild young man, but he was handsome in those days and charming too. No servant girl was safe from him. Then one of the maids came to me in tears, confessing that she was with child. At first she refused to name the father, but eventually I managed to drag the truth from her, and she admitted that she had allowed Joseph to have his way with her. When I realised that the baby would have Damerell blood, I saw a way out for my lady, and she jumped at the chance of proving to the world that she was not barren and giving her husband an

369

heir. It was easy enough to fool people into thinking that she was with child. Sir Hector was away in London for most of her supposed pregnancy, and she delighted in her condition, even though it was purely imaginary. I made a bargain with Zolfina, the girl's mother, and, soon after you were born, I smuggled you into the house. After that it was simple.'

'So that is how you did it.'

'You are as much of a Damerell as if my lady had given birth to you. I see no difference.'

'You may not, but others will. Don't you realise that it makes me a bastard? I am a nobody now, and I'll be shunned by polite society.'

'Only if they find out.' Hickson's eyes narrowed and she moved a step closer. 'Take my advice. Carry on with the pretence.'

'How can I when the whole village knows and half the county too?'

'Then you'd best get that wedding ring on your finger before your fiancé finds out. When you're married, he'll have to abide by his vows, no matter what.'

Josie shook her head. 'It's not that simple. Harry doesn't really want me. I tricked him into proposing.'

'I'd say he's too much of a gentleman to back out now, so it's up to you to make a choice. Marry a man who doesn't love you, or declare a truce with Sir Joseph. After all, he is your father.'

'I – I can't. You don't know what he's like.'

'Of course I do. Joseph Damerell is a lecherous old dog, and incest is an ugly word, but it happens in more homes than you would imagine. If you don't want it to go on, you've got to stand up to him.'

With Hickson's words ringing in her ears, Josie went to find the man who had fathered her. He was not in the dining room and Toop informed her that the master had only just rung for his shaving water. Without stopping to change out of her riding habit, she made her way to the bedchamber where she found Sir Joseph being shaved by his valet.

'Leave us, Frith,' Josie said curtly. 'I wish to speak to Sir Joseph.'

At a sign from his master, Frith hurried from the room.

'This is all very dramatic, my dear.' Sir Joseph wiped shaving foam from his cheeks. 'What is this all about?'

'You and me,' Josie said, folding her arms across her chest and glaring at him. 'You are my father. The gypsy woman said so, and I've had it confirmed by someone who knows.'

'I knew that the old bitch wouldn't be able to keep her mouth shut.'

'Don't blame Hickson. I made her tell me.'

'She's just trying to make trouble. There is no substance in a story concocted by a lying old didicoi to extract money from our family.'

'Farmer Coggins also confirmed her story, or at least part of it. He admitted that Kate was not his child. The Romany woman, Zolfina, said that Kate and I were born on the same day, in the same place. You knew that didn't you?'

'Certainly not.'

'But you did seduce Zolfina's daughter when she worked here as a servant.'

'I can't remember.'

'I don't believe you.'

'All right, I can see you'll give me no peace, until I confess. That part is probably true. I vaguely remember the girl, but it was many years ago. I've had more than a few romantic encounters since then, and probably fathered several more blots on my escutcheon. As I see it, Josie, none of this matters. I am master here now, and you couldn't inherit the estate, even if you were my legal offspring, because you had the bad luck to be born female.'

'That's not the matter in question. Only last night you insinuated that I must pay for my board and keep by allowing you to take liberties with my person, whenever it takes your fancy.'

'I would say that it's an easier way of earning your bread than labouring in the fields, or washing clothes and whatever the servants do to make our lives pleasant and easy.'

'You are a foul, disgusting man, and I hate you.'

'No one can prove that I am your father, Josie. You could be any man's by blow. In all likelihood we are not related at all.'

'I would have the devil for a father rather than a pig like you.'

'You have spirit, which makes you all the more of a challenge, my dear.' Sir Joseph rose from his chair and came towards her with a lecherous gleam in his eyes. 'Come and give me a kiss. I'm quite certain that you'll grow to enjoy my attentions. They all do. I am an expert in the art of lovemaking. It will be our little secret. No one need ever know.'

With the flat of her hands on his chest, Josie pushed him away from her. 'I would rather die.'

'We'll see,' he said, chuckling. 'You'll change your mind.'

'Never!' Josie ran from the room, almost knocking Frith over in her haste. She knew then that he must have been eavesdropping and that soon this whole sorry tale would be the gossip of the servants' hall. There was only one person who could help her now. She needed desperately to speak to her mother.

She discovered her sitting up in bed sipping a cup of hot chocolate. Hickson was standing at the foot of the bed, hands folded meekly in front of her but with a martial gleam in her eyes.

Josie paused in the doorway, taking in the scene. She might have guessed that Hickson would run straight to her mistress, no doubt justifying her part in revealing her ladyship's secret. Marguerite's eyes were huge in her pale face as she stared anxiously at Josie.

'I want to hear it from your lips,' Josie said coldly. 'I've heard it from an old Romany woman, then Farmer Coggins and finally Hickson. Are you my mother?'

Marguerite did not answer immediately. She placed the cup and saucer carefully on the table at her bedside, avoiding meeting Josie's eyes. 'I have always loved you, Josie,' she said softly. 'I loved you as much,

or even more than a birth mother could love her child.'
She raised a pair of tortured blue eyes to Josie's face.
'It is a terrible thing for a woman to be barren. I
suffered dreadfully for years, and then I had the
chance to have a child. You can't imagine what that
meant to me.'

Josie remained unmoved. 'Did you buy me, then?
Did my real mother sell me to you?'

Tears trickled from Marguerite's eyes. 'Don't speak
to me in that tone, Josie. I don't deserve that.'

Josie turned to Hickson. 'Well, madam. You've been
unusually silent. Did money change hands?'

Hickson glanced at her mistress and she bowed her
head. 'There were expenses.'

'So, I was bought. Like any commodity, I had a
price, even then. And now, if we are to stay in this
house, I am to trade my favours for our board and
lodging. Did you know that, Mama? Or should I call
you, my lady?'

'How can you be so cruel to me?' Marguerite sobbed,
wiping her eyes on the silk sheet. 'Why do you make
up these dreadful stories? Joseph would never do such
a hateful thing. Hickson, my smelling salts. I feel faint.'

Hickson hurried to a side table and produced a
vinaigrette from a tray filled with medicine bottles.
She shot a resentful glance at Josie as she returned to
the bedside. 'See what you've done. You're upsetting
your mama.'

'She is not my mother. The Dowager Lady Damerell
has just admitted that.' Josie pushed Hickson aside
and leaned over the bed. 'If it's true that the Romany

woman is my mother, then who was my father? Who am I?'

Marguerite shook her head, falling back against the pillows. 'I never knew. Believe me, Josie. I didn't know and I didn't even care. For my part I loved you, and you were my little girl. Can't we forget that this has happened, and go back to the way we were?'

Hickson held the vinaigrette under Marguerite's nose. 'You're upsetting her, Miss Josie. Leave her now and continue this talk later on, when she is feeling stronger.'

'No. This has gone too far. I can't rest until I know the truth of my parentage, and I can't live beneath the same roof as the man who might be my father, but who treats me like a whore.' Josie looked down at the woman whom she had loved as her mother, and saw a pale-faced stranger staring back at her. 'I'm sorry, but there is only one person left who can tell me who I really am.'

Marguerite struggled to sit up. 'Don't go like this, Josie.'

Shaking her head, Josie backed away from the bed. 'I have to discover the truth. It sickens me to think that that lecherous old dog, Joseph Damerell, might turn out to be my father. Either way I won't live under the same roof as him. I would sooner throw my lot in with the gypsies than see him every day and have him lusting after me like a slavering beast.'

Chapter Twenty-two

Smothering a sigh, Kate picked up the canvas bag at her feet. 'I'm sorry to have bothered you, Farmer Cobb.' It had started to rain and she could already feel the dampness seeping through her clothes.

'I'm sorry too, Kate, but I have no need of a dairy-maid or a girl to help in the house. I really can't help you.'

Molly caught him by the sleeve as he was about to close the door on them. 'Please, sir. I'm Sal's friend. You wouldn't like it if someone turned her away when she was in need, now would you?'

He frowned. 'My Sal has a job up at the big house, and you know it. Why not try there, maidy? You're both used to hard work if I know Robert Coggins.'

'That's right, Farmer Cobb,' Kate said, unwilling to give in so easily. 'You know my father well, and I daresay he has done you favours in the past. Couldn't you find us some work on the farm, and give us a bed in one of your barns? I can dig potatoes or pull turnips. I'm not afraid of hard work.'

'The things that gypsy woman said are common knowledge now, Kate. You know how quickly gossip spreads.'

'Have you thought that it may not be true? You've

known me since I was a little girl and I am still the same person.'

'I'm not a hard man, and I hope that I'm a good Christian, but I can't take you in. If Robert has sent you packing, then you'll not find anyone round here eager to take you on. I know it's difficult for you, but all I can suggest is that you try for work in another part of the county, where you are not known.' Farmer Cobb went to shut the farmhouse door, but Kate put her foot over the sill.

'Why? Why are you treating us like this? Neither me nor Moll has done anything wrong.'

He stared at her for a moment, as if pondering his reply. 'You were found by the gypsies. You could be one of them for all I know, and you might bring a curse down on our heads if I take you in. When your kind curse a farm the cows stop yielding milk and the hens don't lay; the crops fail and the livestock sicken. I can't take that chance. Now take your foot from my doorstep and leave me be.'

Kate removed her foot just in time as the door slammed in her face. Molly began to whimper. 'What's to become of us, Kate?'

'We'll try Farmer Samways. He's a sensible man. I'm sure he won't worry about silly superstitions.' Kate gave her a hug. 'Come on, Moll. It's a fair old walk, but at least it's not raining.'

It was exactly the same story at the next farm, and the next. By late afternoon Kate was footsore and exhausted. Molly was close to collapse, and it had begun to rain again. They were both soaked to the skin and bedraggled, and the hems of their skirts were thick with mud. Kate fingered the leather pouch in her skirt pocket. She had counted out the coins when they had stopped to eat their lunch of bread and cheese at midday in the shelter of a gnarled oak. If she was very careful, there was enough money to feed and lodge them for a week. Molly had begun to cough, and Kate knew that if she did not get her out of her wet clothes and into a warm bed, Molly's weak chest would lay her low for the rest of the winter. They were on the outskirts of Dorchester by this time and it would soon be dark. She hitched Molly's arm around her shoulders. 'We'll spend the night at the Antelope Inn. Things will look better when we're warm and dry and have a hot meal inside us.'

'C-can we afford it, Kate?' Molly murmured through chattering teeth.

'Of course we can,' Kate lied. 'I wouldn't suggest it otherwise. If we hurry we can make it before dark.'

They had just reached the bridge over the River Frome, where Kate had once stopped to rest on a bright autumn day, although that seemed like years ago rather than a few short months, when the sound of footsteps coming up behind them, made her glance over her shoulder. Two men had appeared seemingly from nowhere and they were advancing on them in a purposeful way which did not bode well. Although it was too dark to see their faces clearly, she sensed danger, and the smell of their unwashed bodies was sickening. 'What do you want?' she demanded, pushing Molly behind her.

'Give us your purse and we'll not harm you.' The taller of the two men spoke with an accent that Kate recognised instantly. These were not simple country folk; they were villains who were far from their native East End, and probably on the run from the police.

'We have no money,' Kate said, praying silently that they would believe her.

'She's lying.' The other man grabbed her by the arms. 'Search her pockets.'

Molly lashed out at him with her hands and feet, but the bigger of the two men threw her to the ground, where she lay winded and gasping for breath. He turned his attention to Kate, who was being held in a vice-like grip, and he slid his hand beneath her shawl, groping her breasts with a grin on his face.

'Give over, cully. We ain't got all night,' his accomplice muttered, tightening his hold on Kate.

She kicked her attacker on the shin and with a growl of pain he punched her in the face. The blow stunned her momentarily and she felt blood trickling from her nose into her mouth. He uttered a cry of triumph as he found what he was looking for and ripped the pouch from her pocket. 'Liar,' he said, grabbing her by the hair. 'I'll have to teach you a lesson, girl.'

'There's no time for that,' the other man said, releasing Kate with a shove that sent her sprawling onto the grassy verge. 'There's someone coming. Scarper, mate.'

Kate lay for a moment, dazed and in pain. She could hear the sound of horse's hooves and the rumble of cartwheels. She raised herself and crawled over to where Molly was lying on her side, clutching her stomach and gasping for breath. 'Are you all right, Molly?'

'I – I think so.'

The horse-drawn vehicle was almost upon them and Kate leapt up, waving her arms. The beam of light from the carriage lamps dazzled her, but the driver had seen them, and a familiar voice called out, 'Kate, is that you?'

Shielding her eyes with her hand, she saw that it was Squire Westwood, and sitting beside him was the achingly familiar figure of her father.

Edmund drew his horse to a halt and Robert climbed to the ground, barely waiting for the vehicle to stop moving. 'Kate, are you hurt, maidy?'

'Father!' The word came out on a sob.

He tilted her chin, examining her injuries, and his ruddy complexion paled. 'What happened? Who did this to you?'

Edmund alighted more slowly and he helped Molly to her feet. 'Are you hurt, child?'

'Not much, sir. I was just winded.'

'We were robbed,' Kate said, holding her hand to her swollen lips and feeling the sticky blood on her fingertips. 'They took all our money.'

'The brute hit her, Squire,' Molly said angrily. 'Punched poor Kate in the face, he did. I tried to stop them but they threw me to the ground.'

Kate was trembling from head to foot, but memories of earlier in the day came flooding back to her and she drew away from Robert, squaring her shoulders.

'I'm all right now, thanks to you, but we must be on our way.'

'Don't talk to me like I was a stranger, maidy,' Robert said, wincing at her tone. 'I know it was hard to turn you out as I did, but believe me, I couldn't do no different. I still cares for you, Kate.'

Edmund took a handkerchief from his pocket. 'Here, take this, my poor darling.'

Kate chose to ignore the term of endearment. They were safe now, and that was all that mattered. 'Thank you, sir. It was lucky for us that you chanced to come along.'

'It was no coincidence,' Robert said with a vague attempt at a smile. 'I've been searching for you all day. When I discovered that Farmer Cobb had turned you away, I was frantic with worry, especially when he mentioned all that nonsense about gypsy curses and the like. I've been scouring the countryside ever since, going from farm to farm and always just too late to catch you. Then I came upon the squire in the lane outside the cottage and he too had been out looking for you.'

Kate dabbed at her bleeding lip. 'You shouldn't have bothered. We'll find work somewhere, I am certain of that.'

'For the Lord's sake, Kate,' Robert said, giving her a beseeching look. 'Have a heart, maidy. Let me help you. I was wrong to act as I did. Won't you forgive me?'

She raised her eyes to his face and saw the man whom she had believed to be her father, but his recent harsh treatment had left a gaping wound in her heart. 'I can't – not yet. And it changes nothing. You have your wife and your new family. Knowing what we know now, there's no place for me in your plans for the future.'

He bowed his head and began to walk away, slowly, like a very old man.

'Wait, Coggins. Let me take you home in my carriage,' Edmund called after him, but Robert did not stop.

'Pa.' Kate fought back the ready tears that sprang to her eyes. She was still shocked from the attack and on the point of exhaustion.

'Let him go, my dear,' Edmund said softly. 'You must let me help you. I can't allow two young females to wander the countryside alone and unprotected, especially at night. Where did you think you were going?'

'We were going to take a room at the Antelope Inn. If you could lend me just enough money for a night's lodging, I'll repay you as soon as I find work.' Kate held her breath. Even before he spoke, she knew what his answer would be.

'You will do no such thing. I won't hear of it. Tonight at least you and Molly will be my guests at Westwood Grange. Tomorrow we will discuss your future.' He laid a finger gently on her bruised lips. 'Don't try to argue with me, Kate. My mind is made up.' He turned to Molly with a kindly smile. 'Get in the carriage, my dear. We'll soon have you safely tucked up in a nice warm bed and my housekeeper will take care of you.'

*   *   *

382

The Grange was set back from the road and approached down a narrow lane. Kate had visited it once or twice with her father, but never as a guest. The stone-built Elizabethan house had been added to in the succeeding centuries, giving it a slightly eccentric but friendly appearance, as if its studded oak front door was always open to the weary traveller. Diamond-shaped beams of candlelight flickered from the lattice windowpanes, and the gravelled carriage sweep was illuminated by flambeaux outside the stable block. It seemed to Kate that the house was waiting for its master to arrive, lighting his way and welcoming him home.

Next morning, she awakened to find herself in a light airy room. Sunlight filtered in through the leaded lights, reflecting off the highly polished burr walnut furniture. The floral-patterned curtains had been drawn back and a maidservant was standing by the bedside holding a tray of tea. 'Good morning, miss. Would you like me to bring a jug of hot water now?' She placed the tray on a table close to the bed.

Kate raised herself on her elbow, yawning and stretching luxuriously. 'Yes, please. I didn't realise that I had slept so late.'

'You haven't, miss. I mean we don't keep farm hours here at the Grange. The young ladies don't normally rise until mid-morning now that their governess isn't here to make them do their lessons. Will that be all, miss?'

'Yes, thank you.' Kate sat up and reached for the dainty bone-china cup and saucer. She sipped the hot, sweet tea. This was luxury indeed, but it would not last. If Squire Westwood intended to win her with pampering, he had almost succeeded. After the humiliation and disappointments of the previous day, it would be all too easy to be seduced by the promise of comfort and security. But there would inevitably be a price to pay, and the squire had made it clear that marriage was no longer an option. She might start off as paid companion to his daughters, but she suspected that it would not be long before he wanted more from her than she was prepared to give, and she would hardly be in a position to refuse.

When she had washed and dressed, she went to Molly's room and found her still in bed. Her cheeks were flushed and her eyes suspiciously bright.

'I don't feel too well,' Molly said hoarsely. 'I think I've caught a chill.'

Kate laid a hand on her forehead. 'You are a bit feverish. You should stay in bed.'

'But we must be on our way. You don't want to be obliged to the squire, I understand that well enough.'

Kate smiled, tucking the coverlet up to Molly's chin. 'Don't worry about anything. You just get well, and then we'll talk about moving on.' The smile died on her lips as she left the room. If Molly went down with inflammation of the lungs, they could be here for days, even weeks. The longer they stayed, the more difficult it would be to leave this comfortable home. She went downstairs and was wondering where she might find the squire when the maidservant emerged from a room on the far side of the entrance hall. She bobbed a curtsey. 'The master is just finishing breakfast, miss. He asked if you would join him when you came downstairs.' She ushered Kate into the room and left, closing the door behind her.

Edmund rose from his seat at the head of the table. 'Good morning, my dear. I trust you slept well?'

'Thank you, yes.'

'You will have some breakfast, won't you, Kate?'

'Just some toast, please. I'm not very hungry.'

Frown lines deepened on his brow. 'You are not ill, are you? Perhaps I should send for Dr Smith.'

Kate smiled in spite of her worries. 'I'm in perfect health, apart from a bruised face and hurt pride. But I am a little concerned for Molly. She seems unwell this morning, and I told her to stay in bed. I hope you don't mind. We didn't intend to impose on your hospitality, but I'm afraid we might have to for a day or so.'

'You know my thoughts on that subject, Kate.' He pulled out a chair. 'Sit down and make yourself comfortable. I want you to make your home here, and when young Molly is well again I am sure that my housekeeper can find work for her.'

She met his eager gaze with a straight look. 'I am truly grateful to you for taking us in last night, but you know that I can't accept your offer.'

His knuckles showed white as he gripped the back of the chair. 'I know that I am many years your senior, but I want you more than I have ever wanted any woman. Despite what I said yesterday, I might even be prepared to put aside my scruples

385

and marry you if that is the only way I can keep you with me.'

She dropped her gaze, but it was pity that surged through her veins. 'I am truly sorry, but I don't love you. I can't marry you, sir.'

'Is there someone else?'

'Please don't press me for an answer.' She made a move towards the doorway. 'I don't want any breakfast. I've lost my appetite.'

'I didn't mean to distress you.'

'If you don't mind, I would like to walk to Damerell Manor. I need to see Josie and make certain that she's all right.'

'You don't have to ask my permission, and if you wish to see your friend I'd be more than happy to drive you there.'

She was about to refuse, but he looked suddenly like a shy schoolboy and she had not the heart to dash his hopes yet again.

'Allow me to do this for you, my dear,' he added hastily. 'I take pleasure in your company, even if you do not enjoy mine.' He smiled ruefully. 'Indulge me in this, just for today.'

It was impossible to refuse him, and Kate nodded her head. 'Thank you, sir.'

They arrived at Damerell Manor to find it in an uproar. Sir Joseph was standing in the main entrance issuing instructions to a party of estate workers, gardeners, gamekeepers and stable boys. He stopped speaking when he saw Kate and he pointed a finger at her. 'You, come here, girl. Tell me where I might find Miss Damerell.'

Kate alighted from the dog cart and walked slowly towards him. 'I came to see Josie. Isn't she here?'

'Don't play the innocent with me, you little bitch. Did she come running to you last night?'

Edmund stepped between them. 'That's no way to talk to a lady, Damerell. Miss Coggins is a guest in my house and neither of us has seen Josie. She is the reason that Kate came here today.'

Sir Joseph raised his riding crop, shaking it at the men who were awaiting his instructions. 'You know what you have to do. Go about your business.'

They hurried off, spreading out in different directions. Sir Joseph slapped the riding crop against his palm. 'Well, Westwood. I see the little trollop has got you where she wants you. I hear these Romany girls are a good lay.'

'No wonder Miss Damerell ran away from a foul-mouthed, evil-minded wretch like you,' Edmund said icily.

Kate grasped his arm. 'Don't demean yourself by stooping to his level, Edmund.'

'Edmund, is it?' Sir Joseph thrust his face close to Kate's. 'I was right then. You are a wanton little thing. But she's comely enough, Westwood. When you've finished with her you can send her to me. I hear that Challenor had her first. When I see him again, I'll ask him how he rated her.'

Kate's hands flew to cover her mouth, stifling a cry of protest.

'You'll apologise for that, Damerell,' Edmund said through gritted teeth.

'I don't apologise for speaking the truth. I'll wager she's no better than she should be. You can break her in for me, Westwood. I like them tamed and submissive.'

Edmund's fist landed squarely on Sir Joseph's flabby jaw, felling him in a single blow. 'You asked for that, Damerell. You are a disgrace to the family name. If I do discover Josie's whereabouts, I'll be damned if I'll tell you.' He placed his hands firmly around Kate's waist, and with a surprising show of strength he threw her up onto the driver's seat. 'We're going home, my dear.'

She turned her head to catch a glimpse of Sir Joseph being helped to his feet by one of the footmen. He was purple in the face and she could see his mouth working, but thankfully, she could not hear his words. No doubt he was screaming obscenities at them. She glanced up at Edmund's craggy profile as he urged the horse to a trot. He seemed to sense that she was looking at him, and he smiled. 'I'm not so aged that I can't stand up for the woman I love, Kate.'

'None of it was true,' she murmured. 'He was lying.'

'But Challenor has your heart. Don't deny it. I saw the look in your eyes when his name was mentioned.'

'He is going to marry Josie,' Kate said, turning her head away. 'I expect she has gone to him. Where else would she go?'

'You're right. She would naturally go to her fiancé, and no one could blame her.'

She had nothing to say to this and they drove on in silence. The fields and hedgerows were bathed in warm sunlight, and the air was sweet with the scent of wild dog roses and honeysuckle, but Kate was oblivious to everything except the pain of knowing that Josie must have run to Harry, and that they were in all probability reunited now and planning their wedding. Both of them were lost to her and she was alone in the world, except for Molly, who must be cared for at least until such time as Sam returned to them.

She realised with a jolt that the dog cart had entered the gates of Westwood Grange. Before a groom had time to run from the stable yard to hold the horse, Edmund had alighted and come round to her side. He held his hands out to her. 'My dear, I think I know how you must be feeling. Believe me, I do understand.'

His kindness was more upsetting than if he had ranted and raged at her. She could barely hold back the tears that threatened to engulf her. She nodded wordlessly.

He lifted her down from the vehicle but he did not release her immediately. 'My feelings have not changed, Kate. I am a patient man, and if you are willing to stay on here, just to keep my daughters company, I won't impose myself on you.'

She could not look at him. 'Thank you, Squire.'

He placed his finger beneath her chin and tilted her head so that she had to meet his gaze. 'I'm ashamed of the way I behaved yesterday. My head was ruling my heart, but last night, when I saw you beaten to the ground and bleeding, I knew that I had to look after you and care for you, if only you would permit me to do so.'

'Please say no more, sir.'

He shook his head, but he was smiling gently. 'My offer of marriage still stands and you can have as much time to think about it as you need. In the meantime, we will tell the world at large that you are working for me. I will protect your good name as if it were my own.'

She felt the fight draining from her. She was suddenly tired and dispirited. 'And if I wish to leave?'

'You may do so at any time, of course. But I would insist that you had somewhere to go. I won't allow you to roam the countryside like an itinerant farm labourer.' He raised her hand to his lips and kissed it. 'There is just one condition.'

'What is that, sir?'

'That you continue to call me Edmund, as you did in front of that scoundrel Damerell.'

Even if Kate had wanted to leave Westwood Grange, it would have been made impossible by Molly's condition worsening from a mere chill into pneumonia. Kate nursed her devotedly, sleeping on a truckle bed that the housekeeper had brought down from the old nursery and placed in Molly's room. Dr Smith called daily, but there was little that anyone could do except watch and pray. For days Molly's life hung in the balance, and at times Kate almost gave up hope, but

Molly had youth on her side, and her condition slowly began to improve. Kate was awakened one morning by the sound of her voice asking for food. After that her recovery was surprisingly rapid and soon she was able to get up and sit in a chair by the window, where she had a view of the dovecot and the rose garden. By the middle of June, Molly was almost completely well again and able to go out for short walks in the grounds.

One afternoon they were returning from one of their excursions when they met Amy and Letitia, who were out riding. Amy reined her horse in so sharply that it caracoled, sending a shower of dried mud over Kate's skirt.

'Oh, dear,' Amy giggled. 'Now you'll have to change your clothes, Miss Coggins. And you have so few.'

'It doesn't matter,' Kate said evenly. 'Dirt will brush off.'

'No,' Letitia said, wheeling her horse round so that its flaring nostrils almost brushed Kate's face. 'Mud sticks, Miss Coggins. Or so I've always been told.' She curled her lip. 'But then, you aren't really Miss Coggins, are you? You don't know who you are.'

'And Papa saw fit to take you into our home,' Amy chortled. 'You must have bewitched him, Miss Kate Nobody.'

'Yes,' Letitia added gleefully. 'They say you are part gypsy and you can foretell the future.'

'And put curses on people,' Amy said, pulling a face. 'Why don't you go and join your gypsy folk,

Miss Nobody? They're camped near Maiden Castle. Papa says they should be moved on, so why don't you go with them?' She dug her heels into her horse's flanks and rode off down the lane at a gallop.

Letitia leaned over in the saddle, eyeing Kate with contempt. 'My sister is right. Why don't you run away and join the travelling people? Now that your little playmate is recovered, there is no need for you to stay on at the Grange. Neither Amy nor I want you here, and if you choose to stay, I promise you that we will make your life utter hell. Do I make myself clear?' She urged her horse forward and made use of her crop to encourage the animal into a trot and then a canter.

Molly stared at Kate in dismay. 'Why are they being so horrible to you, Kate?'

'They're just jealous, although they have no need to be, Molly.' Kate took her by the arm. 'Let's get you back to the house. You mustn't overtire yourself.'

Molly fell into step beside her. 'Are you going to marry the squire, then?'

'Whatever gave you that idea?'

'It's what the servants are saying below stairs.'

'No wonder Amy and Letitia resent me so much. I had no idea.'

'It was cruel of them to say nasty things to you. They're just hateful, spoilt girls.'

'Yes, they are spoilt and spiteful, but I can't altogether blame them for not wanting me to marry their father,' Kate said, recalling her father's wedding to Honoria. 'It is not easy having a stepmother come into the home.'

'Maybe not, but that doesn't excuse their treatment of you, Kate.'

'But they are right in one thing. I don't know who I am. All I know is that my mother was a lady and my father a soldier, or so the Romany woman said. It is a very strange feeling to discover that you are not who you always thought you were.'

Molly stopped, holding her side. 'It's just a stitch. It will pass.' She leaned on Kate's arm, taking deep breaths. 'That's better.'

'We've walked too far today,' Kate said, feeling guilty at the sight of Molly's pale cheeks.

'I know the answer,' Molly said, grinning. 'You must pay a visit to the gypsies before they go away, or you may never have another chance to find the old woman and make her tell you what she knows about your mother and father.'

Kate thought hard. The squire had gone to Poole on business and was not expected home until late evening. Amy and Letitia were out riding and would be unlikely to notice that she was missing. This might be her one and only opportunity to discover her true identity. She hugged Molly. 'I'll do it.'

'And I'll cover for you. If anyone asks where you are, I'll say you have gone into Dorchester to get me some more linctus.'

Chapter Twenty-three

Edmund had generously put a suitable mount at Kate's disposal, although she had not so far ventured out on her own. One of the under grooms saddled the animal for her without question and she was barely able to conceal her relief as she rode out of the stable yard. She took the back lanes, avoiding the main road as much as possible as she did not want to be seen and give rise to even more gossip. Edmund would find out soon enough that she had disobeyed him, but she did not care. Her need to discover more about her parents was greater than her fear of censure. She simply had to see the old gypsy woman, who might not reveal anything more than she had at the hiring fair, but it was worth a try. She flicked the reins and encouraged the horse to canter.

She could smell the scent of woodsmoke from the camp fires long before she saw the caravans and the sturdy piebald ponies grazing at the roadside. As she rode into the encampment, Kate was aware of curious glances from the Romany folk, but no one approached her. She dismounted and tethered her horse to a fencepost. A small child was watching her and Kate went up to her, smiling. 'I am looking for a woman called Zolfina. Do you know her, little girl?'

The child turned and ran towards a woman who had just stepped down from one of the vans. 'Excuse me,' Kate called out. 'Can you tell me where to find the woman Zolfina? I must speak to her.'

The gypsy came slowly towards her. 'I saw you at the hiring fair. You are so like your mother, it gave me quite a turn.'

Kate's breath hitched in her throat. 'You were with the gypsy woman who told me about my real mother.'

She came closer. 'Yes, I am her daughter. My name is Dena, and you are Katherine.'

'You must have known my mother. I'm desperate to know more about her.'

'Come to the vardo,' Dena said, beckoning to her. 'We can speak privately inside.' Without waiting for a reply, she led the way with Kate following close on her heels. '

The inside was spotlessly clean and Kate was amazed to see how much could be stowed in such a small space. Dena motioned her to take a seat.

'Please tell me all you know.' Kate sank down on the padded bench as her knees suddenly refused to support her. Her hands were damp and her pulses racing. 'My mother – who was she? Please tell me everything you know about her.'

'I know very little, except that she was a lady and her name was Clara. You must understand that she was in a bad way when my mother found her by the Winterbourne river. Who knows what the poor lady had been through, or why she was wandering alone in her condition.'

'She must have told you something. Her surname, for instance?'

Dena's lips curved in a wry smile. 'You have never given birth. It is not the time for making small talk. She was very weak and I think she knew that the end was near.'

Kate's throat constricted and she swallowed hard. 'Did she know that she had a daughter?'

'She held you in her arms, and she asked my mother to bless and name you. She wanted you to be called Katherine, after her own mother.'

'And my father? Did she tell you who he was?'

'Your father was called Alexander. He was an army officer, and he was killed in the Crimea. They were not married, but I think that, according to your customs, they were engaged.' Dena went to open a small wooden cupboard. She took something out of a box and laid it in her palm, holding her hand out to Kate. 'This was on her finger. She begged my mother to keep it for you, and we have honoured her dying wish. I knew that one day you would come to claim it.'

Kate took the ring, hardly able to believe that she held something which had once belonged to her mother. She could barely focus on the heart-shaped emerald surrounded by fiery diamonds. Her eyes misted with tears. 'This was hers?'

'It was the only thing of value she possessed. She slipped away soon afterwards, but peacefully and with your father's name on her lips.'

Kate slid the ring onto her finger. 'I feel so close to her that I can almost see her.'

Dena angled her head. 'As I said before, you are very like her.'

'Such a sad and lonely end.' Kate kissed the ring. 'My poor mother.'

'In a way she was lucky,' Dena said bitterly. 'My mother brought you into the world shortly after my own child was born. My baby was taken from me when she was less than a day old.' She covered her face with her hands. 'I still feel the pain of it. I wished that I could lie down next to Clara and join her in the world of the spirits. I did not want to live on without my little girl.'

'But you did, Mother. You survived and lived on to become queen of the Roma.'

Kate turned her head and saw Josie standing in the doorway. 'Josie! I can't believe it. What are you doing here?'

Josie smiled. 'As you see, I have joined my people. I have discovered my roots, Kate. I always knew that I was different, but I did not understand why. Now I do. I am more my mother's daughter than I am my father's child.'

'Then Sir Joseph really is your father?' Kate stared at her in disbelief; she could hardly take in Josie's altered appearance. Her long, dark hair hung loose around her shoulders and framed her oval face. She wore a simple gown of dark green calico with a brightly coloured crocheted shawl wrapped around her shoulders, and she looked happier than she had in a long while.

'I was very young,' Dena said swiftly. 'He was like a god to me in those days, and I gave myself to him willingly. I thought I was in love, but I have paid dearly for my folly. Now I have my first born back again, and my life is full once more.'

Kate leapt to her feet and threw her arms around Josie. 'Oh, Josie. I am so happy for you, but – I thought you and Harry . . .'

Josie's dark eyes brimmed with remorse. 'I am so sorry, Kate. I lied to you again and again. I don't deserve your friendship.'

'I thought you had gone to him. You told me that you were getting married.'

'Lies, Kate. It was all lies. Well, most of it anyway.'

'He didn't propose to you?'

'I tricked him into it. He never wanted me. I knew that he was in love with you but I allowed him to think you were a wanton and had run away with Sam, and when he discovered that was a lie I told him you had gone to live with the squire. I admit it all, my dear. I was an evil person then. I sent Sam away from me, even though it broke my heart, and I was mad with grief. I barely knew what I was doing, and I wanted you and Harry to suffer as I was suffering. Can you ever forgive me?'

Kate sat down again, dazed and hardly able to believe what she was hearing. 'You were my friend, Josie. How could you do such a thing to me?'

Dena poured some dark liquid into a cup and thrust it into Kate's hands. 'Drink this, child. It is a cordial made from herbs and roots; it will not harm you. It will revive your spirits. Don't be too hard on Josie; she has suffered too.'

Kate sipped the sweet but slightly bitter brew and

found it surprisingly refreshing. She put the cup down on the table, giving herself time to gather her scattered wits. 'I do forgive you, Josie. But if what you say is true and Harry loves me, why did he just take your word for it? If he truly loved me, wouldn't he have tried to win me?'

Josie's eyes filled with tears and her lips trembled. 'He thought that you were beyond his reach, and it was all my doing.'

Kate closed her eyes in an attempt to blot out Harry's face. 'He is still engaged to you, Josie.'

'You must go to him,' Josie said, taking both Kate's hands in hers. 'Go to Copperstone and tell him that everything I said was untrue. Tell him that I've run away to be with my own people and that I release him from his promise to marry me.'

'Don't be ridiculous,' Kate cried, snatching her hands away. 'How could I face Harry after the lies you told him about me, and why would he believe me anyway? That is the most stupid thing you've ever said.'

'If you're too cowardly to take the initiative, don't blame me if you never see him again.'

'Sometimes I almost hate you, Josie.'

'Stop.' Dena stepped in between them. 'Squabbling like two little girls won't help. If anyone should speak to him it is you, Josie. You made the mischief and you should make amends for your cruel lies.'

Josie threw up her hands and laughed. 'My mother is my conscience, Kate. I expect she is right. I will think about it, but first there is something that you can do for me.'

'You have a strong streak of Damerell in you, my child,' Dena said, pursing her lips. 'I fear that you are more like your father than you are like me. But I will leave you to sort this matter out between you.' She nodded to Kate as she left the vardo, giving Josie a stern look as she went.

'It's true,' Josie said, shrugging her shoulders. 'I am more like Joseph than I would care to admit, but I am not a bad person. I will ride to Copperstone, Kate, and I will confess my sins to Harry . . .'

'No, don't do that.' Kate shook her head. 'I was born out of wedlock, and I know now that I have no hope of discovering the true identities of my poor parents. I am not a fit bride for a man in his position.'

'I won't have that. You are a far better person than I.'

Kate smiled reluctantly. 'Squire Westwood has made it clear that my birth makes it impossible for a respectable man to marry me, although he is prepared to make an exception in my case.'

'I heard that you were living at the Grange,' Josie said with a roguish smile. 'You aren't going to marry that old man, are you?'

'I don't want to, but what choice do I have? Thanks to Sir Joseph and the man I thought was my father, I can't get work because they have spread it around that I am part gypsy and might curse them. Then I have Molly to consider. She is still little more than a child, and I owe it to Sam to take care of her. If I marry the squire we will have a roof over our heads and food in our stomachs.'

'And you will have his two horrible daughters to make your life a misery. Don't do it, Kate.'

'What would you have me do? Run away with the gypsies like you?'

'No, but there must be another way.'

'If there is I cannot think of one, Josie. Perhaps I am a coward, too afraid to face a life of poverty, but the squire is a good man and he says he loves me.'

'You must do what you think best, but I'm of the opinion that you ought to go to Copperstone and tell Harry everything. You love him as much as I love Sam – loved Sam.' She broke off on a sob.

'Why did you send him away, Josie?'

'Because I was a fool and I put money and status above everything. I was wrong, so very wrong. I said dreadful things to him. I deliberately hurt and humili-ated him and I hate myself for it.'

'Then you must seek him out and tell him just that.'

'Don't you think I haven't thought about that? I went to Weymouth just last week and had doors slammed in my face. They are suspicious of gypsy folk and no one would tell me anything.' Josie eyed Kate thoughtfully. 'I couldn't get any information out of the townsfolk, but you might be able to learn some-thing. They wouldn't turn you away.'

'I wouldn't know where to start.'

'You could speak to the masters of vessels in the harbour. You could go into the taverns and alehouses to make enquiries.'

'Edmund would be horrified if he found out that I had gone into places like that on my own.'

'You sound as though you are already married. I thought you had more spirit, Kate.'

'My life is already difficult enough without you adding to it,' Kate said angrily, but she relented when she saw Josie's downcast expression. 'Perhaps we could do it together. If you've kept some of your old clothes and dress as you used to no one would link you with the gypsies.'

Josie beamed at her. 'Why didn't I think of that? I still have the garments I wore when I left home. You were always the cleverest one, Kate. We'll go into Weymouth together. It's market day tomorrow and we can mingle with the crowds.'

'I'll help you, but only if you promise that you will make no attempt to speak to Harry on my behalf. You should release him from your engagement and let him find a bride from his own class. He'll forget about me, if he has not done so already.'

'And you will marry the squire and regret it for the rest of your life.'

'He's a kind man, Josie. He's offered me everything, and I, as his wretched daughters pointed out, am no one. I don't even have a name. You at least have found your mother and now you have a family and an identity. I really am a nobody. Harry was right in the first instance.'

'I have half a dozen half-brothers and sisters now, but none that I love more than you.' Josie linked her arm through Kate's. 'Before you go, you must meet them. Tomorrow we will seek news of Sam, and if I ever see him again, I'll go down on my knees and beg him to forgive me.'

'You won't need to. He'll take one look at you and all will be well.' Kate smiled, stifling a sigh. If only her own future looked so rosy.

Next day, they rode into Weymouth together. Josie wore her black velvet riding habit and a top hat with a lace veil. The moment she put it on she seemed to Kate to become a different person and her free spirit was instantly tamed. She was once again Miss Josephine Damerell of Damerell Manor, but despite her prim exterior, her sparkling eyes gave her away. She could not conceal the fact that she was in high spirits, and bubbling with excitement at the prospect of hearing news of Sam. Kate was a little more circumspect. Her own life seemed much more complex than Josie's relatively free existence with the gypsies.

After her visit to the Romany camp the previous day, Kate had managed to slip into the Grange unnoticed, and she did not seem to have been missed. Only Molly knew where she had been, and her eyes had widened in shock when Kate told her that she had found Josie living with the Romany people, although she had omitted any mention of Sam's name. It would be too cruel to raise Molly's hopes if their mission to find him was unsuccessful.

Kate had seen Edmund briefly at breakfast that morning and she had sought his permission to go riding, although he had been insistent that she should not go too far from home, and that she must be accompanied by a groom. She had nodded her head in a vague acknowledgement of his wishes, but his proprietorial attitude did not bode well for their future together. She had had a sudden vision of herself as his young bride. He would be kind and considerate, but his affection for her might prove to be cloying and overpowering. She would be the virtual prisoner of his overprotective love.

She had left the table as soon as she had bolted down a few mouthfuls of toast, which she had not wanted, but Edmund had insisted that she must eat more if she was to undertake vigorous exercise. For a horrible moment she had thought he was going to accompany her to the stables, but he had not, and she had made her escape, riding out alone to meet Josie on the road to Weymouth.

When they reached the town, they left their horses in a livery stable and continued on foot, going first to the harbour where they questioned the captains of every vessel that was moored alongside, without success. They knocked on the doors of lodging houses in the area frequented by sailors, and then they tried the taverns on the harbour side, but no one seemed to have heard of Sam Loveday. Then, just when they were about to give up, Josie was leaning against the window of a pawnshop in a side street, when Kate glanced over her shoulder and uttered a muffled cry. 'Look at that billycock hat, Josie. I know there must be hundreds of them much the same, but I could swear that that one belonged to Sam.' She pointed at the jay's feather stuck in the hatband. 'I remember the time he found it.'

Josie peered through the green-tinged window glass. 'I suppose it could be Sam's hat, but I'd no idea he'd kept the silly feather.'

'No, you were always too bound up in your own affairs to think much about Sam. You took his devotion for granted, never giving a thought to his feelings.' Noting the startled look in Josie's eyes, Kate bit her lip. 'I'm sorry, but it is true. You always were a spoilt little madam, Josie.'

'I expect you're right, but never mind that now. I'm going inside to find out who pawned that hat and when. If Sam is desperate for money I must do something about it.' Josie barged through the shop door, leaving Kate to follow her.

A gaunt man, dressed completely in black, appeared through a curtain at the back of the shop. 'What can I do for you, young ladies?' He gave them a calculating look. 'Do you want to pawn a keepsake? Or those fine kid gloves, for instance?'

Josie shook her head. 'There is a billycock hat in the window. Do you remember who left it with you?'

A glimmer of cunning flickered in his beady eyes. 'I might, or I might not, miss. What is it to you, anyway?'

Kate put her hand in her pocket and took out a silver florin. 'Will this help you to remember?'

He pocketed the coin. 'It might. Do you want to buy the hat?'

Josie edged Kate out of the way and she leaned across the counter, speaking in a confidential whisper. 'I think that the man who pawned this might be my maid's brother. He went to sea and nothing has been heard of him for weeks. The poor girl is out of her mind with worry.'

Kate took out her last sixpence and pressed it into his hand. He gave her a gap-toothed grin. 'I do remember him, as it happens. Sam Loveday rented one of me rooms upstairs for a couple of days afore he found a ship. Bad business that.'

'What do you mean?' Josie demanded breathlessly.

'A coffin ship, that's what everyone said the *Kimmeridge* was, but the fellow couldn't get another berth and he was in urgent need of money. The ship was bound for Guernsey with a cargo of coal. She went down with all hands in a terrible storm. No one was saved.'

Kate stifled a cry of horror, but her first concern was for Josie who had paled alarmingly and was swaying on her feet, staring at the pawnbroker in stricken silence. Kate took her by the arm. 'It might not be Sam, Josie. He might not have been on board that ship, and anyway he's a strong swimmer. Even if he was part of the crew, he might have swum to safety.'

Josie stared at her as if she were speaking in a foreign tongue. Her stillness was more frightening than any amount of hysterics. Kate squeezed her arm. 'Say something, Josie. You're scaring me.'

Josie's eyes were glazed and her lips moved but she uttered no sound.

'Best get her outside in the fresh air,' the pawnbroker said, scowling. 'I don't want a swooning woman on my hands. It's bad for business.'

Before Kate could answer him, Josie let out an animal-like howl. She broke free from Kate's grasp and wrenching the shop door open she ran into the alley, shrieking at the top of her voice.

'Oh, my God!' Kate ran after her, but Josie had a head start and she was racing towards the harbour. Her cries were attracting a great deal of attention from passers-by, and people stepped aside, staring at her in dismay, quite obviously thinking that she was a mad woman.

Kate picked up her skirts and tore after her, pausing to catch her breath as she rounded the corner onto the quayside. She could see Josie in the distance and her intention was patently obvious when she stopped abruptly, balancing precariously on the edge of the harbour wall.

Petrified with fear, Kate saw a group of well-dressed gentlemen coming out of the harbourmaster's office. She shouted at them, waving her hands frantically in an attempt to attract their attention. 'Stop her. For God's sake, don't let her jump.' Galvanised into action, she broke into a run, but one of the men leapt forward and grabbed Josie round the waist just as she was poised to throw herself into the swirling water. His back was to Kate, but he obviously had Josie in a firm grasp, even though she was screaming hysterically, kicking out with her feet and flailing her arms in an attempt to break free. Kate stopped just yards from them, and her heart did a somersault inside her chest as he turned his head to look at her. His name was torn from her lips in a shuddering sigh. 'Harry!'

He gave her a cursory glance, but Josie was struggling like a wild creature, and he was having difficulty in restraining her. He called to one of his companions, and together they managed to subdue her. As Kate hurried towards them she realised that the man with Harry was Charlie Beauchamp, who had been one of the shooting party when Sir Hector had met with his accident.

He grinned, tipping his top hat and almost losing his grip on Josie. 'This is a fine how-do-you-do and no mistake, Miss Kate. What happened to upset her so?'

'Never mind that now,' Harry said brusquely. 'We'd better get her somewhere quiet, well away from the water's edge.'

Kate avoided meeting his eyes. Her heart was beating so fast that she could scarcely breathe, but her concern for Josie was paramount. 'She's had a terrible shock. Perhaps we could take her into the harbour-master's office, just until she calms down.'

Josie slumped against Harry's shoulder and her whole body was racked with sobs. Charlie loosened his hold on her, setting his hat straight. 'Must have been something dreadful to send her off into a fit of hysterics. If Harry hadn't stopped her I really think she would have jumped.'

Harry lifted Josie up in his arms. 'The George Inn isn't too far away. Go on ahead, Charlie, and see if they have a private parlour. Tell them to light a fire and have a bottle of brandy at the ready.'

'Right ho.' Charlie strode off towards the public house a little further along the quay.

Josie buried her face against Harry's shoulder, but at least she seemed quieter now and her sobs were inter-mittent. Kate fell into step beside him, stealing a glance at his stern profile. As if sensing that her eyes were upon him, he turned his head to give her a questioning look. 'What happened to put her in this state?'

Kate dared not mention Sam's name for fear of upsetting Josie all over again. 'She had some truly dreadful news,' she said vaguely.

'It must have been very bad to make her attempt suicide.'

His eyes seemed to bore into her soul and she looked away, biting her lip. Why, of all people, did it have to be Harry who had saved Josie? 'A very old friend was lost at sea,' she replied in a low voice.

'He must have been very close to have caused her so much distress.'

'She's supposed to be your fiancée,' Kate said with a touch of asperity. 'Perhaps if you'd stood by her she might not have got herself in such a stew.' She dodged onto the narrow pavement to avoid being run down by a horse-drawn wagon, heavily laden with barrels, and his answer was lost in the noise of the rumbling wheels and clatter of the Clydesdale's hooves.

They reached the George and entered the taproom, where they were met with the aroma of roasting meat mingled with that of hot rum, tobacco smoke and tarred rope. Dock workers, sailors and fishermen leaned on the bar or sat around tables, smoking, drinking and chatting. Charlie beckoned to them from a doorway at the back of the bar and led the way to a small parlour. Harry set Josie gently down on a chair. 'Sit there and rest a while.' He poured a tot of brandy into a glass and placed it in her hands. 'Take a sip of that, Josie. Slowly, mind.'

She did as she was told, moving like an automaton. She coughed as the spirit hit the back of her throat, but she said nothing as she stared blindly into the fire.

Charlie poured a measure of brandy and gave it to Kate. 'Here, my dear girl. You look as though you could do with a drink. You're pale as a ghost.'

Harry pulled up a chair for her. 'Sit down and tell us what happened. Who was this man who meant so much to Josie?' He gave Kate a searching look. 'To both of you, it seems.'

She sipped the brandy and felt its fire flowing through her veins and straight to her head. 'It was Sam. He was on the *Kimmeridge* when it went down with all hands.' She bowed her head, staring into the amber liquid in her glass. The fumes were making her dizzy, or perhaps it was the proximity of Harry that made her head spin.

Harry raised his eyebrows in surprise. 'Loveday? What was he to Josie?'

She raised her eyes to his face. This was not the time for lies. 'She loved him.'

'I still love him,' Josie cried passionately. 'I've always loved him and now he's dead and gone and I can't tell him.' She wrenched off the engagement ring that had replaced the cigar band and she hurled it at Harry. 'There you are. Now you know the truth and I release you from your promise, although I don't think you had any intention of marrying me.'

'You engineered the situation to suit yourself, Josie.

As a gentleman I could hardly tell the world that you were lying, but I knew you were capricious and I hoped that you'd see the error of your ways and change your mind.' He turned to Kate with a rueful smile. 'I'm truly sorry, Kate.' He touched her briefly on the shoulder, and then jerked his hand away as if the mere feel of her had burned his flesh. 'You must be suffering too, but then you hide your emotions so that a man has no idea what you are thinking or feeling.'

For a wild moment her spirits had been raised by the sympathetic look in his eyes, but the bitter note in his voice brought her back to reality. 'It's true,' she murmured. 'Sam and I were close, although not in the way you were led to believe. Nevertheless, his loss is a bitter blow.'

'But not fatal, I think.' His smile faded. 'I called in at your father's farm on my way to Weymouth. Your step-mother told me that you are now living with Edmund Westwood, and that you're going to marry him.'

'No doubt Honoria told you everything about me.'

'She took pleasure in it.'

'As I knew she would. Yes, I am living at the Grange, but I am employed as a companion to the squire's daughters. And, yes, he has proposed marriage.'

'And what will you say to the good squire?'

'What I will say is for his ears only.' She struggled to hold onto her last ragged scrap of pride. If Harry was prepared to believe the worst of her, then there was no hope of their ever having a life together. Honoria would have revelled in telling him that her stepdaughter was the illegitimate child of a disgraced gentlewoman, as well as being an ingrate and a troublemaker.

Josie groaned, and with a sudden movement she tossed the empty brandy glass into the fireplace where it shattered into tiny fragments. She buried her face in her hands and gave way to a fresh bout of weeping. Kate moved swiftly to her side and put her arm around her shoulders. 'There, there, Josie. Don't take on so, my dear.'

'My life is over,' Josie wailed. 'If Sam is dead it's all my fault. If I hadn't lied to him – if I hadn't sent him away . . .'

'He went freely, Josie. It was his choice.' Kate smoothed Josie's tumbled curls back from her face. Her hat had been lost somewhere along the way and she must, Kate thought inconsequentially, have left a trail of hairpins in her wake.

'I was hateful to him,' Josie sobbed. 'I said terrible things. I wish I were dead too. You should have let me drown.'

'We must get her home to Damerell Manor,' Harry said, frowning.

'I'll never go back there,' Josie wailed.

Kate put her arm around Josie's shoulders. 'It's all right. No one will make you do anything against your will.'

'What did I say?' Harry demanded. 'Why doesn't she want to go home?'

'You don't know then?'

He shook his head. 'Know what? What don't I know? Tell me, Kate.'

Chapter Twenty-four

'There was a family row,' Kate said, choosing her words carefully. 'It's not up to me to tell you Josie's business, but she doesn't live there any more.'

'I say,' Charlie whispered. 'This sounds like a three-act melodrama. What on earth could have happened?'

'All I can tell you is that Josie can't return to her old home.'

'It's all right, Kate,' Harry said, shooting a warning look at Charlie who had opened his mouth as if about to question her further. 'I wouldn't expect you to break a confidence.'

Kate could have hugged him for being so understanding, but she masked her feelings with a curt little nod of her head. 'I'm truly grateful for your help, Mr Challenor. But it might be best if you and Charlie were to leave us now. I can take care of Josie.'

He held her gaze for a moment and then he turned to his friend. 'Be a good chap and send for my carriage.'

Charlie's shoulders sagged and disappointment was written all over his face. 'Must I, really? This was just getting interesting.'

Harry raised an eyebrow and Charlie backed away towards the door. 'All right. I'm going.'

Despite the tension of the situation, Kate couldn't

help thinking that he looked like a sulky schoolboy. If matters had not been so serious, she might have laughed at his downcast expression. He left the room, muttering to himself. She turned her attention to Josie, who had curled up in a ball and refused to look up when Kate asked her if there was anything she could do to help.

'Leave her, Kate,' Harry said gently. 'Let her come round in her own good time.'

She felt her resolve weakening. She longed to tell him that she loved him and that everything he had been told about her was a pack of lies, but even if he believed her, it would not alter anything. She must hold onto her dignity and pray for her sanity. She gave a start as he laid his hand on her arm.

'Kate, I'm assuming that you came here on horseback, but it's quite obvious that Josie is in no state to ride.'

She nodded dully. He was right, of course, but she wished with all her heart that he would leave now. His continued presence was a bitter-sweet mixture of delight and torture. 'Yes, we left our horses at a livery stable on the edge of town.'

'Just tell me where Josie is staying and I'll take her home. You too, if you will let me. I can arrange to have your mounts brought along later.'

'I don't know . . .' Kate murmured, glancing anxiously at Josie.

'Leave me alone, Harry,' Josie muttered, raising a tear-stained face to glare at him. 'I ran away from the Manor and I live with the gypsies. Does that satisfy you? I am one of them. Kate is too loyal to tell you, but

I am not ashamed of it. I am Joseph Damerell's bastard daughter, and my mother is the queen of the Roma.'

Harry shot an enquiring glance at Kate 'Is this true?' She nodded her head. 'It is.'

'Then we must take her back to her people,' Harry replied calmly. 'Where are they camped, Kate?'

Josie sat up straight. 'You can stop talking about me as if I weren't here,' she said with a hint of her old spirit. 'I'm going nowhere. I won't leave Weymouth until I know for certain what happened to Sam.' Taking a hanky from her skirt pocket she blew her nose. 'Anyway, they're moving on tomorrow and will be heading for Devonshire. I cannot go with them. I won't go.'

'Don't get upset again, Josie,' Kate said hastily. 'We must think of Molly now. She'll need all our love and care. Try to put yourself in her place.'

'I can't think of anything but my Sam.' Fresh tears spurted from Josie's eyes. 'I killed him. It is all my fault.'

'Perhaps Harry – I mean Mr Challenor – will take us as far as the Grange,' Kate said, turning to him. 'I'm sure Edmund won't mind if Josie stays with us for a while.'

He stared at her, frowning thoughtfully. 'And you will be even more in his debt. Tell me honestly, Kate. Do you love this man?'

'That's none of your business.'

'I'm making it my business. Am I not your friend?'

Josie uttered a loud groan. 'I could shake the pair of you. If my life wasn't completely over, I would bang your silly heads together.'

'She's feverish,' Kate said hastily. 'Don't listen to her.'

'I think I have the solution.' Harry laid his finger on her lips, smiling.

'And that is?' If only she were stronger she might be able to crush her feelings for him, but when he was so close to her all her resolve seemed to evaporate like morning mist. She cleared her throat, praying that he had not noticed that she was trembling uncontrollably. 'What do you suggest, Mr Challenor?'

'You used to call me Harry.'

She made a vague movement with her hand. 'Please, not now.'

'Very well, but you and I have unfinished business, Kate. I'm not a man to give in easily.'

'For pity's sake, you two, go away and sort yourselves out.' Josie half rose and then sank back on the settle. 'I can look after myself. I'll find lodgings in the town.'

'You'll do no such thing,' Harry said firmly. 'It isn't practical for you to stay in Weymouth on your own, but I think I may have the answer.'

Josie wiped her eyes on her hanky. 'Go on,' she said suspiciously.

'How would it be if I took you to my old friend, John Hardy, in Puddlecombe? You stayed with him once before, as I recall, and I'm sure he would be delighted to have your company.' He turned to Kate. 'Of course you would have to go with her, Kate. John's parishioners would be up in arms if he were to entertain an unaccompanied young lady, but if the two of you were there . . .'

'I couldn't leave Molly,' Kate interrupted. 'And Edmund . . .'

'Damn Edmund,' Harry said with feeling. 'That man has taken advantage of your situation and forced you into a position where you had little choice but to consider his proposal. I think it would be to your advantage to put some distance between you.'

Kate hesitated. Part of her longed for the peace and serenity of the old vicarage, and long talks with kindly John Hardy, but she could not abandon Molly or leave the squire without a word of explanation. 'It's up to Josie to decide whether she wants to go with you, but I must return to the Grange. I can't just walk out on Molly or my employer.'

Harry gripped her by the elbow, his fingers pressing into the soft flesh of her upper arm. 'If you had any tender feelings for him, would you speak about Edmund Westwood simply as your employer? No, don't look at me like that, Kate. I admire your loyalty, but I suggest that a few weeks away from the good squire will give you time to think about your future.'

'He will never agree to it. I cannot ask him . . .'

'Then I will. If you do this, I promise to do everything I can to find out what happened to Loveday. I have ships that do a regular trade with the Channel Islands and I have many friends there. Take Josie to Puddlecombe, and young Molly too, and leave the rest to me.'

Josie rose unsteadily to her feet. 'I'll agree to go, but only if you come with me, Kate. I have to know whether Sam is alive or dead and Harry is in a better position to find out than anyone else.'

'All right,' Kate said slowly. 'I can't fight you both.'

Harry gave her an approving nod. 'Then it's settled. We'll go to the gypsy encampment first. I'm sure Josie will want to see her mother and explain why she isn't travelling on with them. And then we'll go to the Grange. You can leave the good squire to me.'

'You must do as you see fit, Kate,' Edmund said stiffly. 'I can't force you to stay here against your will.'

'She's been using you, Papa,' Letitia said with a spiteful sneer curling her lips. 'I always thought she was a fast cat, and now I am certain of it.'

'Yes,' Amy added, simpering. 'You'd think that butter wouldn't melt in her mouth, but underneath that goody-goody exterior she's a scheming little minx.'

Kate opened her mouth to protest, but Edmund turned on his daughters. 'Hold your silly tongues. This is between Kate and me.'

'I am truly grateful for everything you have done for me, Edmund.' Kate had seen the pain behind his brusque manner and she was well aware that she had hurt him, but she was desperate to escape. 'But I must keep Josie company at least until we know for certain what has happened to Sam, and I promised him that I would look after his sister. I must stand by my word.'

Letitia and Amy had subsided into sulks, but Edmund managed a smile. 'I understand, and I beg you to take no notice of my naughty girls, Kate. They don't really mean what they say, and, if you decide to return, you will be welcomed with open arms. I can't say more.'

Harry had been standing quietly behind Kate, but now he stepped forward to shake Edmund's hand. 'I will see that no harm comes to her.'

'You had better, or you'll have me to answer to,' Edmund replied gruffly. He shook Harry's hand, but his eyes were on Kate. 'Goodbye, my dear. Remember, if you ever change your mind . . .'

'I think you know the answer to that. I am so sorry, Edmund. It just wasn't meant to be.'

'But, my dear . . .' He lowered his voice to a whisper. 'You cannot stay in the vicarage forever. What will you do when Josie returns to her people?'

'I don't know, but I'll find work as a governess or a paid companion. You must understand that it would be impossible for me to return here. It wouldn't be fair to you, or your daughters. I'll always have warm memories of your kindness to me.'

'Ahem.' Harry cleared his throat, breaking the ensuing awkward silence. 'We'd better make a move, Kate. Josie and Molly are waiting for us in the carriage.'

Kate took one last look around the wainscoted morning parlour of Westwood Grange with its solid oak furniture, glowing gold in the sunlight streaming through the open window. The scent of roses and lavender wafted in from the garden and the air smelt of newly cut grass. All this was a far cry from her early days spent in the squalid mews behind Bedford Square. She could have been mistress of the gracious old house and wife of the man who stood before her with sorrow in his eyes. She was leaping into the unknown, but she knew that this was the path she must take.

'Goodbye, Edmund. Thank you from the bottom of my heart for taking me and Molly into your home. I wish it could have ended differently, but this is for the best.' She turned on her heel and hurried from the room.

'You did the right thing,' Harry said as they left the house. 'He's a good man, but he's not for you.'

'I don't want to discuss it. My concern is for Josie now and Molly too. Please don't make this harder for me, Harry.'

He smiled. 'You've forgiven me then. You called me Harry.'

'There was nothing to forgive,' she murmured as the coachman leapt from his box to open the carriage door. 'We are friends.'

'Yes, we are.'

As she climbed into the carriage she found that Josie was either asleep or pretending to be, but Molly moved up to make room for her. 'Isn't this exciting, Kate? I've never been further than Dorchester in my whole life.'

'Yes, Molly. It's very exciting.'

Harry climbed into the carriage and sat down next to Josie. 'Drive on when you're ready, Sweatman.'

'Yes, sir.' The coachman folded the steps and closed the carriage door. Moments later they were on their way.

Harry settled back, giving Kate a reassuring smile. 'I'm certain that John will be delighted to have some feminine company other than the redoubtable Mrs

Trevett. I sent Charlie on ahead to warn him of our coming.'

Kate nodded her head, unable to find words to express the emotions which raged in her breast. She cast an anxious glance at Josie, who had opened her eyes and was staring moodily out of the window.

Harry frowned. 'Are you all right, Josie?'

'Leave me alone,' she muttered. 'Perhaps I should have gone with my people after all.'

Kate reached out to give her hand a reassuring squeeze. 'Dena knows best, Josie. She was convinced that we would hear good news about Sam, and if you believe in the Romany power of foreseeing the future, then you must trust her.'

Josie turned her head away. 'I think he's dead, and I wish I was too.'

'You mustn't give way,' Harry said gruffly. 'I'll do everything in my power to find out if he survived the shipwreck. I leave for Guernsey first thing in the morning.'

'All hands were lost.' Josie closed her eyes with a deep sigh. 'But I suppose there might still be hope.'

'Dena gave her something to calm her,' Kate said, smiling. 'She said it would give her ease for a while at least and that it would make her sleep.'

Harry tucked a travelling rug around Josie. 'I was impressed with Dena. She seems like a very sensible woman, unlike her scatterbrain daughter. I think Josie has inherited some of her wildness from her father, although everyone will always blame her gypsy blood.'

Kate relaxed against the padded leather squabs. The

luxurious interior of the carriage cocooned them against the outside world, and she found herself wishing that the journey would go on forever, but it seemed no time at all before they arrived at their destination. A velvety dusk was enveloping the countryside as they drew up outside the vicarage. The front door opened spilling a beam of friendly light onto the garden path as John Hardy came hurrying to greet them. 'You made good time. Charlie and I thought you might be much later.' He held out his hand to help Kate alight.

'It's good of you to put us up at such short notice, John.'

'It's a pleasure to see you again, Kate.' He glanced over her shoulder at Josie's prostrate figure. 'Is she all right?'

Molly clambered stiffly from the carriage. 'She's been sleeping like a baby, your reverence. The gypsy queen gave her a potion.'

Kate could see that Mrs Trevett was less than impressed. She frowned at Molly, shaking her head. 'The least said about that the better,' she said in a low voice.

Harry lifted Josie from the carriage. 'She's drugged,' he said, ignoring Mrs Trevett's disapproving sniff. 'Her mother, the Romany woman, concocted a sleeping draught to calm her. The poor girl has suffered a terrible loss and she needs rest and quiet. I knew that she would find it here with you.'

'Gypsy spells and potions,' Mrs Trevett said icily. 'No good will come of this, your reverence. I always suspected there was something not quite right about that young person.'

John frowned. 'We won't have any of that talk, thank you, Mrs Trevett. Miss Damerell is a lady and a guest in my house. She will be treated with respect, or I will want to know the reason why.'

Mrs Trevett turned on her heel and marched back into the house.

'It seems as though we've been here before,' John said, smiling as he ushered Kate into the house.

'Last time it was Josie's ankle. This time I fear it is a broken heart, and that will take a lot longer to mend,' Kate replied sadly.

Mrs Trevett sent Molly off with Hester and she addressed herself to Harry. 'If you would follow me, please, sir? It would be best to take the young person straight to her room.' She headed towards the staircase and Harry followed her, carrying Josie who was still heavily sedated.

John helped Kate off with her mantle. 'Charlie told me as much as he knew of her story,' he said softly. 'It seems that the poor child has had much to bear.'

'I'm sure she will tell you everything when she feels able. I'm most grateful to you for taking us in.'

'It's the least I could do in the circumstances. I am very fond of Josie and you too, of course. You are both most welcome to stay for as long as you please.'

'I love this house,' Kate said, smiling. 'It feels like coming home.' She looked up as Harry appeared at the top of the stairs, and her heart swelled with love at the mere sight of him.

'Should I send for the doctor, Harry,' John asked anxiously.

'Perhaps you should wait and see how she is in the morning. She's sleeping soundly at the moment. Whatever was in that potion was very potent.'

'Then we'll wait until tomorrow. Will you stay and have supper with us?'

'Thank you, no. I must get back to Copperstone. I have paperwork to go through and I'll have to leave early tomorrow morning. I promised Josie that I would initiate enquiries about Sam Loveday.' He turned to Kate, taking her hand in his. 'If he is alive, I'll find him.'

Looking into his eyes, Kate felt something pass between them that sent her spirit soaring towards the heavens. She could scarcely breathe. As his fingers curled around her hand, giving it a gentle but firm squeeze, it seemed as though they were the only two people on the planet. She saw herself reflected in his eyes and it was as though their two souls met and united. She knew in that split second that her love for him was reciprocated and she wanted to cry out for joy. But it was a fleeting moment and when it had passed, she was not certain whether or not she had imagined it. He raised her hand to his lips and kissed it. 'I'll return as soon as possible, and I hope I may have good news for you. Goodnight, my dear Kate.'

He was gone. The candle flames guttered in the draught from the open door, burning brightly again as soon as it closed, but it felt to Kate that darkness enveloped her soul, and she had to stop herself from running to the door and calling him back. John placed his hand beneath her elbow and she realised that he was speaking to her. 'I'm sorry,' she murmured. 'What did you say?'

'I simply suggested that you come into the drawing room and rest until supper is ready, my dear.'

'Thank you for being so understanding, but if you don't mind I would rather go to my room.'

'Of course,' he said, nodding. 'You must be exhausted. I'll ask Mrs Trevett to send up some supper on a tray.'

'You are a very kind man,' Kate said with feeling. 'I feel as if I've known you all my life.'

'And I you, my dear Kate. Mrs Trevett has prepared your old room for you. Can you find your way?'

She smiled. 'I'm sure I could find it blindfolded.'

'Goodnight then, my dear. I'll see you at breakfast.'

'Goodnight, John.' Kate made her way slowly up the gently curving staircase.

As she opened the door to her room she was welcomed by a waft of perfume. Moonlight poured in through the open window and she realised that the scent came from the sweet eglantine rose that clambered up the outside wall. She lit a candle but it guttered in the breeze and she set it down on the washstand, away from the draught. Its flame lengthened and seemed to grow brighter, illuminating the portrait of the young woman hanging from the picture rail. Tired and emotionally drained, Kate found herself staring at the youthful face with the large wistful blue eyes, but it was the left hand of the lady that caught her eye. In particular it was the emerald and diamond ring in the unusual heart shape that fixed her attention. She glanced down at her right hand, where she now wore her mother's engagement ring, and gasped in amazement.

She stood for a moment in a state of shock and disbelief. Surely it must be a coincidence, and yet she had felt a strange affinity with the portrait from the first moment she had seen it. She reached out and traced the outline of the girl's rounded cheek, and the tender lips that smiled gently at her as if acknowledging the inescapable truth. She took a step backwards, shaking her head. Could it be that the answer had been here all the time? Had some strange quirk of fate brought her to this house? There was only one person who might be able to answer those questions.

She left the quiet serenity of her room and ran downstairs. There was no sign of John in the drawing room or the morning parlour and she went next to his study. She knocked on the door, entering without waiting for a response. This was not the time to stand on ceremony. It was as though her whole life depended on what happened in the next few minutes.

He was seated at his desk poring over some papers, but he looked up as she burst into the room. 'Kate, my dear. Is something wrong?'

She held out her right hand. 'Take a good look at this ring. Have you ever seen it before?'

Chapter Twenty-five

John rose slowly to his feet. 'It certainly looks familiar. How did this piece of jewellery come into your possession?'

The mere fact that he seemed to recognise the ring was enough to send her senses whirling. She was not certain what she had expected him to say, but now she felt dizzy with expectation. 'I – it's a long story,' she murmured.

He guided her to a nearby chair. 'Sit down, my dear. You look as though you've seen a ghost.'

'Perhaps I have, John.' She stared down at the emerald surrounded by tiny diamonds. 'The portrait in my room.' She held her hand towards him. 'It's the same ring.'

He perched on the edge of his desk, peering at her through the thick lenses of his spectacles. 'It looks quite similar. But you haven't answered my question. Where did you get it?'

'Did Harry tell you about Josie and the Romany queen?'

He nodded. 'Briefly, but Charlie had already told me as much of the story as he knew. My heart aches for the poor girl, and I can see that you are also very troubled.'

'It was the Romany queen who gave me the ring.' Kate hesitated, feeling suddenly faint. 'May I have a glass of water?'

'Of course.' He reached across the desk to tug at the bell pull. 'Take your time, Kate. Tell me everything.'

Once she had begun the words came flooding out. She told him everything she knew about herself and how her past and Josie's had been intertwined from birth. He listened intently and when she had finished speaking he took both her hands in his. 'I can't be absolutely certain, but I would say that this ring is identical to the engagement ring that Alexander Carstairs gave to my sister Clara on her eighteenth birthday. It was a family heirloom, commissioned for his grandmother from Rundell and Bridge. There are unlikely to be two the same.'

'The Romany queen told me that my father was named Alexander, and that he was killed in the Crimea. Surely that can't be a coincidence?'

John stroked his chin, frowning. 'And your name is Kate, presumably short for Katherine?'

'My mother's dying wish was that I be named after her mother.'

'My mother was also called Katherine. But my poor Clara died in a sanatorium in Switzerland. She couldn't have borne a child, and yet . . .' His eyes searched Kate's face. 'I always felt a fondness for you, Kate, but I . . .' He broke off, turning his head away.

Touched beyond measure, Kate was close to tears. 'I want it to be true, but it would be impossible to prove one way or the other.'

He met her anxious gaze with a steady look. 'I was a blind fool not to have seen it before, Kate. The resemblance between you and Clara is marked. The old saying that blood is thicker than water is certainly true in this case. My dear girl, I can't tell you how happy you've just made me.' He knelt beside her, raising her hand to his cheek and smiling.

'I c-can't believe it,' Kate murmured. 'I always thought I was Robert Coggins' daughter, and when that woman turned him against me I was so deeply hurt, but now I understand him a little better. He loved me as much as he was able – his cuckoo in the nest.'

Just at that moment, Mrs Trevett marched into the room and stopped short when she saw them, clearing her throat loudly. 'You rang, sir?' Her voice vibrated with disapproval.

John rose somewhat unsteadily to his feet. 'Yes, Mary. I was going to ask you to bring a glass of water for Miss Coggins, but perhaps I should change that to champagne.'

'You're pleased to make a joke of things, your reverence. But supper is served in the morning parlour. Will the young person be joining you after all?'

'Yes, Mary. Thank you.'

'Very good, sir. I'll tell Hester to lay another place.' Mrs Trevett sniffed and turned on her heel, every inch of her body quivering with affront as she left the room.

Kate stifled a giggle. 'Oh, dear. Whatever will she think?'

'The worst, I'm afraid, but it doesn't matter, Kate. She'll understand when we reveal the truth of the matter.'

'Perhaps it would be better to keep it to ourselves, at least until Josie is more herself?'

'I agree. Moreover, I want to take you to meet my elder brother, Sir Philip Hardy and his wife, Marjorie. They live on the family estate near Wareham. If anyone can shed a light on what happened to poor Clara, I have a feeling my brother will be that person.'

Kate glanced down at her shabby, much-darned gown. 'I can't go anywhere like this.' She frowned as the practicalities of their situation became clear to her. 'Josie has only the clothes she is wearing. She left everything behind when she ran away to join the gypsies.'

'Don't worry, my dear. I may not have had the advantage of being a married man, but I realised last night that you travelled very light. Harry told me that he planned to visit Damerell Manor to tell the family that Josie was safe and well, and I suggested that he might ask the Dowager Lady Damerell to instruct a servant to pack a few things and send them here.'

'You think of everything, John.'

'It comes with the job, Kate. A country parson has to deal not only in the spiritual side of things but also in the practical.'

First thing next morning Smith, the coachman from Damerell Manor, arrived bringing with him a large brass-bound cabin trunk filled with Josie's belongings. It took the combined efforts of Hester, Mrs Trevett and the stable boy to heave, push and pull it upstairs to Kate's room. Since Josie declared no interest in what she would wear that day or any other until Sam returned from the dead, Kate unpacked the garments and put them away in the antique clothes press which stood in the corner of her own room. She set aside one of Josie's less ornate gowns in a fresh cotton print, but when she asked if she might borrow it Josie turned her face away telling her she could have the whole lot if only she would leave her to mourn in peace. Kate's patience was tested to the limit. She felt like shaking Josie and telling her to pull herself together but instead she walked away, leaving her to wallow in self pity.

John had sent for Dr Drago, and when he finally came, explaining that he had been attending an urgent case, he examined Josie, agreeing that a mild sedative was probably the most efficacious form of treatment for her at this particular time. He sniffed the bottle of elixir that Dena had made up and tasted it, nodding his head. 'This herbal brew won't harm her, and if it is doing her good I see no reason to prescribe laudanum, which can become quite addictive in this type of case.'

'She is naturally very upset,' Kate said. 'She feels things deeply, but she will recover soon, I hope.'

He sucked in his cheeks, shaking his head. 'I have seen young ladies simply turn their faces to the wall and pine away for a lost love. We don't want that to happen to Miss Damerell. Even the strongest amongst us can collapse under severe emotional strain. Keep her quiet and sedated and let nature do the rest.'

'Don't worry, David,' John said, showing him to the door. 'Miss Damerell will receive the best care possible.'

Kate was suddenly anxious as feelings of guilt assailed her. She had been impatient with Josie when she should have shown more understanding. 'Maybe we should postpone our visit to your brother's house, John? I think I ought to stay with Josie.'

'I don't think that's necessary. Molly can sit with her in our absence. After all, it is her brother who is presumed drowned, although she seems to be taking it extremely well.'

Kate said nothing, but she knew that Molly's apparent lack of concern was due to the fact that she steadfastly refused to believe that Sam was dead. Kate could only hope that she was right.

When it was put to her, Molly was only too happy to sit with Josie, leaving Kate and John free to visit the Hardy family home. Kate rushed up to her room to change out of her workaday clothes. The print gown fitted as though it had been made for her, and she borrowed one of Josie's straw bonnets trimmed with pink satin ribbons. Draping a lacy shawl crocheted from the finest lambswool around her shoulders, she hurried downstairs to find Mrs Trevett standing by the open front door, arms folded and lips set in a thin line. 'The Reverend is waiting for you,' she said, bristling with disapproval.

Kate murmured her thanks and ran down the path to where John was waiting beside the gig. She was not certain whether she was shaking from terror or excitement at the prospect of meeting Sir Philip and his wife, but she had a feeling that something momentous was about to happen. She knew she was smiling like an idiot, but it was almost impossible to remain calm. One look at Mrs Trevett, who was standing in the doorway, glaring at them, was enough to bring her back to earth with a bump.

'I'm sure that your housekeeper thinks there is something going on between us, John.'

He helped her into the vehicle. 'Mary has been with me for so long that she thinks she owns me, but she means well.' He climbed up to sit beside her and flicked the reins.

Kate clutched the side of the gig as it swayed into motion. 'I'm sure she does, and I don't blame her for being protective towards you, but I'd rather we kept this to ourselves, John. If Puddlecombe is anything like Kingston Damerell, rumours spread faster than a heath fire.'

'Don't worry, Kate. We'll tell everyone when we are good and ready.'

She sat in silence while he drove through the village, tipping his hat to his parishioners and greeting them cheerfully. She could see that he was a popular priest and much respected, and a warm feeling of belonging enveloped her. A playful breeze tugged at the ribbons on her bonnet and the azure sky above them was cloudless. The fields were filled with ripening corn and Kate breathed in the plum-pudding scent of the damp earth beneath the green hedgerows. It was a glorious summer day and she felt as though her life was just beginning. John was convinced that she was his flesh and blood, but much depended on how she was received by the head of the family.

'We're here,' he said, as he reined in the horse and the gig ground to a halt outside a pair of tall wrought-iron gates. Peering through them she could see a long avenue leading up to an imposing building. The gatekeeper emerged from his cottage and unlocked the great iron gates, waving them through with a respectful bow.

The parkland seemed to stretch as far as the eye could see and beyond. Deer grazed beneath stalwart oaks and Kate caught a glimpse of formal gardens through a topiary arch at the side of the Jacobean mansion. 'This is your family home?'

John turned to look at her and he smiled. 'Our family home, my dear. In a few moments I will introduce you to Philip and Marjorie, and I hope that we will get some answers to our questions.'

Kate was even more nervous and slightly overwhelmed as they entered the great house. So much depended upon what she would learn from Sir Philip and Lady Hardy. Her whole future was hanging in the balance. Would she emerge as Kate Hardy or Miss Nobody?

Seeming to sense her anxiety, John slipped her hand through the crook of his arm, giving it a gentle squeeze. 'Chin up, my dear. They won't bite.'

She twisted her lips into a smile, but she really did feel as though she were entering the lion's den as she stepped into the oak-panelled entrance hall. But despite the grandeur of its architecture, she was surprised to find that the mansion had a warm and welcoming atmosphere. The great fireplace, which in winter would greet visitors with a welcoming blaze, was partly concealed by a needlepoint fire screen. Copper pots filled with roses, delphiniums and lilies made bright splashes of colour against the dark oak panelling. Highly polished suits of armour stood guard at the foot of the staircase, but even they had a benign appearance. Crossed swords and shields decorated the wall above the fireplace and portraits of long dead ancestors stared at Kate from gilded frames.

Their feet echoed on the darkly gleaming floorboards as the butler showed them into the drawing room. A Great Dane lumbered towards them, sniffing at John's hands, obviously recognising a friend, and Sir Philip rose from his seat by the carved stone fireplace. 'John, this is a pleasant surprise, and I see you've brought a guest with you.'

Sir Philip Hardy was so like his brother that they might have been twins. Kate took an instant liking to him, although she was not quite so certain about his wife. Marjorie Hardy was reserved to say the least. When Kate had been formally introduced and the usual civilities exchanged, John explained the reason for their visit. Sir Philip seemed stunned at first and then shocked. Lady Hardy appeared unconvinced. 'It seems that there are far too many coincidences,' she said, eyeing Kate with unconcealed suspicion. 'And poor dear Clara died of consumption in a Swiss sanatorium, so I am afraid you must have been misled, young lady.'

'Did she, though?' John turned to his brother. 'I wasn't here when Clara was sent away, but you were, Philip. Did she go to Switzerland?'

435

'Of course she did, John,' Lady Hardy said hastily, before her husband could open his mouth. She gave Kate a penetrating stare. 'Have you any proof of your identity?'

Kate took off her mother's engagement ring and handed it to her. 'No, ma'am. I only have this ring, which the Romany woman gave me just a short while ago. She told me that my mother had asked her to keep it safe for me.'

'Huh! A likely story coming from a gypsy. If it is Clara's ring, then it was probably stolen and the whole tale fabricated to extract money from us.'

'Let me see the ring, my dear,' Sir Philip said, holding out his hand. 'If this is Clara's ring, it was a family heirloom made for Alexander's grandmother, Lavinia, and I seem to remember that it was engraved with her initials.'

Lady Hardy squinted at the inside of the ring. 'I cannot see anything other than a hallmark, Philip. I think the whole story is a farrago of lies.' She tossed the ring at him and he caught it deftly in one hand.

'My eyesight isn't what it was, but I'm sure I can make out the initials,' he said, holding the ring up to the light. 'This certainly looks like poor Clara's engagement ring.'

'But it could have been stolen,' Lady Hardy insisted. 'You men are so easily deceived, and it doesn't alter that fact that Clara was mortally ill. It's insulting to the dear girl's memory to suspect that she had had an illicit liaison with Alexander and bore a child out of wedlock, quite unthinkable in a girl of her breeding.'

Kate dug her fingernails into her palms, holding her tongue with difficulty, but John laid his hand on hers with an encouraging smile. 'Don't be upset, my dear. We will get to the bottom of this, and I think Philip holds the key.'

'I'm afraid it's true, Marjorie,' Sir Philip said with a sigh. 'Clara and Alexander were engaged to be married and then that trouble broke out in the Crimea. As Alex was a serving officer it was inevitable that he would be called upon to fight. They wanted to bring the wedding forward but Papa put his foot down and forbade it. He said that he didn't want his only daughter widowed before she was twenty, and so Alexander had no choice but to leave for the Crimea with his regiment. I'll never forget the day when the news of his death in battle reached us. Poor Clara was beside herself with grief. She was so distraught, we feared she might lose her mind. She took to her bed and the doctor was sent for. He told our parents that Clara was with child.'

'Philip!' Lady Hardy exclaimed angrily. 'How could you have kept this from me for all these years? How could you allow me to go on believing that Clara died of consumption?'

'I'm sorry, my dear, but my parents were as one in their decision that the birth must be concealed from the world. They knew that no man of any consequence would want to marry Clara when they learned of her disgrace. They decided that she must be sent away, and the child, when born, should be adopted by some respectable family whose silence could be bought.'

437

John stared as his brother in disbelief. 'And you even kept it from me?'

'You were at Oxford, John. You were sitting your finals and Papa did not want to involve you, especially in view of your chosen profession. I wasn't consulted in the matter.'

'I understand, old chap. But how did Clara come to be wandering about alone, at night and exposed to the elements? If it hadn't been for the Romany women, she would have given birth on that hillside with no one to help her. Kate would have died too in all probability.'

'And the sad story would have also died,' Lady Hardy said acidly. 'Now it will all come to light and the scandal will be terrible. I won't have my children suffer for what Clara did all those years ago.'

'My dear, you're over-reacting,' Sir Philip said mildly. 'Helena and James will be delighted to discover they have a cousin.'

'You fool,' Lady Hardy hissed. 'Do you think that anyone of note will want their sons and daughters to marry into our family if word of Clara's fall from grace comes to light?'

Kate could stand it no longer. She leapt to her feet and faced them all with her hands clenched at her sides. 'Shame on you. Have you no thought for the poor young woman who was turned out by her family and died in that lonely place? What must she have suffered?'

'Believe me, Kate, if I had known any of this the outcome would have been different.' John's voice cracked with emotion. 'I loved Clara; she was the dearest, sweetest sister any man could have. I would have left Oxford and forsworn the Church if it had meant that I could care for Clara and her child.'

'And I tried to find her,' Sir Philip added hastily. 'Clara was sent to stay with her old governess in a village near Weymouth, and arrangements were made for her child to be adopted. Then I received a letter from her, shortly before she disappeared. She begged me to come for her and to find her a cottage or lodgings where she could have her baby and keep it. Alas, I didn't receive the letter until it was too late. I rode to Upwey where the governess lived, but she said that Clara had gone missing the previous day. She had sent men out to look for her without any luck. I too scoured the countryside, but in the end I had to return empty-handed. It seemed that Clara had vanished into thin air.'

'No,' Kate said slowly. 'She died giving birth to me and is buried somewhere on a cold, lonely hilltop without anything to mark her grave; only the gypsies know for certain where she lies. I don't know how you can live with yourself, Sir Philip. You stood by and allowed your family to crucify my mother and her only crime was that of loving the man she intended to marry. I'm ashamed to be part of this family. I would rather be plain Kate Coggins than be accepted by those who treated my mother so cruelly.'

No one spoke and all eyes were upon her. Kate faced them with a defiant toss of her head. She had never

been so angry in her whole life. She could feel her
mother's presence in the room; it was so real that she
could almost reach out and touch her. 'You killed her,'
she said slowly. 'All of you were in part responsible
for her death. I don't know how you can live with
yourselves.'

Lady Hardy opened her mouth and closed it again.
She looked to her husband, but Sir Philip and John
were staring at Kate.

John was the first to speak. 'There. Do you doubt
it now, Philip? That could have been Clara speaking.'

'I am convinced,' Sir Philip said, rising to his feet
and walking towards Kate with outstretched hands.
'If I had any doubts initially, they are gone now. What
you say is true, Kate. Perhaps I could have done more
to save my little sister, I don't know, but I've mourned
her loss every day for the last twenty years. Can you
ever forgive me, my dear?'

She went into his arms and he held her in a close
embrace. 'I should not have said those things, Uncle.'

He held her at arm's length, smiling. 'Uncle! That
has a nice ring to it. Welcome home, Kate.'

John clapped him on the back. 'Well said, Philip.'

'Aren't you forgetting one thing?' Lady Hardy rose
to her feet.

Sir Philip turned to her, his smile fading. 'What's
that, Marjorie?'

'The girl might be Clara's daughter, but she is still
illegitimate – a living reminder of Clara's disgrace. No
decent man will want to marry her and she will ruin
our daughter's chances into the bargain. Think of the

scandal. Think of our good name. You must not acknowledge her, Philip. I forbid it.'

'She will come round,' John said, urging the horse into a trot as they drove away from the family home. 'Marjorie isn't a bad person, Kate. I daresay it was the shock speaking.'

'She didn't like me,' Kate said. 'She made that quite clear.'

'My sister-in-law may have slightly old-fashioned ideas, but give her time and she will see sense.'

'I don't know about that, John. If the family recog nises me, they will have to acknowledge an old scandal. I do understand that, and I can't blame Lady Hardy for putting her own children first.'

'I think you're worrying unnecessarily, my dear. Helena and James won't give a second thought to the circumstances of your birth, of that I am certain.'

'I hope not.' Kate fingered the emerald, staring into its green depths and the diamonds winking and sparkling in the sunlight. 'But whatever happens, I am glad that I know more about my mother. I'm just sorry that she suffered so much, and it hurts my heart to know that I was responsible for her death.'

'No, I won't have that, Kate. It wasn't your fault, and Clara loved you even before you were born. She must have been desperate to keep you, and that's why she ran away. She would have been so proud had she lived to see you grow to womanhood. One day you will have a daughter of your own, and you will understand.'

Kate shook her head. 'I shan't marry. You heard

what Lady Hardy said. I'm illegitimate – no decent man will look at me twice. At least,' she added with a wry smile, 'not with marriage on his mind.'

'You haven't lost your sense of humour,' he said, reaching over to pat her hand. 'That's all to the good, and I think there is a man of some standing who would not give your circumstances a second thought.'

Kate stared at his profile as he concentrated on the road ahead. 'And who might that be?'

'A blind man could see that my good friend Harry is head over heels in love with you. And I think that you love him too.'

'It doesn't matter how I feel. The circumstances of my birth would always come between us.'

'But, Kate . . .'

'No, my mind is made up. Please don't tell anyone about this, not even Josie. I'll stay until we know for certain what happened to Sam, but when Josie is fully recovered, I'll look for work somewhere far away from here. If I can't find anything else, I might even accept the position of companion to Squire Westwood's horrible daughters, but that won't include accepting his offer of marriage. I'd rather die.'

'My dear girl, I think you're taking this all the wrong way.'

'No, John. I'm being realistic. I must make my way on my own.'

'There are many of us who love you. You can stay at the vicarage for as long as you want. Forever, if you wish.'

'And what would your bishop think if he knew my history?' Kate chuckled in spite of everything. 'And Mrs Trevett might have something to say if I sullied the name of the Reverend John Hardy.'

'Ah, yes. Mrs Trevett. We must not upset her, must we?' He threw back his head and laughed. 'We'll say nothing for the present, but the truth will out, and the sooner the better, in my opinion.' His smile faded and he gave her a searching look. 'I've heard your reasoning, Kate, but now that my brother has confirmed the gypsy's account of events, I don't entirely understand why you want to keep this news from those closest to you, especially Harry.'

She clasped her hands tightly, staring at the road ahead with unseeing eyes. 'I'm no good for him.'

'Shouldn't he be the judge of that?'

'He's never spoken to me of love, and he was engaged to Josie. He must have had some feelings for her, because I don't believe he would marry simply to further his ambitions. His passing fancy for me would fade away if he did the right thing by her. If she were to go home now I'm sure she'd be welcomed with open arms. With all that wealth and the protection of her family name the scandal surrounding her birth would soon be forgotten. It's different for someone like me. The same rules don't apply.'

He flicked the reins so that the horse moved on at a trot. 'I don't agree with you, Kate. I think you're making a terrible mistake, even though I admire your selflessness. You are my niece, I'm absolutely certain of that. You are my dear sister's only child and I want

443

to see you happy. Don't throw away your chance because of misplaced loyalty. Josie is much stronger than you think. Can't you see that she's manipulating us all, even as we speak?'

'No,' Kate cried passionately. 'That's not fair. She's loved Sam since we were children. Her heart is breaking and I owe it to him to look after her.' She held onto her bonnet as they rounded the corner at an unnecessarily fast speed, narrowly missing a rider approaching from the opposite direction. Both horses came to a stop outside the vicarage and the rider, a messenger in uniform, leapt to the ground, shaking his fist at John.

'What sort of speed is that, guvner? You could have killed me.'

Visibly shaken, John climbed slowly from the driver's seat. 'I apologise for a momentary lapse of concentration on my part.'

The realisation that he was addressing a man of the cloth dawned on the man, and his expression changed subtly. He doffed his cap. 'Begging your pardon, your reverence, but you was driving like a madman.' He pulled a packet from his inside pocket. 'I've got a message for a Miss Kate Coggins. I was to see that she gets this urgent like.'

Chapter Twenty-six

While the messenger was revived with hot tea and slices of Mrs Trevett's apple cake in the kitchen, Kate took the sealed packet into the garden where she sat on the wooden bench in the shade of the oak tree and opened it with trembling fingers. She had known at once that it must have come from Harry, but as she studied the closely written copperplate her feeling of relief was swiftly followed by disappointment. She was delighted to have news of him but disappointed by the tone of the letter, which was formal and to the point. He might as well have been addressing a board meeting rather than writing to the woman who loved him with all her being.

After the briefest of introductions, he went into a detailed account of the information he had discovered about the wreck of the *Kimmeridge*, which had been blown off course during a terrible storm and dashed on the rocks in Cobo Bay. It was thought, he wrote, that all hands had been lost, but it was just possible that some might have been swept ashore and cared for by local families. At least Sam's name was not on the list of bodies that had so far been identified. There were some whose identity still remained a mystery, but Harry was certain that none of them fitted Sam's description. He concluded with a promise to keep up the search until there was proof either way, signing himself, Your devoted friend, Harry Challenor.

She sighed, folding the letter and tucking it into her pocket. The only comfort she could draw from it was that he had written to her and not to Josie, but even that could be easily explained. He had known of Josie's delicate mental state and he would not have wanted to distress her further. She looked up as she heard soft footfalls on the grass and saw John walking slowly towards her.

'Is it bad news?'

She shook her head. 'Not exactly, but Harry still hasn't found any trace of Sam.'

'Then there is still hope. I think you ought to go and tell Josie. She must face up to reality sooner or later.'

Kate stared at him in surprise. She was well aware that he had harboured tender feelings for Josie in the past, but this was the second time that he had criticised her behaviour. 'Are you sure that's a good idea? I mean, the doctor said . . .'

'David is an old fusspot.' He smiled gently. 'I believe that we must all take responsibility for our own actions, and much as I care for Josie, I think she has been pampered and pandered to for most of her young life. She's no longer a child and I think she ought to start behaving like a responsible adult, instead of running you and Molly ragged.' He patted her hand. 'Go to her, Kate, and don't stand any nonsense. Remember that you are a Hardy by birth. You are subordinate to no one, except perhaps her majesty the Queen.'

Kate rose to her feet and kissed him on the cheek. 'Thank you, Uncle. I'll try to remember that.'

Surprisingly, Kate's sudden change in attitude seemed to spark some kind of reaction from Josie. Whether it was surprise or curiosity, she sat up in bed and demanded to read the letter for herself. Then, putting her head on one side like an inquisitive robin, she wanted to know what had occurred to make Kate think she could boss her about. She would not let it rest until she was told everything down to the last detail.

'Well, you are a dark horse,' she said, chuckling. 'So I really am the gypsy's child and you really were born a lady. Who would have thought it?'

Kate stared at her in amazement. 'I'm glad you think it's amusing, but as far as I can see we're equals. We were both born on the wrong side of the blanket, although your misfortune need never become general knowledge if you choose to return home.'

'Everyone in the village knows about me, and probably far beyond.' Josie threw back the bedcovers. 'Anyway, I won't live under the same roof as that dreadful creature, even if he is my father.'

'But Lady Damerell must be broken-hearted. She adored you, Josie. Haven't you any feeling for the woman you thought was your mother?'

'Of course I have, but I always knew I was different, and now I understand why that was. I can't go back, Kate.'

'Not even if it means you could have Harry? If you marry him you would be mistress of Copperstone Castle. Isn't that what you always wanted?'

Swinging her legs over the side of the bed, Josie planted her feet squarely on the floor. 'I thought it was, but now I realise that I was deluding myself. All I really want is to spend my life with Sam. If he's dead then I don't care what happens to me. I'll go to Devon and join my people. I was never meant to be a lady, Kate, but you were. I know how you feel about Harry, and, as far as I'm concerned, he's all yours.' She stared at Kate's gown. 'Isn't that one of mine?'

'It is and I asked your permission to borrow it, but you said you didn't care.'

'It looks better on you anyway. You can have it. Where are my clothes? Ring for Molly, there's a lamb. I feel like getting dressed and I'm starving.'

This was so like the old Josie that it made Kate laugh. 'You're incorrigible, Josie Damerell. And please remember that Molly isn't your servant.'

'No. She's my devoted slave.' Josie stood up and reached for the bell pull. 'I don't want that Hester person anywhere near me. She has hands like a bare-knuckle fighter and breath that would stun a donkey. I think I'll come down to dinner tonight. Will you tell John? I'm sure he'll be delighted to see me up and about.'

Kate made a move towards the door. 'Don't you dare flirt with my poor uncle. You almost broke his heart last time we were here, although I believe he's recovered now. I think he's seen through you at last.'

Josie tossed her head. 'Well, I don't intend to stay here much longer, so you needn't worry about him.'

'What are you planning in that devious mind of yours, Josie?'

'Harry says in his letter that he's returning soon. I'll insist that he takes me to Guernsey so that I can search for Sam. I haven't any money for the trip, but he has plenty. I think he owes me that much.'

'He owes you nothing. It was you who broke off the engagement.'

'And he should thank me for that. He never loved me. I was a ninny to think that wealth and position meant everything, but I've learned my lesson. Now where is that girl? And you'd better choose another of my gowns, Kate. You can't come down to dinner looking like a milkmaid. Did Hickson pack my peach tussore? I think that would suit you nicely and it makes me look quite sallow.'

With Josie fully recovered it was just a question of awaiting Harry's return. The hours could not go fast enough for Kate, but after a day or two the strain was beginning to tell. Everyone else had gone to Matins on Sunday morning, but Kate had slept badly and had awakened with a headache. She would have accompanied them to church, but John insisted that she stay at home and rest. Unable to sit and do nothing, she was darning a hole in one of her stockings when a loud knocking on the front door startled her so much that she pricked her finger on the needle. She set aside the mending and went to answer the urgent summons.

'Kate, I heard you was here.' Robert stood on the doorstep, clutching the bowler hat that Honoria had insisted was more fitting for a man in his position than a cap. He shifted from one foot to the other. His face was flushed and beads of sweat stood out on his brow. His Sunday best suit fitted so tightly round his corpulent belly that the buttons strained and seemed in imminent danger of flying off in all directions.

'You'd best come in,' she said, holding the door open. 'What do you want?'

He stepped inside. 'Can we talk in private, maidy?'

'Come into the parlour.' She led the way in silence, waiting to speak until he was seated somewhat uncomfortably on the edge of a chair. 'Can I get you some refreshment?'

He stared up at her with a sorrowful expression. 'Time was when you called me Pa.'

'You turned me out of the house to please Honoria. Why have you come here now?'

'I've come to beg your pardon, Kate. I wronged you, and all because of that woman.'

She took a seat opposite him. 'Do you mean Honoria?'

'I was an old fool, maidy. Taken in by her flirty ways and flattered that a younger woman wanted me. But she tricked me – led me up the garden path, she did.'

'So what happened?'

He reached out and clasped her hands in his. 'The child was not mine. She had been with a man afore she went with me. The long and the short of it is that he come for her the day afore yesterday. His regiment had just returned to Dorchester barracks and he come riding into the farmyard on a big black horse in his scarlet uniform with brass buttons a-blazing like the sun. For two pins, I think he would have run me through with his sword, but then Honoria goes all limp and floppy-like, swooning in his arms and telling him as how she thought he had deserted her. That woman could have earned her living on the stage, she could. Then she turns on me: "You poor old fool," says she. "Do you really think I'd choose you over my brave army sergeant? I had to have a father for my baby and so I married you." Then he steps forward, grabs me by the throat, and tells me that we wasn't married at all. He had married her a full year before I even asked her to step out with me.' Robert hung his head and his tears splashed onto Kate's fingers.

She saw him then as he had always been: her kindly Pa who had raised her as his own. Even in the bad old days when his drinking had sometimes led him to extremes of temper, she had known that he loved her. She threw herself down on her knees and hugged him. 'Oh, Pa, I am so sorry. Truly, I am. You didn't deserve such treatment.'

He wiped his eyes on his sleeve. 'I was a besotted old fool, Kate. I treated you bad. Can you ever forgive me?'

'Of course I can, Pa.' She released him, allowing herself to smile for the first time since he had arrived. 'You were a good father to me, until Honoria came into our lives.'

'I'm sure I don't deserve your forgiveness, maidy, after what I did to you.'

'I know that you always loved me, Pa. You raised me, and if you hadn't come looking for me I might have been murdered on the road to Dorchester. You just married the wrong woman and I'm glad she's gone, but I'm sorry she took your son.'

'I never had a son. Like I said afore, it was his, the big burly army sergeant's, and she wasn't in the family way for a second time neither. That was all part of her scheming to get you out of the house. I only ever had one child, and that is you, Kate.'

She rose to her feet. 'I'm going to make you a nice cup of tea. And then you can stay for Sunday luncheon and meet the Reverend John Hardy, who has been kindness itself.'

'Thank you, but no.' Robert stood up, reaching for his hat. 'I've made my peace with you, maidy, so I'll be on my way. I can't face other folk, not just yet.'

She laid her hand on his arm, gazing anxiously into his face. 'But you will be all right, won't you?'

'I will, in time.' He managed a crooked smile. 'And if you ever wants to come home, you'll be as welcome as the first swallow in summer.' He hesitated on the doorstep. 'And maybe you could sort out that mad Nanny Barnes. Sir Joseph has put her in the pigman's cottage because she was driving them all daft up at the big house. Now she haunts me day and night, sometimes turning up in her nightgown or taking a bath in the cattle trough with all her clothes on. I'd give anything to have you and young Molly back on the farm, if only to take her in hand.'

'I'm sure that Molly would be glad to have the cottage back, Pa. Nanny Barnes just needs company, that's all.'

'And I'll always need you, daughter,' he said gruffly. 'Remember that.'

She reached up to kiss him on the cheek, but she could not bring herself to tell him that she knew the truth about her parentage; that would keep until another time. When all was said and done, Robert Coggins was her father and always would be. She owed him a debt of gratitude and love. Her real parents were simply shadows from the past. Their sad story would always be a part of her, but they were as much strangers to her as were Sir Philip and Lady Hardy. She would always be glad that she had met and come to know John, but she was still Kate Coggins at heart. She waved goodbye, feeling suddenly at peace.

She did not mention Robert's visit when everyone returned from church. Josie appeared to be in a buoyant mood, and Kate did not want to spoil things by reminding her of times past. John went straight to his study and Josie sent Molly to the kitchen to fetch a jug of lemonade. She drew Kate aside. 'Guess what?'

Kate shook her head.

'Harry's back at Copperstone. Charlie Beauchamp was in church and he told me afterwards that Harry had returned last evening. I'll lay odds that he'll visit us before the day's out. If he doesn't come today I'll borrow John's horse and ride over to Copperstone and demand that he take me to Guernsey. You'll have to come too, or it will look very odd.' She took off her bonnet and tossed it so that it landed on the hall stand. 'Pack a few things in readiness, Kate. I have a good feeling about this. Perhaps I've inherited some of

Dena's second sight.' She danced away, leaving Kate standing in the hall. The thought of seeing Harry again filled her with misgivings. Suddenly she wanted to go home. She longed for nothing more than to disappear into the anonymity of living and working on the farm.

She barely managed to eat a thing at luncheon, but Josie ate ravenously and Molly ran her a close second. John hurried through his meal and retired to his study to prepare for Evensong. Having scraped her plate clean, Molly decided that she would go for a walk, but Josie said that she did not feel very energetic and had decided to while away the afternoon playing the pianoforte. 'One of the few things I miss from home,' she said as she parted from them in the hallway.

'Well I want some fresh air.' Molly rammed her bonnet on her head and rushed out into the sunshine.

Kate followed at a slower pace, heading for her favourite spot beneath the oak tree. She sat on the bench, closing her eyes and listening to the strains of a Chopin waltz floating through the open drawing room windows. The music, together with the hypnotic sound of bees buzzing in the rose bushes, gradually lulled her to sleep.

'I hope they're sweet dreams, Kate.'

The sound of Harry's voice awakened her with a start. She leapt to her feet. 'How long have you been standing there?'

'I'm sorry. I didn't mean to wake you, but you make such a pretty picture with the sunlight shining on your hair. I couldn't take my eyes off you.'

She felt the blood rushing to her cheeks. 'You are

such a tease, Harry. My shoes are dusty and my hair is all over the place, and . . .'

'Kate, you are quite adorable as you are.' He did not let her finish her sentence. He swept her into his arms, holding her so tightly that she could scarcely breathe. He brushed her lips with kisses until they parted with a sigh. She slid her arms around his neck and gave herself up to the sweet sensation of their first kiss, returning his embrace with an ardour that both surprised and shocked her. He drew away just enough to allow her to catch her breath and his eyes were dark with desire. 'I've wanted to kiss you for so long, Kate. You wouldn't believe how much willpower I have had to employ to stop myself from doing just this.'

She was drunk with delight. She felt as if her head was in the clouds. She ought to resist, but being held in Harry's arms was like coming home. She laid her head against his shoulder with a deep sigh of contentment. Her heart was so full that she couldn't speak.

'I love you, Kate. I've loved you for a very long time but I couldn't say anything before. Now I know that Josie is genuinely devoted to Loveday and expects nothing from me, I'm free at last to tell you how I feel.'

Reality smote her like a thunderbolt and she raised her head to look him in the eyes. 'This is all wrong, Harry.'

'Why do you say that? There is nothing to keep us apart now I know that you love me. You do, don't you?' A frown creased his brow, but he held her so close to him that she was not sure whether it was his

455

heart she could feel thudding against her breast, or whether it was her own.

She tried to pull away from him but his arms held her like bands of steel. 'I do love you, Harry. But there are things that you don't know about me.'

'I know that I worship you, Kate. Isn't that enough?'

'No, it isn't. I mean – please, Harry, just take my word for it. There can never be anything more than loving friendship between us.'

'That is the most ridiculous thing I've ever heard. I love you to distraction, I can't get you out of my mind, and I think you feel the same about me. Why, for God's sake, are you putting obstacles in our way? I want to marry you, Kate. I want you with me for now and always. Do you understand?' He held her by the shoulders, giving her a gentle shake.

'You don't understand . . .'

'I bloody well don't understand, and I'm not apologising for swearing. What in hell's name could keep us apart?' His fingers dug into her shoulders and his eyes hardened. 'Unless you are already married? You didn't have a change of heart and accept Westwood, did you? You haven't secretly married the damn fellow in my absence?'

'No, never. It's not that.'

His tone gentled and the angry look faded from his eyes. 'Then what, sweetheart? What is so terrible that you cannot accept me as your husband?'

'I've only just found out who I really am. I was born out of wedlock. The Coggins brought me up but I wasn't their child.'

456

He drew her back into the haven of his arms. 'Is that all? Have you been resisting me because of a stupid convention? Do you really think I care about details like that?'

'You – you don't mind?' She blinked hard; surely she was dreaming? He looked almost boyish in his enthusiasm as he clasped her hands, lifting them to his lips and kissing them.

'I don't care who your parents were or whether you were born in or out of wedlock. I want to marry you, Kate, not them.'

'Good man. I knew you were a fine fellow, Harry.'

Kate spun round to see John standing a little way from them down the path with Josie leaning on his arm. Both of them were smiling. 'You've been listening,' she breathed. 'How could you?'

John held up his hands. 'No, believe me, Kate. We only heard Harry's last words to you, and I wanted to applaud his good sense.'

'It was my fault,' Josie said hastily. 'I saw you from the window. When Harry kissed you I knew that you had sorted yourselves out at last. We came out to congratulate you.' She ran to Kate, hugging her until she could hardly breathe. 'I am so happy for you.'

'You don't understand,' Kate said, pulling away from her. 'I've just told Harry that I can't marry him.'

'And I won't accept that.' Harry caught her by the hand. 'I don't care if your parents were tinkers, tranters or felons – I love you, Kate, and I want to marry you.'

'And you have my blessing,' John said, laying a hand on each of their shoulders. 'Kate, if you don't tell him that I am your uncle . . .' He broke off, laughing. 'Oh dear! I've let the cat out of the meta-phorical bag.'

'Uncle?' Harry stared at him in astonishment.

'It's a long story,' John said, nodding. 'I suggest we go indoors out of the hot sun and allow Kate to tell you everything we discovered about her past, and how we are connected.'

Harry slipped his arm around Kate's waist. 'With all due respect, John, I think this is between the two of us. Come, Kate, we'll go for a walk by the river and you can tell me in your own way.'

It was over an hour later when they returned to the vicarage. They entered the drawing room, hand in hand.

Josie leapt to her feet and ran to them. 'Well, then? What's the news? Are we to congratulate you?'

Kate felt herself blushing. 'Yes.'

'I am so happy for you both,' Josie cried, flinging her arms around Kate's neck and hugging her. 'I am really, really glad.' She turned to Harry. 'And you'd better look after her, Challenor. Or I'll want to know the reason why.'

John rose from his chair to shake Harry's hand. 'Well done, my friend. I couldn't be happier.' He kissed Kate on the cheek. 'I hope you will allow me to perform the ceremony, my very dear niece.'

'I wouldn't want anyone else to do it, Uncle. But we have agreed to wait until we find out what happened to Sam.'

Harry turned to Josie with a glimmer of a smile. 'I

don't want to raise false hopes, but there is a slim chance that Sam might have survived.'

She sat down suddenly, the colour draining from her face. 'What are you saying?'

'I have a ship leaving for St Peter Port in the morning. Kate has agreed to come with me.'

'Then I am coming too,' Josie said firmly. 'You're not going without me. I'll find my Sam or die in the attempt.'

'And I.' Molly rushed into the room, her bonnet strings flying. 'I heard what you just said, Harry. You can't leave me behind.'

'I wouldn't think of it, Molly. You must come too.'

'I'll start packing right now.' She took off her bonnet and flung it into the air. 'Sam is alive – I've never doubted it. When do we leave?'

'As soon as possible.' Josie rose to her feet and the colour came rushing back to her cheeks. 'I'll come with you. I don't trust you to put the right things in my valise.' She hurried after Molly who had raced from the room.

John moved slowly to a side table and picked up a decanter, pouring sherry into three glasses. He handed one to Kate. 'Here's to your future happiness, and to success in finding Sam.'

Kate raised the glass to her lips, but her happiness was dulled by the hint of sadness she saw in his eyes. 'I'm so sorry, Uncle,' she whispered. 'But there has never been anyone for Josie other than Sam.'

'I know, Kate. And I suppose I am a crusty old bachelor at heart, but I'll be here if she ever needs me.'

Harry's ship, its hold filled with a cargo of corn, docked in St Peter Port harbour late next day. A carriage was waiting to take them to the house that he owned in Hauteville. Everything was so new and strange to Kate. Even at first sight, the island of Guernsey had totally charmed her. Perhaps, she thought dreamily, she was seeing everything through the eyes of a woman deeply in love and secure in the knowledge that her feelings were returned. She tried hard not to appear too happy when Josie and Molly were around, but inside she was bubbling with joy, and yet a little afraid that it was all too good to be true and might suddenly end.

After they had enjoyed an excellent dinner prepared for them by the caretaker's wife, Harry took them to the drawing room on the first floor, but it was not long before both Josie and Molly retired to bed, saying that they wanted an early start next day.

Standing by one of the windows, Kate gazed down at the harbour filled with sailing craft of every description. The house was high up on a hill and the lights of the town twinkled below them. The masthead lamps of the moored vessels cast dancing reflections on the dark water and to Kate it looked like fairyland. Harry came up behind her and took her in his arms, turning her so that their lips met in a long and languorous kiss. 'I can't begin to tell you how happy

I am, my darling, Kate.' He smiled into her eyes as he kissed her forehead, the tip of her nose and, last and more lingering, on the lips. 'I do love you so.'

'And I love you, Harry. I can't believe that we're here together like this.'

'We'll be married as soon as we get home, sweetheart. I'll get a special licence and then I'll take you back to Copperstone as my bride. There is someone there who can't wait to see you again.'

'Really? I can't think who that could be.'

'A young man by the name of Alfred, or Alfie as he prefers to be called. You'll know him better as Boy.'

'Alfie.' She repeated the name, smiling. 'Of course I remember him. Is he doing well?'

'He's settled in splendidly. My cook has great hopes for him, and it was he who gave Alfie his name, after a mishap with some overcooked cakes, so I've been told.'

'Alfred the Great.' Kate chuckled at the notion. 'How apt. But didn't Boy – I mean, Alfie – mind?'

'Not at all. He's really happy.'

Kate gazed dreamily into his eyes. 'As am I. I didn't know that such happiness could exist. If we could just find Sam everything would be perfect.'

Next day, Kate came down to breakfast to find that Josie and Molly had already eaten and were dressed in their outdoor clothes, eager to begin the search for Sam. Josie paced the floor impatiently while they waited for Harry to join them. Kate nibbled a

461

croissant and sipped a cup of coffee, but she was too nervous and excited to enjoy her meal.

'Where is he?' Josie demanded angrily. 'Why isn't Harry here, ready to go out and look for my Sam?'

Before Kate had a chance to comfort her, Harry entered the parlour brandishing several copies of the *Star* newspaper. 'We have to start somewhere,' he said, eyeing Josie warily. 'I suggest we each take one of these back copies of the local newspaper and go through them thoroughly.'

'What?' Josie screeched. 'Sit about reading newspapers, when we should be out there looking for Sam? You told us that you had news of him, which is why we came here. Were you lying to us?'

'Take off your bonnet and sit down, Josie,' Harry said calmly. 'I've had people searching for him since I first learned of the tragedy. I may have discovered something, but if not I don't want you to be there when it turns out to be another wild goose chase.'

'Then why did you bring us here?' Molly's eyes filled with tears. 'That was cruel.'

'Harry's right,' Kate said calmly. 'He might do better on his own. We'll search through the newspapers, just in case something has been missed.'

'Give them to me.' Josie ripped off her bonnet and flung it across the room. She snatched the newspapers from Harry. 'You go with him, Kate. I'm sure that's what he's hoping for. Go off and enjoy yourselves, while Molly and I do all the hard work.'

Kate opened her mouth to protest, but Harry took her by the hand. 'Come, Kate. I have other plans for us.'

'I'm sure you have,' Josie said acidly. 'Go on, get out of here. I'm beginning to think that you only brought us here to make your romantic tryst with Kate look respectable.'

Muffling a sob, Molly sat down at the table and bent her head over a newspaper. 'I hate you, Harry.'

'And at this moment, so do I,' Josie said with feeling. 'Go then, but don't come back unless you've found him.'

Kate was about to leap to Harry's defence but he ushered her out of the room, closing the door behind them.

'Did you do that deliberately, Harry?' Kate followed him downstairs to the entrance hall. 'You know that Josie is a bundle of nerves.'

'My enquiries have turned up something at last, but I thought it best if you and I went to investigate on our own in the first instance. Who knows, if it is Sam, he might not want to be discovered.'

'You deliberately provoked Josie, knowing that she would react in that way.'

'I had the measure of your fiery friend a long time ago, Kate. I know that she explodes and says the first thing that comes into her head and is then very, very sorry.'

'You are so clever,' Kate said, reaching up to brush his lips with a kiss. 'Where are we going?'

'There's a small island off the west coast which is accessible by a causeway at low tide only. We must leave now or we will have missed our chance to get there today. I'll tell you all about it when we are on our way. I sent for my carriage and it should be waiting outside. I had the maid bring your bonnet and shawl from your room,' he added, taking them from the chair by the door.

She smiled. 'You think of everything, and you presume a lot. What would you have done if I'd insisted on staying to comfort the girls?'

'I'd have been very sorry to have missed the opportunity to be alone with you, my love.'

As the carriage manoeuvred through the narrow cobbled streets of the town, Kate leaned against Harry listening intently while he told her his plan. He had learned from one of his contacts on the island that monks from the Benedictine priory of St Mary on Lihou had found a man washed up on the causeway the day after the great storm. They had thought at first that he was dead, but by some miracle he had survived, although he was seriously injured. He had nothing on him by way of identification and it was several weeks before he was able to tell them the full story.

'But is it Sam?' Kate demanded, clutching Harry's arm. 'He must have given them a name.'

Harry shook his head. 'The name he gave was not Sam Loveday. But there could be any number of reasons why he kept his identity to himself. We'll soon find out, Kate. Be brave, my darling.'

Once they were outside the town, the horses picked up speed and Kate held onto Harry as the carriage swayed from side to side on the uneven road surface. She prayed silently that the man whom the monks had saved would turn out to be Sam. It seemed like a slim chance.

The green hedgerows, wooded valleys and pastures with tethered cows grazing the lush grass flashed past the windows as they cut across country. Kate felt that she had died and gone to heaven as she sat close to Harry, in the luxurious confines of his private carriage. She prayed that the man in question would turn out to be Sam, but she could not help wishing that the journey would go on forever. All too soon they were speeding along the coast road. The golden sands were licked by white crested waves and the majestic pink rock formations stood out against an opal sky.

'There it is,' Harry said, leaning forward and pointing to a small island off the headland. 'And it looks as though we are in time. I can see the causeway.'

'I feel sick,' Kate said breathlessly. 'I want it to be Sam so much. What shall we do if it turns out to be a stranger?'

Harry squeezed her hand. 'We'll go on searching, my love. We'll stay on the island until we know one way or the other.'

The coachman drew the horses to a halt as close to the causeway as was possible without the carriage wheels sinking into the wet sand. Kate clung to Harry's arm, holding her bonnet on with one hand as they crossed the windy pathway that would soon be covered by the incoming tide. Men were working on the foreshore, picking up what looked like seaweed and dropping it into rush baskets. They were so close now that she could see that some of them wore monks' habits, but others were obviously laymen, clad in breeches and fishermen's smocks. One man in particular caught her eye and she came to a sudden halt. He was bent over his work, but she would have known him anywhere. 'Sam!'

He raised his head and Kate broke away from Harry. She ran, slipping and sliding on the slimy wet stones, calling out to him. Her voice was carried away by the wind and her bonnet flew off her head, landing with a splash in the water, but she did not care. She waved her arms frantically, screaming his name. He dropped his rush basket and picked up a crutch, leaning heavily on it as he limped towards her.

'Sam. Sam – I can't believe it's really you.' Kate flung herself into his arms, sobbing for joy. 'You're alive – it is you!'

He crushed her to him, rubbing his cheek against her hair. 'Kate. Dear Kate.'

'Why didn't you let us know that you were alive?' she demanded, pummelling his chest with her fists. 'How could you let us suffer torments thinking you were lost at sea?'

He shook his head slowly, glancing down at his twisted limb. 'I didn't know where I was, or who I was, for weeks. The monks found me and took me in. They brought me back from the dead, and they did what they could for my leg, but it will never be right.'

'As if that matters. You're alive and that is all we care about.'

Harry had stopped to speak to one of the monks,

but he now approached them smiling and holding his hand out to Sam. 'We'd almost given you up for dead.'

Sam tugged his cap off, clutching it tightly in his hands. 'I would have been if the monks hadn't taken me in. I was lucky to be washed up on the island. Not that I remember much about it.'

Kate shivered. 'It's a miracle. I can't wait to tell Josie.'

'Is she here?' Sam's dark eyes widened and his lips trembled. 'I don't want her to see me like this.'

'Nonsense, man,' Harry said impatiently. 'The girl has been out of her head with grief. She wouldn't care if you had lost both legs. She loves you, you fool.'

Sam's eyes were bleak. 'But she married you, or she's going to.'

'No, my dear. That's not true.' Kate slipped her hand through the crook of his arm. 'It might be what she told you, but she didn't mean a word of it. Josie has always loved you, and you love her. You were meant to be together. Even as we speak, she's searching through the local newspaper for clues as to your whereabouts. She almost died from shock when she heard that you were lost at sea. You have to believe me.'

Harry took a gold half-hunter watch from his waistcoat pocket. 'The tide will be on the turn soon. We must leave now, or we will be stuck here for another twelve hours. I've had a word with Brother Michael.' Harry jerked his head in the direction of one of the monks who was standing a little way from them. 'He said that you are free to leave whenever you choose.'

'I owe them my life,' Sam said, rubbing his hand across his eyes. 'I have been working the vraic – or seaweed, as we call it – in order to repay them for all they have done for me.'

'But you will come with us, Sam?' Kate looked up into his face, suddenly fearful. She had not imagined that he might want to stay.

He met her eyes and his mouth twisted with pain. 'Look at me, Kate. I'm a cripple. I can't go back to farm work. Who would employ a one-legged man? I'm not educated or clever. What else could I do? How could I support a wife?'

'I can find work for you,' Harry said, glancing anxiously at the waves lapping at the causeway. 'There's plenty for you to do on my estate or on the docks in Weymouth where my ships are berthed.'

'I appeal to you, sir,' Sam said, turning to Harry with a desperate look on his face. 'Man to man. You must understand that I could never marry Miss Josephine Damerell of Damerell Manor, not now, or ever. I couldn't drag her down to live with me in rented rooms or a tied cottage. She is a lady, born and bred, and deserves better than a crippled beggarman.'

Kate tugged at his sleeve. 'You fool, Sam. Josie loves you heart and soul. You must come back with us. Once you see her and hear what she has to say, you'll change your mind.'

Sam's jaw stuck out in a stubborn line. He shook his head. 'You must go, Kate. The tide is on the turn so you must hurry.'

'Listen to her, Sam,' Harry said urgently. 'Kate is right. You should at least give Josie a chance to speak for herself.'

'I can't see her; it would break my heart. I want you to go, please. Leave me here with the monks. They were willing to let me stay on as a lay brother. I can do this work and earn my keep. I want you to go back home and forget all about me.'

'But Molly is here too,' Kate cried in desperation. 'You won't abandon your little sister, will you, Sam? She was always certain that you had not died.'

'You will look after Molly, I know that, Kate. I can do nothing for her, and she might end up having to look after me. Let them think that I am dead.' He turned his back on them and hobbled away towards the priory.

Kate would have run after him, but Harry stopped her. 'Let him go, my love. We can't do any more here and we must hurry or the causeway will be under water.'

'I won't let him do this,' Kate said, clenching her hands. 'I'm going to tell Josie everything and we'll take him home. I swear to God that we'll make him change his mind.'

When Kate broke the news to Josie and Molly there were tears of joy, and then, as they realised that Sam had meant what he said, there was astonishment followed by anger. Josie stared at Kate in disbelief at first, but then her stubborn jaw stuck out in a mirror image of how Sam had looked earlier in the day. 'Stay with the monks, will he? We'll see about that. Harry, I want you to take me to this place now.'

'Unless you can swim like a porpoise, you haven't a hope of getting to Lihou until tomorrow morning.'

'Then that's when we will go. I'm going to bring

Sam back. I don't care if he is a cripple, I love him and I won't allow him to hide away in a monastery.'

'But Josie, dear, what will you do?' Kate asked gently. 'How will you live?'

'I can work,' Molly said, jumping up from the window seat where she had been quietly listening to all that was said. 'I can earn money.'

'I'll take him to my people,' Josie said firmly. 'You can come too, Molly, if you wish. My mother is queen of the Roma, and she'll help us. All we need is a vardo and we will live as the Romany people do. They look after their own.'

Kate moved a little closer to Harry on the sofa. She curled her fingers around his hand and felt a comforting pressure in response. 'I would do the same,' she murmured. 'If circumstances were different, I would work my fingers to the bone for you, Harry.'

Regardless of their audience, Harry drew her into his arms and kissed her. 'There's no need for anyone to suffer hardship,' he said, punctuating his words with kisses. He turned his head to encompass Josie and Molly in his smile. 'You will always have my help. Whatever you need, you will have. And if it had not been for you Josie, I would never have met my darling Kate. For that I owe you everything.'

Josie tossed her head, laughing. 'I'll hold you to that, Challenor.'

Next day, at low tide, Harry and Kate stood on the sand watching Josie and Molly striding out purposefully along the causeway towards the priory.

'Do you think they'll manage to persuade him?' Harry asked, wrapping his arm around Kate's shoulders and holding her close.

'I don't doubt it for a moment, Harry. It's amazing what one determined woman can achieve, let alone two. Sam won't stand a chance.' Kate raised her face to gaze into his eyes, and she sighed with happiness. 'Perhaps we could have a double wedding?'

'Absolutely not. I won't have you jumping over a broomstick, or whatever the gypsies do. I am going to marry you with all the pomp and ceremony I can muster. I will have your snooty Aunt Marjorie eating wedding cake out of my hand with a slice of humble pie for good measure. We'll honeymoon in Paris, or Monte Carlo, or anywhere you choose.'

Kate smiled, shaking her head. 'I would like to honeymoon here, in this enchanted island, where we have all found happiness.'

'Then we will. That is a promise, my love.'

Author's Note

I have taken liberties with the history of Lihou, an island off the west coast of Guernsey, in that the priory, established by Benedictine monks in the twelfth century, would have been a ruin in the nineteenth century. However, vraic (seaweed) was harvested on the island but the industry ceased during the German Occupation.